I0687125

Her Heart's Liege

Olivia Fields

Published by **Rogue Phoenix Press**
Copyright © 2015

Names, characters and incidents depicted in this book are products of the author's imagination or are used fictitiously. Any resemblance to actual events, locales, organizations, or persons, living or dead, is entirely coincidental and beyond the intent of the author or the publisher.

No part of this book may be reproduced or transmitted in any form or by any means, electronic or mechanical, including photocopying, recording, or by any information storage and retrieval system, without permission in writing from the publisher.

ISBN: **978-1-62420-126-4**

Credits
Cover Artist: **Designs by Ms G**
Editor: **Sherry Derr-Wille**

Acknowledgments

Heartfelt thanks go out to Ashley, Jeri, Molly, David, Rhonda, Jan, and Jennifer for their varied inspiration, help, advice, editing, and general support in writing this book. Without my friends, I would never have had the guts to get so far. ☺

Chapter One

A bell on the wall clanged harshly, and Alex Bonham glanced up from polishing her boots. She stifled a sigh, frowning down at the brush and the cloth in her hands, and gave the boot a final quick buff before jamming it on her foot. She strapped on her sword belt and tossed back her long, dark braid. Darting a quick glance at the mirror to ensure she was presentable, she hurried out.

She trotted up the spiral stair to the royal apartments, wondering what the prince wanted her for this time. He probably hoped he could convince her to sponge his back in the bath. It wouldn't be his first saucy request, if so.

The guards she'd posted earlier in the afternoon still stood on duty, and they saluted her, swinging the door open without waiting for her to knock. The king's voice penetrated out to the hall, raised in a hectoring shout. Grimacing, Alex went in and waited against the wall, poised and correct in the face of family conflict. She should have expected this. The gossip had already traveled everywhere.

"I swear to you, Holden, if you embarrass the family name again, I'll have you flogged in the public square," King Anselm lowered his voice a few moments too late for privacy. He sat behind the prince's writing desk, leaning his chin on his silver-shod walking stick. His unruly shock of hair was pure white, his face heavily creased with age. He was thin and no longer steady on her feet, but his voice was still firm, his jaw square and steady. His thick brows were currently drawn down, scowling over a stare as intense as an eagle's. Though he was an old man, he was obviously the source of his son's good looks.

"She's just a scullery maid." Prince Holden, a slender, upright man of thirty winters or so, stood at the window, gazing out and stroking his mustache rather than looking at his father. The light caught in his red-gold hair and his neatly trimmed beard, setting them ablaze, and sparkled off his golden coronet. As always, he wore his best, his slim body clad in a flattering brown and green silk shirt with gold embroidery in a pattern of brambles twining down the sleeves. He wore close-fitting brown hose and low suede boots. The prince began to turn his gold signet ring absently on his pinky finger, another visible sign of his discomfort.

"The entire city knows the sordid tale. Every tongue in the capital is busy telling how she's to be sent home for confinement with a pension for life. What did you expect, since the baby has begun to show in her belly?"

"Who's to say it's mine?" He shrugged, so unconcerned Alex knew he hadn't heard her come in. He usually tried to hide his callousness around women he wanted to seduce. "The child could belong to anyone, really."

The king stared at him, exasperated. "You've no compassion at all, do you?" He crumpled a scrap piece of parchment in his fist. "I curse the day the plague killed your mother. Maybe she could have taught you some responsibility, or at least given you a conscience. Obviously, I've failed."

The prince slouched his shoulders, pulling slightly into himself as his father's words scored a hit. He turned, seeming ready to argue the point, but fell silent when he caught sight of Alex. He abruptly pulled himself upright and put on a winning smile in order to show himself off to the best possible effect.

King Anselm scowled at him savagely. "Don't even think it." He limped over to Alex, so angry his hands shook. "Thank you for your promptness, Captain." He glanced back toward his son. "I've a mission for you. Take His Highness down to oversee Mary's departure. Ensure he is polite, and see to it he gives her this writ. She'll need the document to draw her pension." He handed her a sealed letter. "I thought it best if he delivered the writ." He slid a threatening scowl at the prince.

"No worries." She saluted stoutly. "I'll manage him."

"See that you do." King Anselm gave her a slightly worried look. He seemed more troubled than he had since the day she was first promoted to Captain of the King's Elite Guard. He hesitated for a moment, then let himself out.

Alex could easily guess at the reason for his concern. Rumor among her jealous peers claimed she'd been elevated to her current rank on the prince's insistence, to make his pursuit of her more convenient, or possibly so he could enjoy looking at her in trim, fitted brown leather armor, the uniform of her position. Certainly Prince Holden seemed inclined to take advantage of the situation, if she would let him.

However, Alex hadn't ever been attracted to the prince, and the rumors she'd earned her rank on her back were spiteful and untrue. Despite Holden's lusty, appreciative gaze, Alex deserved her promotion to the rank of captain, and King Anselm would not have appointed her if she were not highly competent at her duties. As a female, first in the army and later in the king's elite guards, she'd spent her life fighting for every achievement tooth and nail, proving herself twice as good as her male peers time and again. In spite of that, sometimes she could still see King Anselm's reluctance to trust her.

Given the number of girls from the palace staff Prince Holden ruined, perhaps the king's worries weren't so unreasonable. He would doubtless endure trouble and embarrassment if he needed to replace her, should she turn up in a family way.

The prince pouted irritably after his father as he wandered across the room to rummage in his wardrobe. He pulled out a leather doublet embossed in gold, one that particularly enhanced his slender build. He hooked the thing on and donned a green velvet capelet. He checked his hair in the suite's full-length mirror, ensuring it was still artfully tousled and standing on end, as he liked best.

Alex eyed him, amused, as he prepared himself. Everything about him projected vanity, from the ornate embroidery on his shirt to the tailored waist, flared shoulders, and flirty peplum of his doublet. Even the cape he wore was cut artfully short enough to show off his pretty behind. She had to admit, he was a fine eyeful: trim and handsome, well favored in nearly every possible way, with a charming, roguish smile. He seemed quite a catch, at least until you discovered the spoiled brat who lurked behind the good looks. Afterward, he lost much of his appeal.

He'd be dangerous indeed, if she didn't know all his tricks.

When he judged himself ready, he turned to her, swiping his fingers through his hair one last time, and pasted on a smile. She ignored it, saluting. "Shall we go down now, Prince Holden?"

He let her lead him down to the kitchens, where Alex put the king's writ into his hand and made a quiet inquiry with the cook. She gestured them toward a curtained alcove.

They entered to find Mary waiting in a straight chair, her eyes on her toes. Sure enough, her belly was prominent and round below her bodice, a telltale message of guilt, only half her own. Alex eyed the girl, taking a place against the curtain. Mary seemed composed, but Alex spotted a tremor in her hands. Her jaw tightened as the prince stepped forward, his manner careless and dismissive.

"Your writ of pension," Holden said briskly, and put the parchment in Mary's hands. "In reward for good service."

Mary's gaze darted to the prince's face, agonized, and her cheeks flushed crimson. Alex cleared her throat, giving quiet warning of her aggravation with him.

"To the king's household, I meant." Holden patted the girl's shoulder, awkward. "I wish you well, Mary. You should be amply provided for."

Mary's lip trembled and she wrung her hands, crumpling the bit of parchment.

"Here, easy now." Alex interposed herself between them. "Don't spoil that, lass. You'll need it."

The prince stepped out hastily, and Alex seethed, keeping her face smooth with an effort. "Find yourself a good man after you go," she told Mary softly. "Look past his face to his heart next time." She hugged the girl, trying to comfort her, but there was little more to be said.

The cook bustled in, twitching aside the curtain. "The footman says Mary's father has arrived in the courtyard."

They'd best be going before the man spotted the prince and she was required to stop a fight. "Chin up, lass." Alex squeezed Mary gently and stepped out to find the prince waiting for her in the kitchen, idly scratching the little terrier that usually turned the spit. He wore a frown on his handsome face.

"I heard you, you know."

"I regret my indiscretion." Alex touched her forelock politely, but refused to offer any further apology. "Let's get going."

"You think I'm not a good man?" The prince's heavy brows sank down to shadow his blue eyes. He was building up as fine a sulk as she'd ever seen.

She tried not to let her annoyance show. Of course he wouldn't let her off the hook so easily. "My duty is to guard you, Your Highness. Not to blow smoke up your arse. Begging your pardon." She preceded him up the stair, back toward the main levels. "I've a meeting with General Bonham in twenty minutes. Carl will take over for me."

She delivered her charge to Carl and slipped away with relief. She was glad to leave the prince and eager to go see the general, her father.

Chapter Two

General Bonham sat at his desk across from Roger, Duke of Fakenham, the king's steward. He was also attended by his military secretary, the three of them going over a column of figures. Alex thought the general looked quite exhausted.

She stood in the doorway for a long moment, unseen, watching them. Though he was a good twenty years younger than King Anselm, General Bonham had already started to show his age. His once jet-black hair showed more than a hint of iron gray at the temples, and not long ago, he'd been forced to let his armor out to accommodate a hint of paunch.

The general held up his palm, gesturing for Alex to wait as he listened to Fakenham, who leaned forward over the figures, gesturing to one of the totals. "This is far too much. The king's budget won't accommodate such wasteful spending."

Her father swallowed and remained calm, but his lips turned white as he struggled hard to restrain his temper. "Does the king expect our troops to subsist on imagination and rainwater? We must feed them enough they can stand on their feet to fight."

Her heart went out to her father as she watched the ensuing argument. His job had grown increasingly difficult over the past few years. She was glad he was safe, or as safe as he was likely to get in these troubled times, but far less of his work was in the field now than he would like.

"Very well." Fakenham finally yielded with ill grace, his lips drawing back over his teeth as if he smelled something highly unpleasant. "You may have that total for provisions, but you will have to take the extra money from elsewhere in your budget. The king specifies the army cannot have any additional money. This campaign is already draining an excess of funds from the treasury." He patted self-consciously at his long yellow hair and straightened his surcoat. Scooping up the parchments, he strutted out, barely bothering to give Alex a nod on his way past.

Her father's gaze finally rose to her, and Alex saluted. "Reporting as requested, sir."

He smiled at her, breaking formal decorum. "Thank you, Captain." He pushed away the stack of parchments lying before him, and several scrolls toppled off the table. "Deal with those, would you, Walter?" He flicked his fingers at his secretary, a sickly-looking, black-haired young corporal barely out of puberty, with a harelip from a cleft palate. Walter was so scrawny he almost seemed he would vanish if he turned sideways. He bent over, his breath whistling through his harelip, scrabbling with the dropped documents.

Bonham put his hand on Alex's arm and led her into an antechamber. "I have important business with the captain of the guard," he told Walter. "See to it we aren't disturbed."

Unfortunately, Alex could tell whatever her father wanted wouldn't be pleasant. The general pulled out Alex's chair for her, but instead of sitting too, he closed the door and began to pace with agitation.

"The situation on the coast is growing worse. Crown Prince Gavin reports more invading ships and requests additional men. We have no more trained soldiers to send." His frown drew down so fiercely his bristling brows nearly touched. "I've advised the king to send Prince Holden to the interior, away from Norwich. We can't repel the Danes at the coast for much longer.

7

The battlefront is too extensive, and the defense is costing a fortune. We'll have to draw back and fight them on a united front."

Alex bit her lip. "I'd heard the war was going badly, but as poorly as this?"

"Worse, I'm afraid. We've already been taking refugees into the city, housing the able-bodied men here and funneling the women and children farther inland. The inns are already full. I fear the Danes mean to besiege Norwich. I'm having extra provisions brought up as we speak." He came to sit across from her and rubbed his forehead, looking as if he had a fierce headache.

"Prince Gavin is valiant. He won't want to retreat."

"He'll retreat if he has to. It's the best way to save his men, and we'll need every single one of them here, if a siege occurs." Her father hesitated. "I'll be sending you with Prince Holden, Alexandra."

"But I want to stay here and fight." Outraged, she slapped her hand on the table. "I won't tolerate being shipped away with the women and children."

"I need a trustworthy guard for the prince, one who won't let him run roughshod over her authority. You hold the position you do for a reason, you know. The prince's blandishments and threats don't work on you. I'll send your lieutenant, Carl, along with the two of you. He's a good soldier." He looked at her, his expression sympathetic. "I know this doesn't please you, Alexandra, and you're as valiant as anyone who will stay here to defend the city. But someone must go, and I've chosen you. If Norwich falls, you'll be the last line of defense for what remains of the royal family." His voice fell and he looked toward the door. Rising as stealthily as he could in his rattling armor, he padded over to the door and peered through the keyhole.

"Walter?" he bellowed, ramming the door outward abruptly. Walter cursed and fell onto his bottom, rolling across the floor clutching his temple, which had taken a sharp blow from the latch and was already bruising. "What have I told you about listening at keyholes, you worthless fool?"

He ran the man out, blustering and snarling, locked the exterior door, checked all the chambers carefully, and made sure they were empty before returning to Alex's side.

"Should those who hold the city perish, Prince Holden will stand to inherit the throne. Should he die, you will be the last survivor of the line of High King Wilhelm." He resettled himself and leaned toward her. "We do not speak of this often, I know." He steepled his fingers and rested his elbows on his thighs. "But I confess, I have always hoped you and Prince Gavin might form an attachment and unite the two branches of the line once more."

"Prince Gavin has no eye for me," Alex patted her father's hand, smiling. She liked her second cousin, but there was no spark between them. "Though he is a good man and a fine warrior, I have none for him."

"I hope you have better sense than to turn your eyes to Prince Holden." Her father scowled. "He seems determined to tup his way through every woman in the king's employ, if not every comely lass in Norwich. I know he's had his damned eye on you since before you ever came of age."

"I'd sooner roll naked in a gorse-patch, sir," Alex told him earnestly. The prince was comely enough, but he'd never been anything but a good-for-nothing and a user of women. She'd be a fool to think she could persuade him to act otherwise. "I have goals of my own, and they don't include raising a bastard child. Not even one with 'Fitz' attached to its name."

"Good. For he'd never claim the babe, and he'd leave you husbandless. By the love of all that's holy, never let him touch you." General Bonham laid his open hands palm-down on the table. "Queen Eleanor would have wept to see him grow up such a rake and a wastrel."

"He's never had reason not to be as he is," Alex pointed out. "With Prince Gavin set to claim the throne, so wise in the ways of ruling and so valiant in battle, the prize of their father's eye, what was left for Prince Holden to become? What need was there for him to become anything at all?"

Bonham scowled. "I do not like to hear you defend him, daughter."

"I'm not defending him. I'm making an observation." Alex smiled, hoping to reassure her father. "I have compassion for the prince, but that's all."

"Then you'll go?"

"I will do as you and King Anselm command." Alex frowned. "But in truth, I think I'll have a harder time on the road with the prince than you will here."

"I don't envy you, I admit." He chuckled, but grew sober. "Alexandra, take care of yourself."

"I will." She touched his cheek, saddened almost beyond bearing by the fear she might never see her father again. "When must we depart?"

"The sooner the better. The prince has not been informed of the plans we've discussed. Don't let him out of your sight after he is, or he's likely to send the whole city into a panic by flapping his jaw about fleeing before the invaders."

"I'll sneak him out after midnight tonight." Alex hugged her father and went to relieve Carl, putting a quiet word into his ear about arranging provisions, a wagon, and a team of mules.

Chapter Three

When Alex went to give Carl his orders, she found the prince still sunk deep in his sulks, preoccupied with his own thoughts. Mercifully, he didn't seem inclined to talk to her. She assumed her post outside his door, standing watch quietly.

After a couple of hours Carl, ever thoughtful, brought her some bread and meat from the kitchens. He relieved her briefly, taking up the watch himself. His consideration gave her a much-needed break to pack her own things and carry them down to their wagon.

Alex didn't take long to ready her gear. An experienced campaigner, she preferred to travel light, and she always kept a bag packed in her room, ready to grab quickly if she needed to travel.

Choosing the party's weapons consumed more time than picking out clothes. She carefully filled a capacious chest with swords for the three of them, several knives and daggers, wooden training swords to keep herself and Carl in practice, three heavy crossbows and a number of bolts, caltrops, thieves' picks, and a few other wicked surprises she thought might come in handy. She added a first-aid kit with a bit of willow-bark and some bandages, a poultice or two in wax-sealed jars, and a needle and thread.

An oiled leather wallet lay waiting on her bed, and she inspected the contents, finding documents from the king: notes good for claiming coin from the royal coffers upon presentation of the prince's personal seal, letters of introduction should they visit the monarchs of neighboring lands, and various other necessaries. Good. She tucked it inside the chest too. Finally she added a change of shirt and breeches and some packets of herbs for brewing her favorite drinks. Finishing, she turned the key in the lock and looped it onto a leather thong. She hung the thong between her breasts for safekeeping.

"Carry the chest down to the stables," she directed a handful of guards, and she followed them down to leave her pack in the wagon. She snooped a little, peeping into the bags that were already waiting, pleased to find one contained disguises for them all. She slung the bag over her arm and returned to the prince's room.

Prince Holden raised a brow, surprised to see her again, and lounged back in his chair, his posture lazy and inviting. "Come to see me to bed, have you?"

"Ash is ill," she said mildly. She forbore to mention a man of Holden's age should not require a guardian around the clock, or to point out he wouldn't have to keep a guard from sleeping if he were capable of leaving the maids alone. "Carl and I will split his watch."

"How fortunate for me you're to take the first stand." He favored her with his most winning smile, his hand sliding down the inside of his thigh, and Alex had to restrain herself from rolling her eyes.

"Flirting will get you nowhere," she advised him, and he pouted. He rose and began to strip for bed as if he were indifferent to her presence. She turned her back resolutely, having endured that particular trick before. She knew she'd have the last laugh this time, though. The prince would be most displeased to garb himself as a simple farmer.

Unable to interest her in himself, Holden finally rolled into bed and Alex settled in to wait for midnight, allowing herself to rest in one of his armchairs. Guards did not often remain inside the prince's chamber at night, but evidently he had chosen not to question her presence. She reckoned he must think her resolve was weakening. She hoped he would fall asleep quickly and leave her alone. She needed her rest. The night was not going to be short, and if she didn't get a chance to snatch a nap, she'd be dead on her feet by morning.

When the prince finally began to snore, she let herself relax and drowse.

Carl shook her shoulder to wake her. She checked the prince's water clock, which indicated middle-night was already past. Carl offered the pack with her disguise, and Alex accepted, putting her finger over her lips. She hastily changed, putting on a nondescript, dirty dress. She added a rumpled pinafore and dismal calfskin shoes. The clothes hung on her like a sack. There was also a rough linen shirt and breeches, which she planned to keep for later.

As Alex dressed, Carl pulled out the prince's clothing. He was to wear a stained shirt and tabard with a wide leather belt, rough-tanned leather trousers, and hobnailed boots that had seen better days. His slouch hat looked like nothing so much as a lumpy felt bag.

Alex chuckled to herself and laid the whole lot out on the foot of the prince's bed.

"Your Highness, wake up."

He blinked his eyes open slowly and focused on her; a slow smile spread across his face. "Captain Alex. To what do I owe the pleasure?" He stretched, sinuous and suggestive, his eyes dark.

"We're going on an adventure." She made her voice tart. "You and me and Carl. Now get up and dress. We're going in disguise."

He hopped out of bed brightly enough, but scowled when he saw his clothing. "Where in the world did you find this trash?"

"Put them on," she tossed the shirt into his arms, implacable. "Your father wants you out of the city before dawn."

"Whatever for?" He dragged on the trousers warily, as if he feared something might be living inside them. They fit him loosely, bunching up at the crotch. They looked quite uncomfortable.

Alex shot a sidelong glance at Carl and began gathering a few of the prince's things, including his straight razor, a comb, a scissor, and other personal necessaries, stuffing them all carelessly into his bag. "To get you out ahead of the Danish invasion force that's coming behind your brother's impending retreat."

His eyes flew wide as he worked for a moment to parse her meaning. His brow crimped into a frown. "That's not very damned funny."

"No, it isn't. Now finish putting your breeches on so we can get out of here before dawn."

Holden frowned at her, belting on his rough trousers and shoving his feet into the muddy boots. "Why are we leaving? We should get ready to fight, instead."

She'd seen Holden fight several times, but he was a fencer, not a true swordsman. His rapier wouldn't do much against an armored man with a Danish axe or broadsword. "King Anselm has given me the charge of keeping you safe in case he and Prince Gavin are killed in battle."

He scowled at her words, stripping off his nightshirt. She studied him wryly. His body was slender and lithe, but not at all muscular. He could be strong, but instead, he'd stayed soft and lazy all his life.

"I'll make you a deal," she offered with sudden inspiration. "Beat me in a contest of strength, and we'll stay. If I can beat you, you'll do as you're told and we'll go."

He stared at her as if she were mad, and perhaps she was, but she'd also spent hundreds of hours drilling with a sword, and he had not. Even his fencing bouts were few and far between lately, and were usually conducted against an instructor rather than a genuine opponent.

Alex went to the prince's writing table and moved the few documents that lay there, sitting and putting her elbow up, ready to wrestle. He eyed her narrowly and approached without bothering to put his shirt on. "That's a deal," he said softly and sat, extending his hand to grasp hers.

His hand felt soft and warm clasping hers, no calluses at all. It would feel like a noblewoman's hand if his palm were not broad and firm. Instead he felt distinctly masculine, more so than she'd anticipated. She shifted uneasily.

Perhaps she could blame her discomfort on the sight of his bare, cinnamon-furred chest across the table, distracting her.

She felt the prince's eyes on her, and grew aware of his self-satisfied smile. Damn the man. Recalling herself to the moment, she pushed him into approximately the correct position and grasped his free hand with hers to prevent him from trying to cheat by grabbing the table for extra leverage.

There was a certain amount of risk in this, of course. He had a slight advantage in size, and even lazy men usually developed a certain amount of muscle without trying--more so than women, at any rate. Still, he'd never worked to build strength, whereas she'd spent her time fighting for every ounce she could get. Her preparation should suffice.

She couldn't remember ever taking his hand before. She'd always avoided touching him, knowing contact would encourage him to no good purpose.

He began to smirk as she settled her palm in his. His smug look annoyed her. She decided she'd be damned if she'd let him win. Of course, he wouldn't be likely to, not this first time. He would be almost certain to underestimate her strength.

She set her elbow against the table, bracing carefully. "Ready?"

"Ready." The smirk lit his eyes as he curled his fingers around hers. Carl watched them both with astonishment as they faced off, Alex glowering at the prince across their clasped hands.

"Carl?" she prodded him.

"On your mark." He held up his hand. "Get set." Alex felt Holden shift his feet, bracing himself. "Go!" Carl dropped his hand.

She was ready for the first burst of the prince's strength, and endured easily. He frowned, the smirk fading off his face as he failed to push her arm over right away. She leaned into the contest, and suddenly he began to struggle. His eyes widened and he pushed back harder, but Alex was not expending all her strength, not yet. Even as he tried to bring his reserves to bear, she was already shoving him out of true, over and back, and he couldn't get enough leverage to work against her. He began sweating suddenly, his

15

fingers digging into her left hand as he tried to recover, but he was already beaten. She banged his hand down onto the table and raised a brow at him.

He looked sheepish. "Best two of three?"

"Put your shirt on." She smirked at him. "Let's get moving."

The prince obeyed with a certain amount of ill grace. He nearly balked again when confronted by their ungainly wagon with its team of long-eared black mules, but she finally maneuvered him into the back and jammed his hat down on his head. She had Carl take the reins and drive them out of the back gate of the palace into the sleeping city. They passed through the near-empty streets without a fuss, rattling out over the drawbridge and suffering a jaw-shaking lurch as they thumped onto the hard-packed south road.

They trundled on in silence until they passed the abbey standing a couple of furlongs outside the city wall, tucked into an elbow of the River Yare. Alex climbed over the top of the wagon bed and settled herself onto the seat at Carl's side.

"We should have had him shave," Carl muttered in her ear. "The whole kingdom knows his little mustache and goatee."

"He'll have to comb his hair like a normal man, too," she grinned a little. "If I have to hold him down and force him."

"What's that?" The prince popped his head up, suspicious.

"Nothing at all." She tossed the words lightly over her shoulder. "Lie down and get some rest. You too, Carl."

Carl climbed into the back and joined the prince. Alex clucked to the reluctant mules and headed west when the road split. She managed to ride sentry until dawn. After nearly falling asleep at the reins, she lay down for a rest in the back of the wagon while Carl and the prince rode up front.

"This seat feels like it's made of stone," the prince shifted and squirmed in his place. "Isn't there some way to stop the jolting?"

Alex finally gave up listening to him and dug her spare shirt and tunic out of her pack. She jammed the cloth against her ears so she could sleep.

Really, she had no idea what in the world the maidservants saw in him.

16

Chapter Four

"These trousers are itchy."

The litany of Prince Holden's complaints woke Alex. She unwrapped her head and yawned, sitting up and checking the angle of the sun. Soon after midday, if she was any judge. Carl wore a thunderous expression, so she guessed the complaining must have remained a constant feature while she slept.

It was time to do something about the prince's attitude.

"Pull over at the next copse, Carl," Alex ordered. "The prince's disguise needs adjusting."

She dug into Prince Holden's pack, which he'd not yet bothered to open. She'd packed a straight razor and soap, a shaving brush, a bone comb, and a whetstone along with a change of clothes. She dug out the shaving supplies and tested the blade. It felt nice and sharp to her questing thumb. She tucked them in her pocket, and after a moment's thought, she added the comb.

The prince climbed out of the wagon painfully, walking spraddle-legged, and Alex had to choke back a giggle at his stiff, awkward posture. Already he represented quite a departure from the neatly turned out dandy she was used to guarding. He lowered himself onto a stone and winced. "All right, so this rock *is* harder than that wagon seat. It was an honest mistake." He stood back up hastily and kneaded his arse with both hands, groaning.

"Carl, light a fire. We need to heat a kettle of water. I'll boil enough to make an infusion." Alex planned to heat enough for shaving, too. She went to the wagon and pulled out her store of herbs, sniffing the bag of anise and discarding it in favor of mint. She fished out four mugs and went to a nearby stream to fill the kettle. The prince paced, working the stiffness out of his muscles and staring at the trees and plants as if he'd never seen anything like them up close before. Perhaps he hadn't.

Alex waited until the water boiled, then poured some into one of the mugs, handing the pouch of mint to Carl, who was used to her strange habits. He began brewing the infusion of mint without question.

"Sit down," Alex ordered the prince, and drew the shaving soap out of her pocket. The prince sat as directed, eyeing her advance with some confusion and with growing alarm.

"That's shaving gear. What do you think you're doing?"

"You're going to shave before we have a drink."

"Oh no." He launched himself right back up. "You won't touch my beard."

"You need to be in disguise. People know your look. You'll make us a target for every highwayman and ruffian in East Anglia."

"I'll comb my mustache differently." He backpedaled, glaring at the bar of soap in her hand. "And my hair. But no shaving. Shaving gives me a rash." He shook his head with indignant force. "I won't give up my routine of daily tonsorial maintenance. A man has to have standards."

"There'll be next to no hot water for shaving, no hot towels, and no barber to do all sorts of daily maintenance," Carl commented with a snicker. "Captain, you should have him grow his beard out altogether. That'd be easiest, and it'd change his looks as much as anything."

"Growing his beard would take time." Alex relented reluctantly, but in truth, she wasn't eager to try shaving the prince herself. She might slip and cut his throat, especially with him refusing to sit still.

She rummaged for the comb instead and handed it to him. "Flat like Carl's," she pointed.

With ill grace, the prince complied. "There's no mirror," he fussed, trying to part his hair and failing rather spectacularly.

Alex moved to help him, drawing the comb along a neat line down the left of his skull and separating his hair to either side. It lay soft and thick, and would soon grow long. That too would change his looks considerably, over time. She anticipated a difficult period until his beard came in, during which he would still be easily recognizable.

Well, perhaps an altercation or two would help persuade him to cooperate with shaving.

Carl served up the mint infusion and Alex accepted her cup, pouring out the shaving water and putting the dirty mug aside for rinsing. She drank a sip and murmured with pleasure. The prince glared at his mug with rebellious suspicion. "This is medicine."

"It's good," Alex told him calmly. "My mother used to swear by drinking an infusion of herbs and honey to help with a cough, but she also drank it for pleasure. She didn't care for wine and she said boiling the water made it safer to drink." She shrugged. "I never saw her get sick after drinking water she boiled."

"I don't want to drink medicine." He bent forward to his mug, touching the tip of his tongue to the steaming liquid, and wrinkled his nose. "There isn't any piss in this, is there?"

"Did you see me squat down over the pot?" Alex asked, exasperated. "No alchemist's nonsense. Either drink up or go get the wineskin out of the wagon. Or you could go take a drink straight from the stream and enjoy having the scours, after."

She went to the wagon and fetched out a loaf of bread while Carl busied himself carving three generous wedges from their wheel of cheese. She passed out the food, dividing the loaf with her dagger. "Eat up, Your Highness. We need to get right back on the road if we're to reach an inn before nightfall."

The prince ate his meal and he eventually drank his mint decoction, though he did so under protest. After they cleaned up their gear, they trundled back out to the road. He chose to sit up front again with her while Carl spent the afternoon in the wagon bed, sleeping with his head pillowed atop his pack.

"Today is a jolly day for a trip." The prince looked about them, squinting across the landscape.

Alex had to admit he was right, at least for the moment. The sun was shining brightly, and spring still held sway over the land. Gorse bushes bloomed on the hillsides and in the fields, making the whole countryside gleam like burnished gold.

"We won't think it's so jolly when we're riding in a storm." Alex clucked to the mules, trying to edge the wagon around a mud hole, a mute reminder of the frequent rains that swept East Anglia's quiet countryside.

"You don't like me much." The prince changed the subject without warning. He looked at her full on, with frankness and calm, his self-possession surprising her.

"My duty is to guard you, not to judge you." She shrugged and looked ahead, watching the road as though it might wander off if she turned her attention away for too long.

"As a person, I mean." Holden fidgeted with his tabard, trying and failing to scratch out a spot where something or other stained the fabric. "Not as a duty."

Alex considered, but decided against trying to explain the difference between respect and liking to the prince. Truth be told, though he amused her, she didn't have much of either for him. "Your Highness, I don't have to like you to do my duty."

"This trip would be much nicer if you did." He looked at her for a long moment, his eyes sober.

"Liking you wouldn't necessarily mean I'd agree to sleep with you." She evened out the wagon and set the brake as they headed down a hill. The road meandered lazily down toward a town alongside a small river that stretched in gleaming coils through a wide plain. Clouds had begun to gather on the horizon, and she could see the slanting gray lines of rain falling from them. A wet night lay ahead. It would be a good time to sleep under a roof. "I'm not going to, regardless of whether I like you or not."

"I'm not as bad as you think. Mary had round heels. Half the castle staff bedded her before I ever approached her."

Alex gritted her teeth. She'd seen the genuine anguish on the girl's face when she looked at Holden. Perhaps Mary *had* bedded others, but she'd clearly given her heart to the prince along with her body. Still, Alex had to phrase her response in terms he was prepared to understand.

"If that's true, maybe you should have been more particular than to bed her yourself. Afterward, she could claim her child was your by-blow regardless who fathered it. If she'd named anyone else as the father, the man might have been persuaded to wed her. Your indiscretion caused a long-term drain on the king's coffers." He was listening, she realized, taking her words to heart with unaccustomed seriousness.

He stared at his knees. "You're right, of course. Gavin would never have made the choice I did." His voice sounded bitter.

Alex released the hand brake as the road leveled out and waited to answer until she finished guiding the mules over a wide stone bridge, a remnant of Roman times. "Instead of fretting about what Gavin would or wouldn't have done, maybe you should think about who you'd like to become."

"Someone you'd like. And respect."

She glanced at him, a little discomfited by the intensity of his focus, and raised a brow at his unexpected insight. "I'm hardly St. Peter, consulting the holy book at the gates of Heaven to judge who's good enough to go in and who's not."

"Your respect is a good enough goal for me, nonetheless." He firmed his jaw and started to rake his hand through his hair to make it stand up, stopping his hand belatedly, in mid-motion.

Well, he has to start somewhere, Alex supposed.

"Wake up, Carl. We're nearly in town," she called. "We'll not have to sleep on the ground tonight."

Alex sent the prince inside with Carl and watched over the inn's two lanky stable boys as they stowed the wagon and put the mules in a stall. She insisted on filling the water trough and the manger herself. Best to do that personally, or the boys might skimp on the animals' feed.

"Carry this trunk up to our rooms," she told them instead, and she followed, the packs slung over her arm. She blinked to help her eyes adjust as she entered the dim, noisy common room.

"The place is nearly full. I'm afraid we must share," Carl told her.

"That's for the best. One of us would've had to stay with him anyway. Preferably you, since you slept all afternoon." Alex left Carl with the prince again and pursued the puffing, grunting stable lads up the stair and into their room, eyeing the single bed. She lifted the coverlet to look at the sheets and the lumpy straw mattress. The bedding looked cleaner than she'd expected. She set their packs down atop the weapons chest, locked the door, and went back downstairs, checking to be sure her purse still lay in her pocket.

Prince Holden was already waiting at the inn's best table, sitting behind half a flagon of ale.

"You there. Bring food for me and my guards," he called, his manner peremptory, and Alex could have groaned as she watched the surly innkeeper's fingers go white around the handle of his stout oaken cudgel. So much for pretending to be simple farmers.

The innkeeper's wife studied Holden, her look shrewd, then whispered urgently to her husband. Alex couldn't hear most of what she said, but she made out the word 'rich,' and she grimaced. Yes. Enough money could excuse nearly any amount of rude behavior.

The innkeeper listened to his wife. He put away the cudgel and shouted for maids to come serve their guests. Everything fell into place all too smoothly. A girl hurried to place ale in front of Alex, giving her an obsequious bow. Another provided the same for Carl. Prince Holden regarded the serving wenches regally, puffed up with his own importance, proud of making the staff jump to do his bidding.

Alex and Carl exchanged dismayed glances, but it was too late to undo the damage the prince had already done.

A few of the tavern's regular patrons slunk out, discomfited by the strange, badly dressed nobleman in their midst. After half an hour or so, Alex realized the people who hadn't left represented only the inn's staff and a few scowling toughs. The bravos sat at a table on the edge of the room. They tried and failed to look nonchalant, watching Holden drink with ill-concealed, predatory interest.

Alex surveyed them carefully, which was easy to do under the cover of her femininity. In her experience, men nearly always underestimated a woman.

She didn't like what she saw. Several of the men looked like serious trouble, but the prince remained oblivious to the aura of threat. He was far too busy making himself look grand in front of the barmaids, soaking up their giggles and simpers in a properly pompous, lordly fashion.

Alex noticed one of the farm lads lingering with the toughs, scowling bitterly at the prince whenever he flirted with a plump blonde serving girl with a dimple and a shy smile. She was endowed with ample curves and a flattering tongue. No doubt the farmer's betrothed, or near enough.

The trouble was going to start there, Alex judged. The lad would be easily manipulated into starting the row the ruffians obviously wanted.

She caught Carl's gaze with her own, tilting her head to draw his attention to the farmer boy. Carl joined her in watching as the young man drank himself drunk. A couple of his companions kept filling his flagon, making sure he never reached the bottom of his ale.

Alex shook her head in despair at Carl, watching as the boy's scowl deepened. Prince Holden had already drunk too much as well, completely unaware of the impending violence.

Finally the lad's patience crumbled when Holden pulled the girl into his lap, and he shoved himself upright, staggering a bit. Alex dropped a hand on Carl's shoulder to forestall him, rising to her own feet. She could still avert disaster, if she played her cards right.

She beat the lad to his feet and advanced on Holden, swaying and lurching as if she too had drunk most of a hogshead of ale. She scowled at the barmaid and jerked her to her feet. "Go get him another mug," she slurred, and dropped herself into Holden's lap instead. "Why are you wasting your time on those girls when you have me?" She dropped her tone to a wheedling singsong.

Holden's eyes popped. He was quite drunk enough to buy her act, and his arms encircled her with rapid enthusiasm.

"Don't know," he murmured, confused but obviously delighted. "Didn't think you were interested."

The prince abruptly sprouted as many hands as any six men she had ever met, and every one of them gleefully began wandering all over her. She resisted her instinct to slap them away.

The farm lad subsided reluctantly, and the toughs scowled at one another behind his back.

"Let's go upstairs," Alex murmured theatrically in the prince's ear. She let her lips touch the lobe, and she breathed warmly against him. "I've had enough of this place, haven't you?"

He staggered to his feet, almost dropping her, and she leaned against him as if bracing herself, but she was actually supporting him as they staggered across the floor. He still managed to keep at least a dozen hands on her at every given moment. He nuzzled at her ear, and she made a flirty pout at him, trying to haul him bodily up the stairs without being obvious.

They left the disgruntled toughs and the crestfallen barmaid behind them. Alex fumbled for the key to their room. Her hand closed on it as his arms wrapped around her and his mouth dipped to take hers.

His lips were warm and soft, and in her surprise, she did not manage to close her mouth in time to block him out. His warm tongue swept inside, touching hers, and his lean, slim body pressed her against the door with unexpected aggression.

Alex struggled to escape, caught entirely off-guard, but her arm lay pinned between her body and the door. With one hand still on the key and the other trapped, she could not shove him away easily.

She made a furious sound, which he echoed with a low, contented murmur from deep in his throat. He tasted of ale and of something better, something she'd never tasted before. He had the mouth of a devil, skillful and wicked, making her gasp with the intensity of his passion. His tongue tickled at her palate, teasing sweetly against hers. The kiss ignited a low flare of desire in her belly, tempting her to respond in kind.

Alex blinked, suddenly struggling, her unexpected response making her desperate to escape the kiss. Though he was only one man with a single set of hands, one of them had already dipped inside her dress and curved warmly about her breast. The other slid behind the small of her back, drawing her against him. He was hard for her, his cock pressing eagerly against her hip. He made that low, sweet sound again, both vulnerable and urgent, and kissed her as if he would gladly drown in her mouth.

She managed to haul out the key and rip her mouth away, finally breaking the kiss. She jerked loose long enough to turn in his arms and shove the key into the latch, finally forcing it to turn. The latch clicked open as he grasped her again and tried to push her up against the door for another kiss. He stumbled and nearly fell when the hinges swung inward, dumping them inside the room. She very nearly escaped him, but he was relentless. He caught her again when she paused to shut the door behind them.

"Alex," he moaned. She heard the tenderness in his voice, sweet and aching with passion even though he was drunk as a lord. His hands trailed flame over her, finding their way inside her clothes again, and she realized with dismay how much her body wanted him to continue.

She shoved him as hard as she could, and he fell on his arse, blinking up at her with stunned failure to understand, one hand still outstretched.

"Let's get something clear right away, before this goes on for another second." She wiped her mouth, proud she was still able to speak and to move without shaking. "You were about to start a riot in the common room by flirting with that barmaid, and this was all I could think of to get you out of there without a fight. I didn't want to kiss you, and I didn't want you to kiss me. If you don't behave better than this next time, there won't be another time after, because we'll never stop in a town or stay at an inn again.

"What's more, I'll thank you not to play the grand, pompous lordling when we're supposed to be posing as farmers. Even worse, you seem determined to drink until you can't stand up. What did you mean to do after those thugs attacked you, I'd like to know?" She knew her voice had risen from a hissed whisper to nearly a shout, and with an effort, she forced herself to stop yelling. As she stood there glaring at him, she despaired of saying more. She could tell the only thing she'd driven through his drunken skull was the realization she didn't mean to let him have her after all.

Carl burst in, and Alex didn't think she'd ever been more relieved to see him. "Let's get this royal lout of ours out of his boots and put him to bed so he can sleep off all the ale he's drunk." Prince Holden was no slouch at undressing a lady when his mind was set, drunk or not. Her dress hung askew, its fastening hooks undone, the cloth entirely pushed off one shoulder. Her mind insisted on reminding her his hands had been on her, all over her breast, nearly ravishing her with pleasure. She swallowed hard and straightened her clothes quickly.

As Carl reached for the sitting prince, he blinked up owlishly and quite gently toppled over backward, insensible.

"God's wounds." Alex uttered a dire oath and helped Carl wrestle the prince out of his boots and haul him up onto the miserable straw mattress. "That man has as many hands as a battalion of troops who've been quartered away from camp followers for a year," she muttered irritably. She should take a lover to keep Prince Holden from agitating her so badly. She needed to get her passions worked out of her system safely and remember why he wasn't worth her time.

"Those thugs know he was all but passing out on his feet, and they think you were, too," Carl muttered. "They'll be along after the inn settles, you mark my words, hoping for easy pickings."

"Should we wait or go to ground, do you think?"

"It's a damned wet night, and we can't move the chest without help, plus there'd be His Highness to carry. I don't think we want them to follow us out into the countryside. Who knows how many of them there are? I say we fight here. They won't expect either of you to be able, and they'll think they can take me. They'll be careless."

"We'll keep watch then and wait."

Alex seated herself in a chair next to the door with her sword across her lap and waited to find out whether Carl was right. She was drowsing lightly when the click and scrape of lock picks roused her. She eased herself up without making a sound, standing next to the door and waiting for the soft creak as it swung inward. She slid noiselessly behind the lead man and neatly brought her blade up against his throat.

"I don't believe you were invited," she murmured, pushing her sword up tight below his chin. "Would you like to leave quietly and keep your head, or would you prefer to leave noisily without it?"

"Lads," he called in a throttled, desperate whisper. "Lay off, lads!" Alex heard a frantic clatter as the rest of the ruffians fled down the stairwell before Carl lit the lamp, most of the brigands vanishing without ever being seen.

"Abandoning their leader to his fate," she mocked him. "You never even got near his purse. What kind of worthless highwayman are you, anyhow? You may want to think twice in the future before troubling travelers." Alex released the lead thief, giving him a none-too-gentle shove out into the hall. She re-locked the door in his wake, glad to have accomplished the encounter without bloodshed.

She yielded her place to Carl in case the thieves returned and lay down on the floor to get some rest.

Prince Holden slept through the entire affair.

The prince awoke in the morning looking obscenely cheerful, completely without the hangover he so richly deserved, at least in Alex's judgment. He apparently had no memory of having groped her, either, though he had been so thorough her skin still tingled, remembering the warm caress of his hands.

"Let's put this town behind us," she muttered irritably to Carl. "Then I'm shaving him even if we have to hold him at sword-point."

Holden skulked out to the wagon behind the stable boys, who carried their chest of weapons. He looked appropriately chagrined as Carl filled him in on all the various parts of the evening he did not remember.

He remained quiet during the day, whether sitting in the back of the wagon or taking his turn on the seat. The mules wouldn't let him drive them. They grew fractious the second he touched the reins. They pulled against one another in the traces instead of drawing the wagon, balking and kicking.

"They can sense fear," Carl commiserated, taking the reins back from him. "Or possibly inexperience. You have to hold them like you know what you're doing, see?"

Holden nodded unhappily and subsided, staring down as the road slowly rolled by. He looked so miserable Alex very nearly felt sorry for him.

Chapter Five

When they stopped for the night by the roadside, Holden offered no further objections to Alex's plans to shave him. She heated the water and fished out the shaving kit while Carl went off to hunt game for their supper. She lathered the prince's beard carefully and maneuvered the razor over his face, taking great pains not to cut him. He sat quite still, mournful, his hair combed down flat onto his skull as if to make him as unattractive as possible.

When she finished, she patted his face clean of lather with a bit of cloth and eyed him critically. He stared up at her sheepishly, running his hand over his bare face. She was forced to admit she'd hardly have known him without his beard.

She hadn't been quite sure what he'd look like without his characteristic goatee, but she should have known he'd be just as attractive without any beard at all. His skin was blemished with a few scars, but somehow they managed not to look like flaws. Instead, they left him seeming rugged and strong, rather than looking like a pampered aristocrat or dandy. His jaw was nicely turned and square, his chin neatly cleft. Without the beard to distract the viewer, his blue-gray eyes were even more striking, smoldering out of his smooth face with a blatant challenge that felt distinctly sexual. Looking at the results of her handiwork made her feel more than a little uncomfortable.

"Well?"

"You'll do," she said shortly. "You should let your whole beard come back in on its own. You won't be so distinctive without the goatee. If people keep recognizing you, we'll be fighting robbers all the way to Eire."

"I don't want to leave East Anglia." The prince firmed his jaw and glared up at her. "I want to stay and fight to defend the kingdom."

Alex packed the shaving gear away. "Carl?"

"Yes?"

"Get into the chest in the back of the wagon." She pulled the rawhide loop from around her neck and tossed him the key. "Get out the wooden practice blades."

Carl obeyed Alex's command, fetching back the wooden swords. He smirked a little, though he looked like he was trying not to.

"Why do we need those?" Prince Holden looked disdainfully at the wooden blades. "Shouldn't we use real ones?"

"To keep anyone from getting hurt," Alex said tartly. Carl tossed her one sword, then passed the other to the prince, who swung it contemplatively and barely managed not to whack himself in the shin.

"Point taken." He gripped the hilt as if holding a rapier.

"Being able to fight would be a good thing, regardless whether we stay in East Anglia or go farther abroad," Alex told him. "Are you up for a lesson?"

"I'm quite a good fencer."

"I'm sure you are." She held up her blade, demonstrating the correct grip. "Hold the hilt like so." She waited for him to imitate her and saluted him, then set herself in a ready position, waiting until he did the same. "Not like that," she corrected his grip again. "This isn't a rapier. It's much heavier and less nimble. Hold it that way, and you'll soon have your blade knocked right out of your hand. The broadsword has sharp edges, and can even be used as a club. The whole thing is a weapon."

She could anticipate how he would fight. He'd be prone to use the body of his blade for blocking and would think of scoring mainly with the tip. He'd want to dance all over the place, and would wear himself out in the process.

He wouldn't be as strong as he expected. His shoulder and arm would tire. Soon afterward he'd run out of air and grow weary from dancing about. He'd skitter around like a spinning top, and last nearly as long.

She let him wear himself out, twitching aside from his triumphant lunges, watching him circle and dance as she easily slapped away all of his attacks. She suppressed her smile. Fencing in a mask didn't teach him to govern his face, and he gave every feint away by looking in that direction before he moved. She could easily anticipate each attack he made before he ever launched it.

He finally wore himself down without conclusive results and glared sheepishly at her, a little embarrassed and flustered.

"You're trying to fence with a broadsword," she told him gently. "You're going to have to unlearn some old habits and learn some new ones to replace them. Carl?"

Carl accepted the wooden sword from the prince and faced her. They traded a few blows at half-speed. "See how he's standing his ground?" she pointed out. "You need to move like he does--much less than you do to fence. Watch how he uses the edge of the blade both to deflect and to attack." She let Carl touch her with the edge of his practice sword. "Like that. The broadsword's weight also makes it useful for battering. Full speed, Carl. Watch."

They spent a while fighting hammer and tongs. Alex loved the exhilaration of battle. Carl had always been one of her favorite practice partners, and he knew her so well he could beat her two times out of five on most days. Quick, dogged, and strong, he was the epitome of a good, solid soldier.

Distracted by calling advice to Holden, Alex found herself on the edge of Carl's blade over and over again. The last time she hit the turf hard, but sprang back up sturdily, lowering her sword. "That's how it's done. If you try hard, we might get you minimally competent inside a couple of months. Right now, you'd be all right against a rank amateur, but you'd be in serious trouble against anyone with training. The first problem is your eyes." She moved up to the prince. "I'm going to quarter-speed. Where am I going to tap you? Tell me as soon as you know."

He answered slowly, lagging until she launched each blow before responding, and she shook her head. "No, sooner than that. Watch my eyes."

"Right arm?" He followed her eyes this time as she targeted him, deliberately telegraphing her intent through her gaze.

"Good." She pulled back. "That's what you're doing. You give your plans away with your eyes every damned time, including when you're trying a feint. Your body moves left, but your eyes are moving to the right. That's how I always know where you're going to end up. That's one of the worst bad habits you need to break. Ideally, you should keep your eyes on your opponent's face as much as you can, to read his intentions and hide your own." She tossed him Carl's sword again.

"Now try to fool me."

Holden accepted the sword, trying to incorporate all her advice at once. His struggle proved moderately successful. He managed to fool her once or twice before he grew so tired they had to stop. They went to sit before the fire to rest. Carl sliced bread and cheese from their meager stores while the prince flexed his arm, grimacing.

"You're right. That thing's heavy."

"A real one is much heavier." She wasn't wearing her sword, or she'd have handed it to him to heft. "We won't be sparring with those until you develop some skill or until you actually need to injure an opponent."

He grew still, considering. "How many opponents have you killed?"

She looked soberly into the fire, and Carl did too. Both of them had killed men in the past, though Alex hated to do so. "Probably around ten. Definitely four." She reached out and poked the fire, sending up a shower of sparks into the night. She hooked the kettle with the sturdy stick Carl had cut for a poker, pouring herself a steaming mug of water for an infusion of herbs.

"What's killing a man like?"

"Ugly and terrifying. The fight moves faster than you can think, mostly. I'm afraid battle isn't a place for compassion or hesitation. In battle, you kill or get killed." She put a pinch of aniseed inside a thin linen pouch and laid it in the water, waiting for the infusion to steep. A pleasant scent of licorice filled the camp. "How's your arm?"

"Sore."

"If you cramp up, stretch the muscle away from the pain. Don't curl around it." She demonstrated. "Try pinching your lip right under your nose, too. Don't look at me like that. Both those things often help a cramp release. You should work to build up the muscles in your arms. You can use either or both of them to wield your sword, and we'll want to balance your physical training in any case." She gazed at the liquid in her cup instead of meeting his eyes. His handsome face, shorn of the familiar goatee and mustache, still made her feel uncomfortable.

"My hand hurts worse than my arm," he said wryly, working his fingers while rubbing the muscles in his palm with the thumb of his left hand.

"We'll have to get you some good gloves. But even so, if you train hard, you'll blister. Then the blisters will break, at least until you build up a layer of callus." That would probably make him give up. She wondered if he'd ever carried through with anything that actually proved painful. She looked at him quietly and drank a sip of her aniseed brew. The infusion was a little strong, just the way she liked. "How sincere are you about learning to fight, Prince Holden?"

He looked down at his hand, making a fist, then flexed his fingers. His mouth set in a firm line. "We'll have to get gloves."

Alex glanced at Carl, who maintained a steady, neutral expression. They would have to wait and see if the prince had the strength of character to persist when the going got tough. She drank her infusion and gazed into the flames, aware of Prince Holden's eyes on her. She didn't acknowledge his gaze, eating slowly and neatly. She savored each bite of her supper, then cleaned her plate and mug, setting them aside to wait for breakfast.

She could sense the prince brooding, and wasn't surprised when he sidled a little closer as Carl excused himself to answer the call of nature.

"I apologize for last night."

She blinked and leaned back a little. That wasn't what she'd been expecting, not at all.

"I don't suppose I was thinking clearly. I haven't been out among the public very often. I didn't realize drinking was unwise, or understand I was being indiscreet." His cheeks colored; this was clearly a difficult admission for him. "Carl told me we were attacked, and I slept right through it. I don't suppose drinking so much ale will do anything to convince you I'm a good man."

Alex put a stick on the fire, wondering what to say. "Not much," she hazarded at last. "Nor will pawing me within an inch of my life."

He colored to the roots of his hair. "I don't remember that."

"Little wonder. You were very deep in your cups."

"I wish I remembered." His voice was hushed, and she felt his gaze caress her. "Touching you isn't something I would have wanted to miss. I would very much have wanted to do it right."

"You weren't any slouch." Her voice came out very dry. "Another few seconds and you'd have had me out of my frock. Right in the common room, before I could get you to safety." She exaggerated, just a little, to make her point.

He flushed. "That doesn't sound like me. I've always prided myself on," he swallowed audibly, his cheeks still flushed. "Being quite good."

She looked up, catching his gaze, ignoring the *frisson* it gave her. "My mother once told me 'a man is only as good in bed as he is out of it.'" She watched him narrowly to make sure he marked her meaning.

"I suppose I deserved that." He looked away, awkwardly reaching for the kettle. She stopped him irritably and gave him a bit of cloth to pad the hot handle before he could burn himself. She watched him fill a mug and add mint leaves, pulverizing them between his fingers before putting them in the straining pouch. He made a mess, of course, and he would be drinking plenty of stray leaf fragments. She let him fumble, listening for Carl to return and hoping he'd be back quickly.

The prince sat up with her and Carl until the fire burned low, not talking much as they discussed their next day's route. They eventually bundled into the wagon bed for the night, Carl in the middle despite the prince's best efforts to make other arrangements. Alex took the first watch, staring up into the stars and watching wisps of mist pass across the sky. The moon was nearly full, bright and soft. She wondered if Prince Gavin had already pulled his men back into the city. The Danes could be conducting a siege already. She would have to venture back into the towns as they traveled and gather all the gossip she could. She'd need to visit some towns anyway when the time came to buy provisions.

Humoring the prince with battle lessons was all very well and good, but she knew she mustn't allow his training to distract from her primary goal. She must take him west, out of harm's way, no matter how fiercely any of them longed to stand and fight.

Chapter Six

"Three. Two. Six. Good," Alex called as the prince performed the appropriate parries. He showed no signs of giving up his attempt to learn swordplay, though he'd sprouted a fine crop of blisters, just as she'd predicted.

Dealing with defeat was no easier than nursing his sore hands, either. At first losing plainly rankled the prince, and she could easily provoke him to anger. His annoyance made him forget all his lessons and resulted in an even faster defeat the next time. To his credit, he'd gradually learned not to sulk too much about being beaten time and again. After a while he began to firm his mouth and continue on without complaint after a thrashing, which surprised her a little. She didn't say anything, watching him suffer and testing his resolve.

She wasn't raised to be cruel, though, so she bought a bottle of balm from a healer in a small village that lay along their path. She waited until lunchtime to bring it out, when they were all hunkered around the cook fire. Holden ate slowly, painfully trying to manage his knife and his plate with cracked and bleeding hands. They were in poor condition, especially the right hand. She'd been watching earlier when Carl's blade bounced off the hilt of the prince's sword and smashed his forefinger. His fingernail had already turned black and looked as though it might eventually come off. He made no complaint.

She pulled the balm out when he finished his food. "Set your plate aside and let Carl tend to the washing." That represented a reward of sorts. She'd insisted from the beginning they each take their own share of the domestic chores. However, this mercy was well earned, and she didn't like to make the prince put his raw hands in the filthy dishwater. "Hold out your hands."

He did, and she poured a dollop of salve into his right palm. The medicine smelled of herbs and clean things, mainly comfrey and arnica. She'd made sure the healer wasn't some self-styled alchemist with a penchant for filthy chemical potions that did more harm than good.

She began rubbing the salve into his skin, gently rather than briskly. His palm was a ruined mess, cracked and crusted, oozing blood. "You'd never done a lick of hard work in your life. Look at this. You had soft hands like a woman's."

"They won't be for long," he said quietly, turning his palm over so she could reach the back. "They're nothing like yours, either, though perhaps they soon will be."

She couldn't be sure whether he intended his words as an insult or a compliment. Before she could stop herself, her gaze flew to meet his. He looked quietly back at her, inscrutable. His beard had begun to come in well, stubble thick and heavy on his jaw. The hair caught the firelight, glowing red-gold. Christ's blood. Was there anything that didn't look good on the man?

"I've had a sword in my hand all my life," she muttered, defensive.

"I know." He let her begin on his left hand. "I used to see you drilling with the soldiers when you were small."

"Father was kind enough to indulge me, yes. I think he hoped I'd grow out of being a tomboy," she said shortly. "But after mother died, learning to fight was the obvious way for me to stay near him." She surveyed his hands and re-corked the bottle. "Take this and use it every day. We'll give you a day or two off from sword drill. Those hands won't ever harden if they don't get a chance to heal." She watched as he stowed the salve in his pack. "Besides, I need to take us into the next town and sound out the gossip. We can suspend your training for a couple of days."

"You're taking me along?" He spoke slowly, surprised. She'd strictly declared towns off-limits after the attempted robbery, and he hadn't seen one at anything slower than a jog since their first disastrous night nearly two weeks ago.

"You've earned it. You've been working hard." She looked away. "I'm rather hoping you'll stay sober, though."

"All right," he agreed easily. He continued looking intently at her, and his gaze made her nervous. She found she was quite glad of Carl's presence.

"I think I'll go out and try to shoot something to cook for supper." She unlocked the weapons chest and pulled out a crossbow. Looking up, she flinched a little to find him at her shoulder, staring curiously into the box.

"May I come with you?" He picked up one of the crossbows for himself before she could shut the trunk. "I'm a decent shot."

"Can you be quiet?"

"I can."

"Then come on." If he didn't stay quiet, she'd send him to scout one way and go the other way herself.

He remained quiet at first, staying at her side. His hobnailed boots weren't well suited for stalking game in silence, but he had enough sense to step lightly.

She scanned the fields for hares, moving slowly, but her concentration was off. She knew the prince must be up to something. He was incapable of innocence. Since he'd arranged to be alone with her, she suspected he had plans to make a pass.

Hoping to disrupt his intentions, she found a place for him to settle, a stony outcrop looking down into a bit of grassy valley where rabbits were likely to have a warren. "Stay here and watch for rabbits while I go try to startle a pheasant or something at the edge of the wood."

"I make you nervous." The corner of his mouth quirked up, self-deprecating.

She didn't try to deny the truth. "You do. Any time someone treats me like prey, I get uneasy."

To his credit, he didn't attempt denial. "I don't usually pursue women."

"No, they jump into your bed all by themselves." She gave him a wry stare.

He shrugged, equally off-hand. "Near enough."

"Then all you have to do is find a bed and wait. I want no part of it."

"I'm tired of prey that doesn't put up a struggle." He looked briefly away from her, and she could see something almost weary in the set of his shoulders.

She raised a brow at him. She'd believe him on a cold day in Hell.

He shrugged, seeing her disbelief, and shifted uncomfortably. "Serving girls and barmaids are all very well and good for a night's pleasure, but they have nothing to offer afterward. All the ladies at court are shallow and dull." He pulled a wry face. "I'd rather court a girl with something to her. Like you." They sat silently for a long moment. Alex resisted the desire to squirm uncomfortably under his warm regard. "The problem with me," he said at length, his brow furrowed, "is that everything has always been too easy." He leaned toward her, intent. She could sense how important this was to him.

She looked down at his damaged hands, which gave silent evidence of perhaps the first thing he'd ever done that was difficult. He reached out to her and touched her cheek lightly with his fingertips. "But you aren't easy at all, and I find I quite like it."

"You're going to have to learn some things aren't just hard," she said gently. "Some things are actually impossible."

Like shooting game, evidently. She left him to watch for rabbits and wandered along the forest's edge until nightfall, but neither of them spied anything to shoot at. They returned to Carl empty-handed, and all they had to eat was hardtack. The prince chewed his without complaint, if without pleasure, and drank his mint infusion. There were fewer leaves left floating in his cup this time, Alex noted, and he'd swiftly learned to use a pad on the handle of the kettle. She'd almost trust him to brew the infusion for all of them now, but instead each of them made a cup independently, self-reliant.

Carl seemed to sense the tension crackling in the air, and nobody talked much as they sat around the fire under the stars.

At bedtime, Alex spread her blankets under the wagon bed instead of on top with the prince and Carl. When the prince gave her a sidelong look as if he meant to join her, she bared her teeth at him with enough ferocity he stayed where he was, reluctantly spreading out his blankets next to Carl's. He could like her indifference as much as he pleased, but it was about time the man learned he couldn't have everything he wanted.

That, too, should be good for him.

Chapter Seven

The next day they rode into Tanton, which was a nice, large town, almost a small city. They arrived about an hour after dawn. The town square was turned out for market day, stalls displaying a variety of wares. They immediately bought a large quantity of cured meat. After their skimpy supper the previous evening, the meat looked like a feast. The all tucked a few strips into a convenient pocket and began to chew their way through them. Breakfast of hardtack could keep a soldier marching, but it wasn't particularly enjoyable, and failed to satisfy the belly's craving for something with substance.

Alex gave Carl her purse. She directed him to purchase a variety of foodstuffs, plus more dried mint and aniseed for infusions. She wanted a pot of honey, as well. She watched over the prince, who was quite happy to wander through the nooks and crannies of the market, examining the various wares for sale. He seemed particularly interested at the booth in front of the smithy, picking up hand-tooled daggers and examining them wistfully, putting them down again with great reluctance. Alex knew he had one of his own tucked away in his boot, though she suspected he believed she had no idea he'd sneaked a weapon out when they left his room at the castle.

She chattered with various merchants and customers, eager for news of the capital, though she didn't glean much of use.

Things went well at first. The prince kept himself on his best behavior, subdued and following her lead. However, as he trailed her through the market on the way back to the livery where they'd left their wagon, a girl hawking for customers in front of one of the stalls spotted him and gave a startled little squeak.

She was loud enough to draw a variety of curious stares. The girl ducked her head and fled back into the stall, hiding in the shadow of a truly enormous man.

Alex frowned. The stall was a butcher's, selling fresh meat. It was too late to slip away. The man squinted at them and scowled as he spotted the prince. He stood behind a wooden table, clutching half the skinned carcass of a sheep in one hand and a cleaver in the other. Ribs lay on the table, neatly chopped in segments and ready for cooking. Fresh blood stains were spattered thickly across his apron and more dripped from the edge of his cleaver.

"Is that who I think he is?" He demanded of the girl, who covered her mouth and turned away.

"Who is she?" Alex hissed to Holden with alarm. "Is she one of your paramours?"

"I...I don't know. I don't remember," he stammered. Alex squinted at the woman, who quite looked the part of a wronged maiden, hiding her face and blushing miserably.

"You," the butcher snarled at the prince. His loud, hostile voice drew a large and interested audience immediately. "Are you the knave from the castle who ruined our Sal?"

Alex groaned to herself. There could be no denying who the prince was, not with the girl standing right there.

"Good sir," she tried to calm him, "let's discuss this over an ale. I'm sure we can arrive at an understanding."

"Hiding behind a lady's skirts. She would be your guard, then?" The man snapped at Holden, turning his unfriendly snarl momentarily on Alex. He didn't put down the cleaver. "I care not whose son you are. You are no man."

42

She glanced at Holden, worried his temper would flare at the provocation, but he wasn't paying attention. He looked stricken, his eyes fixed on something else, something at the back of the stall.

She followed his gaze to a small boy with red-gold hair and a terrified expression, barely old enough to wear breeches instead of an infant's long, loose shirt. The lad stood clinging to one of the stall poles, visibly trying to decide whether to cry or keep watching.

The butcher brandished his cleaver and maneuvered his muscular bulk out from behind his wooden table.

Alex stepped forward. "Please. Not in front of the little boy."

That made the man waver. He glanced back. The additional weight of his attention decided the child, who darted forward and buried his face in his mother's skirts, wailing.

"Come forward and fight me," the man hissed at Holden. "If you have any honor at all."

Alex winced. She couldn't allow a fight to happen, no matter what. She reached for the prince's arm as he pulled the dagger from his boot and started to step forward, bristling. She shook her head.

"You don't fight." She kept her voice flat and businesslike. "That's my job." She turned to the man, keeping a sharp eye on his cleaver.

"I can take him," Holden insisted, close to her ear. "Give me a sword."

"What will you do with it? Kill the family's chief provider, leaving your son to starve?" She hissed the words as quietly as she could.

Incredibly, that silenced the prince. The fight flowed out of him, and he bent to tuck his dagger back into his boot.

Alex turned to the man. "He will not fight, and I would rather not, either." She spread her open hands. "We'll be glad to leave a gift of money for the child and his mother."

The man's attention wandered, his eyes sliding to Alex's right. She realized suddenly the prince had left her elbow. He stepped forward, bending to one knee next to the little boy, who glanced up at him, his little red face wet with tears. The prince's hand went into his pocket and came back out holding a strip of cured meat.

He extended the tidbit in his fingers, and the boy's hand darted forward to grab it, his tears suddenly forgotten. He crammed it into his mouth with all possible haste, his eyes round as he looked up into the prince's gentle gaze. Holden reached out, tentatively, and ruffled the untidy red-blond hair, studying the little lad's face with a stunned expression.

Before anyone could react, Alex stepped up next to him and pulled her purse out of her pocket. There wasn't much inside, perhaps two or three sovereigns, but she knew she had more on hand than Holden himself. She proffered the open purse. After a shame-filled glance at the furious butcher, the boy's mother snatched the money out and tucked it away hastily inside her bodice.

Her action deflated her protector, who scowled bitterly as Alex carefully gathered the prince's collar in her fist and tugged him to his feet, then backed them away. There would be no more attempts at newsgathering, not in this town.

Alex was uncomfortably aware of hostile eyes still watching them, so she hurried to reunite with Carl and get back to their camp. Happily, they managed without further incident.

"Let's put some leagues between ourselves and this place before they decide to send out a lynching party," she suggested quietly.

They packed up their camp quickly and returned to the road. The prince remained absolutely silent as they rattled along, brooding in the back of the wagon.

Glancing at his sober face, Alex realized this was the first time he'd ever seen one of his by-blows. Perhaps this was the first time he'd ever understood they were real, and his.

Chapter Eight

Alex went into the next town alone. The prince didn't protest or ask to go along, helping gather wood as soon as they stopped, then hunkering down with Carl next to the fire.

She was relieved beyond measure to be on her own after so long a time spent in the prince's company. Carl didn't grate on her, at least not often, but Prince Holden represented a constant drain on her. She had to keep her guard high around him and remain wary at every moment. Walking down the road alone, with a dagger concealed inside her vest, she felt as if she could breathe freely for the first time in days.

The town seemed peaceable enough, if not as large and prosperous as the one they'd fled. She soon found a tavern and ordered a flagon of ale. She took care to sit down with her back to a wall, sipping cautiously.

As the afternoon wore on and faded, men began to drift into the tavern. She overheard much talk about the lack of rain, whose wife had cuckolded him with another man, and other matters of no import to her. She also overheard occasional discussion of the Danes. She pricked up her ears, listening carefully. A little knot of men discussed how Prince Gavin had retreated to Norwich, leading his troops, but the Danes had not responded as predicted. They'd showed little interest in confronting the massed army at Norwich. Instead, they separated into small raiding parties and dispersed into the countryside, where they went about plundering and pillaging homesteads, terrorizing small towns to their hearts' content.

The news troubled her more than a little. She frowned, pretending to sip her ale, and dipped her fingertip into a puddle on the table, drawing runes absently.

For a woman to travel alone was unheard of, so she drew interested glances from many of the men. Some looked a little disapproving. Others were obviously intrigued. As the evening drew on, she realized one young lad in particular was lingering in the tavern longer than his fellows, eyeing her with open appreciation.

He was comely enough, tall and dark. Once he'd seen her returning his stare, he smiled at her and stood up, approaching her in an easy amble. He moved gracefully for a farmer. He didn't have the predatory glide of a good soldier, but moved with a solid confidence she found quite charming. She'd been meaning to take a lover ever since Holden started getting under her skin. This should be as good an opportunity as any.

Alex smiled at him and pushed out a chair with her foot. He rested his hands on the back of it.

"Hello. What brings a lady to our town by herself?"

"Business." Alex remained friendly even though she declined to be more specific.

"Can I buy you something?"

"I have plenty." She didn't want any more ale. "But you're welcome to stay and talk." She watched him take his seat. "Crops need rain?"

He laughed, showing strong white teeth. "Always." He had a mug of his own, and he swallowed a gulp of his ale. "But you're more interested in tales of the Danes, if I'm any judge."

"Observant." She laughed softly. "I have kin in Norwich, and I'm concerned for their safety."

"You have the Norwich accent. I should have guessed." He smiled at her, which looked quite good on him.

"Do you own a farm hereabouts?"

"My father does. I work the land with him and my brothers." He hesitated. "I'm the youngest. They married all the decent lasses in the area, and left none for me."

"You've the same chance at an inheritance as at a lass, I suppose."

"True. Now you know, you won't give me the time of day, will you?"

"I don't care what you stand to inherit," Alex laughed. "You're quite well-set-up, it appears, from where I sit."

He blushed, a bit shy, but modesty was to be expected of a country boy. "Are you going to be in town for long?"

"A while, I think. As long as this town suits me, anyway." Alex slid her gaze at him, flirtatious. He resembled the prince not at all. He would do very well indeed. If she were a town girl, she'd be over the moon for him. She didn't know when she'd passed a more pleasant quarter of an hour.

"Then I hope it suits for a good long time." His eyes were merry.

"I'm Alex."

"Edgar," he answered, and inclined his head, tapping his mug lightly with hers. "It's getting late. If I don't get home soon, my father will give my share of supper to the sow."

"Then go. I suppose I might see you, if I come here again." She gave him a slow smile.

"I suppose you might."

"Bring your supper with you next time," Alex teased, and he grinned.

"I'll be here, without a doubt."

She waited until he was gone, finishing her ale before she went out herself, strolling down the road. She was whistling by the time she entered the camp, and found Prince Holden sitting watch, struggling to keep himself awake.

"You're late returning. I was worried."

"I've been gathering gossip," she shrugged, dismissing his concern. "Nothing much I liked, either." Except for Edgar, but there was no need to mention him.

"Oh?" Her diversion worked. He went for the bait and forgot her personal business. "What news of Norwich?"

"Your brother retreated to the city, but the Danes didn't follow. They've spread out instead to terrorize the folk who live in the countryside."

He scowled and poked the fire savagely. "Now what?"

"I'm not sure. I suppose Prince Gavin will lead a squadron out and challenge any of them he can find."

"That doesn't sound promising."

No, but she was a little surprised he understood. "That's how warfare goes. You make a plan, your enemy responds, and you have to adapt."

"I suppose." He sipped his aniseed infusion, making a face and adding a bit of honey. "Shall I make you a cup?"

"I've drunk enough," she refused politely.

"I still don't like you going off alone."

"Carl will look out for you."

"Believe it or not, I'm not concerned about myself." He gave her a wry look. "What would we do if you disappeared? We should stay together."

"You don't blend well in a town, as we've seen too many times already." There was no way she was going to accept him as a tag-along on her next trip to town, not after arranging to meet Edgar.

"If you were set on by brigands, you'd be glad to have me there."

"No, I wouldn't. I'd have to watch out for you. If I'm alone, I can take care of myself instead of worrying about your safety."

"I'm no more than a burden to you, then." He picked at a scab that was beginning to peel off his knuckle.

"You're my duty." It was a kinder way of saying the same thing, she supposed. "My mission, my responsibility."

"Your friend?"

She frowned, feeling vaguely guilty. "I can't say I've ever thought of you as such."

"Why not?"

She resisted the impulse to roll her eyes. "I don't think of your father or your brother as my friends either, if that helps. You're my employers."

"I guess we are." He laughed at himself, a little gruff. "I've been thinking, Alex."

She bit her tongue and didn't make the smart comment already waiting behind her lips. "Oh?"

"About the little lad." His brow wrinkled.

"He looked quite like you." She kept her tone very gentle, glad she hadn't given in to her impulse to taunt him.

"Yes, he did." The prince fed the fire soberly. "I'll never know who he is or what he does with himself. Or the others, either."

A worrying number of them might exist, she knew.

"Do you think that child will grow up hating me like his family does?" He scratched at his beard, a little nervous.

Hatred was a likely outcome, though she hesitated to say so. "He was glad to have the meat." If the prince were Carl, she'd reach and pat his hand or put her arm about his shoulders to comfort him. But he wasn't.

"What about the others, those I haven't seen?"

By-blows often grew up to haunt their fathers; primogeniture worked that way. Still, he was not in line to be king, and they shouldn't be a factor in the succession. "I can't say." She wished she'd accepted the offer of a hot drink; brewing it would have given him something useful to do.

He sat there quietly, still fidgeting with his hands. She could tell they pained him.

"Carl has the next watch?" she asked at length.

"Yes."

"I'll turn in, then."

She curled up beneath the wagon, uncomfortably aware she'd abandoned him, somewhat forlorn, to wrestle with the demons of his conscience alone throughout his watch.

Chapter Nine

Alex slept soundly. The prince slept not at all. He never woke Carl, but sat watch the whole night through. She found him still sitting by the fire, shivering a bit with his chilled hands wrapped around a mug of his preferred mint infusion, when she opened her eyes in the morning.

While the prince went to tend the call of nature, Alex roused Carl and told him she planned to return to town in the evening, not to return before the following morning.

He glanced aside at the prince, who was emerging from the bush and bracken a short distance from the camp, and winked. "I'll sit on his head to keep him here, if I must."

"He'll be too tired to argue." She picked up her training sword. "I'll see to that."

She worked him hard all morning long. His reflexes were slow from lack of sleep. She beat him repeatedly, but he refused to surrender, his jaw set. She thumped his ribs quite sharply once. She knew she'd bruised him, but he remained stubborn. He merely lifted his blade to endure another thumping.

She pondered him as they sparred. He was getting better. He'd stopped dancing around like he was fencing. His strength had developed rapidly. At Carl's suggestion, she'd set him to doing the heavier physical tasks as their trip progressed. He kept busy moving their baggage, chopping up trees for the fire, and carrying water. All the hard work showed in more than the poor condition of Holden's hands. He could fight much longer without succumbing to exhaustion, and he could hit harder. His strength had grown quite satisfactorily.

They'd been forced to start giving him a larger share of the food, also. He'd been working hard, and he needed red meat to help him build muscle. She made sure he ate as much as he needed, though she also had to start watching their money with some caution. The countryside was gripped in an unseasonable drought, and hunting was quite poor for early summer. They'd need to find a larger town soon, one where they could cash in one of the notes the king gave Alex and get coin in exchange.

Distracted by her worries, Alex failed to anticipate a feint, and Holden caught her arm sharply with his wooden blade. She yelped and dropped her sword. His settled at her throat in an instant. Wonder and shock dawned on his face.

"Did I hurt you?" He dropped his sword, too, and reached for her arm, pushing up her sleeve, concerned.

"Only a bruise, no worse than I've given you." She shook out her arm with a bit of a grimace. "I let my attention wander, and you took advantage. Just as you should."

"I won!" A grin split his face, radiant. "For once, I beat you!"

She chuckled in spite of herself. "You did. Fair and square."

He beamed at her, his weary face transformed, and he laughed aloud, delighted. She thought for a moment he might sweep her up in his arms and swing her about, like a sack of meal.

Alex's belly flip-flopped unexpectedly, warm and dizzy. She stepped back, delicately swift, before he could touch her. "Congratulations, Prince Holden." Oh, yes, she would meet her farm boy again tonight. It was past time she cared for her needs. "We'll celebrate a bit, shall we?"

She pulled out a skin of wine and poured him a cup, then one for herself, as well. He would soon be ready to have a go with a real sword, and begin to get used to its weight. She thought he was ready enough he wouldn't be likely to hurt himself.

"Shall we go into town together tonight?" He asked her, smiling. "Have a proper meal, one we don't have to cook for once?"

"I'm off by myself this evening. Still gathering news," she watched his smile fade and swallowed a pang of guilt. "Maybe at the next town."

He watched her as she kitted herself out to go, but he didn't speak again, his celebration spoiled. Carl waved at her from behind the prince, and she saluted them both soberly, setting out.

Guilt gnawed Alex's belly as she rented a room in the town's single inn and ordered her first real bath since leaving Norwich. It was purely impossible to bathe adequately under the prince's alert and interested eye.

She luxuriated in the washtub, dipping her head under the hot water as completely as she could and washing out her long hair. Rinsing was a hard task without help, but she managed. Finishing, she wrapped her hair carefully in a bit of toweling to squeeze the excess water out, and scrubbed her body with care.

She judged she should be all right for a bit of fun. Her moon time was newly past. She smiled at the faded shard of mirror she carried, pleased at being clean, and combed out her hair until it dried, then re-wove her braid and went out to wait in the tavern.

Edgar walked in through the door shortly after dusk, and Alex greeted him with a smile. He came to join her, ordering a mug.

"I'm glad to see you here. I was afraid you'd reconsider." He seemed a little nervous, fidgeting with his hands, and she covered one of them with her own.

"I'm afraid I must be moving on very soon. But not without meeting you, as I promised."

Disappointment rose in his eyes, but he rallied well, raising his mug to her in toast. "We'll have to make the most of our time together, then."

"Yes," she said softly. "I have a room at the inn. Would you like to visit?"

He drank deeply from his mug and set it aside. "Very much."

She laid her palm on his arm and they strolled through the streets together. The lamps hanging outside houses and businesses cast a comforting glow on the street, creating little pools of light to hold the darkness at bay. She liked the feel of his arm under her palm, and enjoyed the comfortable quiet between them.

They ate supper together in the inn's common room, and Alex insisted on paying.

"This is good." He scraped up a last spoonful of stew and wiped out his bowl with a bit of bread.

He was right about the food, but Alex also realized she missed the camaraderie of listening to Carl and Holden grousing over how best to cook their latest rabbit. They could never agree on how long to fry the bacon, either. Carl liked his chewy, but Holden wanted his seared crisp. She smiled at Edgar nonetheless, and finished her own bowl neatly.

"Shall we go up?"

They did, and Alex laughed softly at the moment of awkwardness between them when the door of her room thumped shut.

"Alex."

"Shhh." She walked over to him and opened his leather coat button by button, smiling up into his face. "Let tonight be what it is."

Edgar chuckled along with her, then folded her against his chest and kissed her.

Alex went willingly, twining her arms behind his neck. She opened her mouth and touched his tongue with hers, luxuriating in the unaccustomed closeness. She had let far too much time pass since she had a man. Her body was already eager, growing slick and ready for him.

"What did I ever do to deserve you wandering through my life?" Edgar murmured against her mouth.

"Something very good, I'm sure." She reached and tugged his shirt upward, pulling it over his shoulders and head, then let him shake it off his wrists. His body was pale except for his neck and arms, which his clothing didn't cover. He was faintly smudged with dirt. She didn't care. She let her hands wander over his firm chest, savoring the feel of muscle under her fingers. The prince wouldn't be so tall, and not yet so firm. He would be lithe and warm, though.

She drew back, frowning a little at herself. "Come to bed," she urged Edgar seductively, pulling her own shirt up and off her body, revealing her breasts to him.

He inhaled softly, a sweet breathy sound, and followed her as she lay down on the bed, sinking onto the mattress. He moved to cover her, his hands shyly tracing the curve of her breasts. "Beautiful," he mumbled, his eyes hazy with desire, and he lowered his mouth to suckle at her nipple.

Alex writhed luxuriantly, curling her hand behind Edgar's head to encourage him, working to banish an image of the prince's tawny head in the same position. Curse him, anyway, what right had he to intrude on her pleasure?

She dragged Edgar up to her mouth and kissed him hotly, wriggling her hand into his breeches. Oh, yes. He felt sweet and hard in her hand, his long, slender cock capped with a thick, strong head. Alex purred into his mouth as he gasped, and stroked him slowly. He should be good for several rounds, if she was any judge of youth.

He was too shy to manage her skirts as swiftly as she wanted, so she slipped out from under him and got up. She pulled off the dress herself, stepping out of the puddle of cloth seductively. She stood bare before him.

Edgar rolled onto his back with a groan, his cock pushing at the fabric of his breeches, insistent and eager despite his inexperience.

"Off with those," she murmured, and when he obeyed, she settled over him, one thigh on either side of his. "Mmmm," she purred. "Ready?"

"Yesss." His voice fell to a hiss, and she lifted his shaft in her hand, then moved to sink right down onto him. His head tipped back, exposing his beardless throat, and she leaned in to kiss him, loving the feeling of his hard cock piercing deep inside her.

"Oh, that's good," Alex purred. She moved her head deliberately, tickling his chest with the end of her long braid. She raised herself, and his hips came up to meet her as she thrust back down.

Finishing didn't take him long at all. He lasted for couple of dozen fierce strokes, then spent himself with a groan and a curse. Alex chuckled throatily, feeling him go. She knew he'd be better for more the second time.

"Damn it," Edgar sounded sheepish. "I'm sorry."

"Don't be. We have all night," Alex nipped at his lips and rolled off him. She reached for his wrist, guiding him to touch her. "Let me show you what to do."

His callused fingertips were a little rough, but they slid well enough in the slickness of her body, and Alex moaned her appreciation. He watched her, wonder on his face, as she gasped and cried out for him, shifting against his fingers as he stroked her.

"Beautiful," he muttered, and she managed a smile for him, gasping abruptly as he touched exactly the right spot.

"There," she writhed, gasping, and he worked his fingers with growing confidence as she shivered and whimpered, kindling at last for him. She clutched at his wrist and jerkily lifted her hips. "Yes, yes, *yes*!"

He was ready again by the time she shuddered herself to rest, blinking contentedly up at him. He rolled her under him, spreading her thighs, and slid into her easily.

"Mmmm, slow," Alex suggested, her voice throaty. She licked his neck happily, tasting salt. He pressed his hips forward and she lifted hers. They began to move together, seeking a rhythm, leisurely and sweet.

Edgar lasted much longer the second time. He was young, strong, and fit. He was quite acceptable, she decided some considerable time later, after he finally gasped his way to a halt and slumped over her, his harsh breath starting to subside.

"I'll never manage again tonight," he gasped, nuzzling at her ear.

"Oh, we'll see about that." If she couldn't suck another erection out of him before they slept, she'd eat her best frock. She smiled wickedly and started working her way down, settling for a moment to torment his nipples, a little disconcerted to see they were dusky olive instead of sweetly pink. Damn it, the prince again. Curse him.

Alex attacked her work with renewed determination. "Catch hold of the headboard and don't let go," she purred at Edgar. She began to bite and suck the little peaks, making him groan until their neighbors must have thought a pig was being killed. His cock finally stirred under her, and she grinned at him, victorious.

"There you go," she told him, and cradled it in her palm, then licked the head, broad, swirling swipes of her tongue, tasting his bitterness and her own salt on his skin. Edgar cried out, startled, and his hips lifted by instinct. She slid her mouth over him and began to suck hard, rewarded when he firmed on her tongue.

"God!" he keened. She purred, making him whimper, and decided to bring him off this way, even if it cost her another good hard ride.

She pulled off all the way to the crown, swirling her tongue, then pushed down, taking him deeply into her throat. Edgar wailed, thrusting up, and she rode him easily for a few moments before she pulled off him entirely. "Stand up," she commanded. When he did, she knelt before him and sucked him in again. She cradled his smooth white arse in her hands, urging him to thrust.

His legs were wobbly, but he managed, taking her mouth slowly at first. When she blazed a challenge at him with her eyes, he moved faster, sliding across her tongue and down her throat.

She loved making men lose control, watching them fall apart for her, and this was one of the best ways. She hollowed her cheeks, sucking hard, watching his Adam's apple rise and fall as he swallowed convulsively.

His hands knotted to fists in her hair, and he gave himself over to her, a little rough, making her eyes water. Perfect. She slid her fingers between his thighs and up to his taint, making a fist. She pressed one knuckle there, pushing quite firmly.

"Jesus Christ!" Edgar yelped, and she felt his hips start to jerk. She drew back, taking his come into her mouth, and milked him dry, then bore him back onto the bed. He collapsed easily and she offered him a kiss. His eyes flew open wide when he tasted his seed. He made a startled sound, but she kissed him insistently, pushing her slick tongue into his mouth and giving him back the taste of himself.

He gentled under her, accepting, and kissed her back. Alex drew back at length, smiling, and wiped her lips.

"Now the same for me," she purred, hopeful. "Will you?"

His eyelids were drooping, but he roused himself, and she helped him adjust his position, moving him to lie between her legs, where he lay gazing hesitantly down at her.

"Lick me where you touched me with your fingers," Alex murmured. "Or if you'd rather not, you could touch me again." Once more, and she could sleep like a baby.

He opened her, and she watched his nostrils flare as he caught her scent. Slowly he lowered his head and favored her with a tentative lick, sliding his forefingers along her center at the same moment, spreading slow fire through her.

"So good," Alex purred, and he tried again, more confidently. She was melting already, incredibly sensitive. A shiver slid through her from fingertips to toes as he settled his mouth over her, sucking and licking. He put his fingers inside her, stroking them in and out of her slick, willing body.

This time was perfect, Alex's nerves melting in pure fire as her lover's tongue played and circled. She arched as his fingers opened and filled her. She cradled his head, whispering words of encouragement and passion, until she finally shattered for him, moaning his name. Pleasure crested in an overwhelming wave and rolled through her, destroying sanity. It left her gasping and spent, barely able to move.

Edgar slid up along her body and held her in his arms, mouthing at her cheek. She nuzzled his face clean with little kitten licks, tasting them both as consciousness started to ebb away.

"Who is Holden?" Edgar murmured after a moment, and her eyes flew open with dismay.

Shit. Alex dithered for a moment. Had she said his name instead? She must have.

"It's all right." Edgar sounded a little wistful, and as sleepy as she. "I know you're off in the morning, and this was only for one night."

"I'm sorry, Edgar," Alex said softly, and gathered him close. "That was incredibly rude of me." She'd have to spend some time thinking sternly about why she'd made such an unforgivable lapse, but for now she was exhausted and badly needed to sleep.

She made sure to rouse him early the next morning, and coaxed him erect with kisses to make up for her rudeness. She let him ride her, slow and tender. This time she made sure to say the right name when she came. However, he seemed a bit subdued as they dressed, giving her a sad smile when they parted.

Alex rubbed her eyes till they sparkled behind her eyelids and stared at herself in the mirror for several minutes after he'd gone. He'd been a nice fellow and a good lay, but she felt vaguely foolish nonetheless. She called for another bath. It wouldn't do to go back the prince reeking like a camp follower the morning after payday.

Edgar was long gone off to his farming by the time she emerged, her collar turned up to hide a deep purple love-bite. She paid her bill before walking out into the countryside to return to Carl and the prince. The morning was cool and fresh. She had a spring in her step by the time she arrived at camp.

Her good mood vanished when she spotted Prince Holden's face. He was worn with fatigue, deep shadows under his eyes, and she could tell he'd barely slept for a second night in a row.

"What news have you gathered, Captain?" A muscle in his jaw jumped as he spoke to her. "I trust you had urgent news indeed, for it to keep you from us overnight." His eyes studied her face and his lips compressed. She realized her collar had fallen, revealing the mark on her throat, but she refused to compromise her dignity by snatching to pull it back up.

"The crops need rain and the Danes are still working their way inland. Prince Gavin's troops are engaging them wherever they can, but the enemy has a nagging tendency to melt away into the countryside." She tossed her braid back, defiant. "Carl, it's your turn to take a bit of time off at the next town." She met the prince's glare steadily. "Your Highness, you had your recreation at the first town we passed, if you remember."

"I rather think I didn't," he said slowly, his eyes narrowing at her. "I believe that unlike you, I was misled by a false offer. My enjoyment was cut considerably shorter than I'd hoped."

Alex colored, but didn't back down. "Unlike you, I neither precipitated an attack nor invited the attention of thieves. Nor did I leave a bastard child behind me." She refused to feel guilty for this, not after all the maids she knew he'd bedded and left. She would *not*.

He left the fire ring without another word and wrapped himself in his blankets to sleep. Curling up in the bed of the wagon, he turned his back on them both.

Carl pursed his lips and whistled silently, perhaps in admiration of her nerve or possibly in disapproval. Alex didn't ask which. She merely sat there, feeling wretched.

Eventually she made herself useful. She pulled out their swords to tend them, sharpening the edges and scouring away any specks of rust from the blades. She oiled the steel and tucked them away safely in their scabbards.

She'd crossed a line and pushed too far with her last jibe, she knew. She should apologize. However, she couldn't see her way clear to doing so, not without surrendering too much of her authority. She would have to find another way to make things right.

Maybe the prince would brighten up when she let him practice with a real sword.

Chapter Ten

Prince Holden's sulks were not as easily mended as Alex hoped. He accepted the real sword grimly and began working drills, as instructed. However, he did not smile or look her in the eye.

Alex and Carl packed up their camp without his help while he worked the drills she'd set, then they moved on, passing through the town without her laying eyes on Edgar again. The shadow did not rise from the prince's face. As the next few days passed, she realized he'd stopped speaking except in response to others' remarks. He'd also stopped laughing entirely.

In spite of his depression, he worked even harder than before. He did not complain about the lack of drink or salt. He remained silent and did not make his customary complaints about the constant need to gather and cut wood for their fire. He began spending a considerable amount of time away from the campsite, so Alex followed him when he slunk away one evening. She watched him curiously as he filled their buckets with water from a nearby stream. He stuck a branch between the handles so he could lift them. He took his time, raising them to his shoulders and standing up with their weight across his back, then putting them down on the ground, repeating the exercise again and again.

She slipped away before she could be seen.

"You've really lit a fire under his arse, haven't you," Carl commented softly when she told him what she'd seen. "I'd say his determination was a good thing, and yet, I've never seen him so sour. Not for so long."

"He's left a good deal of unhappiness behind him in his day." Alex added honey to her mint infusion. "Having a bit of sorrow for himself will teach him compassion for others."

"I think he quite fancies you. More than the norm. Lovesick, he is."

She scoffed and swallowed a mouthful of the infusion. It was still too hot, burning her tongue. "Don't be a fool." She very carefully refused to think of her lapse with Edgar, when she'd foolishly used the prince's name at her moment of climax.

"Don't you be, either," Carl warned her, serious. "Don't think he's not human."

"I think he's a devil even if he doesn't have cloven hooves and horns."

"I had all I could do to keep him in the camp that night." Carl kept his voice cautiously low. "I told him you said you didn't plan to return. He kept worrying that perhaps you'd been caught off-guard and robbed. He made to go in to town, but then I asked him if he had any idea where to look for you when he got there. Of course he didn't. I finally persuaded him to stay up and watch." Carl smiled a little. "He's really quite protective of you."

"Well, I suppose it's nice to be valued."

"He's working his arse off to impress you."

"Good. I don't care why he's working, as long as he works."

"Why? Are you training him with an eye to actual fighting?"

"Of course not. Still, he needs something to do. This will be a valuable skill for him to learn. Sword training gives him a sense of purpose. It lets him keep his pride in the face of running for his life while his father and brother stay behind to fight."

They fell silent as the prince emerged from the bushes and drew near. He held the yoke of buckets easily on his shoulders. The sun slanted in behind him, catching his hair, giving him a halo of burnished gold. He swung the buckets down easily, without spilling a drop. He was much stronger now than at first, when he'd labored under the weight of a single one. Alex swallowed and buried her nose in her mug of herbal infusion. The prince sat down, listless, and picked at a new callus on his palm.

"We'll stay at an inn when we reach the next large town," she said after a bit, hoping the news would cheer him. "We'll cash one of your notes there, Prince Holden, if that's agreeable to you."

"It's fine." He sat quietly with his arms clasped loosely around his knees, looking soberly into the fire. "Then Carl can have his evening off."

"Yes," she agreed, poking at one of the rabbits. Clear juice ran out. "These are done, I think."

They ate in silence, Carl shooting her significant glances. *Lovesick, eh? That'll last until the prince first lays eyes on a pretty barmaid, no longer.*

But Alex was wrong.

They found the inn, as she'd planned, but the prince sat at the table with her all evening, barely glancing at the barmaids who brought their food and served them ale. He stirred himself from his taciturn retreat and tried to talk to her instead about news of the Danes, about hunting, and about his own sword training.

After a while, she observed he did not draw unwanted attention, perhaps because he didn't look like such an easy target anymore. She realized his shirt had drawn tight over his shoulders, stretched by a layer of new muscle. His face had also grown harder, or maybe his lengthening beard made him look more intimidating. He wore his sword in a scabbard at his hip. The blade looked well used even if he was not perfectly comfortable carrying it.

Alex sipped her ale thoughtfully. "You should go and have a bath. I'll come up after you've finished."

He yawned a little. "Very well." He went out, leaving a coin to pay for his meal, and she swallowed the last of her ale, pondering the changes in him.

Carl was correct, it seemed. She frowned and swirled the dregs in her mug. She could never enjoy being the source of anyone's unhappiness. Her concerns didn't end there, either. She'd been aware of the prince's attractive looks long before they left Norwich, but since this journey began, she'd noticed him more and more frequently. Worse, her night with Edgar had whetted her appetite. All day she'd found herself being startled by the prince's handsome face and by the changes in him.

That thought was a mistake. Her imagination formed a picture of him, unbidden. She could just see him sleek and wet in the bath, naked as the day he was born, with droplets of water gleaming on his chest and in his beard. He was never particularly shy, and he'd often paraded himself before her in various states of undress while she guarded him back at the castle. He'd undressed with her nearby several times as they traveled together this summer, too.

She made a soft grunt of annoyance and put down her ale. Curse him. No, curse herself for a fool. She was the one to blame here. This was her own lack of self-control. Her father had tried to warn her. Even the king's doubts were justified.

Alex stared miserably into her mug. She had to get herself in hand, right speedily.

Chapter Eleven

When Alex finally went up, she found Prince Holden squinting into the cloudy tin mirror hanging on the room's wall, working to neaten his beard a bit with his razor. Trimming himself evenly appeared to be an uphill battle, one in which he was achieving limited success at best. He'd bathed, but he hadn't bothered with a shirt, though he'd put his breeches on. His feet were bare.

She pitched his shirt at him and he caught it, tossing it aside with a grunt. She looked wryly at the room's single bed. She decided to unroll her blankets on the floor, positioning herself where the door wouldn't open without disturbing her. She lay down, covering her eyes with her arm.

He put his things away, stowing his sword in their weapons chest, which she'd made the innkeeper's sons carry up earlier. He sat down on the edge of the bed and stared at her. She could feel the weight of his gaze even though her eyes were covered, and hoped her pose couldn't be construed as a provocative one, but she refused to move.

"Alex, I want to return to Norwich." His voice was steady and resolute.

"So do I." She left her arm over her face. "I'm afraid it isn't my choice to make."

He chewed on that for a moment. "No, I suppose not." His voice was thoughtful. "I suppose it isn't."

His tone alarmed her. She moved her arm and peered at him suspiciously. "It isn't yours, either. Your father wanted me to take you west. I'll do as ordered, if I have to bind you and haul you in the bed of the wagon."

"I'll arm wrestle you again. You win? We go west. I win? We go east." He looked at her evenly.

She considered the wager, remembering the ease with which he'd lifted those buckets, estimating the new strength of his sword-arm. "I think not." She might still beat him, with luck. But then again…

He chuckled, and she felt a flare of irritation.

"I'll wrestle you for a lesser bet," she snapped without thinking, and he tilted his head, raising a brow.

"That's a deal." He rose, moving to pull the room's single small table away from the wall and over to the bed. There wasn't much space, and there was only one straight chair; he had to sit on the bed, leaving the chair to her. "What will you wager?"

"What *is* there to wager?" Their money, the wagon, the lodgings, the weapons, and even their food were all community property.

"A kiss." He challenged her with his eyes.

"You haven't changed at all." Alex rolled her gaze to the heavens. This was madness.

"I wouldn't agree." He put his elbow on the table, flexing his fingers. "Do you accept the wager?"

She wondered if she could still beat him. They'd both be motivated to do their best, she was certain. "No."

"You're afraid I'll beat you." His eyes were hot, and his mouth curved upward.

"I'm afraid we're well-matched enough one of us will hurt the other."

"You're afraid to kiss me."

"I don't want to kiss you. There's a difference."

"You'd chance the contest if you weren't afraid."

The bastard knew how to get under her skin, no doubt. She scowled at him.

65

"After all the times you've thrashed me with your wooden sword."

"Will you give over and be satisfied if I agree?"

He tilted his head at her. "Satisfied? I can't promise that."

She bared her teeth at him, feeling trapped in this little room without Carl to act as a buffer between them. "Carl isn't here to start the match."

"We don't need him."

How did he manage to advance on her even when he remained seated and unmoving? She had no idea. But the more she dithered, the worse her authority suffered.

Furious, she slammed herself down in the seat. "Fine. Let's get it over with."

He clasped her hand, moving rather more slowly and deliberately than she liked. He moved his left hand to grip hers. She scowled at him, settling into position, planning her strategy. She could use her nails to aggravate the healing blisters on his hands, but that wouldn't be sporting. She'd have to take the advantage early and never let him recover.

"Ready?" he asked, voice soft.

"Ready." She wasn't. She drew a deep breath.

"I'll count down. Three. Two. One."

She set her shoulder, prepared for the force of his initial push, anticipating his strength. He was more powerful than she'd feared. His brow creased, and he held her first counter-surge.

She wasn't going to win.

She fought him valiantly, but she didn't have his weight, and he'd been working hard. Their hands quivered, and her muscles started to burn.

His eyes darted up to hers. She saw anticipation of victory there, along with surprise and pleasure.

She would have to cheat.

Still managing to hold him somehow, Alex slipped her foot hastily out of her low boot. She could feel her balance slowly giving way as she divided her attention. He began to push her down. The seconds she had left dwindled fast.

She pointed her toe, sliding her foot seductively up Holden's ankle and into his breeches, her toes stroking his calf.

His eyes flew wide with shock and she exploded into motion, forcing his hand away. The back of it struck the table and she pulled away, chest heaving for breath, her muscles quivering from the strain.

"You cheated!"

"I won." She put her foot back into her boot and massaged her arm. "All's fair on the battleground. Winner takes all."

"You owe me a forfeit."

"I don't."

"You do." He stood, pushing the table aside, and reached for her arm. He began to rub her quivering muscles gently. He tugged her toward him, up and out of her chair. "Rules of honor."

"No honor on the battlefield."

"No?" His eyes were very blue. "Then I could kiss you as much as I like." Both his hands rested on her forearms, and began sliding up toward her elbows. She could kick him. She'd not even begun teaching him hand-to-hand combat, and he knew nothing of street fighting or wrestling. She could grip his thumb and push it back and have his ear pinned to the floor in half a second. She could make him beg forgiveness before she let him up again.

She stepped back once, then again. He followed. His hands rested on her shoulders now, and he was smiling.

"I'll bite," she threatened.

"Will you?" His eyes fell to her mouth. Her back struck the door. There was nowhere left to retreat. His face was very close to hers now. She could feel his breath on her cheek.

"I will," she threatened, and realized how breathless she sounded. Damn it all, she wasn't even fighting. Some part of her wanted him to take the kiss without permission, so she wouldn't have to admit she was willing.

There was only one right choice.

Alex moved her right hand six inches to the left and closed it quite firmly on him.

That brought him up on his toes sharply, his eyes wide.

"I'll bite, or I'll do even worse," she pointed out, punctuating the words with a squeeze. "No forfeit."

"No forfeit," he agreed, a little breathless. "All's fair on the battlefield."

"Good boy." She pushed him back, detached from his arms, and let go. "Next time I'll make that seem pleasant by comparison, and I won't give warning." Good God, she was out of breath and she was starting to shake. Even worse, she was so aroused she was quivering in her boots. If he had any idea how wet she was for him...

Hell.

"I find I want some air," she snapped, and made her escape.

She sat down in the common room for a few minutes and ordered a mug of ale to steady her nerves. When she had drunk it all, she stood and headed outdoors instead of going back up. Let him worry.

Once she was outside, an inspiration occurred to her. Redirecting her path toward the stables, she spoke briefly to the chief hostler, then climbed into the loft to bed down there for the night. She found a stack of straw sheaves piled in the loft right above the stalls where their mules were housed, and sat down next to them. She could hear the animals snuffling and thumping softly below, searching for more grain in their empty manger.

The sheaf-stack blocked the worst of the draft, and she decided to bed down in the lee of the sheaves. A pair of doors had been set into the wall nearby to allow stable hands to pitch hay down into the yard. She pulled one open and could see a light at the prince's window. His shutters were drawn, though, and she couldn't see in. She'd left the swords, so he ought to be able to defend himself, if the need arose.

Evil sodding bastard. Her heart was still beating too fast. The situation with him was rapidly getting worse instead of better. How the hell was she supposed to keep him in check when she couldn't even manage herself?

Alex reached for calm, forcing herself to breathe slowly. She couldn't do the situation any good by fretting, so she snuggled down into the straw, mounding up an insulating heap around her, and forced her mind to stillness. Finally, despite feeling a little cold and quite uncomfortable from straw-stalks poking her through her clothes, she fell asleep.

Chapter Twelve

Alex jolted awake, a heavy impact jarring the breath out of her lungs. She opened her eyes, dizzy and confused, her head aching. Rough hands seized her. They ripped her clothes open and slid inside to rest on her chest. Confused and disoriented, she forced her eyes to focus, blinking. The prince knelt over her, both his hands inside her shirt, and rage filled her. She'd warned the bastard, hadn't she?

She coiled herself with an effort and lashed out savagely. Her fist connected satisfyingly with his cheekbone and he fell sideways. "God's blood!" he swore, half-choked.

She rolled over, struggling to her knees, but her legs wouldn't hold her. She collapsed in a fit of coughing. Wrongness began to penetrate her swimming brain. The light was odd, ruddy and unsteady. She became aware of people scampering around like ants from a kicked hill. Shouting penetrated her ears: panicked orders, cries of fear, and horses trumpeting in terror.

She twisted about, her eyes raw and streaming. She stared at the stable, which had somehow transformed from a peaceful, quiet bed to a hell of flames. Horses ran loose, rearing and kicking as they milled about in the street. As she watched, a bucket brigade began throwing water on the smoking thatch of the inn, trying to keep the fire from spreading.

She clutched at her shirt, pulling it closed, and glanced about frantically. Prince Holden crouched on his knees next to her, his hands pressed over his face. He rocked in pain, cursing. She could see blood on his fingers, flowing from his nose. His hair looked scorched and his face was bright red, as if he'd had a bad sunburn.

"Holden?" she couldn't finish the question, coughing horribly instead. Her chest burned with effort. "What...?" She managed to gasp out a word, belatedly realizing Carl was there with them, his hand on her shoulder, steadying her.

"You're welcome," the prince muttered indistinctly, pulling his hands away and looking at the blood on his fingers. He grimaced and Alex winced. He was going to have a hell of a shiner, and possibly she'd broken his nose, though she couldn't be certain without touching his face.

"Move back, move back now," a man bellowed. "That wall's coming down in a minute!"

With Carl and Holden to aid her, Alex stumbled away. They all sank against the brick of a nearby building as the stable wall crumpled, sending flaming debris, coals, and sparks scattering everywhere. Their mules were dancing about loose in the road, rearing and squealing as hot cinders settled on their skins. Carl darted out to catch them and bring them to heel. He bound their halters together with his belt, then stepped over and put the makeshift tether into the prince's hand.

Alex tried to bring her lagging brain up to speed. She could remember bedding down in the loft, and evidently while she slept, the stables must have caught fire. That much she could be certain of, though the prince's role in the events remained unknown. She had a sinking feeling he'd been instrumental in getting her out, for which she'd thanked him by nearly knocking his head off.

She tried to breathe, the thick smoke catching in her throat. She watched blearily as the crowd battled to save the inn and surrounding structures. After ensuring she was all right, Carl ran off to join the bucket brigade. Their weapons chest was still inside the prince's room, after all, filled with all their weapons and nearly all their money.

Alex's front, where the heat from the burning stable baked into her, was very warm, but her backside felt icy cold. She struggled not to cough. She would like to turn to the warmth of the prince's arms, if not for her shame and confusion and his sullen demeanor. He'd managed to stanch his bleeding nose, but his eye was swelling up and darkening rapidly.

At last the inn was safe and the embers of the stable extinguished. People began to file back into the buildings. She, Carl, and Holden went in together. She still endured fits of coughing from the smoke she'd breathed, and they bracketed her on either side, supporting her when she needed help.

Back in the room, Prince Holden poured water from the pitcher into their chipped basin and gingerly dabbed at his face. He cleaned away the blood and some of the soot. His nose wasn't broken, but Alex judged it had been a near thing. Carl stared at her with the intent face of someone who had an urgent communication to make, but wouldn't speak in front of the prince.

Holden looked between them, his mouth pinched. He picked up the basin and pitcher. "I'm going to get some clean water." He stalked out.

Carl frowned as soon as the door closed. "Why did you hit him?"

"He made quite a determined pass at me earlier, which is why I was sleeping in the stable instead of up here. When I awoke, he had his hands inside my shirt. What would you expect me to do?"

Carl winced. "Understandable, I suppose, but I wish you hadn't. You don't know what he did, Captain. One of the stable boys dropped a lantern, seemingly. The little fool was afraid to stamp on it, so he couldn't put the fire out. There being so much hay and straw, the flames spread like mad. I was handy when the alarm went up, so I helped lead all the beasts out. Nobody knew you were inside. You breathed so much smoke the commotion didn't wake you, I suppose.

"The prince came running when they cleared the inn, and he was frantic. He said the two of you argued earlier, and you went out. He didn't know where you'd gone. About that time the hostler showed up and asked if the lady who was bedding down in the loft ever made it out all right, or was she still up there?"

Carl gestured helplessly. "The place was lost, that much was clear, but neither of us was going to give you up without a fight. We ran back in and had a look. The left quarter of the stable was an inferno. A draft sucked the fire through there, roaring like a banshee. Bits of straw were falling everywhere, burning in our hair and clothes. The prince threw his coat in the horse-trough to wet it and covered his head, then pulled his shirt over his mouth. He swarmed up the ladder through the smoke. I climbed up to the top of the ladder after him, but there was so much smoke I couldn't see anything. Men came rushing in to drag me down. They said it was too late. They hauled me out."

Carl cracked his knuckles methodically, his eyes sober. "Then part of the roof fell in, and flames gushed out everywhere. I thought sure I'd lost you both. I didn't know what on earth I'd tell King Anselm. I thought I might as well cut my own throat and be done.

"But then the prince came leaping out of the loft door with you in his arms and his coat afire. He dropped you and threw off his coat. I beat the rest of the fire off you both with my own. He bent over to check whether you were still breathing, and you reared up, fierce as a badger. That's when you knocked him flat on his arse."

"Damn." Alex rubbed her grainy eyes miserably. She reeked of smoke, and no wonder. She heaved herself up, pressing her hand to her chest to forestall a spasm of coughing. "I'd better find him and apologize."

"Yes, Captain." Carl nodded sober agreement.

Alex squared her jaw and stood up. She thought she could walk unassisted now that she'd had a chance to breathe a little, if she didn't push herself too hard. "You stay here."

Chapter Thirteen

Alex slipped down the stairs, moving slowly and leaning on the banister. She found the prince sitting in the kitchen. Other than him, it lay empty. Someone had fetched him a bucket of water, a wooden bowl, and a clean cloth. He'd folded it and dipped it into the water. He sat at a low table, gingerly bathing his swollen eye.

Alex cleared her throat, feeling sheepish, then coughed a bit, unable to help herself. When she recovered, she found him looking at her in silence.

"Carl told me what you did." She stepped forward and removed the cloth from his hand, putting it back in the bowl. "I wanted to apologize, and to thank you." She hesitated for a moment. "Properly." She looked at his abused face and singed beard, her heart aching with remorse.

There wasn't much light in the kitchen, but even so, she could see the skin on his face still looked tight and red. She touched his unbruised cheek lightly with her fingertips. "Does that hurt?"

He shook his head, silent.

"Good." She stepped forward, pushing the table out of her way, and moved carefully between his thighs. Then she gently lowered herself to sit on one of them and reached for his face with both hands. She wondered if he would still want this, after her ingratitude.

She slid her hand into his scorched, brittle hair and guided his mouth to hers, opening softly for him. He allowed her.

She invited him in, her eyes sliding shut. His arms slipped around her, slow but firm, his palms gliding over her waist to rest on her back. His tongue touched hers tentatively, then stroked along her lower lip, sweet and slow.

She let him adjust her until he was comfortable, pulling her close, and after a moment she kissed him back. She would be quite churlish not to, really.

He tasted of smoke and the sweet masculine savor she remembered from before, but without the added taste of ale this time. His hands caressed her back as their mouths touched, parted, and touched again. His breath blew warm on her cheek and his lips teased gently at her. He suckled first at her lower lip, then at her upper one. He slid his tongue slowly inside her mouth, playing a teasing game of tag with hers.

He was good. Much better than good. For a moment Alex might almost imagine she hadn't escaped the stable, and she was going up in flames. Except this fire was made of pure, aching sweetness, and her hands were curving behind Holden's head, pulling him closer. The angle was awkward, so she moved, raising herself, and put her leg over his other thigh, seating herself firmly across his lap. Her breasts pressed against his chest. She kissed him thoroughly, deep, unhurried, and warm.

The kiss slowly faded, leaving them breathless against one another's faces, noses touching and bodies pressed sweetly close. "Thank you for saving me," Alex said, her lips brushing his. "I'm sorry I hit you. I was confused and frightened."

"I forgive you." He nuzzled the words against her cheek. "I should not have pressed you so insistently earlier for a kiss you clearly had no wish to give." He inhaled as if she smelled of the sweetest perfume, not of bitter smoke. "I still have much to learn, it seems."

"You won your kiss fairly, I confess." She withdrew a little. "I can't beat you any longer. Not in a contest of strength. Skill and cunning, maybe."

He chuckled. "I'm going to keep learning."

"Good." She levered herself onto her feet, stepping back a little awkwardly. "You've surprised me, I admit. I'd not thought you would last a week at sword-drill."

"I mean to keep surprising you." His voice sounded husky, and he looked up at her, his eyes soft. "Until you decide I'm a good man."

She flushed a little. "You were not meant to hear those harsh words."

"They were true, and I needed to hear them." He stood, offering his arm. "Shall we go up?"

She accepted the escort awkwardly and slowly walked upstairs with him. Though he offered her the bed, she declined, preferring to lie down on the floor next to Carl, wrapped in her abandoned blankets. It was a good thing she'd left them when she fled to the stables.

Prince Holden pinched out the lamp and lay down on the mattress. She remained awake for a long while, staring at his back silently, her mind conflicted. Finally, she slept.

Chapter Fourteen

They were forced to buy a new wagon before they could depart the town. The old one had perished in the stable fire; all they could find were the warped iron rims that had capped the wheels and the half-melted iron pegs that once went through the axle-hubs.

While Carl haggled over the price of a new wagon, Alex accompanied Prince Holden to meet the town money-changer, who eyed him with dismay and demanded to examine his signet ring. The prince pried it off his finger and handed it over. The money-changer made a great fuss of studying the sigil, taking out a small eyeglass and peering myopically through the lens. All was in order, so finally the changer paid out the money, obsequious but not best pleased to part with so much coin.

They departed from the market and headed back to meet Carl, but Alex felt the hair at the nape of her neck prickle. Something wasn't right. Several men who'd been slouching about the marketplace moved to follow, and as they passed, another one casually fell in behind them. She snarled quietly to herself, glad she'd finally let Prince Holden start carrying a real sword.

"Do not react, do not turn, do not look," she murmured, pointing toward a store sign and leaning near his ear. "But we have a group of robbers after us."

To his credit, he only startled a little, and her hand on his arm kept his palm from going to the hilt of his sword.

"They saw us pick up a large sum of money. If we don't settle them in town, they'll come for us out in the wild. There could be more of them, and we'd have no chance of help. I'll pick a place for the confrontation. Be ready to draw if you must, and remember everything I taught you. Don't think of mercy. Go for the kill." She made a show of laughing lightly and patted his arm as if she were flirting. "Try to stay as close as you can to me. Damn it, we should have drilled on tandem fighting, not always pitting one against the other."

She didn't like that this was coming so soon after her close call with the fire. She was still prone to coughing if she exerted herself too much. However, it couldn't be helped.

She picked a promising alley she'd noticed on their way into the heart of town. The passage was very narrow, with a wood-capped brick cistern they could use for cover. The structure might even serve as a boost up to the rooftops, if they needed to run.

She steered Holden aside quickly, entering the alley's mouth, and hurried toward the cistern. A handful of robbers followed them in, not best pleased to have their trap sprung early. As the men closed in behind them, she heard the scrape of blades leaving sheaths and a low growl of voices.

"Draw your sword," she told the prince, and they put their backs to the cistern. He held his blade steady. The thieves scowled at him and stared at her with amazement when she did the same. One laughed and stepped forward, sneering.

"Your purse, or we kill your woman," he snapped at the prince. Holden raised a brow.

"I'm afraid you've miscalculated badly," he said with cool politeness. "I advise you to reconsider."

They laughed in his face, the whole group pressing forward.

Alex brandished her sword and palmed a dagger, holding it ready in her left hand. She didn't wait to let the thieves get set. She darted out to meet the leader and battered his blade aside before he could launch a strike at the prince. He snarled at her and engaged. The others came stalking up the alley toward them, but the first battle blocked the way. Only one pair could fight at a time.

She struggled to keep from coughing, her breath still a little labored after all the smoke she'd inhaled. Holden cursed, realizing she'd deliberately arranged for him to stay behind her. He cast about for something to do, then jumped up onto the cistern and started throwing half-bricks at the men, plucking them from the top of the adjacent wall.

His aim proved surprisingly deadly. She could hear his missiles whizzing past her, and the impacts prompted shouts and curses. She was glad he'd had the brains to get himself out of the way. The leader turned out to be a good swordsman, a dangerous man and a strong one. Fortunately, his swings were constrained by the narrow alley. She met his blows, parrying efficiently and launching a few shrewd attacks of her own.

Holden soon clipped her opponent over the ear with a well-judged throw. A trickle of blood started to stream down his temple. The blow stunned him for a crucial second, and she scored a cut across his shoulder, making him snarl. He kept fighting, but his men's morale wavered.

They began trading glances and edging backward out of the alley, one by one. The leader glanced over his shoulder to curse at them, then lunged for her, furious and undaunted. He refused to give up and flee.

She sidestepped his thrust and locked his blade, then drove her dagger into his ribs, angled up into his lung. She pushed it in all the way to the hilt.

He crumpled, his face contorting, and landed on his knees, slowly sinking forward, curling around the knife. His breath began to whistle, growing shallow.

She pulled her dagger out and blood gushed from the wound, bright crimson. Prince Holden leaped down from the cistern, but when he saw blood oozing out of the man's chest, his face went white and he swayed a bit.

"Steady," she warned. "No fainting on me, Your Highness." She cleared her throat at length and spat, then cleaned her blade on the ruffian's woolen coat, her motions brisk. She'd seen this kind of injury before, and knew he wouldn't last long with a hole in his lung.

"You chose this narrow alley so they'd have to come through you to get to me," the prince accused her.

"I did," she agreed calmly.

"I am not such a burden as I once was. I could have fought him blade to blade."

"You'll have to fight for your life sooner than I like."

He blinked at her, suddenly uncertain. "When do you mean?"

"Whenever your first unavoidable fight comes." She shrugged. "Thanks for the cover fire. I didn't know you could aim so accurately." She glanced around. "Let's move on before they come back with reinforcements, maybe even archers."

They left the dying thief behind them and hastened to rejoin Carl. Alex paid for their wagon while Carl harnessed the mules, and they rattled out of town at a brisk pace, the wagon so new-made a little sawdust sifted down onto the road as they rolled along.

The prince stayed quiet for a few minutes, thoughtful, before he spoke.

"I suppose we're even now," he glanced at her out of the corner of his eye. "We've each saved the other's life, inside the space of a day."

She hadn't thought of events in those terms, but she supposed he was right. "All in a day's work." She couldn't bring herself to classify fighting off a handful of cowardly ruffians as being on the same level with diving into an inferno.

He shook his head a little, impatient. "I meant to say thank you."

"You're welcome." She couldn't bite back her smile. "Thank you, as well." She flushed as Carl noticed her expression and entirely failed to choke back a smug smirk of his own.

Chapter Fifteen

They traveled several miles before they camped for the night, and Alex noticed a distinct change in the prince's behavior as they set up their campsite. He didn't maneuver overtly in an effort to bed down next to her. He didn't jockey to be seated right at her side when they sat down at the fire. Instead, he ventured his hand at gallantry. He offered her a hand up any time she rose, waited on her by trying to lift down her things before she could get at them, fussed over preparing her food, and was generally as obnoxious as he had ever been before, but in a very different way.

She finally burst out laughing when he offered her a cup of aniseed infusion ready-made and pre-sweetened. He stared at her with chagrin when she began to chuckle.

"Your Highness, stop before I have to slap you." She shook her head at him. "I'm no fragile flower." She accepted the drink and sipped nonetheless. When she finished, she grabbed the camp spade and strolled away from the camp to tend to nature.

She wandered around the edge of the pond where they'd made their camp, and the prince began to speak as she walked, apparently not realizing how well sound traveled over water. She could still hear him as she slipped out of sight into the bushes, looking for a likely spot to dig their privy.

"How do you manage her?" Holden asked Carl, his voice wistful. "She likes you well enough."

"I don't press her for things she doesn't want." Carl shrugged. "You don't give her room enough to breathe."

"I suppose not."

Alex peered through the bushes and across the pond. She could see Holden staring into the fire, his face sad.

"She spitted that thief like a Christmas goose. Like it was something she does every day."

"She's well-trained for her job," Carl murmured, feeding the fire. "She wouldn't be Captain of the King's Elite Guard, else."

"I suppose I never considered her duties in quite those terms. I never imagined her killing someone to protect me. I never thought." He pounded his fist against his thigh, frustrated. "That's my trouble. I've spent all my life thinking with my cock, Carl."

"Most of us lads do our fair share of that." Carl chuckled, sympathetic. "But you can't get away with careless thinking, not with her. She'll see through you in a heartbeat."

"So I've learned." He clasped his wrist in one hand, arms wrapped around his knees. "Too late for her to see me any other way, I suppose."

Carl clucked his tongue, sympathetic. "Your cock didn't send you up into the stable loft. I thought you dead."

"I thought I was as well." He paused, and she stayed still, watching him stare into his mint infusion without drinking any. "I thought her dead, too. But I meant to find her, Carl, if she lived. It's a wonder I ever did. She was all but buried in the loose straw beside a stack of sheaves." The prince's voice dropped so low she had to strain to hear. "The loft door was cracked open. The fire was drawing toward it. The straw wasn't just burning. It was melting, vanishing like it was never there. The flames were about to take the whole loft. I couldn't see much. The place was a living hell. I was crawling on my hands and knees, searching blind, when my hand fell on her boot. Fire was eating through the sheaves at her side when I reached her, and the flames would have had her already, if not for her being tucked away in the lee of the stack. Her bed was the last place in the loft to kindle. Luckily for us both, the door was at hand."

"Would you have given up and jumped down without her?" Carl hesitated a moment. "I'm sorry. I've no right to ask, sir."

"I'm the reason she sought refuge there." Prince Holden's voice was gruff. "You know the answer."

"I suppose I do," Carl murmured, barely audible.

Alex stood where she was, dithering, not certain what she should do. Her hands trembled, and she sank down on a log, wrapping both her arms around herself. She couldn't conceive of the scene the prince described, of him braving such a horrible danger for her sake. She couldn't believe they both came so close to death. She thought of his bruised face and her easy dismissal of his efforts to care for her. Tears welled over her cheeks, silent and scourging.

She stayed gone for a long time, unable to compose herself enough to tend to business and return to the camp. After she did, she made her goodnights swiftly. She rolled herself up in her bedroll beneath the wagon, pretending to fall asleep right away.

She lay very still with her eyes closed until Carl and Holden prepared their places on the wagon bed, where they couldn't see her. Then she opened her eyes and listened as they settled into their bedrolls overhead. She spent a long time gazing up at the rough-hewn planks. Carl took the first watch, and he hummed quietly as he sat, a little off-key. She could picture him sitting cross-legged among his blankets, looking out through the woods.

She wondered if she should say something to Carl about what had passed between him and the prince. She decided not to, understanding he was no longer on her side. She shouldn't confide in him again, at least not about her confused feelings for the prince.

She fluffed her blankets and turned onto her side, resolutely shutting her eyes again. Her turn to watch would come soon, and she needed to be rested in the morning.

She slept fitfully. When Carl woke her, she rolled up her blankets and fed the fire, choosing to spend her watch sitting there. When Prince Holden awoke, she quietly pulled out his mug and poured hot water for him. She added mint leaves to their makeshift pouch and crushed them, then set the infusion to steep as he wandered off to find the privy hole. When he emerged from the brush, she added honey and removed the leaves. She left the steaming cup sitting ready at his place for him.

He looked at it with surprise. He smiled at her, warmth and pleasure lighting his face, leaving him almost as radiant as the rising sun. Alex blushed a little and looked away, preparing her own mug a little clumsily.

"Good morning," he murmured, and drank a sip, his eyes closing with enjoyment. "I've rather grown to like this stuff, you know."

"Yes," she agreed, unable to hold back a smile. "Good morning."

Chapter Sixteen

Alex beckoned to the prince after he finished his drink. "Time to start your combat training in earnest. I like this place. We'll stay here a while. We have cover, there's fresh running water, and it's concealed from the road. This place is perfect for what I want." She unlocked the chest and considered the contents carefully, then repacked everything except for the swords. She sat down on the lid.

She tried not to notice the prince's eye had turned a stunning shade of dark purple, with hints of green and yellow around the edges. It was swollen nearly shut. There was nothing to do but accept her remorse for hitting him and force herself to let her shame go.

"Carl, I want you to work with His Highness on hand-to-hand combat and strength training. I'll handle swordsmanship, archery, and general fitness." She reached into the bag where their provisions lay stored. "Get started now. Go for a run, then make him do some push-ups or chin-ups or whatever you like. I'll make breakfast while you're gone. Well? Get moving."

Carl beckoned to the prince, who gave her a quick grin, then sprinted after him. Carl brought Holden back to camp to do his push-ups, sit-ups, and other strengthening exercises, irritating Alex with the obvious attempt to draw her attention. They shed their shirts and competed to see who could do the most push-ups, using a sandy flat next to the stream that fed the pond. She turned sausages in the pan. She very deliberately tried not to look at Prince Holden's shoulders. If she worked very hard, it was nearly possible to ignore both the new ripple of muscle on his ribs and the way sweat darkened his red-blond hair, then trickled over his chest.

Alex groaned silently to herself in defeat and moved a quarter-turn around the fire circle, putting her back to them. She put the kettle on the coals to brew some more drinks for them all.

In the afternoon she and the prince sparred with metal blades for the first time. He was awkward and a bit slow, unaccustomed to the weight of the sword. She kept him at quarter and half-speed, not wanting either of them to make a mistake that might harm him. Then they switched back to wooden poles and she pushed harder, driving him back. She forced him all the way into the pond, where he snagged his toe on a root and fell over. He came up sputtering, water sluicing off him, slicking down his hair.

His other outfit was burned so badly it was unfit to wear, so Alex had no choice but to have him strip to his breechclout and hover by the fire, shivering as he held his shirt near the flames to steam dry. She wondered for a moment if she'd dunked him on purpose in order to see him strip, and could give herself no satisfactory answer. She knew he could feel her eyes skittering past him as the afternoon passed. He preened a little, unable to help himself.

"You need to work on your legs as well as on your arms. They're scrawny." She toed his shin with the tip of one boot.

He chuffed surprise and studied himself, dismayed. "Are they? I quite like them."

She did too, but she merely rolled her eyes and tossed him his breeches. They weren't very dry yet, but he put them on anyway. She ignored the amusement in his eyes with all the dignity she could manage.

Later she had Carl construct the prince a wooden training target, so he could practice swinging his sword at full strength without worrying about hurting what he was aiming at. He could use the dummy for kicking practice, too.

She wished it weren't high summer. After the incident at the pond, Holden invariably removed his shirt to train. While his skin remained pale, freckled and prone to burning, he started to soak up a little golden color as the days passed. He was also developing more muscle. His appetite grew along with his strength, making it increasingly hard to keep him fed. She knew she'd made a good decision to stay near a decently sized town where she could shop for what they needed.

The days passed slowly as the summer ripened, golden and shining. Apples swelled and started to turn red on the bough. She went in to the town to shop on market mornings, riding one of the mules bareback. She bought butchered sheep, calves, or yearling pigs, chickens, or sometimes a goose. Carrots and onions were available in plenty as well, along with bread, flour, wine, and mead. She bought occasional crocks of milk, too, to keep cool in the stream. She bought a little of everything, and they enjoyed their meals much more than they could while traveling.

Prince Holden soon began to need a better running partner than Carl, whose legs and wind were both short. Alex traded some of the sword-work to Carl and began to run with the prince herself. Running was something she'd always enjoyed, being long-legged and light on her feet.

The runs should have been pleasant, but they weren't, quite. Holden deferred to her, lagging a step or two behind. His presence at her shoulder made her always feel she was running from him, on the verge of capture. His pursuit loaned wings to her feet and pressed her to test her limits.

Her speed pressed his, as well. He began their runs by gasping for breath after a few furlongs, but soon he could run steadily, uncomplaining, for as far as she cared to lead him. They developed paths through the woods, leaping over the trunks of fallen trees, bounding over stone outcrops and hopping through the courses of narrow streams, vaulting over fences, or sometimes winding through a stile, then around the pond and back to the camp. Sometimes they did the whole circuit three times or more, but he never wavered.

She was growing stronger, too, by virtue of the constant work. She even improved her marksmanship while shooting with the prince. His boasts were true. He was a fine natural archer. She persisted in practicing those lessons more for her and Carl's sake than for his.

The prince wrestled with Carl daily. He turned out to be as slippery as an eel and twice as hard to hold. Alex chuckled, watching them. After a week, he could defeat Carl more than half the time.

"You need to teach him more dirty tricks," she told Carl, sipping a cup of milk as she watched him lose. "He needs to learn street-fighting. Teach him about thumbs to the eye, knees to the balls, how to work the joints. Not so much of this brute strength and honor-before-survival stuff."

"I don't want him using aught of that on me," Carl gasped from where he lay pinned under the prince's knee. "He's bad enough as is." He yielded and Holden let him up, smirking a little.

"He is, isn't he?" She surveyed the prince, who grinned at her cockily. He was finally getting good enough his arrogance was starting to resurface. She considered her options. Time to push him to the next level. She'd been delaying with good reason, but the conversation cornered her. She'd finally run out of excuses.

She could hardly make him put his shirt on first, either, given how filthy he already was.

"Attack me," she told the prince, taking the last swallow of her milk and tucking the mug away for later washing.

"I couldn't," he demurred, and she put her hands on her hips, exasperated.

"Stop being a fool." She stood up and shook out her arms, ready. "Come at me like you mean to knock me down."

"It wouldn't be fair. You know what we agreed about contests of strength."

She rolled her eyes. "You weren't listening. This isn't a contest of strength, though what you've learned from Carl is mostly strength-based. What I have in mind is a contest of skill, wits, and know-how, none of which you have. Are you going to attack me, or are you going to give up on your training?"

The taunt sufficed to goad him forward. He lunged, a little half-hearted. She caught his thumb and turned it just so. In half a second, she'd pushed him up onto his tiptoes and jerked his arm up behind his shoulders. His skin was smooth and hot, slick with sweat. He smelled salty and musky, very male in her nostrils.

"What the hell did you do?" He gasped, shocked.

"That is how a woman becomes captain of the king's guards," she told him coolly. "I learned the art from a Chinaman." She let him go. Li had been her first lover, though she wasn't going to tell the prince about him. He'd known more about the motion of bodies than anyone else Alex ever met, either before or since.

The prince's eyes narrowed. She realized she'd let herself slip, revealing a lazy little smile as she started thinking of Li. He'd perceived some fraction of her thought, and instinctively chafed against his unknown rival.

"Show me."

She did, working at quarter speed, showing him where to position his hands and thumbs. Patiently she taught him which direction to push and how hard.

Hand to hand was a difficult craft, not one a fighter could master in a few days. She'd never distinguished herself in unarmed martial arts, not compared to her teacher, but she knew enough to be deadly dangerous to anyone who had no training in combating her techniques.

The lessons turned out to be brutal and exhilarating, exactly as they were with Li. She learned sympathy for her teacher as they progressed. Teaching a novice was a difficult job. She had to balance worrying whether Holden would hurt her in his clumsy eagerness against knowing she could permanently cripple him before he ever realized what she was about.

Within a few days, they both had more bruises and contusions than he'd ever received during sword training.

After another day or two, the two of them were so battered she decreed a temporary halt to the lessons and announced her plans to take the prince into town. Their mules' hooves badly needed trimming, and they needed to be re-shod, as well.

Carl announced he wanted a lazy day of lying about the camp, so they made their preparations without him. Alex climbed on top of one of the team, and Holden caught hold of each of the mules by the halter, drawing them toward the road.

"You have the harder job today," she teased him a little. "Only a month or two ago, they'd hardly let you touch them."

"Like Carl says, the bastards can smell fear," Holden agreed easily. He darted in front of the mules and reached out to the hedgerow at the side of the road. He plucked a wisp of grass, holding it between his teeth as he fell back into step. The road ran straight ahead for a few miles, cutting between hedgerows that marked the boundary of two farmers' hay fields.

"They aren't inclined to respect titles." She patted her mule's neck. "Have you ever been to a smithy before?"

"Not inside."

"The forge will be hot, though I suppose after the loft, the heat won't seem very impressive to you." She flushed, wishing too late she hadn't brought that up. "When he puts the new shoes on the mules, they'll smell horrible."

He squinted up at her and wrinkled his nose as if he could smell burning hoof already. "I'll try to keep my refined palate upwind, then."

She was tempted to stick her tongue out at him, but contented herself with an eye-roll. Riding into town next to him was quite pleasant, the sun baking comfortably into her stiff shoulders, hot on the crown of her head. Maybe she'd buy a straw hat to shade her eyes on the way home, and one for him, too. She laughed softly to herself, picturing him wearing a ragged straw hat with his royal finery instead of his gleaming golden coronet.

"What's funny?" His hand brushed her calf for a moment, then retreated.

"You, of course." She answered lightly. "Wearing a straw hat instead of a crown, with that seed of hay in your mouth, sitting in the palace in Norwich."

He laughed along with her. "That would annoy my father almost enough to make it worth doing."

"He'd be proud of you, if he could see the progress you've made."

He gazed at the ground for a moment, and a frown creased his brow. "I hope he would be." His voice was sober. "I've given him precious little cause for pride thus far."

"He would." Alex tried to sound nonchalant. "I am."

He glanced up at her, but she avoided his gaze, removing a stray bit of leaf from the mule's mane and tossing the stuff aside.

"Your opinion matters a great deal to me," he said softly. "Pull up."

She did, and he struggled up onto the other mule's back, grinning at her triumphantly when he was done. The mule snorted, tossing its head.

"Now who's going to lead them?" She chuckled. "There aren't any reins."

"They won't stray from between the hedgerows," he answered her, still pleased with himself. "I'll get off when we get closer to town. Hup in there." He nudged the mule with his heels, and they were off again.

True to his word, he slid off and caught the halters again when the hedgerows ran out. Alex squinted at the town, shading her eyes with her hand. "I see ribbons tied to the gate-posts," she murmured. "I think there must be a wedding today."

The church bells began to ring even as she spoke, and the prince guided their mules to the side of the road. They watched as a small cart decorated with flowers and ribbons trundled out of the town, slowly toiling up the hill. The newlyweds rolled past with a wave, the blushing bride nestled under her husband's arm. The decor was very simple, with wildflowers starting to wilt on the wagon bed and a few bows tied to the horse's tack. The girl's dress was plain, but her face was radiant. Her new husband wore his Sunday best, looking very red in the face and stiff in his unaccustomed high collar, his skin abraded from shaving.

Behind them, a crowd of walkers began to straggle out of town, children jumping and dancing, ignoring their mothers' warnings about spoiling their best clothes. Other courting couples walked arm-in-arm, and a few dogs frolicked, stirring up butterflies amidst the hay as everyone dispersed in different directions.

The prince gave the groom a wink and touched his finger to his forehead in salute.

"I envy him," he murmured when the newlyweds had passed, and Alex blinked at him with some surprise.

"Surely not."

"Why shouldn't I? He has everything he wants. Look at them." He gestured at the cart, which was already receding into the distance. "Heading home to their little cottage together."

"Where they'll soon have more mouths to feed than they can comfortably manage," she grumbled a little, but relented when he cast her a reproachful look.

"Haven't you ever thought of marrying?" He probably thought he was being discreet, but she could see the hope in his eyes, and his tone was a shade too eager.

"Not in particular." She shifted atop her mule as he danced away from a long-eared hound that went bounding past, gamboling away up the road. *Marriage? **Really?*** She snorted. "Don't even try to convince me you're in the market for a bride."

"Not just any bride. Only the right one." He looked straight ahead, but his ears were pink, and she didn't think it was from sunburn. Embarrassment, maybe. She couldn't be certain what he was feeling, any more than she could identify the nervous flutter in her own belly.

"The smithy is to the left just after we enter the town," she directed him and slid off her mule, landing on the opposite side from him. She led the mule forward through the last few wedding guests, mostly older couples and a few scattered singles who seemed in no hurry to get wherever they were going. She went slowly, making sure the mule didn't tread on anyone with his clumsy hooves.

The smith was busy, fitting a set of wagon wheels with iron, but he let them stable their beasts and told them to return around midafternoon.

She found herself at a loose end, standing out in the morning sunlight with Prince Holden at her side. The hour was still not ripe enough to go to a tavern for lunch and far too early to start drinking ale. Worse, they'd come when it wasn't market day, and there were no open stalls in the town square to serve as a pleasant distraction.

"Let's find a place where we can buy a hat," she suggested, and led him deeper into town, peering into the occasional storefront. He seemed unaware of her scrutiny, lagging a little behind her, but she could see his face reflected in the occasional small, distorted pane of glass, and she knew he was smiling at her indulgently. She obtained her revenge by buying them the widest, floppiest straw hats she could find. When they stepped out into the bright sunshine together, she turned to him and set one on his head, jamming it down over his ears. Then she put on her own.

"I've finally found something you don't look good in," she told him tartly.

His grin deepened, and she realized suddenly she'd given herself away rather badly with her thoughtless comment.

"You look quite nice in yours," he told her, not at all self-conscious.

Her cheeks colored against her will, and she turned her gaze aside. A group of ragged children, still over-stimulated from the wedding, was racing back and forth across the street, the leading one carrying a wilting yellow primrose. That girl was promptly caught and kissed by the fastest of the boys. The flower passed to another, a small boy who panicked as the girls homed in on him. The boy bolted straight toward Holden, who extended his hand and accepted the flower from the lad to rescue him. He smiled down at the posy for a moment, then lifted his gaze to Alex, a laughing challenge in his eyes.

When she didn't scowl, he swept off his hat, then leaned in, bussing his lips lightly against her cheek. She bridled a little but didn't refuse, shaking her head at him, and he passed the flower gallantly to a little girl who stretched out her hand. The girl fled in the opposite direction with the group in hot pursuit.

"Come sit down with me," he suggested, and they settled themselves on the grass next to the town mill, shaded by the trough of the dry millrace. From within, she could hear the occasional bray of a donkey and the soft thud of hooves as it pulled the shaft that drove the grinding stone, since there was no water.

"The summer has been terribly dry," she murmured. "I hope the crops will make enough of a harvest for everyone to survive the winter."

"We've been lucky to find water whenever we needed," he agreed. "Though I confess, I'm selfishly glad we haven't had to sleep out in the rain more often." He leaned back and closed his eyes at the sun, then lay down, shading his face under his new hat.

"Typically selfish," she chuckled, but she'd been glad of the pleasant weather, also, if she were strictly truthful. "I must admit, I've enjoyed being dry."

"I'm enjoying having nothing in particular to do for a whole afternoon." He squinted up at her from under the edge of his hat. "The sun feels good."

She looked at his arms, and could count half a dozen bruises without even pushing up his sleeves. She rolled her shoulders in their sockets, tilting her face up at the sun. He was right, and she shifted, leaning back like he had.

"The ground is soft," he reported, very carefully not looking at her.

Alex yawned and lay down in the grass. She took care not to lie too close to him, but not too far away, either. His company wasn't unpleasant. She closed her eyes. The turf was deep, thick with moss and soft green grass. Lying on it felt much nicer than the hard ground under the wagon in the woods, with its scattering of roots and stones. The millrace had dripped before the stream sank too low to be diverted, so the growth beneath its length was lush, with a few wetland flowers nodding on their stems.

She fell asleep before she ever realized she was drowsy. When she woke, she looked up into the prince's face and realized he was lying on his side next to her, gazing at her with soft eyes. He held her hat up to shade her face and neck. A few brilliant pinpricks of sunlight penetrated the loose weave of straw.

She blinked up at him, stretching luxuriantly, and couldn't suppress a smile. He was quite handsome, and more gallant than she had a right to expect. "The way to a woman's heart is through her sun-shade?"

"I'm willing to give it a try." He handed her the hat as she sat up, and rose to his knees at her side. "You slept for a tidy while. The mules might be shod by now."

"Mmmm." She stifled a yawn and made herself rise to her knees, bracing her hand on the creaky wooden trough of the millrace. A dragonfly darted in front of her face, brilliant iridescent blue.

He stood and reached to help her up. She put her hand in his and let him raise her to her feet, feeling the tips of his fingers trail briefly over the soft pulse-point at her wrist. The contact made her draw her breath swiftly, looking away from him.

"Race you to the smithy." He was away before she could make sense of the words. She blinked at his heels, then bolted after him, the two of them bounding through the streets like children. One old storekeeper shook his fist after them with irritation.

The mules were not quite ready; one stood in a stall, already shod, face buried in a nosebag of oats. The other was nearly finished, standing with one foot raised between the smith's thighs. Prince Holden edged his way in to watch the smith clean the hoof and trim it with his farrier's knife, shaving off curls of horn. He winced to see the man cut so speedily, but the mule never moved, champing quietly even when the smith filed the hoof fiercely with an iron rasp.

He eyed the smith with curiosity. "How do you hold him up?"

"If I don't lean on him, he don't lean on me." The smith chuckled. "If he gets fractious, I give him a good thump twixt the eyes. Haven't had to do that with either of your two. They're well-trained." He tested the cold shoe against the hoof, then replaced it in the coals and began to pump the bellows. He heated the iron till it glowed. He picked it out with a pair of tongs and hammered it against his anvil sturdily, shaping and widening the shoe a little, then applied the hot metal, somehow avoiding the tender frog of the mule's foot.

The prince's nose wrinkled at the stink of burning hoof, and Alex laughed. "I warned you."

"You did," he admitted.

The smith needed a few more minutes to finish, fashioning a toe-cap on the shoe to help hold it on the hoof and quenching the iron in a bucket of water. He nailed the shoe on and bent down the tips of the nails, filing everything smooth to finish.

The prince watched every move with open admiration. "You put on a horseshoe faster than I can eat my supper."

"It's a living." The smith winked at him.

They paid the man for the shoes, the work, and the mules' fodder. Holden bought a short length of rope, too, tying the makeshift lead to one mule's halter. He hoisted Alex onto her mule's back, then took advantage of the mounting stump to climb up behind her.

She chuckled at his persistence, but didn't feel annoyed enough to complain, not even when his arm curled around her waist. He touched the mule with his heels and she guided it out onto the main road by tugging on the halter, listening to the prince singing a very old folk song softly behind her.

My love is far in land.
Alas, why is she so?
And I am so sore bound
I may not come her to.
She has my heart in hold
Wherever she ride or go
With true love a thousand fold.

He had a fine rich tenor voice, warm and sweet. She smiled to hear him, but the love song made her feel shy and uncomfortable. "Don't you know any bawdy songs?" Alex teased him a little and began to sing, trying to cover her discomfort.

"Women, women love of women
Makes a bare purse for some men?
Some are as nice as a nun's hen,
Yet all they be not so?"

He chuckled. "I might have heard that one. It's very naughty."
"I'll bet you have." She grinned. "I daresay you know this one, too.

"Give me loose society
Where the jokes are funny
Love will bring variety
Toil that's sweet as honey.

Down the primrose path I post
Straight to Satan's grotto,
Shunning virtue, doing most
Things that I ought not to."

He joined in for the third verse, and they rode into camp singing lustily in harmony. She and Carl spent the evening teaching Holden all kinds of soldiers' bawdy songs as they sat around the campfire, drinking ale while they laughed together.

Chapter Seventeen

Alex and the prince were easier with one another after their day in town. They continued their sparring matches at regular intervals, varying tandem sword training with hand to hand. The craft of unarmed combat continued to prove frustrating for the prince, especially when defending against her attacks.

"Impossible," Holden lamented one afternoon as she put him on his face in the dirt for the umpteenth time, effortlessly seating herself atop his back. "You can't have done that. Again."

"I'm not using strength." She wound up his arm a bit more to demonstrate. "This is leverage."

"I concede." He went limp, and she sat on him for a moment longer, liking their position rather more than she strictly should. She made herself move before the moment stretched too long, heaving off him, and offered him a hand up.

He reached for her, and gave her no warning whatsoever before yanking hard. Off-balance, she toppled helplessly onto him. He rolled her under his body, pinning her arms with his hands, his waist sinking between her thighs.

"There," he said with satisfaction. "Escape this."

She clenched her fists in exasperation, trying breathlessly to ignore the sensation of his body weighing down on her, pushing her thighs apart and pressing against the center of her. "I haven't showed you everything I know. Not yet."

She bucked her hips up sharply and kicked her heels against the ground, unseating him. They rolled, trading advantage back and forth. He couldn't pin her, but neither could she escape without hurting him. They thrashed about wildly, kicking up dust, dirt, and bracken as they struggled. He clutched her tightly against his chest. He was laughing, and she realized she was too. They abruptly fetched up against one of the log segments surrounding the fire ring, and she found herself lying on top of him, her face a few inches from his.

They froze there, and their laughter faded. He did not try to dislodge her again. His eyes grew warm and deep. He was still smiling, his lips parted slightly. She lost herself in his gaze, wavering on the verge of sinking down to taste his mouth.

She felt his hands settling slowly on her waist, anticipating her kiss. He was smeared with dirt. Bits of dried fern stuck to the sweat on his face and body, tangled in his untidy hair. He looked so good he almost seemed edible. Hypnotized, she was tempted to bend her head and lick a droplet of perspiration right off his cheek.

Carl was watching them, she knew.

"You're a mess," she observed, hearing the breathlessness in her voice. "Get up and wash that dirt off. Carl almost has the supper ready."

The spell was broken.

She climbed off him, briskly dusting all the twigs and bracken off her clothes, using her fingers to pluck what she could out of her hair. It was so bad she'd have to get out her comb and re-weave her braid.

The prince went to splash in the pond, and she disciplined herself not to watch. Carl looked up as she went to the wagon for her comb and returned to the fire.

"One of these days he'll weary of you rubbing his nose in the dirt and give you a right good thrashing," he said amiably.

"On the day he can, I'll be proud of him." She slouched by the fire and began to unravel her braid, all but exhausted. She rubbed her neck, which was covered with grit and dust. That was too damned close for comfort. She'd have to see to it there was no more light horseplay of that sort.

"Ohhh, will you look at him," Carl muttered, gazing past her toward the pond, and Alex barely managed to stop herself before she obeyed.

"Look at what?"

"The results of your handiwork."

She snorted. The prince's idea of modesty still left much to be desired. "Flaunting himself again, is he?" She began combing at the bottom of her hair, slowly working her way up as the tangles came out.

"You might say that." Carl turned the spit where a pheasant the prince had managed to shoot was roasting, dripping juices on the fire and producing a mouthwatering smell. "He would be if anyone were looking, at any rate."

"Well, I'm not." She didn't bother to keep the tartness from her voice. "I wonder why you are."

"Purely to keep you informed, of course." Carl chuckled. "It's the least I can do."

"Let me guess. He has two arms, two legs, and a cock he's rather more than reasonably proud of. Just like any man." She re-wove the braid briskly and tied it with a bit of leather.

"He's sprouted a good bit more muscle than he had in Norwich. I'd have thought you'd appreciate a chance to enjoy examining your handiwork." Carl wasn't at all perturbed by her frank speech. "I believe he's grown a bit more courtesy, as well."

"If he had an ounce of politeness, he wouldn't strip naked and wash in the presence of a lady." She thought of making a mint infusion, then reached for their jug of ale instead and poured herself a mug.

"Well, mayhap if you want to be treated more like a lady, you could act more like one." Carl glanced at her out of the corner of his eye, calculating how angry he was making her. "Instead of like a sergeant at the drill."

"I act like what I am," she muttered.

"You still think he's a devil, after he risked his skin to pull you out of the jaws of Hell?"

"I think he felt guilty for driving me out there, acting as he shouldn't." This was not an argument she wanted to have, especially not where the prince might hear. "I think you're forgetting your place, Carl."

"Your pardon, Captain." He straightened up, indignant. "I feel the need for a day off."

That would leave her alone with the prince. She stared into her mug irritably. Carl deserved a day's rest. She did too, for that matter. The prince did, also.

"Take your time off whenever you will," she muttered. "I'll be his wet-nurse by myself until you care to return."

"Then you don't mind being left alone with him?" Carl pressed his luck, giving her a shrewd look. She knew he'd sensed the changes between them, including the deepening tension, the subtle evidence of attraction on her part, her slow, reluctant yielding to the prince's charm.

"You saw me throw him arse over tip." She shrugged casually. "I'm not concerned for my virtue." She was beginning to wonder if the prince himself asked Carl to leave. If that were so, he'd be sorely disappointed. But no. She already knew Carl was on the prince's side in this. He was more than capable of coming up with the idea on his own. She stiffened her jaw. Let him try to play the matchmaker all he liked. She would not give in.

Alex's neck began to hurt, radiating tension all the way up to her skull. The fingers of a headache spidered out to her temples, throbbing across the center of her forehead and spiking behind the bridge of her nose. She chewed her lip and tried to ignore the pain, taking over turning the spit as Carl readied his gear for his time off while the prince dried himself and finally put on his clothes. She heated water and put a curl of willow bark in her mug instead of mint. The infusion would be bitter, but it should help her head.

Carl departed after supper while she and Holden were still finishing the washing-up. He arranged to return two mornings later. Alex watched him go, trying to hide a certain amount of nervous tension. She noted the prince didn't object to Carl's extended absence, as he would have to hers.

"You should have a wash," the prince told her, his eyes dancing with good humor. "The pond feels good. Exhilarating."

"You'd love a chance to watch," she muttered.

"I wouldn't, if you asked me not to." His voice sobered quickly as he caught her mood.

"You'd look."

He tilted his head at her, reproachful. He looked exactly like a puppy that had been scolded, and she rolled her eyes.

"You'd feel better after a bath."

"I'll have one if you'll let me lock you into the weapons chest while I bathe."

Another reproachful look greeted her comment, and she couldn't help but chuckle at the thought of him curled up inside the chest, his hands bound and his eyes wide, listening to her splash.

She compromised on a sponge bath, and didn't ask him not to watch. He didn't, though, averting his eyes at first and later closing them entirely while she ran the warm damp cloth around her neck and inside her shirt. She kept her eye on him as she washed. His lashes lay flat against his cheeks, his hands demurely resting on his thighs.

She let her eyes wander across the planes of his chest and realized she could no longer deny she found him quite desirable, when he behaved himself. If she was perfectly truthful? He was attractive even when he didn't.

She grimaced and wrung out the cloth. She wiped her calves and her feet. She would not venture any more. She would not remove any of her clothing with him so near, not even if he was behaving.

He was right. She did feel a good deal better after getting some of the dirt off. She frowned, shifting her shoulders and trying to ease the taut muscles there.

"Done?"

"Yes." She rubbed her neck, grimacing a little.

He stood up and moved around the fire circle, kneeling down behind her.

"Let me help." He reached and put his hands on her neck.

Alex tensed, but didn't jerk away. How far could she trust his self-restraint?

He moved her braid aside carefully, draping it over her shoulder, and his hands began to press and knead at her shoulders through her shirt, his thumbs rubbing slow circles over her spine.

Alex exhaled, her head falling forward. Even now, after they'd grown hard and rough, his hands felt sinful, delightful. She shouldn't indulge this, not even for a moment, but she couldn't resist. This was a fair test of him, a test she could end at any time, should he fail.

He didn't. His hands worked their way up and down her back, pressing and kneading wherever they found knots and stiffness, but they did not wander, and he did not speak, neither to taunt nor to pressure her.

Alex felt herself turning to melted honey under his touch, heat surging in her belly, and belatedly admitted this had become a test of her resolve as well. She struggled not to turn to him and knot her fingers in his tunic. She refused to drag him down to cover her right here even though they were alone.

She pulled away subtly and he stopped, taking his hands off her.

"All right?" His voice was slightly hoarse, a little husky. He moved back around the fire to take his accustomed place.

"Just fine." She pulled her woolen coat on. "Much better, in fact. Thank you."

He smiled a little, and she was struck by the note of uncertainty betrayed by the relief in his eyes. He'd been afraid she would not appreciate his touch.

She thought of turning the tables, putting him in front of her, even peeling his shirt off and letting her hands wander over him. She knew his back was smooth, perfect and unscarred, dusted with freckles and starting to grow delightfully solid with muscle. He would obey her. He would welcome her hands on him. She could touch him to her heart's content, and she would not have to stop.

She dropped her eyes shyly and resisted the temptation.

That night, she could not sleep. Every sound from him tormented her; every creak of the wagon as he shifted to stay awake on watch roused her to wakefulness. She twisted and turned miserably, knowing what she needed.

Keeping watch meant he would not sleep and give her privacy, but her desperation grew until finally she succumbed, sliding her hand down stealthily to touch herself.

She continued as quietly as she could, trying to keep her breath soft and even, moving only her fingertip. She was already so aroused even the slightest shifting pressure brought the sweet, tantalizing flare of pleasure she needed.

She closed her eyes, and in her mind she saw him, the sun gilding his skin. She remembered the feel of his hand on her breast. She could all but taste the savor of his mouth. Her hips lifted, urgent, and she bit her lip.

She pictured him bathing in the pond; she had not let herself look, but she could imagine how he must have looked, nonetheless. There would have been dappled sun sliding over the soft velvet of his skin and catching golden-red in his hair, a gleam of diamond-droplets sliding over him, caught in the fur on his chest, wandering slowly down toward his waist, and lower...

She'd seen him naked back in Norwich. She knew the look of his cock, passive but promising, hanging between his legs in its thatch of dark auburn hair. She tried to control her breathing, or at least to keep quiet, her fingertip circling swiftly.

She imagined his cock swelling, lengthening for her, thick and heavy and strong. She knew the feel of his weight sinking between her legs from when they'd wrestled, the press of his hard shaft against her from when he'd drunkenly believed she meant to let him take her. She dreamed of how he would feel pushing in, moving deep inside her. She throttled a whimper before it could escape, imagining his eyes locked with hers as he thrust into her again and again, the sweet half-smile he might wear, how his face would soften and his eyes would close, his mouth falling open as he lost himself in pleasure.

She came with a low gasp he did not seem to notice, and afterward she was finally able to subside into sleep, guilty but relieved.

Chapter Eighteen

The next day dawned a misty gray. The thick, wet clouds that had proved so elusive throughout the long, dry summer swept in at last, under cover of darkness, to hover low over the land. A drizzle of rain had begun to fall an hour or so before dawn, driving the prince under cover of a tarpaulin, and Alex had to admit Carl had chosen his day of rest wisely. She envied him, tucked away nice and dry in the common room at the nearest inn, enjoying a hearty breakfast and good company.

She avoided the prince when she rose, feeling self-conscious after her indulgence the previous night. She wrapped herself in her coat and tried coaxing the last embers of the fire to light. The reluctant flame hissed under the damp sticks, sullen, the smoke clinging close to the ground. Prince Holden stood upwind, tending the unhappy mules. She saw him lift his head and sniff the air.

"I smell smoke."

"If the smell isn't from here, it's probably from a farmstead."

"It's coming from the wrong direction."

"The rain has everything muddled."

"Come here and tell me if you think I'm wrong."

She did, patting the soaking flank of one of the mules. He was right. She could smell smoke, and also cooking meat, coming from deeper in the forest.

"Let's go see where that smell's coming from," Holden suggested. "We'll have a good exercise in stealth, if nothing else."

"Very well." There was little else to do. They could either huddle around the failing fire, squat under the wagon, or slog about the dripping woods together. They might as well have the exercise.

He strapped on his sword and she followed suit. She let him lead. His sense of smell was keener than hers. They broke the path with care, stepping around twigs and on soft mossy patches wherever possible, trying not to leave footprints in the damp earth.

He stretched out his arm and halted her after a time, going to his knees behind a fallen log. She slipped up next to him and they peered over the top of the log and down into the dell below.

A campfire burned sullenly in the center of the dell despite the thick misty rain, and three tents stood in a rough ring. Alex blinked, startled. The men milling about didn't look quite right.

"Listen," the prince whispered, and she realized suddenly she couldn't understand their speech. She watched as a large man came ducking out of the biggest tent. He was tall, blond, and wore a heavy crested helm with a nose-guard. A dull, rusty chainmail coif covered his neck. He issued a command and others scampered to obey. He must be a chieftain of some sort, perhaps the ranking officer in this group.

"Danes," Holden breathed to her, and she knew he was right. Danes, this far inland? This was beyond alarming.

She glanced at the prince, and his eyes were burning, a fierce, angry look she'd never seen on his face before. His hand fell on her shoulder and he guided her to turn and retreat, looking back over his shoulder from time to time to ensure they were not pursued.

"We'll settle them," he said quietly when they were well out of earshot. "We'll arm ourselves and wait until dark, then we'll attack."

She blinked at him, astonished. "Do you really think that's wise?"

"Wise? No. However, there aren't many. I'll warrant we can put a scare into them they won't soon forget, and kill at least a few without bringing any harm to ourselves. We know this area; they don't. That spot wasn't trampled enough to be an old campsite, and we'd have run into them before. They'll be easy pickings."

They returned to their camp and armed themselves, then went back to spy on the Danish camp, moving as stealthily as they could. The rain seemed to have discouraged the Danes, who huddled about their campfire, not bothering to set sentries.

She and Holden prepared their plans carefully. "We need Carl," she murmured.

"There's no time to fetch him." He tightened a knot, lashing a screen of branches across their planned bolthole. "If the rumors we've been hearing are true, this lot has been attacking homesteads ever since they set foot in East Anglia." He glanced up at her. "We should be able to demoralize them easily. I used to pull tricks like this on my guards before I came of age. I was a spirited young lad, and their leader was a hard man, quite humorless. I grew very tired of his constant disapproval, and I used to break away from him and his men whenever I could, especially if we went hunting. I would hide and pick his squad apart with pranks while they searched for me. I may not know much about warfare on the battlefield, but I know sneaking." He looked at her wryly. "A unit of men relies on patterns, chain of command, and predictable routine. Break down their expectations, and chaos follows."

"You make a lot of sense," she admitted. "I'd still feel better if there were more of us."

"More preparation time would be good, too, but we're stuck with what we have. Do you want to sit idle while these invaders burn a homestead?"

No, she didn't.

His eyes glowed hard and fierce, and he held his chin high. Looking at him, she was suddenly reminded of Prince Gavin. There was a new and implacable confidence about Holden. His good nature was still visible in the laugh lines around his eyes, but his jaw was set, and he looked formidable and dangerous.

He drew his plan in a bit of muddy earth as she watched. His idea was quite clever, really. They'd prepared their bolthole, and would string her crossbow and wrap it in oilcloth, then leave it concealed there. After dark, Prince Holden would use his own bow to shoot a bolt into the Danish campsite. He would taunt them, if he had to, to start the pursuit. She would wait in the forest and trigger the first trap, a precarious natural deadfall. He'd trigger the second trap himself while she cut across the wood and arrived at the third. When the final snare had sprung, they would retreat to their shelter. After any remaining hunt died down, they would use their crossbows and their greater knowledge of the terrain to pick off any Danes who remained a threat.

Sneak attack was a good plan. She thought it had a better than average chance of success.

Chapter Nineteen

Alex and the prince closed their coats carefully, covering their pale shirts, trusting the brown of their clothes would fade into the woodland background. They settled in to their bolthole in the woods to wait for nightfall. By the sound, the Danes were drinking, singing around the fire in their sonorous, guttural language. Alex approved. Their drunkenness would hinder them.

Time seemed to crawl, and they could not risk speech. However, Alex never felt drowsy, the adrenaline of impending battle keeping her on edge. When the night reached its darkest point, midway between sunset and moonrise, she nudged the prince and he nodded.

He stood up noiselessly and advanced toward the camp. Alex wanted to linger and watch out for him. However, her role led her away into position by the first trap, where she crouched behind a thicket of concealing brush and waited with her sword ready. This trap had proved the hardest to prepare, and also represented the least reliable of their tricks. She'd spent a long time working quietly with her dagger to notch the dead tree supporting the hillside, while Prince Holden kept watch on the Danish encampment, ready to warn her with a whistle if anyone approached. She hoped her time had been well spent.

She heard a shout go up, then Holden's rapid footfalls passed nearby. The Danes pursued him in yelling disarray, one waving a hastily snatched torch. She kept her eyes off the light, not wanting to let the flame spoil her night vision.

As the Danish pursuit drew near, she lifted her sword and chopped at the last bit of wood supporting the dead tree-trunk, whose branches held back a wall of stone and debris, much of it augmented by her and Holden's patient, silent labors earlier in the day. As soon as the wood fibers severed she darted away, and after a pregnant, groaning pause, the entire hillside collapsed, burdened with stones and weakened by the fresh rain.

She was away well before the falling earth could catch her. Not waiting to see how many Danes were engulfed, she darted through the wood, leaving the main path. The landscape was so familiar from her runs with the prince she knew where to put her feet almost without looking.

The second trap was next. Sharpened stakes and caltrops lay waiting in the path. She knew exactly when the Danes stumbled over the trap from the echoes of their agonized shouting. She hoped none of the noise was coming from Holden. He should have known where to jump and when to dodge, but sometimes accidents happened. She knew she would worry until she saw him safe.

The third trap was a snare. They'd brought the mules in as close as they dared and hauled down a sapling, tethering it down on the ground with a well-staked rope, and laid a net in the path, firmly tied to the top of the tree's trunk. They had tied all their remaining knives and daggers into the rough rope net, which would jerk upright and haul tight when the rope was cut. The blades should shred anyone who was unwary enough to be caught standing atop them.

Holden flashed past, running well, and she let out a breath of relief. Half a dozen men were still behind him. When she cut the rope, three of them screamed. One was thrown thrashing into the night and came down with a thud, then lay still. Two wound up dangling from the tangled net, dripping blood.

Back to the bolthole, then. She melted away noiselessly and sheltered, monitoring the path. She heard another scream. Holden had done for one of the men who'd been caught by the second trap, perhaps. She saw motion and a glimpse of pale cloth nearby; too pale for Holden. She fired her crossbow, but missed.

There was no more light; the Danish raiders had dropped their torch. Men shouted. She heard one, perhaps two separate voices, and another answered them from the camp.

Ten men had quickly been reduced to three. She judged there was little need for her and Holden to take refuge in their carefully prepared hiding place. They would become the hunters now, not the hunted.

A rustle at her ear announced Holden's arrival as he knelt by the mouth of the shelter. Even though she'd expected his arrival, she nearly jumped out of her skin.

"We killed most of them. I finished the ones who were lamed." He kept his voice low. As she'd guessed, he had his crossbow in hand, and was slotting in a fresh quarrel. "Let's go to their camp and split up, one on either side. We'll soon pick them off."

She'd worried about him freezing in battle, squeamish about killing, but his steadiness ended her fretting. She joined him, peeling off to take the south flank when he headed north.

After that, patience was all they needed. She targeted a guard and shot him soon after she settled in to snipe. He finished the other in the resulting confusion.

The chieftain proved no harder to manage. He kicked the fire to cinders and tried to go to ground, but the ruddy gleam of scattered coals on his pale tunic betrayed him, and she heard Holden's crossbow twang a second after her own. The chieftain's body jerked twice and he fell, trying to crawl to the shelter of his tent, but soon collapsed and lay still.

They checked their traps, counting men, and discovered only one couldn't be accounted for. Morning light showed his tracks departing the forest. Every other print was distinct, but his right foot dragged in a shuffling limp.

"He's heading back east." Holden smiled at her, ferocious. His eyes gleamed.

The sky rumbled overhead, lengthy and ominous, and she glanced toward the horizon. Curtains of thick, heavy rain had begun to sweep in from the west, obscuring the landscape. Their celebration would be drowned in short order by a heavy squall.

"Let's get under cover," she suggested, and he agreed, trotting hastily back to their campsite.

They wound up hunkered under both the wagon and their oiled leather tarpaulin, watching the rain sheet down in thick curtains. The mules stood miserably under a nearby larch tree, twitching their ears, water dripping from their tails and bellies and chins.

After Alex and the prince finished analyzing their victory, their tongues lagged and weariness set in, robbing them of anything to say. The growing silence slowly became awkward, and Alex could tell Prince Holden was thinking hard. She wondered if he was pondering the lives of the men he'd killed.

If he was, he spoke no word of them.

The rain proved so persistent they were finally forced to take the privy spade and scoop a trench around the upper edge of the wagon, ditching away the runoff from the sloping ground in an effort to prevent water from streaming into their relatively dry sanctuary. Their efforts occupied a little time, and the prince managed to fill some additional minutes speculating how long the rain would last, but by lunchtime, he was silent again. They ate cold bread and cheese without speaking and listened to the drumming of the rain.

Tired of sitting hunched, they eventually stretched out and stared up at the boards. Alex tried to keep her heart from racing. Being so close to the prince was starting to wear on her. She kept noticing his scent, which reminded her of the taste of his mouth. She couldn't help bumping into his knee or elbow occasionally, which made her pull herself into as little space as she could easily manage so as not to touch him again.

"I'm worried about my father and my brother," he said finally. "We've had little news of either in the last few weeks, and for these raiders to have come so far inland? I don't like it."

She chewed her lip. She'd been worried also, but they were far enough west news from the capital didn't reach here readily. Nor should the Danes, not unless they were running roughshod over the whole land.

When he spoke, the prince revealed his thoughts were following the same line.

"Alex, I will not flee any further." He said the words quietly, but she could hear his absolute determination. He would not be put off easily this time. "Pleasant though it is to camp here with you, my country is being invaded. I will take my stand and fight."

"Your father commanded us to go west."

"He gave you orders. Yes, I know," he said gently. "As your prince, I'm countermanding them." His voice was like steel.

She lay very still, recognizing the definite nature of the statement. This was no sulky whim of a spoiled prince, eager for a shiny uniform and battlefield glory he believed he would win from the back of the fray while his men died in the front lines. This was the determination of a ruler who keenly felt his responsibility to protect his people.

Prince Holden's father never could have anticipated he would learn such authority and purpose. King Anselm might have given different orders if he suspected Holden could come to understand so much of his duty. Perhaps the king would not believe his youngest son could have learned so fast, but he had. She sensed she could not gainsay Prince Holden or buy his distraction. Not this time, not even if she offered herself as a bribe.

She stared up at the bottom of the wagon bed. The saw that had cut the boards was dull, perhaps missing teeth. The cut was indistinct, and frayed fibers made the surface of the wood look rough, almost furred. She studied the texture silently, not knowing what to say, until she almost forgot a response was called for.

He turned onto his side after a time and placed a gentle hand on her arm. "I'm a different man than the one who was sent away. I'm ready, and you know it."

She didn't. She wasn't sure at all. He *was* changed. Perhaps he could fight without being killed, but he still didn't know how to lead men. She hadn't even thought of trying to teach him. She'd never trained him in battlefield tactics. There was only so much she could do in one summer. Would the men of East Anglia follow him? She couldn't be sure. They knew him by reputation, and they did not respect him. Perhaps they could learn to do so. After all, even Carl had slowly changed his allegiance from her to the prince, had he not?

"We should leave soon," he said quietly. "As soon as Carl returns. That escaped man could be trouble."

"He might bring back reinforcements to investigate. Yes." She was frustrated she hadn't thought of it first. The sleepless night was affecting her more than she'd anticipated. "This plan is foolhardy," she said softly. "You're mostly untested in battle, and you still have a lot to learn about swordsmanship. You haven't led men."

"I know," he answered quietly. "I plan to go on exactly as we began last night." He raised himself on one elbow. "I'll gather a small force of men and draw on the locals wherever we go. We'll drive those Danish bastards off one small band at a time. We'll hit them on the fringes of their action. A little here, a little there, before we melt away. After enough attacks, they'll think we're ghosts or spirits. We'll make ourselves a legend of terror. Whenever they get frightened enough to band together, then Gavin and my father can bring in the army and sweep them out."

"It's crazy enough to work," she said slowly. "We'd have to manage our raids with care."

113

"That's where you and Carl come in." His smile turned wry. "I'll need your help and advice, of course. Men will follow me if you and Carl stand at my side." His eyes searched her face, earnest. "Will you help me?"

She closed her eyes and gave the best response she could: a single nod, curt. His hand curled around hers, his fingers settling into her palm and his thumb moving over her knuckles in a delicate caress, but he did not press her further.

They didn't speak much for the rest of the day, each preoccupied with private thoughts and worries, and they prepared to sleep as soon as nightfall drew near. A cold wind sprang up out of the northeast as the sun sank, turning the leaden gray clouds to inky black, and they crept together without discussion, curling chastely close and sharing their blankets against the cold and the damp.

She woke nestled in the curve of Prince Holden's body, seeing familiar boots on the muddy ground inches from her face. The sun had risen and the rain was clearing swiftly. Carl bent to peer tentatively in at them, his eyes curious. The prince's warm arm held her securely. Alex flushed a little, knowing how they looked, embarrassed even though she'd sometimes shared blankets innocently with Carl himself while bivouacking in the cold. This was nothing more, but...

"Good morning, Carl." Prince Holden was already awake. He spoke with quiet authority, as if he had commanded the man for all of his life. "Don't unpack your things. We'll be going now you've returned."

"Yes, Your Highness."

Chapter Twenty

The prince continued as he had begun, surprisingly self-assured in his new role of command, leaving Alex floundering at sea. She had no idea how to relate to his new assertiveness. She couldn't decide whether to challenge him at every turn, or whether to knuckle under and do as she was told.

The latter option rankled more than a little, so she wound up offering him quite a bit of sauce even when she accepted an order, starting right away as they prepared their camping gear for travel. She caught Carl chuckling into his sleeve so often she started to give him dangerous looks, which did nothing but amuse him all the more.

They rode out that first morning through a world washed to shades of velvet green and gold, almost as fresh as the first leaves of spring. However, Alex could recognize the first signs of autumn on the land. The leaves were dark green now, with a few patches turning to yellow and brown here and there, and the gorse was no longer in bloom. Instead, the fields' golden glow came from the fast-ripening grain.

The prince sat on the wagon bench with her, taking a turn at driving the mules while Carl napped in the back. She looked at his hands as he held the reins and clucked smartly to the mules. His fingers and palms were new-callused and strong, no longer cracked and bloody. They held the leather straps with confidence. Where once he could barely steer the mules, which had sensed his uncertainty and balked, he now directed them easily with automatic motions of his wrists.

As they traveled, Alex had plenty of time to brood on her choice to let him assume command and reverse the king's orders. She had the authority, technically, to refuse him. The king's mandate outweighed the word of a mere prince, after all. She knew she would have had to tie him and haul him unwilling in the back of the wagon.

As she'd once told Holden, you made a plan and when the situation altered, you revised your plans to account for the change.

She did not think the king ever anticipated how much his spoiled offspring might grow up in such a short time. He'd misjudged his son, just as he'd miscalculated when he expected the Danes to follow his army to Norwich and provide Prince Gavin the opportunity for a focused battle.

Holden grew aware of Alex's scrutiny and looked up, his brows lifting in a silent question. She hastily looked away, down at her own hands. She needed to clean under her nails with the tip of her dagger, but she knew better than to try while the wagon was in rattling motion.

This new prince was largely her creation. She'd trained him in fighting and led him to re-evaluate and change his behavior. She had to confess her approval of his choices, at least so far. An uncomfortable awareness had begun to form in her mind. Some part of her missed the old prince, the spoiled bratling who was so easy to predict and manipulate...so easy to resist. He'd always amused her. She was quite fond of him, in a strange way.

This man beside her, though...he was an unknown quantity, as confusing and worrisome as he was desirable. She didn't know whether he was changing himself merely to impress her. Would the changes last? Were they superficial? Would he crumple under pressure?

Would he revert to his old habit of going through women like a flame through pine straw?

She remembered her mother narrowing her eyes at the men of the court, steering Alex through the echoing halls of the castle with a firm grip on her hand. "Fops and rakes, every one. You can't redeem them. Marry in haste and repent at leisure." Her mother had been a veritable font of wise sayings, and nearly all of the ones about men were warnings. She'd always encouraged Alex to be self-reliant and securely independent, as sure of herself as any man, and needing no man to be happy.

Until now. She shifted a little, uncomfortable.

If the brat prince drew women like moths to a flame, how would they respond to the kingly man he had become?

She rather thought they would break on him like ocean waves on a rocky shore. They'd be innumerable and beautiful and transient, unable to make any lasting mark on him. She didn't need to steal a glance to know how handsome he was, or how the thought of being one of those discarded, broken women distressed her.

He might think his battle was all but won, and she was nearly his, but Alex knew better. There were still tests he must pass before she would seriously consider his suit. The first of them was likely to come tonight. As they crested a low hill she saw a town in the middle distance, near enough they should arrive at the gates by twilight.

She would be most curious to see how he comported himself around the chambermaids and serving wenches. He could not fail to attract their interest.

"Let's make that town by nightfall," she said casually. "A real bed would feel good after lying out in the cold and the wet last night."

"It certainly would," he agreed with enthusiasm, and clucked encouragement to the mules as they began the winding descent into the valley.

Chapter Twenty-One

Alex's judgment of the distance and their speed proved correct, and they rattled into town as the local lamplighters set out about their rounds. They found the inn easily, and while Carl and the prince saw to the horses and to their possessions, she rented three rooms. The extras represented a bit of an extravagance, but they suited her purposes.

They sat down together to succulent roast chicken with herbed vegetables and bread still hot from the oven. The prince seemed quite well behaved, admirably courteous but largely indifferent toward the girls who served them, so Alex relaxed and ate till her insides ached.

Carl carried the burden of the conversation for the three of them, chattering amiably and not seeming to care who with. He was cordial with Alex, the prince, the serving girls, the few travelers resting for a night along their road, even the local drinkers and farmers. The town had a nice, friendly feel and he fit right in with the common folk, singing and enjoying his ale.

Alex finished her meal and wiped her lips, refusing a third helping. Then, while the men still sat talking over full mugs, she begged exhaustion and made a strategic retreat to her room.

Later she heard footsteps hesitate outside her door. One set continued and one paused. She heard a light tap at the door. Doubtless it was the prince, ever hopeful. She covered a chuckle with her hand, trying not to let him hear.

She did not answer his knock, and after a moment he moved on, doubtless assuming she was already asleep. She heard him enter his room, which lay between hers and Carl's. All the better to spy on the prince's movements. She stood up stealthily, padding across the floor in her stocking feet, and cracked open her door, keeping a sharp eye on the hall.

She waited for nearly two hours and a half while the common room emptied and the place went quiet, the lodgers gradually settling to sleep.

She stifled a yawn and considered abandoning her watch in favor of bed, but footfalls on the stair stopped her. Someone was approaching, trying to be stealthy. Alex pressed an eye to the crack. A pretty wench crept through the hall, glancing about with sly caution. She counted doors to herself as she pattered down the corridor, then tapped at the prince's.

Alex's belly turned to ice and her fist knotted around the door-handle so hard her hand ached, her knuckles white.

The door opened, showing darkness beyond, and the girl slipped inside.

She did not come out again. The walls were thin, and after a few moments, Alex heard the telltale creak of the bedframe and a high-pitched giggle.

She rose silently, closed and locked her door, then found her bed. She lay down and bundled the pathetically flat pillow over her ears, struggling to find sleep. Slumber would not come, and rest still eluded her even when the gray light of dawn filled her window and incriminating noises had long ceased to come from the room next door.

By then, all she could hear were her memories, including her mother and father's voices repeating their stern warnings. They made a bitter trio with her own miserable regrets, all yammering in her aching head, admonishing her for being a fool.

She was too much the mistress of herself to betray her distress publicly, rising and pouring cold water from her full pitcher into the basin waiting on the table. She washed her face to take the redness from her cheeks, then went down to the common room and forced herself to eat a bowl of porridge. She spoke with distant politeness to the prince when he wandered in and sat down at her side, but finished rapidly and went out to tend to the mules before Carl ever managed to make it downstairs.

She sat beside the prince quietly as they rolled down the road, fighting her fatigue. She did not twist at the end of her belt or crease the cloth of her sleeve. She rode patiently and swayed with the motion of the wagon, long accustomed to poor roads, even though she felt like vomiting and clinging to her seat.

She did not look at the prince, and she answered his occasional comments politely but without interest. Eventually he fell silent, catching something of her mood.

She was glad when he left her in peace. Her mind was busy assessing the past months coldly, turning each day over with brutal clarity. She paid particular attention to the last few.

That handful of days had cost her a good measure of her pride and authority. Her dignity was lost with them, and her stature too, at least in regard to the prince. She could no longer even pretend to command him like a subordinate.

Shrewd though he was at reading women, he still could not be certain of her. He might guess her desire had grown, but aside from a single kiss, given willingly in repayment of a wager, she'd never surrendered her body. She'd never given him even an inkling regarding the state of her heart, thank God.

Secrecy was of utmost urgency. She must keep her wounded feelings hidden. He'd grown much more dangerous to her now than ever before, and proved just as faithless as even the worst of his detractors might have predicted. Yet he still commanded her loyalty and service. She vowed he would have those in spite of her disappointment, as her oaths demanded.

Alex spent the morning tucking her wayward feelings into a strongbox inside her heart, battening down the lid, and locking it securely. By the time they stopped for lunch, she felt herself fully able to fulfill her duties as a guard to the prince. She spent the halt setting a perimeter around their temporary camp, currying the mules, accepting a mint infusion from Carl, and sipping as she worked. She hunted a few strips of dried meat and a chunk of bread out of her pack and ate them from the top of a stone outcrop where she sat when all the other tasks were finished, watching the countryside for Danes.

Her position and duties had shifted along with her heart, but the change in them was at least something she had trained for. She ignored the puzzled glance the prince threw at Carl and the shrug he received in return. They were at war, after all. Her caution was admirable and prudent.

This would be the only way she could protect herself now. She wished she'd been more careful from the beginning, as her father warned.

Chapter Twenty-Two

After Alex made her resolution to do her duty, Prince Holden became 'Your Highness,' no more and no less. After an awkward day or three, she became 'Captain.' The word was both a relief and a bitter disappointment when he spoke it, and she burned with secret anger to see him surrender so easily.

In truth, his acceptance was not unexpected. If he was truly growing into a warrior, one who might one day be worthy of the throne, then she could hardly expect him to hang on to his childish ambition of seducing his guard. That was to be expected, particularly since she refused to give him any further encouragement in the matter.

Carl watched them both with troubled eyes, but kept his mouth shut. He was no longer required as a buffer between them. Alex made cold formality suffice.

"Captain, come join us for supper," the prince called to her one evening while she stood watch. "This is a flat plain. Hordes of Danes are hardly lurking behind a tussock and waiting to attack."

"Yes, sir." She approached obediently, stiff, and stood at attention by the fire.

Prince Holden stared at her for a long moment, his mouth narrowing, and tossed his tin plate aside without taking any food. He stalked away to the wagon, taking a deep breath and leaning with both hands braced against one of the wheels. Carl blinked at her. 'Yes, *sir*'? he mouthed, incredulous.

She shot him a savage look and he drew back, serving himself without further impertinence. He began to shovel beans into his mouth. She glanced at the prince, who remained still, hands locked around the rim of the wheel, struggling with some unidentified emotion. He returned after a time, as stiff and constrained as Alex herself, and ate without evidence of enjoyment.

Carl finished first and went to the perimeter to take the first watch, showing no desire to listen to the cold silence around the campfire.

"Mind the cleanup," Prince Holden ordered Alex at length, his voice challenging.

"Yes, sir." She accepted his plate and poured water from the kettle into the washing basin. It was not the prince's place to do the work of a common kitchen drudge, not if he didn't wish to.

He made an aggravated noise. "I command you to come to my blankets after." The order was gruff.

"No, Your Highness." Implacable and resolute, she drew the line.

"I see there's still some fire to you, then."

"I don't know what you mean, sir." She used the words like a weapon, fending him back with her sharp tone.

"Alex." His voice dropped low, a desperate plea. "I had hoped we were becoming friends. What have I done wrongly?" He looked lost, almost her wayward prince for a fleeting moment, then reclaimed his dignity.

"Nothing, sir. It's time we behaved like a proper prince and captain, since you've proved yourself worthy."

"You resent me taking command?"

No, she didn't; he was ready. She kept her face smooth with an effort. This wasn't about command. Curse him! He knew damned well why she was angry.

"No, sir. I don't resent King Anselm or Prince Gavin's orders either." She took a deep breath, struggling to master her anger. She must remember she'd refused his affections, and therefore she had no claim on them. Furthermore, as his subordinate, she did not get a say in whether he chose to bed a willing girl. "A captain yields superior officers respect and obedience in the line of duty, and works to the best of her professional ability. Or the captain isn't fit to hold her rank." She felt her cheeks color; perhaps she *wasn't* fit to serve him while she was still this angry.

"I've heard my father address yours by his given name, in tones of friendship."

"You haven't heard my father use the king's given name to him, I'll wager." She was certain of her guess, and he acquiesced, taking a painful breath instead of denying her claim.

"Solitude is one of the hard facts that comes with royal blood." Alex unbent, very carefully, just a little. "You are a prince of East Anglia, sir. I am your servant to command, within the boundaries of duty." It was true she was his subordinate, but she'd also become his teacher. Part of her duty was to help the prince grow as a leader, and she could not ignore that responsibility, not even if she was furious with him.

She lifted her gaze to meet his. "If you would be a leader of men, you must learn to be absolutely comfortable with giving orders to your subordinates, and with receiving their respect in return as they serve you." She drew a deep breath. "You must learn, as well, what may be ordered in fairness, and what may not. You cannot order friendship, just as you should not try to command more intimate services, though some might choose to obey your wishes. In refusing these things, I serve you the better by teaching."

Not that Alex thought for a moment he'd been serious when he commanded her to go to his bed. He was merely baiting her, trying to provoke her into an argument that would break the ice growing between them. What's more, it was working. Prince Holden might have all the moral standards of a cat in heat, but he was a shrewd tactician.

The knowledge that he'd trapped her so neatly sent a flare of anger thrilling through her nerves. She couldn't keep some of the waspishness out of her voice as she continued. "You will doubtless have no shortage of willing partners without ordering subordinates to your blankets."

His eyes searched hers, wounded, but his jaw stayed firm and his shoulders sank only slightly.

"I had no expectation you would obey such an order. I only meant to..." he gestured with visible frustration. "To rouse your temper, so you would become yourself again." A muscle twitched in his jaw as he sat back, accepting the stalemate with reluctance. "You have been a good teacher, but I will not accept this distance between us. You and I are more to one another than links in the chain of command."

She wanted nothing more than to agree with him, but she must not relent. She had weakened critically in her resolve to withstand his charm. The depth of her hurt over his dalliance was ample proof of how urgently she must resist forming a deeper emotional attachment to him. She could not admit it aloud, not to him, but she needed the protective distance of rank and protocol far more than he.

"The hardest lessons are often the ones we require the most." Her words were cold comfort at best. She'd longed to believe his devotion to her was true, but it was not. Why had she ever let herself come to care for him? She was a fool.

She must learn to be his captain and his teacher again, no more and no less.

"These are not my final words on this matter, Captain." He looked at his hands for a moment, twisting the signet ring on his smallest finger. He opened his mouth as if to speak further, but fell silent instead.

"Go to your blankets. I'll rouse you for third watch," he finally directed after the silence became uncomfortable.

"Yes, sir." Alex obeyed with relief, rolling herself up and turning away from him. She was so tired she fell asleep quickly in spite of herself.

He kept his word, setting his hand on her shoulder after his watch. She blinked up into his pale, unhappy face and sat up, subtly moving away from his hand.

"A moment, please." He raised his palm, stopping her where she sat, still tangled in her blankets. "I have spent my watch thinking, Captain. You may not wish my friendship, but you have it." He pulled the heavy gold ring off his finger. The signet bore the crest of House Stuart, a lion rampant within the circle of a belt and buckle. She didn't know how to read Latin, but she hadn't spent a lifetime in service to King Anselm without learning many things about her superior. She knew the meaning of the letters inscribed in delicate filigree beneath the crest: *Nobilis est ira leonis,* or 'The lion's anger is noble.' Holden turned the ring in his hand, letting her see his name engraved within the thick circle.

"If you are determined to have a lord rather than a friend, then I would still be him." He didn't look at her face as he extended the ring on his palm. "This is a symbol of my regard, of my protection, and of my patronage, if you will. I suppose it isn't needed, but anyone who sees this will know if they trifle with you, they incur my unending enmity. There are those in half a dozen lands who would offer you protection and succor in the name of the House of Stuart if you carried my ring. It's possible that may be worth something to you, someday."

"Your Highness, I can't." She held her hand up, palm out, warding him away. She felt truly shaken. She would never have anticipated such a gift.

"Be silent and take the cursed thing." He made the words a command, his voice taut and unhappy. He caught her hand and firmly pressed the ring into her palm. "It is nothing, compared to my feelings." He stopped himself and grimaced bitterly. "Alexandra. Take my token and throw it in the river, if you will, but I beg you to take it."

Reluctant, she let him fold her fingers over the ring. He hesitated, then lifted her hand to his mouth, pressing a kiss to her knuckles. His lashes closed, surprisingly long and thick, and lay against his cheeks. His mouth lingered for a moment, warm and soft on her fingers.

The gesture was courtly, not at all out of place with such a gift, a symbol of fealty. Asking for hers to him, a vassal to a lord? Certainly. Giving his to her, a man to a woman he desired more than common? Her heart fluttered

126

and raced in spite of everything she knew to the contrary. She had to react to the gift in the most rational way possible.

"I offer thanks for the chance to serve you, my liege."

He let her hand fall and exhaled explosively, plainly relieved. "I accept your service." He reached out, touching her face lightly with his fingertips, then surged to his feet and slipped away to find his blankets.

The ring fit on her forefinger, but she could not display such a token openly. Too many people would misunderstand...or understand all too well, perhaps better than she did. How could he bed a tavern maid so casually, but still retain such a warm regard for Alex? It made no sense.

Alex removed the necklace holding the key to the weapons chest. She threaded the leather thong through the prince's ring and put the lot back over her head.

The ring hung heavily between her breasts, still warm from his hand.

Her eyes filled with tears and she blinked them away fiercely. They dazzled a halo in the light from the fire and eclipsed the prince, who knelt not far away, unrolling his blankets so he could take his rest.

She'd never heard of Prince Holden giving a token to any other living person, male or female. To give a token that bore his family crest? Such a thing was usually done to mark a particularly strong bond, to identify someone he would regard as the nearest thing to kin. This ring marked her as his. It acknowledged her as his guard, his captain, his servant, trusted to speak on his behalf, allowed to claim hospitality or ask succor as if she were a Stuart herself. To deny her anything she requested while holding this ring would be to deny Prince Holden himself, as if to his face.

Even the Danes should respect this. If she were ever captured, they would believe her one of the king's chief thanes, and treat her accordingly. That might mean immediate execution, or possibly a demand for ransom, likely a hefty one. She should be treated honorably, imprisoned or slain as a valiant warrior, rather than enslaved and raped.

There were those closer to home who might accuse her of stealing the ring, and refuse or prosecute her on those grounds. There were also those who would say she'd earned the token on her back with her legs spread.

Those who might question her right to it would be mistaken.

Alex pulled out the ring and closed her fist over it tightly, her heart welling over with fierce pride. The prince, for all his faults, was now her liege lord. Regardless of how he intended his gift, Alex regarded it as a formal pact between them. He'd claimed her loyalty, and she accepted his claim. She would live and die in his service.

As to what more the ring might mean...she swallowed hard and turned her eyes to the prince, who was settling in near Carl's bedroll, wrapping his coat and blankets around himself. Friendship, indeed. She might not accept him as a lover, but as a friend? She might be forbidden to speak plainly of such things in polite society, but he'd earned her friendship long ago. Perhaps she'd always liked him, even before they left Norwich.

Some things, she was forced to admit, were even more important than decorum.

She rose and went to her prince, and she let her hand fall on his shoulder. "You do not have to command my friendship or buy it with a token," she told him quietly, even though his inconstancy had hurt her heart. She did not have to be his lover to be his friend. "You already have it. You will always have it." She squeezed his shoulder lightly and went to take up her duty, hunkering down atop the wagon and keeping watch over them all as the moon rose.

Chapter Twenty-Three

Prince Holden slept poorly, tossing and turning, so Alex let both him and Carl wake up on their own the next morning. They didn't wake quickly. The sun was shining strongly onto Carl's eyes before he stirred, squinting and trying to turn away from the glare. She started frying bacon and sausages in their big iron skillet, and the scent of food brought him the rest of the way out of his stubborn sleep.

The scent of breakfast also roused the prince, who slipped away to tend to the call of nature. Alex turned the bacon as Carl struggled upright, rolled his bedding, and came wandering over to the fireside, reaching for his mug and pouring himself a strong mint infusion.

"You're a sleepyhead," she teased him, adding a stick to the fire.

"I should say so. Didn't get a bit of rest back at the inn." Carl leered a little, giving her a broad wink. "I'm still trying to catch up."

"So the prince and his little miss kept you up as well?" Alex asked, trying to sound indifferent.

Carl blinked at her with surprise. "The prince and...what are you talking about?"

"They were working hard all night." She poked the fire fiercely. "He's not changed a bit, not when it comes to the lasses." She tried to keep the bitterness out of her voice, not entirely succeeding.

Carl stared at her. "Well no wonder you've been acting like you have a poker up your arse."

Alex stared at him with dawning outrage. "What's that supposed to mean?"

"You've judged His Highness for the worst again, without even stopping to ask any questions." Carl pursed his lips in dismay.

"You have exactly two seconds to explain your remark," Alex shot back tightly. "For I saw the girl go into his room, and I heard what happened after."

"That was *my* room," Carl leaned forward and hissed at her, not backing down a hair in his defiance. "He saw she and I were wanting a bit of fun, and he told me to trade with him so we could use the bigger bed."

Alex sat back, her eyes going round, and stared at him. "You slept in the prince's room and spent the night with a serving girl?"

"I did. And I tried to wake you to tell you of the switch when he and I came up, but you weren't answering the door, so I thought you were dead to the world."

Alex's mind whirled and her belly did as well, threatening to make her sick up her hot drink. Her hand flew to her breast, covering the prince's ring. Guilt stabbed her as she remembered the pain in his eyes when she'd begun to treat him with such unwarranted coldness.

"Aye, there, you see what you've gone and done, I'll warrant." Carl shook his finger at her. "I hope you've said nothing worse than what I've heard pass."

She rubbed her palm over her face, which burned with embarrassment. "Shit."

"Why were you watching the hall, if you weren't answering your door?" Carl's eyes narrowed at her. "You set him up to the test, didn't you?"

Alex drew a deep breath, looking away, and breathed out forcefully. "What if I did?" Her own voice fell to a hiss. "You can't expect me to believe a dog can change its spots so quickly, not without a bit of proof."

130

"Hung yourself on your own rope, you did." Carl frowned at her. "I'll note you weren't too proud to have a bit of slap and tickle on the side yourself, not long past."

"That was different." Her protest rang hollow. She knew how her night of fun had made Prince Holden suffer. While she'd never intended to hurt the man, she might as well have deliberately set out to punish him.

"Sometimes I don't know why he likes you as well as he does." Carl glanced to the forest where the prince still could not be seen returning. "You've given him precious little courtesy of late, Captain."

She stared at him, tears prickling behind her eyes. "You know, Carl, we've been friends for more than a decade. There's no other soul in the guards I'd let give me such sauce, not without stripping him of his rank and sending him down to the infantry. You're right, as far as you understand things, but you simply don't realize a woman pays much more dearly than a man if she makes a mistake in who she beds. She has to bear the shame and suffer the pointing fingers and raise the bastard child." Her hands shook as she dragged the frying pan off the fire before the bacon could burn.

He listened to her gravely. "I suppose that's true enough. I don't know what it's like for a woman, but I know you. You don't let people get close to you, Captain. No closer than me, at any rate, and I'm your second in command. We're friends, but you keep me at arm's length, enough I half piss myself when you threaten to pull rank."

She could see his anger and his hurt in the way he put his mug down with care so he wouldn't spill or break it. However, he didn't give in to his temper, reining himself in carefully as he continued to speak.

"You've no friends among the ladies at court, and you don't see your lovers more than once or twice. You've only your father and me to care about you. Us, and now the prince. If I may be frank, I don't see you have the option to treat him and others who love you so careless-like, not if you don't want to spend the end of your years alone." The tone of his voice stayed soft though his words were harsh, and she saw compassion in his eyes when he spoke. "I may know naught of women, but I do know aught of men, and I tell you, that one has fixed his heart on you. You can put an end to his hopes, if you push him away hard enough, but you won't find another like him if you do."

He fell silent abruptly as the prince appeared. Alex scraped the bacon and sausages out of the pan and portioned them out onto their tin plates, trying to keep the mortification off her face.

"Thank you," the prince accepted his portion politely, and rested the plate in his lap while he brewed himself a mug of mint infusion.

"We should move on," Alex murmured at length, struggling to seem normal. "I'd like to inquire at any settlements we pass through and see if they have news of the Danes."

"There was news in the last town, but not of Norwich. Nearly everyone we spoke to after you went up had heard tales of homesteads being looted and burned," the prince scowled. "One of the farmers gave me directions to a town that's been hit more than once. He said we'd get there if we take the first right turn after we get out of these hills, then follow the east road."

Chapter Twenty-Four

They followed Prince Holden's directions, and not two days later, they found themselves standing on a destroyed farmstead. The surrounding countryside seemed abnormally quiet, not even a bird scolding as they stood staring at the charred and gutted farmhouse, which stood open to the air, all thatch burned away. Faint trails of smoke still rose from the ashes of the byre. Oddly fletched arrows stood half-buried in some of the house's crumbling wattle-and-daub walls, and Carl picked up the broken blade of a bronze spear in the sheep-pen. Everything valuable or edible had been taken.

Alex stepped around the corner of the empty house and found the prince standing there with his fists clenched. He moved aside slowly to let her come abreast of him, revealing half a dozen mounds of fresh-turned earth. Three of the mounds were quite small.

She covered her mouth unhappily, turning to him. He held one of the arrows in his fist, his lips drawn back in a snarl. "Let's find the nearest town and see what may be done," he kept control of his voice with an effort.

They followed the lane into town. The citizens there were sober and watchful, wary, and not best pleased to see strangers. With a start, Alex recognized the town where she'd taken her young lover. She glanced anxiously at the prince. It could prove awkward if they encountered Edgar again.

He immediately spied the very inn where she'd once made her assignation, and she sighed, accepting the all-but-inevitable as he hopped off the wagon and vanished inside.

She left Carl in charge of stabling the mules and disposing of the wagon, and went in to arrange rooms for them all. After she finished, she wandered over casually until she was near the prince and sat down at an adjacent table, watching him speak with the locals.

His touch with diplomacy was not particularly deft, and the farmers were clearly uneasy about speaking with a man who was dressed as one of their own but was plainly well-educated and sounded like he came from far above their social station. However, the topic of the raid was a sore one. After the prince bought a round of ale for the house, the locals proved eager to hash the matter through with him even though he was a stranger.

"Where do these Danes come from? They must be encamped nearby."

"Likely in the wood by the old mill," one grizzled elder muttered into his pint. "I saw smoke rising there a few days ago, where no smoke should be. The king ought to be told. He'd send troops to aid us."

"We'll have no help from the king," another old man shook his head, pessimistic. "He and Prince Gavin are busy in their own neck of the woods, and doing naught but flailing, too, it's said. The younger prince is gone, or so the story goes. He's run off to another country to keep his precious arse intact."

That gave the prince a moment of pause, but after consideration, he passed over the unwitting insult without comment. "When there is no army at hand, sometimes good citizens must fight on their own. I heard of a group of raiders near Tanton who defeated a Danish band right handily not two weeks past."

"We've no weapons," a third old farmer shrugged. "Naught but forks for pitching hay, anyhow."

"You know the countryside and all its dangers. You know the lay of the land." Holden leaned forward, earnest. "Moreover, you have something more important than weapons. You have the will to defend your farms and your friends and kin. You don't have to have an army to defeat a foe. Sometimes cleverness and deceit will serve."

"How so?" That was a young lad, his interest piqued even though the oldsters continued shaking their graying heads sagely.

"Shoot a flaming arrow into their tents and run," Holden shrugged. "Leave a pitfall trap on a path they patrol, and embed your pitchforks tines-up in the bottom. Rig a deadfall or a tree snare. Sneak up on a sentry in the night and cut his throat, then vanish like a ghost and leave the rest to find him dead in the morning. They'll soon get the message."

That commanded the lad's attention. He called to some of his companions, who came over to listen. Alex recognized Edgar among them. He glanced toward her and gave a start, then his face warmed with a smile. She blushed in spite of herself, ducking her head.

The prince began to speak with the lads as the older men drifted away, and she could sense their enthusiasm catching fire. They needed a leader to inspire them, and she knew Prince Holden meant to lead.

They soon began to draw crude maps of the countryside on the table for him, dipping their fingers in their beer, and were rapidly buried deep in plans.

Edgar hung back, smiling at her. "Alex? I had not thought to see you again."

She saw the prince's ears prick to points even as he supervised the mapmaking.

"I did not know I would return, Edgar. However, my lord wanted to help these people. He has no love for the Danes." She kept her voice low.

"So I see." He chuckled. "He has the lads afire. I hope he can rein them in before they run off and get their throats cut."

"He will guide them himself. His last raid was successful."

"That's interesting." The way his eyes lingered on her face said he found her even more interesting. "What happened?"

"He used his methods to kill nine of the ten Danes in the party, with no losses on our side." She shrugged a little, uncomfortable. "I was his only aid, and there was little risk compared to open battle. Mind, I don't think our luck can always be so good. Accidents happen, and sometimes the Danes will be better led or better prepared. Still, I'd rather fight than sit still and wait for trouble to come, for it may find you incapable of defending. Preferable to lose a soldier or two than family after family, I think."

"Yes, that may be." He touched her cheek, and out of the corner of her eye, she saw Holden's spine stiffen. "Will you be free from your duties tonight?"

Alex smiled gently. "I fear not. My lord will want me to think through his plan and tell him of any flaws I see."

"Then another time?"

"I don't think so." Alex shifted her weight uncomfortably. "I'm very busy, Edgar."

"I hope you may change your mind." Edgar bowed to her and rejoined the lads. Alex drifted close enough to hear them discussing the local grist mill and its potential as a trap. One lad suggested concealing the millrace beneath a screen of branches and twigs, then leading the Danish troops to blunder across the obstacle, hoping some of them would be hurt.

"As a last resort, perhaps." Prince Holden tapped the table with his fingertip. "Who among you knows the region best?"

"I do." Edgar stood tall, and Holden eyed him speculatively. "My own farmstead is quite close to the one the Danes burned. My family is staying in the town, now, for fear of the raiders catching us at night."

"Can you take me near the Danish camp without being seen?"

"I think so, if they've made their camp where old Aldwin guessed."

"Good." The prince lifted his head decisively. "Take no action, lads, but if you live near the Danish camp, go now and remove your families into town. They are not safe. Meet me here tomorrow morning, and bring your brothers if they're trustworthy and of age. Otherwise mention this to no one, lest the Danes overhear our plans. Tonight we wait and scout. Tomorrow we act." He turned to Edgar. "You and I will go out to scout their encampment."

Alex groaned silently, keeping her face outwardly smooth as the two men eyed one another, both bristling a little, each of them plainly jealous of the other. Edgar and Holden off alone together on a scouting party? She must not let that happen.

Chapter Twenty-Five

Prince Holden broke the charged silence after a moment, clearing his throat, and strode out with Edgar at his heels. Alex followed, pulling her cloak on. "You're taking me also, sir," she told him. This was her prerogative as his guardian, and if he thought he could order her otherwise, he had another think coming.

"Very well, Captain." He gave her a shuttered look, showing little of his normal openness. "The better to help us plan our strategy. We'll leave Carl with our things." He gestured Carl to one side. Carl grimaced behind his back, not liking to be left behind, but Alex agreed.

"You'll be in the thick of things when we attack, I'm sure," she told him drily. "For now, you're backup. Bring as many of the locals as you can gather and come after us if we don't return."

"Captain?" Edgar frowned at her. "That would make you military. In service to...?"

"To the crown," Alex answered shortly. The timing of his insight was inconvenient, to say the least.

Edgar's eyes flashed to the prince, going wide with shock. "Prince Holden?" He pronounced the name with particular astonishment, his eyes flickering back to her.

Alex winced and her cheeks flushed crimson. She wished harder than ever that she had not been so careless as to speak the prince's name while she was abed with Edgar.

Holden inclined his head, curt, unaware of her humiliation. "Keep that under your hat for now. We've a camp of Danes to rout."

Edgar touched his forelock cautiously and fell back, properly deferential. He trailed Alex at a respectful two paces. "You might have told me," he muttered, and she shrugged.

"I had reasons to keep the secret," she equivocated. "Are those the darkest clothes you have? I suppose they'll do." There wasn't much moon, and what there was wouldn't rise for another couple of hours.

They crept out into the woods toward the Danish camp, a much less pleasant prospect in unfamiliar surroundings than at their well-traveled and familiar campsite near Tanton. Edgar went first and Alex put herself third, placing the prince right in front of her so she could keep an eye on him. They followed the road to the mill, which wasn't much used at this time of year. The way was overgrown with grass except in the deepest part of the wheel-ruts. The path allowed for easy going until they reached the little river that turned the millstone.

"Hst," Edgar warned, pointing. They maneuvered up next to him until they, too, could see the light of a fire flickering through the distant trees.

"That will be them," Holden muttered grimly. "They may have sentries set. Any landmarks the Danes might find convenient for posting a watch?"

"The mill itself," Edgar breathed. "There's a bluff ridge on the other side of the river, starting a furlong down or so. The crest commands a wide view of the countryside, looking over the downs toward the nearest farms."

Holden hesitated, then tilted his head at Alex in a mute command to approach the mill and reconnoiter. Though she didn't like the notion of leaving him and Edgar alone together, she approved his choice. She was by far the most silent and deadly of the three of them.

She nodded sharply and vanished, leaving them to await her return. The grass rustled underfoot, but there was a breeze, and her steps were no noisier than the natural soughing of the wind through the hay and through the leaves of the thick oaks towering over the millrace.

She found the sentry easily. He sat slumped on the stoop outside the mill, snoring, his head tipped back against the wall and his hands folded in his lap, nowhere near his sword.

She slipped up next to him and cut his throat to the bone right below his chin with one rapid slash of her dagger. He made a low gurgling sound, hissing, but could not scream, and his twitching body rapidly went still. She stepped away from the gouts of blood, grimacing. That was nasty fighting indeed, the kind she liked least. Still, he was an opponent who had killed innocents, and now he could no longer harm her or the prince.

Such were the fortunes of war.

She wiped her sticky hands on her breeches and scouted the interior of the mill. Once she was sure it was empty, she crept back to the prince and Edgar.

Prince Holden raised his head. She watched as he sniffed the air when she approached. She knew he smelled blood, and he reached for her urgently when she came within reach, touching her arms and her face, exploring worriedly for signs of damage.

"I'm fine," she whispered in his ear, a breath softer than the wind. He relaxed and let her go.

They crossed the millrace stealthily, nearing the camp's now-unguarded flank, and went down on their bellies to gaze into the circle of firelight.

This was a larger group than the last one. It contained twenty or more men, some of them sleeping, others sitting around the fire drinking ale and laughing among themselves. They wore swords and daggers and seemed more disciplined than the other group. Many of them were active, sharpening swords and filling quivers with newly fletched arrows.

Alex traded a glance with the prince, who shook his head. The Danes were too many to attack without more men.

They departed noiselessly with Edgar in tow, and walked toward the town until they found a straw-stack near an abandoned farmstead. They sat down in the lee of the stack to confer.

"My count is twenty-three, sir." Alex told the prince. "Plus another sentry or two on the other side of the camp, at the bluff ridge, probably. At least twenty-five in total, counting the one I killed."

Edgar gulped at the count, blinking at her.

"I picked out at least three officers." Holden chewed at his lip. "They're likely to be more seasoned fighters than the rest, and I thought they had on better armor."

"Most of the rank and file didn't have any visible armor. That's a point in our favor. Two of the officers had leather jerkins with metal plates hanging from them. It isn't true plate mail; it's much inferior. If we must resort to swordplay, they'll be fairly easy to kill. Arrows probably won't pierce the plates, at least not anywhere vital."

Edgar's expression looked squeamish in the light of the rising moon; she realized she was proving a bit more bloodthirsty than he'd anticipated.

"Let's get back to the inn and discuss the terrain to see if their position changes our plans," Holden suggested briskly.

Alex led the two of them back into town, keeping a wary eye out for pursuit.

In their state of heightened vigilance, they all sensed the change at once. The clouds above them lit up with a faintly orange glow, and when they turned back, flames were visible in the distance, licking skyward from a farmhouse near the eaves of the wood: another Danish raid.

"They must have sent out a raiding party just after we left," Alex murmured. "That's why they were readying their weapons."

"Was the farm empty?" Holden asked Edgar, who shrugged, helpless.

"Maybe. Dai was in the tavern. You told him to get his family out, Your Highness. If he didn't, they only have themselves to blame."

Prince Holden frowned, his pleasant face grim. "I wish we could have attacked the whole camp of invaders tonight and prevented this raid. But there just aren't enough of us yet." He set his jaw. "Before they have time to raid more farms, we'll give them something else to chew on."

They reached the inn without incident and went up to the prince's room to draw crude maps and fine-tune their plans. A large camp like this would be better watched and more disciplined than a small one. The prince didn't quite dare to risk such extensive preparations as he'd tried the last time.

"We'll make them fight a war of attrition," he mused, his red-gold head bent over the map next to Edgar's dark one. Alex couldn't help but compare them. Holden's strong, straight nose, his square jaw, and his compact but powerful body seemed elegant and refined compared to Edgar's tall, slender frame. Edgar was young enough he remained a bit gawky about the elbows and the knees, his nose once-broken, his chin a little weak and his beard patchy. She could hardly understand why she'd found him so attractive before.

Edgar was nice enough, yes, and he'd been a pleasant bedmate, willing and eager, ready to experiment. However, he was not what she wanted. Not anymore.

Holden made adjustments to his plan, noting them down on a bit of parchment. When the changes were settled to everyone's satisfaction, he sat up straight and rubbed the bridge of his nose.

"Captain, you're dismissed until breakfast," he said abruptly, his voice quiet. "Use the time as you see fit."

She blinked at him even as Edgar turned his head to grin at her, pleased.

"Thank you, sir." Alex stood and gathered Edgar with a look. The glance was hardly needed, he was so eager to follow her out the door.

"That's a stroke of luck." Edgar reached for her hand as soon as the door closed. "The prince seems a decent enough fellow, despite tales to the contrary."

"Yes." Alex drew a deep breath. "He is." She could not do this to him.

"I'm all over blood and muck, Edgar, and tomorrow will be a long night," she evaded his outstretched hand adeptly. "You should go and check on your family. They'll be wondering what's happened to you."

"I suppose you're right." He looked crestfallen. "I'll see you tomorrow, then."

"Tomorrow," she agreed, and slipped back into the prince's room.

Holden was sitting at his table when the door opened, his head buried in his hands. He looked up with bleary eyes, blinking with surprise to find her standing there.

"I sent Edgar off to his family, sir," Alex reported, her spine straight, very correct and dutiful. "I'll not leave you alone with all those Danes camped less than five miles from here." She lifted a brow at him, wry. "You might get foolish ideas about creeping back out to take them on all by yourself."

He raised his head, his smile widening. "You know me too well, Captain." Happiness warmed his voice and set up an echo of sweet heat in her belly. She knew she'd pleased him beyond expectation, even beyond measure, and done so in a way consistent with her duty. She should not have returned to his room, certainly not so swiftly. Nevertheless, her heart was made glad by the look on his face. His joy might almost make her believe Carl was right.

"I've been harsh with you of late," she whispered. "I am not so cruel as to go with him and leave you here to suffer."

He rose gracefully and approached her, his eyes still smiling even though his face was now earnest. "You care for me well." He touched her shoulder, his palm curving over her in a light caress, his thumb stroking softly.

Yes. Yes, she cared deeply for him. Alex blushed, her belly fluttering. "May I borrow your wash-basin, sir? I'm sure I'm a mess."

"You are," he agreed, smiling at her again, joy in his eyes. "Take all the water you like, Captain."

She washed the blood off her skin as well as she could, dabbing gingerly at her face and hair until the worst of the mess was rinsed away. There was nothing to be done about her clothes, not until she could contrive to wash them or replace them.

Holden was still smiling at her when she finished, and she blushed again, feeling self-conscious and grubby, but also inexplicably pleased.

"Rest well," he urged her as she shed her bloody surcoat and curled up in her blanket-roll. "Tomorrow will be long and nasty."

Chapter Twenty-Six

Prince Holden rose with the dawn and Alex woke when he stirred. They went down to breakfast with Carl, then out into the country along with the first of their lads. Edgar was an early arrival, and the prince singled him out for responsibility.

"Edgar, I want you to direct the remainder of the troops out to meet us." Holden settled him at a table near the back of the common room. "Come along with the last ones. I've a feeling we'll be needing every man we can muster."

Alex formed the men into crude ranks and started them marching. She was an old hand at recruitment, and began her morning assessing the boys' skills. By the time the sun was well over the horizon, everyone they expected had come, Edgar arriving with the stragglers.

Several of the lads turned out to be decent archers, able to group their arrows neatly near the center of a target, which pleased the prince. Edgar was one of those, and he also proved quite fleet of foot.

The prince counted skill sets and retreated for a few minutes while the young men rested. Alex went to watch him draw on his maps and fine-tune his plans while Carl rode shepherd over their troops.

At length he finished, frowning, and put away his quill. "Archers to me." He gathered them around his documents, showing each one his place. "You'll be stationed here," he assigned each man a carefully chosen location in the woods. "When we go, I want you to pick good cover where you can lie concealed and shoot. You won't see much in the dark, but the last of our men will give a whistle when he passes. Then you can shoot anything that moves. Preferably everything." He set them to practicing shooting from cover, then turned to the rest.

"Now we'll see who's the fastest of you." He set them a course over broken rocks and streamlets, amidst trees and over logs. He stood aside with Alex and Carl as the men ran, noting not only the speed of the runners, but also who was most nimble. These he counseled in stealth and night running, drilling them in recognizing Edgar's landmarks. They would lead the Danes forth, luring them between the ranks of the archers like animals to the slaughter.

"The rest of you are our muscle, our strong arms. If it comes to a melee, you'll join the fight." A few of them had brought scythes and pitchforks. He distributed a variety of weapons to the others judiciously from Alex's weapons chest, then delegated the men to Carl, who led them out and employed them in digging a deadfall at a narrow place in the road, where wagons had worn a deep cut between two ridges on their way to and from the mill.

They lined the pit with sharp wooden spikes and covered the hole with branches and straw, making the trap all but invisible to anyone who might pass in the dim of night, a deadly hazard to anyone moving at speed, and a final barrier to any Danes who survived the archers' barrage. Alex stood a careful watch over the group as they worked, but saw no sign of the Danes. They apparently preferred to remain concealed in the wood, wary of sending scouts too far from their camp after losing the one at the mill.

Following their busy afternoon, Holden marched his men back into town and treated them all to a good meal in a private room at the inn, where he stood up to toast them. "This enterprise is dangerous, but you stand to ensure the safety of your families and friends, and when you do so, you will earn the thanks of all the citizens of East Anglia, and of King Anselm. When we succeed, I will guarantee any of you admission into the king's army, if you want it." He glanced aside to Alex, who had carefully coached him, helping choose his words. "This I promise you on my honor, for I am Holden Stuart, Prince of East Anglia."

A startled buzz of conversation arose from everyone but Edgar, who smiled a little and sat quietly, sipping from his mug of ale.

"A toast to our prince!" One voice spoke up spontaneously, and all the lads enthusiastically joined in. They rose in a ragged wave, bowed to Holden, and raised their mugs to honor him. Alex smiled privately. Not one of them balked or mentioned the prince's unsavory reputation. If this venture succeeded, he would have established both the foundations of respect and the seed of an army, one he could build and grow to serve both him and his father.

She hoped fortune would favor their enterprise, and luck would be with the prince in his plans.

They crept out of town under the cover of darkness after agreeing on signals and reviewing the maps, going over the chosen places for battle and rendezvous.

"Edgar, to me." Holden called to him. "You know the land hereabouts, and you've seen the Danish camp. I want you to lead the archers out and settle them in their places. I'll send the runners ten minutes behind you, so don't dally."

"Yes, Your Highness." The archers gathered their bows, and Alex watched Edgar lead them out and vanish into the night. She stood next to the prince and struggled to keep her face smooth and calm when in truth, she was nearly beside herself with worry for all the lads. They looked so young, all but untrained, with the whole of Holden's hopes riding on them.

"They'll do well," Holden spoke softly. "Runners, you know your business. Stay in a group if you can, and you," he indicated one of the group. "Be the last man. Whistle for the archers when you've passed their position. If any of you are hurt, get to the side and lie flat on the ground so you don't get shot. Let the enemy pass, then make your way to the rendezvous as stealthily as you can. If not, get out of the way and lie low. We'll come hunting you as soon as the battle is through."

The runners slipped away, and he moved among the remaining men. They waited, shifting a little nervously, armed and ready to do battle. "Chin up, lads. We'll make our stand beyond the deadfall. Let our runners pass, then step into the road and block the Danes' way. We're the final guard. The captain and the lieutenant and I will take the lead in our fighting."

~ * ~

Alex stood shivering with her heart beating hard as the first alarm arose from the Danish camp. The shouts were swiftly followed by the signal whistle, then by panicked shouting and agonized screams. At last the sound of running feet grew audible through the woods, and their runners lightly vaulted over the deadfall trap.

Danes plunged clumsily after them, and the thin layer of branches gave way, resulting in more screaming. Alex and the prince waded in to confront the remaining few Danes, who were winded and badly demoralized. The battle proved quick and dirty work, and fortunately their untrained young lads hardly had to strike a blow before the remaining enemies lay silent on the bloody ground, the single sound a faint whimpering from a survivor in the deadfall pit.

Alex gave the survivor mercy with a scythe borrowed from one of the boys. By then the archers had begun to arrive, and Carl set a sentry to warn if the remaining Danes rallied, then took stock of their casualties.

Only two lads were injured, neither fatally. One of the runners had taken a graze from a Danish arrow and was bloodied. Another man, a runner, was missing, and he was the subject of great concern until he limped into the rendezvous point alone, using a branch as a makeshift crutch after turning his ankle while he ran through the woods. All their troops had managed to evade capture or serious harm.

A body count showed all but a quarter of the Danes were accounted for. Alex's cautious scouting revealed their six remaining fellows showed no sign of wanting a fight, hastily working to pack up their camp and retreat.

Holden and Alex stalked the Danes through the night, picking off three more of their number, and the first light of dawn saw the survivors fleeing eastward, vanishing into the ground-fog in different directions at a desperate run.

Holden's men marched back to the inn in excellent spirits and Alex roused the staff to give them breakfast. The prince went round as they ate, congratulating each man personally. One of the lads went to fetch a healer, who tended the wounded with a good deal of fussing and clucking, though her smiles reassured Alex their hurts were minor.

After a rest, their troops gathered in the village square, and they marched out to burn the dead Danes in a heap well away from the town. Townspeople tagged along to watch and small family groups trooped by on the road, glad to return to their abandoned homes. They cheered for the prince, who waved graciously to each group, causing much fluster among the womenfolk.

When Holden prepared to leave town, a handful of the best lads decided to accompany him, mostly good runners and archers, several of them younger sons of many brothers. Edgar was among those, which caused Alex no small worry. She was concerned that he had misplaced hopes of winning her; she didn't doubt his prowess in battle. His aim was true. No fewer than six Danes were discovered with his arrows in them, the kills proved by the fletching.

That had made his face turn white as he looked at the men who lay dead by his hand, but he'd eventually squared his jaw and manned up. He did not waver as the men readied themselves to march out of town together, their bows and packs slung at their backs.

As much as she was concerned for Edgar, Alex was even more concerned for the prince. He now bore a great deal of responsibility on his shoulders, and his money would not last indefinitely. Even more, she worried how he might react when things did not go as well as they had the previous evening. Failure was inevitable. He would lose men sooner or later. Her father had always found casualties one of the sorest trials of command, and she'd suffered the loss of a subordinate a few times herself. It was the worst thing she'd ever endured.

She hoped Holden would have the strength to bear the responsibility, when the time came.

"What's this?" She glanced up to find him approaching, leading two horses. "Have you been spending money?"

"We need them. The men will ride in the wagon now." He handed one of the lead ropes to her, and she patted the horse's nose. The beast wasn't the best mount Alex had ever seen. Closer inspection showed her to be a mare, but the animal was fit enough, with a lively spark to her. She danced a little, then settled as Alex breathed soothing words to calm the animal, putting her face close and letting the mare get to know her by scent.

"Thank you." Riding would be better than walking, and they'd move a good bit faster if no one had to go on foot. She vaulted up, using the stirrup for a boost, and settled herself in the saddle. The prince did likewise and clucked to his gelding, reining the horse around and guiding their wagon out through the square onto the road. He waved to the onlookers who came out to watch them go, then settled into his saddle, his back straight and proud.

"If we're to maintain a force of men and feed these horses, we'll soon need more money than we have notes to claim," Alex warned.

The prince patted his flat purse ruefully. "We'll have to take a fairly direct route back to Norwich. I plan to petition my father to commission a special branch of the army for me to lead in these covert actions, and to fund us."

"A good plan." She wondered uneasily how well King Anselm would respond to his youngest son's return, and to his tales of victory in battle. She could not be sure he would like the idea Holden wanted a little army of his own. She also doubted the king would welcome a force of untrained lads in ragged homespun, half of them armed with crude farming tools. She hoped he would take his son seriously, but she feared he would question Holden's loyalty and blame her for his rash actions.

"I'll protect you from his wrath," Holden said softly. "He will see I gave you no other option."

"That wasn't my chief worry," Alex confessed. "My concern is for you."

"I can manage the king." Holden smiled a little, rueful. His eyes wandered past her, back to the wagon, where Edgar sat with Carl on the driver's bench.

"Your Edgar is valiant," he observed, nodding toward the wagon.

"He is not 'my' Edgar." She shifted in the saddle, uncomfortable.

"He follows you, not me."

"I'll send him home, then."

"He won't go," Holden predicted, both confident and wry. "I'll wager you a shilling."

She accepted his wager with a curt nod and fell back, motioning Edgar out of the wagon. He obeyed and she dismounted, taking up the reins in her left hand. She fell in at his side, walking quietly for a moment while she considered her words.

"Edgar, I fear I've lured you out on this adventure under false pretenses," she said quietly. "You did not know I was Captain of King's Elite Guard until yesterday." She colored, realizing she was not as blameless as she'd once imagined herself to be. "I fear I took advantage of you when we met."

He blinked at her a little, chuckling, but his tone was wry. "I did realize I'm in a bit over my head when we started killing invaders, yes."

"That may be true, but it's not what I meant. I'm not free for you to court me," Alex confessed quietly. "My duties do not leave me free, Edgar."

"I can see what quarter the wind blows from." He looked quietly toward the prince. "I don't have to guess at how matters stand on your side, and plainly he wants you for his own. How can I blame him if he doesn't want anyone to poach his claim on such a beautiful lady? Yet I think he is a fair man," Edgar continued quietly. "He hasn't shown me any resentment or ill-will. He would have let us have an evening together, had you wished." His smile turned rueful.

Alex stilled her hand before it could move instinctively to cover Holden's ring, which still lay concealed inside her shirt. She tried to repress a flare of anger. Embarrassment colored her face at the truth in Edgar's words.

"Whether you are right or not, we would not be able to continue as we began, for you're my subordinate now," she said softly. "I'm sorry. I wanted a night of pleasure with you then, but no more." At least she didn't leave him with a babe to feed. She flushed, bitterly ashamed of herself. She was no better in this than the prince once was, not really.

"I already knew your heart was given elsewhere." He looked sad nonetheless. "I can't say I'm not disappointed. You're very beautiful, Alex." He paused. "Captain."

"Captain," she agreed, and touched his hand, regretful and ashamed. She tried to ignore her embarrassment. Would her feelings be so obvious to everyone? Worse, were they obvious to the prince? "From now on."

"Yes, Captain." He saluted her clumsily, inexpert.

"You can go back, if you like. No one would blame you."

"I would blame myself." He glanced toward the prince. "There's little enough for me at home, and this work is important. I would have come even without you to tempt me, I think."

"The prince said you would remain with us."

Edgar blinked at her with some surprise. "Did he?" He studied her for a moment, thoughtful. "He's a good judge of character, then."

"Maybe so." She let him fall back and climb onto the wagon, then she re-mounted her horse, spurring ahead to fall in at the prince's side, where she belonged.

Prince Holden grinned at her, expectant, and she dug in her purse for a shilling, flipping it to him. He chuckled and snatched the coin out of the air with one fist, then put her money in his pocket. "I wouldn't give up on you so easily either, Captain."

She flushed. "You don't know the meaning of the words 'give up,' Your Highness." She made her voice very dry, but she knew her eyes were smiling at him.

"As it should be," he said with a grin, and turned his gaze to the road ahead.

Chapter Twenty-Seven

Holden's first casualty came unexpectedly, a result of bad luck rather than poor planning. His scouts missed a sentry party that heard the commotion when their camp was roused and managed to get in the way of the group's retreat.

One of the Danish sentries drew his bow, shooting with deadly accuracy. His arrow struck the chest of Holden's foremost runner, who fell and tripped two others. With the main band of Danes in hot pursuit and closing fast, the commotion was disastrous.

Prince Holden stopped and drew his sword, Alex hastily skidding to a halt and returning to stand at his side. They engaged the pursuit together, giving their men time to flee, but after their troops scattered to all sides, it was too late for them to do likewise.

Metal clashed behind Alex and she swore, turning aside a heavy blow, unable to look to see how the prince was faring. She had all she could do to parry the attacks of two adversaries, with more arriving every moment and the sentries with their bows closing in fast.

She heard the twanging of a crossbow. *Carl's*, she thought. The bark of the shot sounded like a heavy, military-grade weapon, and she blessed him for running far enough to get out of sight, then turning back to help. The quarrel caught one of her assailants in the neck, and he fell out of the fight, cursing in his strange, guttural tongue.

A barrage of arrows whistled through the air immediately after, the sound making her flinch, but fortunately they were friendly. They struck Danish soldiers, including most of those who held torches, and the volley dropped the two sentries whose unexpected arrival had spoiled the plan.

The dropped torches didn't go out, still casting enough light to fight by. She managed to steal a glimpse at Holden, who bore up sturdily under a savage blow from the chieftain's bulky two-handed sword. He wouldn't be able to take many blows like that, not without getting his arm beaten numb or possibly broken from the force of the impact, even if he parried successfully.

No more men arrived, but they were outnumbered and apparently their own troops had run out of arrows, or they simply couldn't get a clear shot. Several torches had been lost when the Danes closed in around Alex and Holden. Alex gritted her teeth, finding a seam in one man's leather armor and cutting his belly open for him, leaving him to sink to his knees, trying to hold his guts inside himself. She retreated to put her back against Holden's, covering them both from rear attack, and parried furiously as another Dane fell victim to a crossbow quarrel.

Holden's body struck hers, flung back by the force of the chieftain's latest strike. He wasn't making much headway. His foe had on a chainmail shirt, and while the blows he'd managed to land were well aimed, they had little effect on his enemy.

She was glad of their many hours of practice, which now included tandem fighting. They could read one another like a book, and when she leaned on his left shoulder, he gave way, letting her spin and strike at the chief's undefended legs while he parried her startled opponents' attacks, keeping them both off guard.

Given time, with no other opponents, they might beat the chief by sheer stubbornness. They could play him back and forth between the two of them until they let him wear himself out. However, they didn't have time. The ragged handful of Danes who remained were bloodthirsty, and one of them had already stepped aside to string his bow.

Prince Holden scored then, with sudden, unexpected grace. The chieftain's heavy sword proved slow to reverse after a swing, and the delay left him an opening. He made a savage thrust, forcing his blade through the eye of the Dane's iron helm. The metal scraped harshly until his sword could go no farther, but the man was already dead, his weight slumping forward so suddenly his fall tore the blade from Holden's hand.

"Run!" Alex barked, and they fled in the confusion as the Danes leaped to aid their fallen leader.

An arrow flew past Alex, nicking her ear, but by then they were already out of the light and running well. Their practice in sprinting stood them in good stead as they fled like hares, outdistancing the brace of Danes pursuing them. The foreigners were slow and fell back quickly, soon vanishing amidst the thick trees. Alex aimed for one of the boltholes they'd prepared before embarking on the skirmish, and for a wonder, they found the sanctuary empty of any of their own troops. She scuttled into the ditch under the low branch platform as hastily as she could, and the prince followed her, struggling to squeeze in at her side even though the shelter was designed for only one.

Alex and Holden held their breath. They could hear the heavy boots and rapid puffing of their pursuers, and the gabble of their harsh language. The Danes paused to look about, standing almost at the mouth of the tiny hiding place. Alex sniffed. She could smell blood on the prince, and prayed he was unharmed.

She stayed as still as she could, her heart pounding so loudly from the chase she was sure the men must hear her. The prince's arm tightened around her, and she could sense the rage of battle in him, still unquenched. They could take these two men, all other things being equal, but the others were still nearby, and Holden had no sword, just his dagger. He stirred slightly. Alex put her palm over his mouth to quell him, silently imploring him not to move, not to get up and try to fight.

He subsided, his reluctance eloquent in the tension still thrumming through him. She could see his eyes moving, searching as the men's feet edged nearer, breaking branches and twigs and stirring the leaves and bracken as they considered their next move. The Danes paused right in front of the shelter, so close she could have reached out and touched one man's ankle, and another pair of searchers came stamping through the brush to join them, starting a quiet conversation.

Their voices were low and tense, but unintelligible. Their tone revealed the thread of their argument without need for a shared language: they had no idea where to find their quarry. Finally one gave a disgusted hiss and stalked away, leaving Alex and Holden lying undisturbed. The prince exhaled a long-held breath and tension flowed out of him as all of the men followed the first one, trampling noisily back toward their dead leader.

Alex sagged with relief and let her hand fall.

After a judicious time, she and Holden slipped out of the ditch and made their cautious way to the pre-arranged rendezvous. They were last to arrive, and when they stepped into the quiet, unlit circle of men, Carl nearly collapsed as his worry dissipated.

Alex put her finger to her lips and marched them away in single file, moving beyond the fringe of the wood and through a grassy plain until they reached the ravine that held their temporary camp. They did not speak until they reached safety, and even then the men remained quiet, looking at one another with stricken expressions as Carl quietly ordered them to set sentries and bed down for the night.

Holden was silent as well, his face drawn and weary as he went to retrieve his blankets. A trickle of blood was drying at his hairline. One of the arrows must have grazed his scalp, or perhaps he'd struck a branch as they fled. Alex put her hand on his shoulder and turned him to look at her.

"Losses happen," she said softly, "though no good commander likes to see men die. We lost only one. The casualties could have been worse."

He acquiesced, but his frown didn't lessen. He reached for her hand and pressed it tightly against his chest.

156

"You acquitted yourself well. You beat your first swordsman." Alex drew him aside, keeping her voice very soft. "Their leader." She turned her hand and clasped his, firm and reassuring. "You avenged Jon and protected the others, Your Highness. You gave our troops the time they needed to recover and escape."

"His family will wonder what happened to him." Holden's voice sounded tired and lost.

Her eyes prickled with tears. "Yes, they will. However, they and other families are alive thanks to his bravery." She knew words were insufficient comfort. There was never enough consolation when one of your men died. "Let me tend that scratch."

The prince meekly followed her to the fire. She heated water and bathed his temple, examining the wound. It was merely a scratch, very shallow, but after the manner of scalp wounds, it bled freely when she cleaned the blood and dirt away. She tore a strip off her shirt to bind a pad of cloth against the cut.

When she finished he laid his head against her, and she slipped her arms around him, holding him tucked snugly below her breasts. Her eyes filled with tears, and she stroked his hair softly. There was nothing sexual in this. He needed comfort, and he trusted her to care without condemning him for weakness.

"My liege, you should rest." She stroked his cheek.

"Yes." He stood, leaning to touch his forehead to hers. "Not until after I tend your hurts, though. You fought valiantly, my captain." He refused to go to his bedroll until he'd washed the blood from her ear, bathing her skin and applying a clean bandage, pinching it onto her ear between his fingers until she stopped bleeding.

He lay down, staring up at the sky without blinking. She thought perhaps he slept after a time, but not well. He remained sober and hollow-eyed when he arose for breakfast.

They went into the nearest village in the morning, and the villagers greeted them eagerly, so stirred by their story they seized scythes and pitchforks and marched out *en masse* to finish off the remaining Danes. The last few men fled when they saw the furious, bristling crowd arrayed against them, leaving their dead and their belongings behind.

Alex directed the lads to dispose of the corpses, taking the valuable mail shirt from the dead chief before the bodies were tossed onto a pyre to burn. She and Carl decided to award the spoils to Edgar, who had become a leader among the men, having made the most kills in nearly every raid. The mail would not be useful for stealth work or speedy retreat, but the reward reinforced the chain of command, and the well-deserved honor pleased everyone. Prince Holden stirred himself and rose when Edgar laid the shirt atop his pack, and went over to him.

"You're a good fighter," he said, and slapped Edgar's shoulder briskly. "This honor is well-deserved."

"Thank you, sir." Edgar lifted his chin, and his eyes shone with pride.

"The rest of you, take what you want from the Danish gear," Holden directed the men. "Arm yourselves. Carl will help you choose the swords with the best balance. We'll load the remainder of their gear onto our cart."

Alex smiled a little to herself, careful not to let her expression be seen.

The prince was quiet all day, and for several days thereafter. She made sure he ate and drank when he should, and watched to be sure he slept enough. He would simply have to come to terms with the cost of war if he meant to continue leading troops in battle.

She offered what little comfort she could.

After his moment of weakness the first night, he did not let the men see him suffer. He would let down his guard only in front of Alex, who gave him all the small reassurances she could. She patted his shoulder when he sat silent and apart, or took him a cup of wine when he was tired after each long day in the saddle. She stayed near him, letting him draw strength from her support.

Each time she saw how sad and careworn and human he was, something melted a little more inside her. She tried to deny her feelings, but some part of her knew nonetheless. She was losing her heart to him by slow and inexorable degrees, however hard she fought not to.

Chapter Twenty-Eight

Prince Holden became increasingly uneasy as they drew nearer to Norwich. The gossip grew more detailed, and yet none of the news was good. Scuttlebutt had King Anselm and Prince Gavin at odds over policy, with Gavin annoyed at being pulled back from the coast for nothing. Meanwhile, King Anselm refused to send the army out of the city again because there was no unified group of Danes to confront. Apparently he had other plans. No two accounts agreed on what they were, but the Danish attacks on East Anglian citizens continued unchallenged except by Prince Holden's team.

Prince Holden's arrival in the capital would throw a millstone into the fishpond. That much was certain.

They kept moving and raiding, riding out the last days of golden summer. They arrived at the final town before the capital a couple of weeks before Samhain. They rode in late one afternoon and lodged at a sprawling inn, which was bustling with travelers. There wasn't much money left, so they had to share rooms, but at least those rooms were well appointed and clean.

Carl gave Alex a sly wink and said his duty required him to stay close by the men, leaving her to bunk down alone with the prince. She glared at him. His insolence in the name of matchmaking had grown to intolerable levels, and if he were anyone else, she'd demote him. However, Carl had been her good right hand for many years. He was entitled to tease her if anyone would ever be. He was the closest thing to a brother Alex had, and he knew her much too well.

She had to concede he'd arrived at the right estimate of the prince long before she did. Prince Holden proved a surprisingly good leader. He cared deeply for the welfare of his men, and turned into a shrewd planner and a valorous fighter. He still needed the occasional nudge in the proper direction. Sometimes inexperience left him with the odd blind spot. However, he had Alex to help when that happened, and she assisted him as well as she might.

Their losses continued to grieve him. She saw this more clearly than anyone else, even Carl, for she was always with the prince. She'd learned to read volumes from the small expressions on his face, or from the set of his jaw and shoulders. He constantly questioned his role in their mistakes and worked himself to exhaustion trying to prevent more.

She told him gently, again and again, how a commander must suffer such losses at times regardless how well he led his men. In truth, their losses were astonishingly few. But he cared about each of his men and worried about them, even those who were merely wounded.

She watched every evening as he fretted, writing the names and hometowns of the dead men down on a list he carried with him always. She knew he meant to send word to their families, along with such compensation as a regular soldier of the king's army would receive after being slain in battle.

On the last night of their long journey, they sat up in a common room together, keeping the squad company as they celebrated their latest victory. The inn was lively, and the barmaids bustled around in a frenzy of haste, trying to keep everyone served. The men behaved well under the prince's sharp eye, and he seemed content.

"One more round, lads, then off to bed. We'll march right after dawn." He arranged with the innkeeper for porridge to be ready before the sun rose, then departed for his room, leaving the merriment behind.

Alex followed after pausing for a final word or two with Carl. She was looking forward to getting back to the castle again, where she could have fresh clothes and hot baths. She longed for clean linens to wear against her skin. She stifled a yawn against her palm, tapping at the prince's door, and went in. She felt a little shy as she prepared to take her place on the floor.

The last skirmish had been a bloody one, and she'd seen many such. Her clothes were stiff and sticky with blood and dirt. She'd spent many nights sleeping in mud and dust and straw. She'd made sure the prince received luxuries she didn't, including a bath or two when she'd had none, and she stank so badly it was a wonder anyone could bear to be in the same room with her.

She wondered if Holden looked forward to the creature comforts of home, or if he dreaded meeting his father so much his worries drove everything else out of his mind. She shrugged off her coat and grimaced wryly. Maybe she'd arrange to have it burned as soon as she arrived in Norwich.

The skin on the nape of her neck prickled, and she glanced up to find the prince watching her, his eyes soft, a small smile lingering on his face. She flushed a little at his fond expression, looking back down at the ruined cloth in her hands.

"I'll call for one of the maids to wash your clothes." The prince jerked at the bell-pull before she could protest. "You don't have a clean change, I know. That's fine." He rummaged in his own pack and pulled out his cleanest shirt. "Put this on instead. I'll pay the chambermaid to have your laundry ready first thing in the morning."

Alex opened her mouth to protest, but the maid's knock sounded at the door before she could choose her words.

The prince let the girl in. "We need these cleaned and dried by morning. Here, for your trouble." He handed over a sovereign, and the girl's eyes flew wide. The coin was worth more than the price of a single room and meals for a week.

"Th-thank you, Your Highness. They'll be ready, sir!" She stammered, reaching for Alex's filthy coat with trembling fingers.

Prince Holden turned his back on them and went to lie down on the bed with his arm politely flung over his eyes.

Alex stared at him, defeated. She had little option other than to peel off her clothes and hand them to the maid, along with the other dirty clothing from her pack and a heap of the prince's as well. The maid might as well earn her riches.

"Bring a basin of hot water for her to bathe in before you go, girl," Prince Holden directed.

The girl scurried out and returned promptly with a steaming bucket of water, and Alex sponged herself clean hastily, her skin vibrating with her awareness of the prince's quiet presence on the bed. The room felt very cool, especially since she was wet, and all she had to put on when the girl vanished was the prince's nearly clean shirt.

The garment barely came down below her bottom in back, and an inch or two down her thighs in front. The cloth smelled of him. The shirt tied rather than hooking or buttoning, so she lapped the front over and loosely knotted the flap shut.

"Dressed?" He asked at length when she grew quiet.

"Yes." She tugged the hem down as far as she could. She couldn't appear less professional and reserved than this if she were naked. Was all her good work toward keeping him at arm's length to be undone so easily? She felt her heart racing, and knew her color must be high.

He lifted his arm and sat up. Her blanket-roll lay next to the bedstead, and he toed it over toward her. "There are no fewer than six encampments of Danes within easy walking distance," he mused. "I feel as if I could vanquish them all."

Alex chuckled ruefully. "That's why I'm staying with you, not off with Carl and the men." She felt very shy, and tried to cover her nerves with bravado. "I can't let you kill all the Danes yourself and take the glory. Someone has to look out for the troops, and make sure they get their share."

She felt her breath coming short in her chest; there was a look on his face that made her quiver down to her very toes.

"Will you bed down in front of the door, or are you afraid I'll make an escape through the window?" His eyes danced at her. Her legs prickled with goose bumps as she felt his gaze slide over them.

"If I didn't trust you so implicitly, I suppose I'd have to take the front half of your bed and imprison you against the wall," she told him dryly.

"I'm extremely untrustworthy." He pulled back the coverlet of the bed. The mattress looked soft and inviting. It was a featherbed, an unexpected luxury. "I always have been. Ask my captain."

She was alarmed to discover how much she longed to lie down at his side. What's more, she could do whatever she liked, then forbid him to touch her. She knew he would respect her wishes.

"I'll sleep on the floor by your bed, then, Your Highness, so you'll stumble over me if you try to escape." She was flirting, and she shouldn't, but she was helpless to resist the temptation of his slow smile.

"You'll find your bed very drafty on the floor wearing that short shirt, Captain."

She blushed in spite of herself. He was right. She'd be cold even wrapped in her blankets. "Don't push your luck," she told him and reached for the knot holding her blankets tied together in their neat roll.

"Alex." He slid to the back of the mattress. "We've slept in close quarters before. You'd be foolish to lie on the floor and shiver all night. This bed is quite large enough for us both. Besides, your blankets are filthy. We should have sent them out for laundering as well. I promise I won't attempt to seduce you." He chuckled, a little sadly. "At least not tonight."

"This from a man who named himself untrustworthy only a moment ago."

"You know I won't break my word once I've promised."

"If I don't agree, you're going to argue all night instead of letting me sleep, aren't you?"

He grinned at her, something of her familiar brat prince peeking out from behind the new heavy beard and strong body, mischief dancing in his eyes. "If arguing will get me what I want."

She scoffed and scrambled into the bed without letting herself think again, her heart pounding. "Touch me, and I'll tie your privates in a knot."

"I wouldn't dare." His voice was smug. She knew this was a mistake. She *knew* it, but the bed was comfortable, and a very long time had passed since she slept in one. The sheets and blankets felt clean, warming quickly around her.

She turned onto her side, facing away from him, carefully keeping close to the front edge of the mattress. Her hand closed over his ring. She craved an excuse to snuggle back against him. She could almost feel his warmth against her skin, but she must not give in.

"Goodnight, Captain." His voice sounded very close to her. "Sleep well."

She did, and she dreamed quite vividly of his warm, hard body pressed up against hers, his new-callused palm sliding up her waist under his shirt to caress her skin. In the dream, his hand stroked back and forth along her ribs, his soft rough voice whispering tenderly to her as his lips dragged slowly along the skin of her shoulder and her throat. "Alex, my captain. My own."

She never knew afterward whether any of her dreams were real, but she woke once, briefly, to find him properly chaste, lying on his own side of the bed. He was drowned deep in sleep, rasping his usual appalling snore.

She closed her eyes and slipped away again, and afterward, she didn't dream.

She woke to the sound of motion and lay still, feigning sleep. She felt disoriented. She lay in a soft bed, not on the ground under the wagon. The bedding against her skin was not her own familiar blanket.

Memory flooded in suddenly, and she slitted her eyelids open. The prince was already up, crouching over his pack and preparing to dress, rummaging through what remained of his clothing. He was as bare as the day he was born, his nightclothes carelessly tossed over the room's single chair.

For once, she thought, *he hasn't done this deliberately, intending to goad me to admire his body.* And so she did, drinking her fill of him through half-closed lashes.

He was beautiful, excruciatingly so, glowing golden in the light of the single candle he'd lit and placed in a sconce on the wall. She saw him as she had never seen him before. He was not posed, not flaunting himself while aware she was watching. He moved with unconscious grace. One knee was bent nearly to the floor, and the other leg supported most of his weight. His back was stretched forward, and the taut muscle over his ribs rippled in the light as he dug through his pack.

She could glimpse his manhood hanging free between his legs, and her eyes locked there, going wide. He chose a pair of breeches and stood up to put them on, shaking them out, revealing himself entirely. She'd seen him naked before, but Carl was right. He had changed, his body growing harder, his muscles lean and perfectly defined, moving sleekly under his skin. The glow of the candle cast him in golden tones of light and shadow.

She swallowed hard without meaning to, drawing a breath. His head lifted in surprised response to her low gasp.

They froze, their gazes locked. She knew her face was unguarded, her want written all over her. Her breath came swiftly in her chest, and she couldn't look away.

He dropped the breeches and stepped forward, predatory, lean and lithe like a cat, all smooth-flowing grace. Her breath quickened. She knew she should bolt out of his bed, out of the room, out of the inn. She should not stop running until she reached the sea.

She lay still and let him come to her instead, her whole body trembling. He went to one knee beside the bed, his gaze searching her eyes. His hand reached out and lifted her braid, letting it drop behind her shoulder.

He leaned in, hesitating before he touched her lips, giving her a chance to protest or escape.

When she did not, he kissed her.

Alex could have wept for mingled relief and reluctance and sweetness and shame as his lips closed over hers. His hand rose to stroke her cheek, curving around her jaw.

He tasted her, slow and careful, his hand sliding the blankets down from her shoulders to her waist, then tugging at the tie binding his shirt on her. The garment fell open, baring her breast, and he drew back, sweeping his eyes along her body, a heated caress she could all but feel. Her skin tingled and she moaned softly. She hadn't the strength of will to deny him, not with that melting, tender look in his eyes. She lay still, trembling, wanting more of him.

He rose from his knee and the bed dipped as his weight came down, half on the mattress and half on her. His mouth opened hers slowly and his tongue dipped inside. His skin pressed against hers all the way down, delightful. He pulled the blankets up to cover them both and his arms went around her inside his shirt, pressing her bare breasts against the coarse tickle of fur on his chest.

Alex whimpered, her thighs parting to admit his knee. Her head spun dizzily, and she teetered on the edge of abandoning herself, the embrace drowning her good sense in pleasure. She was already all but lost in his kiss, and he *was* good, very *very* good.

She should not do this. She should *not,* but he was strong and warm. His body felt exquisite pressed against her. She wanted only to be with him, here and now, opening her mouth and her body to him, giving herself at last.

Tears prickled at her eyes, sudden and unexpected.

What would she do when he finished with her, when she was used up and no longer a challenge, no longer of interest to him? When she must stand guard over him and keep her chin high as he bedded the next pretty girl who caught his fancy? When he sent her away with his child growing in her belly, to have no more of him ever again than a pension and the bittersweet echo of his memory, captured in her fatherless babe's red hair and blue eyes?

She stiffened and he pulled back, sensing her retreat, his eyes troubled.

"Alex?" He touched her lip with a gentle finger. His hard shaft nudged insistently against her thigh, ready and eager for her, and his skin glided against hers, silk-soft. He felt better than anything in her arms, better than everything. She'd never wanted any man more.

"What's wrong, Alex?"

Her eyes filled with tears, and before she could even think of stopping them, she began weeping silently in his arms. He drew her face against his shoulder and held her. She felt him swallow, his discomfort and uncertainty evident in the way his hands stirred, awkwardly petting her shoulders, no longer as sensual as they were comforting.

"Don't," he breathed, helpless. "Don't cry."

She sniffled and wiped her nose, unable to stop. He kissed at her tears very tenderly, licking them softly off her cheeks. Her hands would fist in his clothes if he had any on, and she'd cling to him. Would he hate being loved so desperately? He needed her to be strong, not weak. Maybe her clinging would confuse him, annoy him, and make him want to push her away.

"Why are you crying?" His soft, husky voice murmured in her ear. "Tell me, Alex. Let me make things right."

When did she start loving him so much? She didn't know. His kisses caused a terrible wound to open inside her, and she was hurting as though she had taken a sword through her middle.

She struggled out of his arms, panicking, pushing him away. "I can't do this. I can't be this to you." She wound up against the wall, fending him off with one hand when he tried to pursue and curl around her again.

"Why not?" His voice ached with tenderness. "I can tell you want to." He tried a wry smile, one that nearly broke her heart with baffled, gentle pain.

"Wanting to isn't enough." She scrambled up and past him, out of the bed, needing to be away before she succumbed. "I have more important things to be to you than just a...a camp follower."

She pulled the open shirt tightly around her, then was relieved to spy her clean clothes lying folded in a neat pile by the door. She dived for them, shoving her legs into her breeches and dragging them up, skinning rapidly out of his shirt and into her own. She fumbled with the hook and eye fasteners, fingers made clumsy by haste.

"A camp follower?" He asked slowly. "You should know you are much more to me than that." She caught a glimpse of his face, of his anguish, his eyes alive with pain. "I understand your reluctance better now." He drew himself up with dignity, the sheets puddled in his lap. "I think you're afraid to believe in your own worth as well as in my devotion."

He rose, ignoring his nakedness, and stepped forward, stopping her where she stood. He laid his palm against his ring, his hand warm on her chest. "I would never give such a token to a woman I thought of as a whore." His voice was still velvet, but now the softness lay over steel.

"No, my liege," she confessed, "I know you would not, but I would not have you come to regret your gift."

"I won't." His eyes turned sad and patient. "I've left the past behind, Alex. I no longer choose to be that man, but you continue to see him." He turned from her and walked to the window slowly, clad solely in dignity. It became him well. Her eyes lingered on the spare curves of his arse, smooth and graceful in the candlelight, so perfect they nearly made her mouth water.

"I'm still learning not to." Alex tried to keep her voice steady. "Forgive me."

"This has been the most important summer of my life." Prince Holden drew himself upright. "Sometimes I forget how short a time we've spent away. You will learn to believe in your value to me. I'll prove myself to you yet." He turned halfway toward her, the candlelight rendering his profile in harsh planes of light and darkness, turning his expression severe, like a hawk's. "I'll prove myself to my father and brother, as well." He went to his pack and picked up his abandoned breeches. He pulled them on, leaving them untied as he hunted his boots and his socks.

Alex stared at him, suddenly desperate, terrified by the distant and resolute look on his face. "You must not endanger yourself out of vanity and injured pride." Her heart pounded. She didn't want him to take foolhardy risks in the name of honor, or of trying to impress her. "I would not have you go to a useless death against the Danes for such foolish reasons." She swallowed hard. "Please. I beg you."

"No," he agreed, surprising her a little. "I won't fight the Danes because I want to prove myself to you, or to anyone else, but because I'm a prince of East Anglia, and the safety of her people is as much my responsibility as my father's and my brother's."

He approached her on bare feet and touched her cheek, his thumb sliding onto her lips, lingering over her mouth. "I think it is high time I told you I love you, my captain, as much as I think you might love me, if you had the courage to admit you do." His eyes fixed hers, bright blue and intense. "Seek your courage, Alex. I know it's there. Consider this a challenge."

She blinked at him with an impossible roil of shock and indignation and fear and sweetness storming through her. He laughed softly at the stunned look on her face. "Think on what I've said," he straightened his spine. "I'm afraid we'll have to go now and talk of this later. The men expect to march at dawn."

She went through the motions of dressing, her mind and heart in turmoil. Carl tapped while the prince was still tugging his boots on, and she opened the door, scowling. "Are the troops awake?" She demanded of him before he could speak.

"Ready and sitting down to breakfast." He glanced inquisitively past her into the room, where her blanket roll still lay tightly tied on the floor, unused. "The two of you had a good night, then?"

She huffed at him, embarrassed, and stamped out to get her own breakfast. The hot porridge smelled good, with honey and fresh butter stirred in. She barely tasted her meal, though, the prince's words still echoing in her mind, keeping her in a muddle of agitation. She finished before he could come down and hastened out into the courtyard to direct the muster.

"Saddle the prince's horse for him, Edgar." She took the time to ensure their wagons were neatly packed, especially the ones carrying the battle trophies.

Those would be needed later.

They headed out as the sun's lower rim cleared the horizon, and she chivvied the ranks a bit to cover her discomfort, making sure no one lagged behind.

The countryside should have been lovely, painted in the waxing colors of autumn, but there were too many signs of battle and raiding. Numerous homesteads lay abandoned, crops going to waste in the fields, never having been harvested. Some of the structures had been burned. Fresh graves lay scattered along the roadside, and a sober mood quickly subdued the men. They marched purposefully toward the capital, trusting in the prince's leadership. From the looks of them, not a single one doubted they would be welcome at court.

Alex hoped they were right.

Chapter Twenty-Nine

The midday sun slid out from behind the clouds and transformed the leaves of the oaks scattered about the plain from dull brown to a blaze of orange and gold as Prince Holden's group arrived at Norwich. Prince Holden gestured briskly to Alex, and she heeled her horse up to the moat, where she called to the soldiers who manned the drawbridge. They recognized her and promptly engaged the winch to let the little company come within the gate.

The first of the prince's troops stood milling on the cobbles, waiting for the rest to cross the drawbridge and looking nervously about. The city was quiet, and all they had to see was the gray stone wall of the city's outer perimeter and the shabby, smoke-stained brick buildings huddling against the city wall. They were still a small group, thirty men plus she, the prince, and Carl. They'd lost some of their group and replaced a few, and turned down any number of others. Those who'd remained from the beginning were becoming good soldiers, tempered in the forge of combat, skilled at stealth and night fighting, each one of them learning tactics and teamwork along the way.

Word of the prince's return spread through the city like wildfire. Everywhere they went, heads turned to follow. The people appeared first in windows and doorways, then in alleys and on sidewalks. They shielded eager whispers behind guarding hands. Alex knew by the time word reached the palace, the rumors would have the prince riding at the head of an army of hundreds.

She wished they looked a bit more impressive. The men had nothing to wear but their worn and filthy traveling clothes, and their troupe was humbly equipped with plow horses and farm carts. They carried stolen Danish weapons and wore no uniforms or livery. However, she was well known by sight, and Prince Holden was also widely recognized. As they wound their way further into the city, the people greeted them with glad cries.

By the time they made their way through all the layers of the city, ascending slowly up to the summit of the ridge supporting the king's castle, a welcome had been prepared for them. King Anselm and Prince Gavin stood waiting on the white marble stair at the head of the main courtyard, with her father standing to their right. Colored banners hung from poles on the battlements and snapped crisply in the autumn breeze, catching the light of the noonday sun. Various retainers and aides assembled nearby. Duke Roger hovered solicitously at the king's shoulder and Walter lingered near her father, nervously adjusting the corporal's insignia pinned to his doublet.

Alex held Prince Holden's horse as he dismounted, then slid off her own and followed the prince to the foot of the stair. Both of them stood upright despite their travel-worn gear and unkempt hair.

"My son." The aged king had taken the time to don his best ceremonial armor, which was a bit too large for him now, but still intimidating. His leather plate mail gleamed with elaborate golden filigree over black. His scarlet plumes blew back from his helm and the breeze lifted the corner of his blue velvet cloak. He looked mildly dyspeptic, and surveyed the small band with an expression of distaste. "I understood you were to go west and await a resolution to this conflict." His austere gaze touched Alex and his eyes narrowed with disapproval.

"With all due respect, I believed I could be of more use here." The prince held his head high, recalling the king's attention to himself. There was no trace of sulkiness or pettishness in his tone or his expression. "I countermanded your orders to the captain."

Prince Gavin raised a brow, eyeing Alex shrewdly. She resisted the urge to shift with discomfort. Her father also watched her like a hawk, and this was no time to betray her uncertainty by fidgeting.

"The rumors suggest you are raising an army. Of sorts." That was definitely contempt in the king's eyes as they ranged across Holden's meager band of farmers and plowboys. "One that sets the Danish raiders quivering in their boots." His tone fairly dripped with doubt.

"We have engaged several groups of Danes, with good success, as I can show." Holden signaled to Alex, who turned back and pointed to Edgar and Carl. They whipped tarpaulins off the nearest two wagons, which were stuffed to bursting with swords, helms, arrows and bows, food, tents, and other plunder from their defeated enemies.

Prince Gavin's eyebrows went up. Alex watched him crane his neck, trying to count swords and estimate how many Danes must have perished to supply such a hoard.

By contrast, King Anselm scowled. "Then it's true. You've attacked Danish camps."

"I have." Prince Holden drew himself straight.

"Quarter your men in the stables. There's no better room for them. Then go get a bath." The king's nose wrinkled with distaste. "Come meet me in General Bonham's planning room afterward. We've a great deal to discuss." He strode off with an irritable flick of his wrists, his formal armor rattling. Prince Gavin nodded politely to Alex and Holden, then followed him. The welcoming committee filed away into an arched corridor and vanished inside the castle.

Holden ran his fingers through his hair, scratching it into disarray. "Well, that could have gone better." He adjusted his belt, his voice dry. "Carl, see to the men, then all of you may as well take the day. Captain, we've been given leave to bathe, and I think we should eat. I suggest you make the most of the time before you meet me at my rooms. We'll go to the planning council together."

"Yes, sir."

Alex trotted into the castle, nodding at the door warden and taking the steep, tapered steps of the spiral stair two at a time. She took a shortcut through the servants' passage into the west tower, arriving quickly at her rooms, which lay a single level below the royal apartments where she was to meet the prince. She closed the door behind herself and let out a long, heartfelt sigh.

Despite the chilly welcome, she was glad to be back in her chambers again. The rooms had a neglected, dusty feel, as if they'd been abandoned for much longer than the three or four months she'd spent away. She summoned servants to light the fires, change the linens, and bring a bath, then peeled out of her traveling clothes and tossed them aside for disposal.

Her bathtub was narrow and not very deep, but it was wonderful compared to the washtubs and basins on offer at roadside inns, or the icy ponds and streams she'd found near their camps. She sank into the hot water with a low groan and began scrubbing herself pink with a linen cloth. Despite her recent sponge bath, the dirt came off her in sheets. She lay back and ordered the maids to wash out her hair, then comb it and wrap it carefully in towels to soak the damp out. Finally she stood and had them sluice clear water over her until she was satisfied all the grime of her travels had been rinsed away.

She went to her closet for fresh clothes, finding them clean and crisp, if a little musty from disuse. She chose her favorite fawn breeches and a tight long-sleeved shirt, then called for a squire to help her on with her formal armor. The boy sorted through the many buckled parts, helping her into her pauldron, breastplate, full arm and leg pieces with joints, and her heavy boots. She inhaled the familiar scent of the brown leather. She ran her palm over the embossed devices on the right arm detailing her rank and accomplishments before pulling on her gauntlets. Everything felt familiar but strangely surreal. Too much time had passed since she wore her proper uniform. She felt uncomfortable when she stood up, heavy and constrained.

She freed her hair and let it fall down her back in a curling torrent to finish drying, tying it back with a single leather thong.

She went searching among her things after she was clean and dressed, and found a sturdy but light chain necklace among her meager collection of jewelry. She removed the tarnished silver pendant and looped the chain around the prince's ring, then hung it about her neck, dropping the ring down inside her armor.

Before she finished, a page arrived carrying a big bowl of stew and a loaf of bread. The bread was day-old, but light and soft. She devoured the food eagerly, sighing with bliss. Being back in the castle and enjoying the familiar comforts of home felt good in spite of the tension between Holden and his family.

She stirred herself, gulping a last swallow of wine, and trotted up the steps to the prince's rooms. He was still dining at his table when the guards ushered her in, and he gestured her to sit down with him, pushing out a chair for her with his boot.

She looked about the place, feeling rather nervous. She'd never been invited to sit and eat with him here before. In fact, the only time she could ever recall being at ease in this room was the night they left the city, when she'd stolen a nap in his easy chair while he slept.

"Sit down, Captain," he said softly, and poured a cup of wine. "Are you hungry? No? I'll be finished shortly." He extended his arm, offering her the drink.

She sat self-consciously, perched upright on the edge of the chair. She accepted the cup and drank a sip to be polite. Their last conversation hung heavily in the air between them. She felt shy and ill at ease. It seemed strange to be here with Holden after so many changes, as if the new prince of her memory were all a dream or an imagining, or as if the old one had been, instead.

Holden ate patiently and neatly, with unexpectedly exquisite table manners. She stole a look at him as she waited. He too seemed oddly out of place, much as she felt in her own quarters and in her own formal armor. He fussed with his napkin, placing it neatly in his lap, and Alex stifled a smile. Perhaps he, too, felt uncomfortable.

Holden forked up the last bite of the meat pasty from his plate and hummed with pleasure, setting aside his napkin and rising to prepare himself for departure. He had bathed and wore clean clothes now, too. They were his own, quite flattering on him even though they'd grown a bit too tight for his newly muscular frame. The servants had trimmed his hair and beard quite neatly. She found him stunning, and looked away from his face shyly, examining his clothing instead.

He wore brown accented with royal purple panels and gold embroidery, with the Stuart family sigil neatly embellished on the right of his chest. A short matching capelet swung at his shoulders and his heeled boots made him stand a little taller than she was accustomed to. He looked formidable and dignified, his back and body straight. Alex's mouth went dry at the sight of him.

He smiled at her a little, flirtatious, and she flushed, caught gawping.

"I suppose we must face my father," he grimaced, bringing himself back to the business at hand. "Let's go."

"Yes, sir."

Chapter Thirty

Alex heeled Prince Holden down to her father's conference chamber, where they tapped at the door and were admitted by a bored young guard. Alex smiled at General Bonham, whose gaze sought hers, soft with relief and welcome. Walter hovered at his side, his thumb and forefinger fidgeting nervously with his harelip. He wore an insolent sneer, twisting his misshapen face into an appalling grimace.

King Anselm leaned stiffly over a map and straightened as they entered, looking impatient and favoring his left hip. Duke Roger rose, putting away the pomander he was sniffing. With an ostentatious flourish, he handed the king his silver-shod wooden walking stick. King Anselm rapped his cane on the stone floor, silencing the low buzz of talk in the room.

"About time you joined us," he grunted, and seated himself in the ornate armless chair Prince Gavin pushed up for him. "Check this map of Danish encampments and tell us of any inaccuracies you may see."

The prince did, moving a few markers and pointing to scattered locations. "There was a Danish camp here. We drove them out. There was one here, and here as well. This homestead was burned. This village was entirely taken. Many more small groups lie scattered about the countryside than are indicated here. We found at least one near every settlement of any size within ten days' march of the coast."

His recitation lasted a dismal few minutes, and Alex did not need to add a word. He was thorough and accurate. When he had finished, Prince Gavin and Alex's father exchanged a quiet but lingering look, one she could not read. Their faces remained absolutely impassive.

"What tactics have you used in battle?" Prince Gavin asked his brother, but his father cut him off with a curt sideways slash of his hand.

"That point is moot." He glared at Holden. "I mean to make peace with the Danes, my son, and your attacks pose a serious obstacle to my plan."

"He has a point," Roger leaned back sagely, toying with the curled ends of his long blond hair. "How can he convince the ambassador his offer of peace is sincere when his own son rides about the countryside, preying on their outposts?"

"Peace with the Danes?" Holden's eyes narrowed. "Preying on their outposts? Rather, say they are preying on our people. Families are slaughtered in their homes nightly. I could only scratch the surface of the problem, given my limited funds and men, but I judged it right to try. I have seen the graves of women and children who were cut down by spears and arrows as they fled their homes. I have seen families who were burned alive and left roasted in their beds. My raids have made the farmers safe again, and I have taught the men and boys of each township I visited how to defend themselves in the future."

"Your raids have increased the very hostilities of which you speak," King Anselm snapped at him, livid. "We can co-exist with the Danes. I mean to set aside a territory where they can settle and live according to their own laws, so they can escape the harsh winter country where they live and can't feed their families. When they have a better place for themselves, they will become valuable trading partners."

"I agree, they mean to send colonists from their lands to settle here. If they didn't mean to disperse settlements throughout the country, they'd fight us openly at the capital and insist we pay tribute, then return to Denmark. Regardless which method they choose to conquer us," Holden insisted, "they will continue to trouble us with violence until we have nothing and are enslaved."

"As if you paid attention to your tutors when they tried to teach you of foreign policy and battle tactics."

"I learned more than you give me credit for." Holden's voice grew icy. "I saw no purpose then in parroting lessons I would never have occasion to use." He considered the map, a muscle in his jaw jumping, and Alex could sense how hard he struggled to rein in his temper. "Tell me, who would you negotiate this peace with?" His eyes flashed to Roger, challenging him as well. Roger merely smirked at him, remaining arrogant and smug. He fished out his pomander and took a pointed sniff, his eyes never leaving Holden.

"King Sweyn Thorssen has proposed peace talks with me," King Anselm scowled. "We were set to meet until rumors reached him that my own son's violent attacks were making a liar of me in my attempts to sue for peace."

"What of the other Danish chieftains? They are a tribal culture. Does he hold sway over them all?" Holden met his father's stare sturdily. "Does he speak for the others? Does he even speak truth? Better we drive them away. I have achieved my victories at the cost of a scant three men dead, and barely a handful were injured. The Danes can be driven out, given enough men and patience."

"He speaks sense, father." Gavin stared at Holden steadily. "I too have wondered if Sweyn Thorssen holds the power he claims, and if his intentions are honorable. If Holden has stumbled on a strategy that could work, then we should use it."

"His strategy is the treachery of an honorless youth, and his efforts are an irresponsible lark."

Alex had difficulty remaining calm upon hearing the pronouncement. She flicked her eyes around the room, carefully noting who agreed and who remained expressionless. As she expected, Roger and Walter both nodded along, satisfied expressions on their faces. Too many of the others looked troubled, as if they were tempted to agree. A few remained stoic, withholding all approval. She noted their names on a mental list as possible supporters.

Holden straightened his shoulders. "You think it honorless to defend the subjects of the crown and keep innocents of the realm from harm?"

General Bonham chose that moment to clear his throat and gather Alex with his eyes. He drew her away from the trio of Stuarts, who began to converse in furious, hushed tones.

"I am glad to have you home again, daughter," he said softly as they pretended not to overhear the argument, which grew more intense and heated by the moment. "Did you have trouble with him?" His eyes were weary and his voice concerned. She sensed she had added to his problems with her return.

"More than you could possibly imagine." She let her glance stray to Prince Holden, who stood scowling, his eyes moving from his father to his brother and back again as their voices drowned his out. "And less than you would ever believe."

"That sounds ominous."

"If not for him, I would not have survived our journey."

"If not for the need to protect him, you would not have been endangered in the first place." He watched her sharply, his eyes keen.

"Being sent out was an awakening for him. He is changing. We have all underestimated him."

"I saw the battle trophies in your wagons. Surely that is your doing more than his, is it not?"

"No." She shook her head. "The prince's tactics are responsible for our victories. I merely worked with him to develop his swordsmanship and his skills in hand-to-hand combat." She looked to the prince, feeling her eyes drawn as if by a magnet. "He is growing up at last, Father. He has lacked only the need to do so."

Bonham cleared his throat, an uncomfortable and disapproving rumble. He whispered his next words, barely audible. "Perhaps he's always needed a strong woman to beat some sense into his thick head."

She kept her voice as low as his. "Perhaps. Even more than that, he's needed something to do and a reason to be—a better reason than tupping the servants." She hesitated. "He needs people who believe in him. His men out in the courtyard? They do. Carl does too, now. You know Carl is a shrewd judge of character."

"And you?"

"I believe he is much better than his father thinks, or than you do." She lifted her chin, defiant. "He's becoming a good man."

Her father raised a dubious brow. "Has he bedded you?" He watched her sharply.

"He has not." She flushed a little at the denial. He hadn't, at least not quite. "Not for lack of trying, I admit." His ring hung heavily between her breasts, a weight that made her feel somehow both guilty and proud. She chose not to tell her father about the token.

"Thank God." Bonham relaxed a little. "Keep a shilling always between your knees around him, daughter, and do not drop it."

"You've listened to nothing I've said," Alex snapped, then bit her tongue, wishing the words back inside her head.

"He may have learned to lead men and grown in battle skill, but a stiff prick has no honor."

"Yours included?" she asked him coolly, and was pleased when his eyes flew wide with shock, then narrowed with anger at her insolence.

"Captain." Prince Holden's voice was brisk but courteous, and Alex found the interruption quite timely. "Please attend me."

"Yes, sir." She left her father behind her, steaming, and moved crisply to the prince's side.

"My father wishes you to set a guard on my rooms and confine me there so I will stay out of trouble until he can accomplish his parley with Sweyn Thorssen." He enunciated each word with bitter precision. "Manage the matter, will you?"

"I'll see to it, sir." Alex drew herself up straight. She addressed her obedience directly to him rather than to King Anselm. Prince Gavin's eyes flickered. He did not miss the subtle distinction. Luckily the king seemed to, subsiding into his chair with a grunt and gesturing for Roger to attend him.

The Duke of Fakenham stepped over hastily and offered the king a cup of spiced wine, which he accepted.

"Thank you, Fakenham. You're most kind. Bonham, we will proceed with our preparations for peace," the king proclaimed, stubborn and proud, his severe dignity spoiled as he gave a great sneeze into his white handkerchief. "Have the scribes draft a call to meet."

Chapter Thirty-One

Alex exited the room at Prince Holden's side. He was so furious she could hardly keep up with him as he strode bitterly along the narrow hallway, his fists clenched. "I should never have come back," he hissed to her. "I could have done more good raiding randomly in the countryside. If I'd had access to money of my own, I'd not have returned here at all."

She didn't have to ask whether the king would be willing to fund Holden's private troops or even repay the outstanding debt they were already owed. She winced. "I'll arrange for my father to pay our men, Your Highness."

"Thank you, since I have not even that much influence." She'd never seen him in such a dark, fey mood. "I am no better than a worthless whelp in my father's opinion. He's always seen me as a nuisance. All my labors are folly. Whatever will you think of me now?" He spat the words with contempt, self-loathing so hot in him it drove a spike of grief through her heart.

"I will think your father has erred." She stared straight ahead as they walked down the long, echoing corridor on their way to the main stair. "He doesn't want to see you are a faithful servant to the crown, a capable leader of troops...and more than worthy of their loyalty."

He inhaled sharply and glanced at her, his eyes searching.

"My liege." Alex spoke very softly, aware her voice would carry along the bare stone. "Do you think I would ever have let your orders outweigh the king's if I did not believe that? If I had no faith in your leadership?"

He stopped, and she halted with him. His eyes caught hers and softened, some of the fury leaching out of him. His voice, when it came, was equally soft.

"You honor me unwisely in setting me above my father."

"I serve His Highness, Prince Holden of Norwich. I bear his token. Will you report me for my treason?" The hall was empty, but Alex knew walls had ears. Still, she offered no great treachery, not one punishable by death. It was merely one that might strip her rank from her, removing her from the king's guards and the army proper. Her heart pounded. The prince's eyes were deep, shining bright, and she met them steadily.

"You know I will not."

"I do. You may rest assured I mean to serve you in any way I may." She held his eyes steadily, willing him to understand.

"Imprison me, then." He swallowed. "For now."

"Yes, sir."

She led him up the stair to the royal hall, where she escorted him to his room, then called for eight of her most trusted guards. She set them to watch him in shifts, reserving herself and Carl for other duties. Two of the guards waited inside the prince's door, and two in the corridor without. She arranged for the other squad to take the night watch, then confiscated the prince's sword.

"I will store this until you require it," she said gently, and he nodded curt agreement.

She left him there with reluctance and went to deposit his sword in the armory. On the way out, she had an idea. She would have books sent up to him. He needed information on warfare and tactics. It would provide a purposeful distraction from his captivity.

She went down to the castle library right away and began scanning the spines of the books to see if she could find anything of use. Footsteps entered the room and stopped behind her, and she glanced up, surprised to find Prince Gavin standing there. "Add this and this, I think." He reached over her shoulder to choose two volumes and set the heavy tomes on a table for her. "They will help him grow even more sly."

She looked at the crown prince with caution. "Your Highness?"

"You are training my brother, obviously." Prince Gavin shifted to sit on the edge of the reading table. "He's twice the man he was when he left. I can see a warrior in him now, in the way he moves and how he wears his sword. He's filled out. He stands up to our father, no longer as a whining boy, but as a man secure in knowing he is right. He's found a different use for his balls, if I may say so." He smiled a little, his eyes alert and thoughtful as he watched her.

Alex was not quite sure how to answer him. Though he'd showed respect for Holden's accomplishments, in the end he'd still supported his father. She could not afford to reveal the extent of her true allegiance, either overtly or by accident.

"Do you believe the peace treaty will work?"

"At the cost of half our lands? Maybe, or maybe not. Thorssen is cunning." Prince Gavin swung his heel thoughtfully. "I don't like father's plan, but I must support my king's authority. I'll be at the parley with a hand-picked force of men-at-arms, ready to rejoice if we agree to peace, or to fight our way out if things go badly."

He was as straightforward as Prince Holden was slippery, and easily as stubborn. Alex considered asking him why he believed he had to support his father, but decided not to.

"Thank you for your recommendations."

"I'll help you carry all those up." He hefted the heavy books, and she chose two slender volumes of poetry to add to them. They climbed up together, nodding to the guards, and carried their gifts in to Holden, who lay on his bed, staring bitterly up at the canopy.

"Brother," he said evenly. "Captain."

"We've brought you something for entertainment," Prince Gavin said easily, setting the books on Holden's dressing table. Though I would have thought you'd prefer a wench, the good captain believes you have more interest in tactics."

"I've done with wenching," Holden said shortly. "I thank you for the books, though."

"I thought you might like to try a bit of friendly swordplay, when I've some spare time," Gavin invited him. "I'd like to see how much you've improved, I confess."

"I suppose I've nothing better to do." Prince Holden's voice sounded bitter. "Other than sit back and wait for my father to make peace with the marauders who are burning his subjects alive."

"Stopping that would, of course, be a condition of the peace treaty he proposes," Gavin said mildly. "The treaty would save bloodshed among the ranks."

"It will cost us half our kingdom."

"Our?"

The temperature in the room dropped suddenly, so quickly Alex blinked with surprise.

"Your blasted kingdom," Holden conceded, tart. "Oh, begging your pardon, but the kingdom isn't yours yet, is it? Father's blasted kingdom." He smiled, razor-sharp. "My mistake."

"With a tongue like that, you'll soon run short of allies." Prince Gavin didn't smile back at him.

"You can't lose allies you don't have."

"Your diplomatic skills still need work." Prince Gavin rapped his knuckles on the cover of one tome to recommend it. "I'll tell your guards to bring you down to the training salon before supper, if you like."

"By all means."

Holden remained still until Prince Gavin departed, then rolled to the edge of the bed and rested his elbows on his knees, putting his head in his hands. "He'll wipe the floor with me, won't he?"

"Not as easily as he thinks." Alex raised a brow. "There's a good chance he won't, if you remember the cardinal rule."

"All's fair on the battlefield," Holden recited softly.

"Yes, precisely." She gave him a sly wink, bowed politely, and stepped to the door. "I'll go see to your men, Your Highness. I'll return and come to the salon in time to stand with you tonight."

"Yes. Thank you." He went to stand at the window, staring away toward the horizon, and she slipped out.

Chapter Thirty-Two

Carl and Holden's troops were still inside the stables, many of them tending their weapons or their gear. A few of them sat grouped around a bale of straw, playing cards. None had left, even though they had the prince's permission to take the day. Alex chuckled wryly, suspecting Carl was to thank. His nose for trouble was usually very good. He looked up at her expectantly.

"Did the meeting go well?"

"About as well as we should have expected." She kept her voice low and pasted a smile on her face for the benefit of the men, knowing he could read her eyes in spite of her cheerful expression.

He kept sharpening his sword, looking down at the whetstone in his hands. He ran it along his blade, making a silky scrape, then set them both aside. "What's King Anselm's plan?"

"A peace treaty, yielding up half the lands of East Anglia in exchange for a stop to the raiding."

"The families on those lands won't want to move. Where will they go?"

"They'll submit to Danish rule if they don't want to move, I suppose."

"Danish rule would mean the king of East Anglia doesn't have any authority over whether they're forcibly removed or not."

"Right."

"What will Prince Gavin do?"

"He'll support his father, though he'd rather stand and fight."

"Where is Prince Holden?"

"In his quarters. Four of the guards are on watch, which frees me to do as I see fit." She removed her sword belt and sat on the end of the wagon next to him. A few of the soldiers had begun taking notice of their conversation, gathering to listen with expectant faces. Edgar's eyes were sharp. The others might not be sure, but she suspected he could tell she wasn't happy.

"We're not needed," he observed, quiet.

"The prince will need us when he's had time to think of a plan." Alex felt certain. "He won't take long to decide on a stratagem, I think."

Carl glanced at her, raising a brow, and she could tell what he had to be thinking. *What* stratagem, precisely? Rebellion against an entire army with only thirty half-trained men? Flight into exile? Becoming penniless outlaws, preying on the Danes by night and hiding from the wrath of the king by day? Knuckling under to Prince Holden's father and being ignored while the peace talks proceeded, and disbanded thereafter?

"Since none of you have taken your day, we might as well march out now to the plains and set up a camp for training," Alex decreed. "Then I'll set you at liberty to explore the city. You should probably avoid the southeast quarter, if you value your purses and your hides." She drew out a bag she had tucked away earlier, and distributed a sovereign to each man from her own private funds. "In earnest of receiving what you're owed." She'd have to speak to her father about their pay sooner rather than later.

The men raised a hearty cheer and prepared to march out, chattering at one another, their spirits high. She shrugged helplessly at Carl and prepared her own horse.

She hoped Prince Holden had something more than his arm up his sleeve.

Chapter Thirty-Three

Alex supervised the creation of the camp and kept the men's afternoon training short, limiting them to archery practice so they could return to the city before suppertime. She left Carl to watch the camp with a handful of volunteers and marched the rest of the men back, then dismissed them to enjoy their time in the city. She thought of changing out of her armor before Holden's match, but there wasn't time. She left her horse with one of the stable boys and hastened toward the training salons, trying to look unhurried.

A large group had already assembled, alerted by the lightning-fast work of the castle's gossip chain, and a good number of them were female. Though most of the women of Norwich had fled the feared siege, a certain number of the ladies in the court preferred pursuit of a husband in the capital to relative safety in the countryside. Many of those who remained had their caps set for Prince Gavin. Though he was well over legal age and stood directly in line for the throne, he had chosen no wife yet. The subtle jockeying to see whom he would wed had long been a battle of epic proportions throughout the upper echelons of the ladies at court.

The women who wanted to catch Gavin's eye maintained an absolute and brittle politeness on the surface, so Alex believed Prince Gavin knew little of the hatred and savage rivalry festering beneath their mild facade. He was a typical male, all but blind to the desperation and the viciousness of women competing over a man.

Alex regarded herself as a special case; she'd never wanted any of the noblemen who were such hotly contested targets among the other ladies. She had occasionally been the object of social snubs and slights for one reason or another, but she'd never had any interest in snaring Prince Gavin. Even before this summer, her responsibility was to be more aware of the ladies who had fixed their hopes on Prince Holden, since he was her charge.

A few of the women who fancied Holden stood scattered amidst the throng, paying court to Prince Gavin's favorites in hopes they might ultimately forge an alliance to their benefit. Some of them, she knew, were Holden's former lovers, though none had ever managed to extract any promises from him. None of them looked at her with welcome.

She felt a little sad to realize Carl was right. She had no friends among the women at court. Her world had always been a man's world, and she'd spent her time in men's occupations instead of joining the ladies at their embroidery or painting or card playing.

She resolved she would work to change that in the future.

Be that as it may, she was glad none of the women who wanted Holden were privileged to go and stand by him now. None could act as his second, as she could. He stood all alone, wearing butter-soft leather breeches and a short tunic that wouldn't hinder his motion. His boots were soft-soled as well, textured to cling tenaciously to the stone floor. All his gear was light, and would serve him well when he needed speed and endurance.

She approved silently, moving to stand at his shoulder and meeting his gaze. She gave him a crisp salute.

The brothers agreed to spar with practice blades, and Prince Holden went to the rack, considering his selection at length. He chose a wooden short-sword with a grip that fit comfortably in his hand. Its balance suited him well. Alex stepped up to tighten the strap of his glove, and he held his wrist still for her.

"Thank you."

"Think nothing of it." She kept her head down, tucking the wayward strap out of sight so the extra material wouldn't hinder him. "Do you have a plan?"

"At least three."

She smiled at him, looking up through her lashes without moving her head. "Luck be with you, my liege." Her voice was barely audible, and her lips hardly moved, but his eyes flashed with pride. He held himself straight as he stepped out onto the floor, swinging his sword in a circle around his hand like a rapier.

Prince Gavin stepped out likewise, sizing up his brother with a speculative look. As Holden lifted his blade, Alex recognized his plan immediately.

Holden addressed the tip of his sword to Prince Gavin as if he was fencing, and Gavin smiled, advancing with a vicious swing.

Prince Holden backpedaled away from him, looking desperate and moving swiftly—again, as if he were fencing, as if he had no better sense than to tire himself out. But Alex knew how far and how fast he could run, and she had no worries on that account.

She watched Prince Gavin instead. He was steadfast, stolid, and heavier than his brother. His tactics were those of patient advance and sturdy aggression. She remembered many other bouts in which he'd relied on building momentum slowly, wearing his opponents out through the sheer stubborn persistence of his attacks. Prince Gavin knew how to accelerate his pace, building deadly strength even as he built his momentum, while his opponents' stamina waned until his implacable force overwhelmed them. He was not a brilliant swordsman, but the crown prince rarely made mistakes with his blade, and his solid persistence usually stood him in good stead.

Holden scored a minor hit on Gavin's wrist with his elbow, almost as if the blow were an accident. Prince Gavin scowled and the ladies gasped, their collective surprise all but sucking the air from the room.

Prince Holden continued to retreat from Prince Gavin's escalating attacks, employing varying degrees of seeming desperation. Alex held her breath, watching closely, but not so closely she missed her father slipping into the room to watch. She wondered if he would be as blind as Prince Gavin. Would he believe she'd trained Holden incompetently, or think he merely hadn't learned what she would have attempted to teach him?

His eyes flashed to her and he raised a brow. He was clearly wondering exactly that. She maintained a steadfast expression, refusing to give anything away.

The two brothers clashed fiercely, Holden intercepting a swing that might have broken his ribs and slapping the blade away with startling strength. Gavin's eyes narrowed, and he stepped back.

"Interesting," was all he said, wiping his brow, then fell into guard position once more. This time he waited for Holden to attack.

Holden obliged him, again leading with the tip of his sword, again up on his toes, moving too much. He drew Gavin out, then dispatched his attack. Again, again. Alex watched, frowning a little, looking for Gavin to leave the opening Holden was obviously baiting him for.

There it was, half a heartbeat. Holden lashed out like lighting. The edge of his fist slid low on the sword hilt. His hand blunted an impact that would otherwise have slammed the hard hilt of his sword savagely against Gavin's vulnerable temple. Gavin staggered and Holden hooked his ankle with his own and yanked. The crown prince went down, flailing, not managing to strike Holden as he fell.

Holden stood back, wiping sweat from his face. He kept his sword raised, wary.

"First touch for Prince Holden," Alex said, and Gavin's second confirmed her judgment.

Gavin shook his head, trying to clear his dizziness, and glared up from the floor. He rose to his feet slowly. "Very well. That was no fencing move. Fight me properly this time."

Gavin was slower than before as they started up, still trying to shake off the blow, but Holden took him at his word and faced him truly. Their blades clattered together with savage force as Gavin parried his swing.

Prince Gavin might have more skill, but he was slower, with a layer of fat around his middle. Holden was younger, fitter, and very swift, evading his attacks at every turn.

General Bonham raised a brow at Alex, conceding her a point, and she accepted his respect with a nod.

This time Holden failed to feint properly, signaling his direction with his eyes, letting Gavin grow confident in the pattern as he barely evaded counterattack after counterattack. Alex almost smiled, waiting for the moment when he would strike.

The opening happened on the fourth pass, and Holden countered his brother's lunge with a riposte that very nearly knocked Gavin's head off his shoulders, striking his left arm instead with enough force to leave a deep bruise. The strike would have been a crippling blow, if the swords were real.

Gavin stood back, shaking his arm and scowling.

"Second touch," Gavin's man decreed, approaching him to examine his shoulder, his expression worried.

"Trickery," Gavin decreed, scowling and working his shoulder. He blew a hiss of pain through his teeth as he tried to shake off the hit.

Prince Holden raised a brow at General Bonham, who exhaled through his mustache. "What rules were specified before the match?"

"Three touches to victory, and no other stipulations," Holden answered steadily. "The rules of honor in swordplay do not forbid a feint, unless they have changed since I last read them."

Bonham shrugged and Prince Gavin growled softly. "You don't fight with honesty."

"I fight to win." Holden raised his sword. "Do you have another in you?"

Prince Gavin gave a curt nod and advanced, guarding his weakened arm. He surged forward, delivering a flurry of blows, determined to take Holden rapidly and by brute strength. Alex blinked. Gavin must be desperate. She'd never before seen him abandon strategy to risk fighting in a way ill-suited to his talents, a mistake that would put him at a serious disadvantage.

Holden suffered a minor hit. "One touch for Prince Gavin," Gavin's second decreed. Holden danced away easily, his soft boots allowing his toes to grip the smooth stone floor, giving him good traction as he dodged and darted. Gavin pressed on, exhausting his strength in a barrage of frenzied lunges and thrusts. Holden went to one knee, rolling, and barely avoided a blow to the shin, but came up behind Gavin to tap his shoulder with the edge of the wooden blade.

"Third touch for Prince Holden," Alex and Gavin's second spoke in unison.

Holden dropped his sword and stooped to rub his knee, and Alex tensed, seeing Gavin's anger manifest in his sudden tension. He wavered, filled with desire to strike Holden while he was inattentive, to take vengeance.

Ever-honorable, he did not.

"Well-fought." The words sounded like gravel in his throat, and a hush of whispering ran through the room like wildfire. "Your win was...not straightforward." He paused. "However, it was fair by the terms of the match."

Alex's father agreed with a nod, confirming his assessment.

Alex exhaled with relief. Gavin's innate sense of rightness had won the day, in the same way Holden's sneakiness had won him the bout. She stepped forward to Holden's side as Gavin's second moved to check his shoulder. Her prince's knee appeared sound through his breeches. He had a slight limp, but she was not about to go prospecting for a look at the bruise on his skin with her father standing by and watching them.

She picked up Holden's practice blade and stepped aside, returning it to the rack. Holden offered Prince Gavin an embrace, and Alex was relieved when he grudgingly accepted. The crown prince smiled a little when they let go.

"My congratulations to your teacher." He tipped his forehead toward Alex, who made a small bow in return. "If she's as devious as you are, then the realm should tremble to see what you'll make of yourself, brother."

Prince Holden smiled a little in return. "I tremble for the realm," he said quietly.

Prince Gavin grimaced a little, accepting the remark as fair. "Come and have supper with me. You come too, Captain. I want to pick your brains."

"Yes, Your Highness." Alex saluted and fell in behind them as they left the salon, working their way through the slowly dispersing crowd.

Chapter Thirty-Four

After the heat of his rivalry with Holden subsided, Prince Gavin proved an amiable host. He was as good as his word. He spent the evening carefully grilling both Holden and Alex, hashing over every possible detail of their encounters with the Danes. The atmosphere felt friendly, and Alex enjoyed her dish of roast lamb with mint sauce, savoring the single glass of good red wine she allowed herself.

Prince Gavin's second also attended, making the group into a convenient foursome so no one would be left out of the conversation. He sat across from her, interjecting polite remarks whenever an opportunity allowed.

"The two of them were quite evenly matched, I thought, didn't you?"

Still as dull as ever. Alex mustered a dutiful smile for him. Ralph was pleasant enough, and she'd known him for a long time. Like many secretaries were, he was a bit boring and staid, nearly as straight-laced as Gavin himself.

Alex had long suspected the man would have liked to wed her, but she'd never found him particularly appealing. Still, he was a polite conversation partner, and Alex gradually relaxed as the evening stretched and the two princes did not start to bicker.

At length they moved to sit around the hearth for port and conversation, and Ralph excused himself reluctantly after Gavin gave him a pointed look.

The crown prince poured each of his remaining guests another tot of the sweet wine, leaning back in his chair. Midway through the glass, he started to grow chatty. "I confess, brother, I do not like our father's plan. Duke Roger's plan, I suppose I should say." He leveled a quiet stare on Alex. "Though I have complained often enough to my father in person, I would not like this repeated outside these rooms."

Alex nodded politely.

"Fakenham's plan doesn't take into account the fate of those people who would be abandoned under Danish rule, even if the treaty accounted for all other factors," Holden agreed.

"That, and more. We'll lose the right to tax them and the ability to draw on them for manpower, as well as leaving them to suffer eviction and uncouth laws." Gavin slapped his knees with frustration. "I do not believe in Sweyn Thorssen's honesty, as our father does. His desperation to end the conflict and the encouragement of his nearest counselors lead him to act unwisely."

"Then what would you propose?"

"We should wait until the treaty fails and drive the Danes out using whatever means are necessary." Gavin filled his cup again. "Straightforward battle tactics don't work the way your stealth attacks seem to. Maybe you can advise me, so my own army can use your methods to root the Danes out a little at a time until they flee back to their own land."

"Send the captain thirty of your men," Holden said slowly. "Have your officers handpick them for cunning and wit and leadership. Speed and stealth wouldn't be bad qualifications, either. They can train with my lads, and when they're ready, they'll be able to lead your men in stealth attacks, or even train others."

"Very well." Prince Gavin stared into his cup for a moment, then frowned, setting it aside. "I would have you at my side when the parley meets, Holden. You seem able to see into the heads of these ruffians. Maybe you can sense whether trickery is afoot."

Alex shifted, not liking what she heard. "For all three of the royal family to be present at such a parley is a terrible folly," she volunteered quietly. "What if an ambush slays you all?"

Gavin shrugged. "That outcome is an unlikely one. We'll have our best generals and men assembled there to defend against attack."

She frowned. "If all our rulers and best generals are there, who will remain behind to command the army proper and administrate the city?"

"You will remain," Prince Gavin pointed out calmly. "As the ranking officer in the city and the leader of the king's guards."

"No. I will go with Prince Holden, as his personal guard."

"You will remain here," Holden disagreed softly. "To discharge your duty to me and to the realm."

"Absolutely not." Their eyes locked, but his were steely, and Prince Gavin's stare joined his. She knew her father would agree with them, as well.

She glared at Holden, but his gaze did not waver. She hesitated, then decided not to push the matter further. After his humiliation at his father's hands, he did not need her to challenge his authority in front of Prince Gavin. Instead, he needed her to support and believe in him.

"Very well." She stared at her half-empty glass, feeling wretched. "I do not like this."

Holden's hand fell on her knee and pressed lightly there. "I don't either," he said softly, his voice sober.

She lowered her eyes, outwardly submissive, but her mind was already racing with plots and plans. She'd be damned before she'd stay in the city, helpless, while Holden went out to risk death on his father's foolish whim.

Chapter Thirty-Five

Within two days, Prince Gavin selected and dispatched his thirty men. They arrived at the stables to find Holden's forces had left, and a messenger summoned Alex, who was out at the camp conducting a stealth attack exercise. She went back into the city to lead the new men out to join Carl and the others in their training camp. She and Carl put their heads together to devise a training regimen, then assigned each of the men a partner and started the process of drills and exercises.

Her next urgent duty was to approach her father on the matter of the troops' pay, so she rode back into the city once more and found him in his private rooms, laid up for the moment with a touch of gout in his left foot. He lay irritably in his bed amidst rumpled sheets and untidy sheaves of parchment, trying to work and rest at the same time. His foot was clad in a sock, and he had propped his leg up on a plush velvet cushion. Walter hovered nearby, chewing on his lip and studying a leather-bound ledger full of figures.

"Set that over here and be gone with you," Bonham told him, and Alex checked the door after he departed to ensure he had actually left.

"The crown prince has authorized me to have my men train a portion of the standing army in Prince Holden's tactics," she reported to her father, after filling his carafe with fresh water and diluting his glass of wine, then setting it within his reach on a bedside table. "Does this warrant an official disbursement of funds to recompense them for services rendered?" Her eyes twinkled at him mischievously.

Her father huffed at her, mildly irritated with her political manipulation. "Daughter, the budget is already stretched thin."

"That's as may be, but these men have done service to the crown. Will there be proper compensation for the families of those who died in service?"

"Very well," he surrendered. "I suppose I can either justify the expense or hide it in the account sheets, if Walter doesn't actually show a copy of them to someone with more wits than he has himself." He put down his quill, shifting his hips. "As he did over the provisions accounting last spring, when he called Fakenham in to bring me to heel." He reached for his goblet, swilling a mouthful between his teeth as she brought him a lap table and his inkwell and pen. He grimaced at the wine. "This vintage is far too weak for my taste."

"The physicians say you should avoid rich food and wine until the attack has passed," Alex reproached him.

"Bah," he answered succinctly and took another swig.

"Finding someone with more wit than himself would be an easy proposition for Walter," Alex joked. In spite of her jest, Walter still worried her. He'd seemed all too cozy with the Duke of Fakenham at the recent council, and that association made her hackles rise.

"Don't I know it." Bonham gestured irritably with his quill. "His stupidity isn't often as convenient as at present." He uncovered a blank piece of parchment and scribbled for a few moments. Finishing, he blotted the page, then handed the document over to her.

"Will that cover your needs?"

"Admirably." Alex saluted him, grateful.

"Prince Holden fought well in his duel against Prince Gavin." General Bonham changed the subject abruptly. He blustered the words a little too forcefully, obviously a bit embarrassed by offering the concession they represented. "Your combat training was effective."

"He is learning," Alex agreed, stifling a smile. "I wish his father could admit it."

"Fatherhood isn't easy." The general gulped more wine, emptying the goblet. "Especially while you're trying to repel half of Denmark." He refilled his cup without diluting the wine, staring moodily into the ruby liquid. "I suppose it wouldn't make any impression if I were to tell you parents try to do what we believe is best for our children, even when they resent our meddling."

"As if I'd ever resented your guidance, sir." Alex looked up through her lashes, trying to seem demure but unable to keep from grinning.

"You're an impudent young lass," he chuckled. "Your mother would flay me if she could do so from the afterlife, I'm sure. She'd have been appalled to see you grow up in the ranks the way you did." He glanced over to where his wife's portrait stood on a shelf, his expression rueful.

"I wouldn't have had any other life," Alex murmured, and put her hand on his shoulder. "I'm happy as I am."

"Good." He covered her hand with his and gave her fingers a squeeze, then reached to his side, chuffing a little with impatience when his fingers stopped short of their goal. "Can you hand me my ledger? I need to see to covering up that draft."

"Yes, sir." Alex gave him the book and made sure to tweak the wine bottle out of his reach before she departed. "Doctor's orders," she explained, giving him a saucy wink on her way out the door.

She carried her draft to the royal coffers immediately and drew the men's pay, then went up to check on Prince Holden. Midafternoon had already arrived, and she hadn't seen him since the evening after the duel.

The constant guard on his quarters proved an irritating inconvenience, the guards formally questioning the reason for her visit. She answered tartly. They should be her men, but she could sense an unfamiliar element of suspicion and mistrust among them. Most of the people she'd seen since returning to the castle acted oddly, as if they were wary of her and Prince Holden. Their attitude must be a result of the king's hostile greeting.

She wished she could have brought Carl with her to help distract them. He could have insinuated himself into their confidence in order to find out if there was a deeper source for their unpleasant attitude, but he could not be present. At least one of Holden's loyal officers had to remain in camp to train the men.

After a short delay, Alex gained admittance to the prince's chambers. She walked in and discovered him half-buried in books and parchments and maps, as if his chamber had become a copy of her father's planning room. She moved to the table and glanced down at his maps, which reflected the most recent intelligence he could gather on the Danish encampments, his own reports included.

She raised her gaze to find him watching her keenly. She left her hand splayed on the page with the camps listed and marked.

"Good afternoon, Your Highness." She spoke blandly, keenly conscious of the guards behind her.

"Good day to you, as well." He matched her formality, standing but keeping well away from her. "I've spoken to Prince Gavin regarding my father's plans." He moved some documents and showed her a diagram. He selected a map with a circle drawn around an open area in the woods not far from the abbey. "The meeting will take place here, do you see?"

"In a clearing surrounded by forest."

"Yes." He traced a hand-drawn tree with his fingertip. "Quite a respectable forest, in fact. The area is served by three roads. It's conveniently neutral, being located several miles from the city proper."

Their eyes met. Neither of them liked the chosen site. They both knew from experience how convenient the cover of woods could be for troops who did not want to be seen approaching.

The prince stepped away from the table, stretching his back and legs with a sigh, and maneuvered a fresh log onto the ornately wrought andirons in his fireplace. The rooms were chilly in spite of the blaze, and Alex was glad he was not sleeping outdoors and awaiting the season's first frost with only a single blanket to warm him.

"My father will take a squad of a hundred men with him to serve as an honor guard. The main army will remain quartered here in Norwich, ready to ride out if anything goes wrong. As we discussed, Gavin plans to petition my father to place you in charge of the army until the parley is finished, and we anticipate his agreement."

Putting her in command was what they'd agreed in their discussion with the crown prince, but Alex secretly planned to renege on her part of the bargain. Nevertheless, her plans would work better if she were officially in charge. "What of you and Prince Gavin?"

"We will ride with my father," Holden's voice was dry. "To mark the sincerity of the Stuart dynasty in offering this treaty, as well as to defend the king."

"Once the treaty is signed, it will be all but impossible to reverse, regardless what treachery the Danes may try afterward."

"That's so." Holden shrugged. "However, I can't make that choice." His gaze intensified, holding hers for a significant moment. "See the key Danish encampments? Here, here, and here." His hands moved across the map, picking out some of the larger dots speckling the surface. She noted an alarming number of them were positioned along the Yare, by far the most easily navigable waterway of the Broads. "These comprise Sweyn Thorssen's headquarters, by all accounts. If treachery is to occur, I would expect an ambush to originate in these areas."

Alex smiled faintly. "I would agree." She marked the positions carefully. The Danes could bring an endless stream of men and materiel up the relatively deep channel of the Yare. There would be very little distance between the debarkation points these camps represented and the planned parley. Anyone with wits should be able to see the jaws of the closing trap.

"I've asked Prince Gavin to place scouts near the larger encampments, to bring warning of troop movements or other indications of aggression." Prince Holden's voice fell a bit. "I'm afraid his men move slowly and know little of stealth." He tapped the map with a neatly tied narrow scroll, then laid it casually on the table, barely touching her fingertips.

She picked the scroll up, twirling it idly between her fingers. "There are dozens of camps. Too many to watch them all." She knew him well enough by now to guess his thoughts: he wanted her to have their men scout the camps and bring early warning of the coming ambush so the parley could be canceled.

"Perhaps fifty good-sized ones are positioned within a day's march of Norwich," Holden agreed. "A handful have the potential to be truly dangerous." His gaze cut towards her, touching hers briefly. She nodded. The timing would be all but impossible, but she would do her best.

She palmed the scroll deftly, sliding it up into her sleeve and covering the motion by turning half-away from him to adjust her hair.

"Carl has begun training Prince Gavin's men. The troops are out on the plain today, running a test encounter in the fringes of the King's Wood not too far from the planned site of the parley." She reported the relevant details of the encampment and the exercises, very correct, aware he was giving them only cursory attention. The important business, the scroll, had already been managed.

"That's interesting." His bored voice gave a lie to his words, but his eyes lingered on her, caressing her as if he would like nothing better than to pull her into his arms. His warm regard threatened to spoil her concentration. She flushed a little and continued her recitation, dogged.

When she finished, his gaze rose to her face, meeting hers. For more than one reason, she wished there were no guards present. A spark jumped between them. Alex smiled a little, wry, and closed one eye in a broad wink.

He gave her a faint nod and took his seat, settling in before a book and giving her a casual flick of his fingertips, acting the part of the bored superior dismissing a troublesome underling. "Carry on, Captain," he directed her, and looked down at the page.

She saluted and marched out, the tight-rolled scroll concealed neatly inside her sleeve. Her heart was pounding. She hoped she understood him correctly.

When she reached the privacy of her own rooms, she shook the scroll out of her sleeve and unrolled it. As she'd expected, Holden had made a small copy of the information collected on several of the maps they'd looked at in his room, with strategic points marked and annotated.

There was no accompanying note, but she felt certain she knew her course.

She set her jaw, re-rolling the scroll, and pushed herself up onto her feet. She pulled the bell and dispatched a pageboy to the stables to order her horse saddled for travel. She would consult with Carl right away, and together they would put Prince Holden's plans into motion.

Chapter Thirty-Six

Alex arrived at the training camp to find the process of educating Prince Gavin's men well underway. Carl sat calmly amidst the new men. He had commanded his untrained troops to remain in camp, and sent his own group out to terrorize them. He forbade them to use arrows. Instead, Holden's squad threw small stones from concealment to demonstrate how effective arrows might have been. As Alex rode in, they took advantage of the distraction and a patter of stones fell, many of them striking the camp's inhabitants.

Gavin's men glanced about, nervous. No sign of Holden's troops could be seen. Alex waited patiently next to the fire, smiling a little to herself, as the sun went down.

Carl refused to advise his men on what to do, and eventually they decided on a sortie. As they prepared to move out, all hell erupted. A barrage of stones struck the camp, leaving not even Alex untouched. Gavin's men drew their swords, losing nearly all their number to 'arrows' in the process.

"The sentries were done for before you ever arrived," Carl murmured to Alex, who felt sorry for the new men in their embarrassment. "Well, what are you waiting for? Get after them. If this were real, you'd already be dead. They've picked most of you off twice over. You show up right well against this fire. See how you do out in the dark," Carl barked.

Men kicked dirt over their fire and ventured out into the wood. Alex did not have long to wait. All were tagged handily and tied up within a matter of minutes.

"Everyone come back to camp!" Carl bellowed after adequate time had passed, stirring and re-feeding the fire. Chagrined men came creeping back with their captors. Each confessed he'd been caught with a wooden training blade at the throat, or hit with an 'arrow' stone, or been taken by surprise while standing sentry duty and neutralized without a sound.

"Well done," Carl praised Holden's men. "Later tonight, we'll trade places and we'll see how our new men do assaulting a trained defense. After that, we'll re-run the exercises, pairing up one new man with one experienced man, so you can learn the right way to go about the drill from either side."

He gazed around at their attentive faces. "The day after, we'll work on stealth techniques. Concealment, constructing boltholes, how to anticipate an opponent and act to confuse him." This speech satisfied the sheepish trainees, who were eager to have a shot at ambushing the victorious veterans. Soon everyone sat down to a hearty venison stew, Carl and Alex sitting a little apart, waiting to be served.

"After a few days of training, we should have some of the newcomers raid a real Danish camp," Carl suggested hopefully.

"We'd best not risk that. King Anselm won't tolerate more attacks. Nonetheless, we'll have to train them swiftly." She showed him Holden's map and brought him up to date on her understanding of the prince's plan. Carl paid strict attention, his face grim.

"I can't believe King Anselm doesn't see an ambush coming. He has his head too set on the treaty to think clearly."

"Prince Gavin sees it, but he thinks mostly of battle lines and pincer movements and plowing through massed enemies with sheer force. He's nervous, but he doesn't know what to do."

"They'll be ambushed and the Danes will crush them, including our prince."

She chewed her lip. "Prince Holden made me promise to stay in Norwich and command the army."

Carl grimaced in sympathy. "He'll need the army to be ready to swoop in and counter the attack Thorssen's bound to launch as soon as the negotiations are underway," he pointed out. "He knows he can trust you to manage things. Of course, he means for us to persuade the king what's coming before the ambush can happen."

"That's how I understood his plan, yes. But the timing is going to be narrow, Carl. We can't send scouts until we know when the parley will start, or there won't be anything for them to find. But if we wait, by the time our scouts find evidence of an ambush, it may be too late for them to return in time to stop the parley."

Carl nodded agreement. "There's a terrible risk in this, especially to anyone who goes to the parley."

"His father won't have things otherwise."

Carl gazed at her soberly. "Is Prince Holden determined to go with the king, then?"

"I think he means to protect his father when things go bad. As does Prince Gavin. Gavin must have gathered most of this information and given it to Prince Holden, Carl. Our prince is a prisoner in his own rooms. I think the crown prince is playing a game of his own, one he's ill prepared to win. He knows Prince Holden has found a tactic that might work, something he can't do himself. He's giving Holden what he hopes is enough room to prevent the ambush from succeeding. He's given him enough rope to hang himself, anyway."

"We'll hang with him if there's no ambush. King Anselm will be furious if he finds out what we've been up to."

"That's right." Alex looked him full in the face, eyes steady. "Would you like to be reassigned before the hangman earns all our boots, Carl? I can make arrangements, if you want."

"No," he said quietly. "I think what we're doing is right."

"So do I." Alex accepted a bowl of stew and dipped her spoon in for a hearty bite.

"Your agreement would please Prince Holden." Carl's voice was deferential, but she sensed an undertone of reproach, and she shifted, embarrassed.

"You think it wouldn't please him so much as something else. I can hear your disapproval." She stared into her stew, her cheeks burning a little. "You think I should go to his bed before the parley." Carl might not know exactly how far things had progressed between her and the prince, but he was plenty shrewd enough to read the signs. He knew she was still making Holden wait.

"I think you should ask yourself whether you'd regret not having gone if something happened to him and you lost your chance." Carl tore off a bite of bread and chewed, not looking at her.

"You've been matchmaking us ever since the night of the fire, I know."

"I think he loves you, as I've said before," Carl's expression was a little exasperated. "You didn't see his eyes when that hostler asked if you were still inside the loft. If I may say so, I think you care rather more for him than you let on, Captain. I've never seen you in such a dither over a man. You've always been as like one of the lads as I've ever seen a woman be. You've taken your pleasure for an evening, then marched down the road afterward with a smile and a whistle. You never looked back. Like with our Edgar." He gave her a sympathetic wink. "You don't do that with the prince. Something holds you back. Now he's taken charge of himself, I think your hesitation must come from how much he's grown to matter to you."

Alex's neck burned scarlet at his frank assessment of her habits. She set her half-empty bowl in her lap and scrubbed her palm over her face, trying to decide what expression to put on for Carl when she was done. She didn't know, and settled for none at all. "The prince needs a captain more than a lover."

"That may have been true at one point. Do you really have to choose between the two now?"

She had no easy answer, so Carl simply finished his stew in a few large bites and went to the pot for seconds, giving her time alone to think. She swallowed another bite from her own bowl and grimaced to realize the food was growing cold. She barely tasted the stew as she finished it off, thinking of Prince Holden's face, his hands, and the sweetness of his sly smile. She could remember every one of his words. She needed to gather her courage and let herself believe she truly mattered to him.

He was right. At some point she had to make a leap of faith.

Alex wasn't a timid woman, and she wasn't a blind one, either. The prince might not remain constant forever, but that was true of any man. He had proven himself time and again. She had no compelling reason to doubt he had chosen her and given her his heart.

Alex scraped the bowl with her spoon, pensive. Prince Holden would be even more grievously lost to her after his death in battle than if he made love to her and lost interest in her afterward. Should she get a child from him...which she might. It was the wrong time of the moon for her to go to a man without worry...she would have at least that much of him left with her for always.

She finished her stew mechanically and chewed her slice of hard bread, washing it down with a gulp from her wine skin. By the time she could return to the castle, the hour would be past middle-night. There would be the matter of the prince's guards to be fooled. If she went barging in and summarily ordered them out, the tale of her assignation with the prince would be all over the city before breakfast. That would do no one any good.

No, to get in and out unseen, she would have to take a leaf from Holden's book of trickery and become invisible.

Alex smiled suddenly, quietly, to herself and called to one of the men to fetch her a second helping of stew.

Carl came back with his own, slumping onto his blanket-roll and digging in as enthusiastically as if it were his first bowl. Edgar brought her bowl back to her, full and steaming, and she thanked him. She began to eat, devouring the stew with renewed appetite. "Thank you for your advice, Carl. You're right, as usual, curse you." Her warm tone took the sting out of her words.

He chuckled. "The prince can thank me later."

She snorted softly and blew on her spoonful of stew, which was piping hot. Food tasted much better now she'd resolved on her course of action.

The men picked up their drilling voluntarily after supper, with the seasoned troops remaining in camp and Edgar leading the others to march out into the night to prepare their assault. Alex saddled her horse to head back to Norwich. "I won't stand about in the woods and be pelted by pebbles again tonight," she laughed to Carl when he carried her empty bowl away. "Thank you, though."

"Have a care on the roads. There may be Danish brigands abroad," he cautioned her.

"I pity them, then," Alex said, giving him a wink.

"I wouldn't want to come between you and Prince Holden myself, not if I had Sweyn Thorssen and all his ancestors behind me," Carl chuckled, then stepped back out of her horse's path as she reined it around. "Never you worry. I'll take care of things here."

Chapter Thirty-Seven

Alex met no travelers, friendly or otherwise, on the road. She stayed slightly to the side, where the turf was damp and the grass muffled the sound of her horse's hooves. The night was silent and dark. The moon wouldn't rise until shortly before dawn.

She was going to have to find allies to help her achieve her plans. Since she couldn't confide in her father…Maybe old Pelley would be helpful. She was always able to twine him around her little finger. She'd been doing so ever since she first wheedled him into showing her how to hide a dagger in her boot. He was a good general, too, even though he'd spent his life in her father's shadow. He could do what she needed, and do it well.

She was smiling as she signaled for the drawbridge to be let down. She gave the password, and she caught herself humming as she guided her horse into the stables.

The other part of her plan would be far less fraught with uncertainty than convincing General Pelley to conspire with her. That was true even though her decision to go to the prince's bed made her heart race as her scheming at the brink of treason did not.

She stopped by the laundry on her way to her room and borrowed a stack of linens, including bed sheets, blankets, coverlets, and pillowcases. She made the pile tall enough to eclipse her face. She also stole a maidservant's shapeless dress, an apron, and one of the charwomen's wimples.

That should do nicely.

She could hardly sleep for nervousness and anticipation, and woke early in the morning, gazing up at the canopy of her bed. She stretched, luxuriant. It was still early in the week for a bath, but she called for one anyway. She took her time, washing with harsh lye soap and rinsing herself carefully. She stepped out of the bath and dried herself carefully with a linen towel, then oiled her skin, applying perfumes she hardly ever bothered with, even when there were diplomatic functions she must attend in a gown because she'd be expected to dance.

She fastened up her hair so the ungainly wimple would cover it all and put on the rough maid's dress. She tied on the apron last, leaving off her underclothing beneath the disguise. The air flowed around her body delightfully under the dress, an unfamiliar feeling of freedom. She didn't have a pair of the servants' sturdy shoes, but her feet wouldn't show under the long skirt, so she stepped into a pair of worn slippers, checked her attire in the mirror, and picked up her stack of bedding.

She had some difficulty sneaking out of her rooms and getting the door shut behind her without being seen, but she managed. She timed her exit so she would be in the halls midway between breakfast and luncheon. Few people other than the domestic staff would be wandering the castle, and those who were would have duties to preoccupy them.

Her heart was pounding by the time she arrived at the prince's door, her face effectively concealed behind her pile of linens. The bored guards swung the door open immediately to admit her, much faster than when she'd entered in her captain's garb. Pulling a wry face, she stepped inside and bustled over to the bed, setting down her bundle and keeping her back to the door, where the second pair of guards stood their vigil.

Prince Holden never looked up from his work as she began to strip the bed. She moved slowly, her hands clumsy. Changing sheets wasn't work she was skilled at performing. She waited for him to look up at her, meaning to catch his eye, but he never did.

A fine time for his new sense of responsibility to show up. She made excessive noise shaking out the sheets and tucking them around the mattress, growing impatient and seeking to disturb him.

"Be done there and go. I've no use for dallying," he snapped at her, never looking up.

"I beg your pardon, Your Highness. I shall be glad to do as you wish." Alex made her voice as sultry as she could, purring, and his head snapped up. He blinked at her for a moment.

"Perhaps I was too hasty." His voice fell to a smoky rumble. His tongue flickered out and moistened his lips. "Guards, leave us."

The guards hesitated long enough to exchange a glance, then clattered out to wait in the hall, well familiar with Prince Holden's habits of old.

Alex flipped the coverlet onto the bed and stood up straight, awaiting the prince's opening move. He also rose, but remained behind his table. "A fine trick," he said softly. "Is there news?"

"Carl is training the new men, as Prince Gavin asked. I watched them last night, and the exercise seemed to go well enough. They were completely lost when our seasoned troops attacked, but I think they learned several valuable lessons. When I rode out, they were eager to try an attack of their own using your methods." That was not important enough to warrant a disguise and he knew it. He waited, expectant.

"Is that all?"

"I missed you." His hesitation let her know she had to reassure him she had come to him for more. She took the wimple off her head and freed her hair, pulling the pins out so it streamed softly down her back as she shook her head.

He watched, his eyes intense, but did not move. "Ah." He had a quill in his hands. He ran his fingers along the edges of the feather and set the pen absently on the blotter, seeming at a bit of a loss.

"I must admit, I'm a little disappointed," Alex murmured.

He blinked back, startled. "What for?"

"Your reputation is rather more astonishing than the reality."

He frowned at her, baffled.

"Here I am, a humble but comely serving maid, offering myself shamelessly to Prince Holden, that fabled cocksman, and I'm not yet on my back in his bed." She brought her hands behind her neck and untied the apron covering her dress.

His eyes popped open wide. He glared at her, but his tongue flickered out again, licking his lips.

"I've an idea the Captain of King's Elite Guard would be quite annoyed with me if I were to take my pleasure with one of the serving girls." He began to drift forward, his confidence growing, though he was clearly not quite sure of Alex yet. "I would not offend her."

Her heart started to hammer in earnest as he passed the table. He moved tentatively, without any hint of predatory intent, but she froze, rooted to the spot, unable to draw enough breath into her lungs. She dropped the apron and it crumpled at her feet.

He stepped forward once, then again, staring at her in the shapeless, dingy dress as if it were lovelier than the finest, most close-tailored silk gown. "If she were here, that would be another matter entirely." He reached for her, his fingertips grazing the rough hemp cloth of her dress. They trailed down and closed around her wrist. He lifted her hand to his face and kissed each knuckle, slow and deliberate. "If you were she, then I might indeed be tempted to forsake my vows of virtue."

Alex shivered, her nipples peaking against the coarse homespun cloth. "So might she," she breathed, and blushed.

"Alex." He tasted her name as if it were infinitely precious and beautiful to him. "Have you…are you…?" He laughed softly, helplessly, his eyes filled with hope. "Listen to the stammering suppliant you make of me." His hands moved up and cradled her face.

"I've found my courage," Alex murmured, holding his gaze. "If it isn't too late."

He chuckled, stroking his fingertips along her cheek. "You have run me around in circles for so long." He leaned in, nuzzling softly at her lips. "Are you certain?" He murmured the words against her mouth, never asking her why she'd made her choice, or why now.

"Yes," she breathed, feeling her whole body resonate with anticipation.

He devoured her mouth, sweet and passionate, opening her and diving in. His lips and tongue explored hers, hot with urgency. She met him equally, surging against his body and wrapping her arms behind his neck. She was no blushing virgin, and now she'd decided to give herself to him, she knew exactly what she wanted.

He sensed her passion, and his hands slid to rest on her bottom, drawing her tightly against him and rucking up her dress. He kissed her harder, maneuvering her up against one of the posts of his bed. His knee slid between her thighs and she rested on him with a gasp. He drew back, his eyes dazed with heat, and dragged her dress up and over her head. He groaned when he realized she was already bare beneath.

She gasped for breath, tingling under the ardent caress of his gaze. She reached and scrabbled at the buckle of his belt. He helped her, yanking it off and dragging his tunic over his head. He stepped forward against her again, and their bodies pressed together. He growled, curling his arms around her and pulling her fiercely against him.

"Your boots," she whimpered, nipping his lip. "Off!"

He released her reluctantly and tried to kick them off, cursing when they clung stubbornly to his feet. She laughed helplessly as he hopped on one foot, clumsily tugging at the heel. Then they were gone and his eyes turned to fire as he advanced on her again. He tugged her tightly against him. She slid her hands down his back to the waist of his trousers and inside, cupping them around the spare curve of his arse.

He groaned and helped her push the trousers down. He stepped out of them and scooped her up, laying her on her back in the bed and following her down, one knee settling between her thighs.

"If you think," he nipped at her collarbone, his teeth stinging lightly, "I will rush this now you are willing," another sweet love bite settled on her throat, and another, trailing up toward the lobe of her ear. "Then you are very much mistaken." His hand covered his ring, which was still on her, still hanging from its chain. He smiled at her, and the tender heat made her throat close with emotion.

He meant his words. He kissed her slowly, working his way over every part of her, exploring with lips and tongue. The bristles of his beard made her moan, or gasp, or even laugh helplessly as it tickled her. The wet velvet of his tongue tormented her nipples at great length as he suckled and licked there, rolling her free nipple between his thumb and forefinger, blissful, his eyes half-shut, his beard harsh against her skin.

She explored him too. The spare lines of him were slender but hard with new muscle. She stroked the rough hair on his arms and chest, then buried her fingers in the longer hair on his head, loving the softness of it sliding between her fingers. Then she trailed her hand down his front to discover the satin-soft steel of his cock, eager and straining in her palm.

"Not yet," he smiled at her. "Much more, and you'll be disappointed indeed."

He slid down her body, tonguing softly at her navel. She lifted herself, opening for him, and his hands began to trail upward along the insides of her thighs.

His fingers parted her and found her slick and ready. He brushed the tips of two of them over her swollen flesh, making her whimper and buck. He chuckled, appreciative, then set about driving her mad, fingering her lightly. At last he knelt between her knees and kissed his way up and down the insides of both thighs before burying his face against her to ply his wicked, skillful tongue there until she thrashed and jerked and gasped and arched against his hands. As she shuddered to completion for him, she was unable to care that the men in the hall must be able to hear her helpless cries of ecstasy through the closed door.

Only when he had satisfied his need to touch and kiss all of her, and after she'd shattered twice, once on his fingertips and once on his tongue, did he move to mount her. He hesitated between her legs, looking down at her with burning eyes and a smile that made her heart flutter.

He positioned them both gently, lifting her thighs and settling himself against her, then pressed, slow and steady.

She trembled, holding her breath as he speared her. His cock felt better than she ever imagined. She could hardly breathe for the sweetness of holding him inside. She clutched at his back and writhed, moaning.

He caught her face between his hands and held her eyes with his as he rolled his hips, sinking all the way inside her. He thrust, riding her firmly, and she wrapped her arms and legs around him, gasping for breath, nuzzling her face against his, mouthing desperately at his cheek and his ear and his throat.

She'd had her share of lovers, but nothing like this. Never had she felt such a devouring passion, filling her with aching tenderness even when the flame burned brightest, awakening effortless sensuality. Their bodies fit together perfectly, and he took full advantage, lifting her hips and bringing her back up off the bed to change the angle as he had her, every touch sparking fire all along her nerves.

She scrabbled at his shoulders, her short nails digging into his skin, and he hissed against her throat, biting her softly. He lifted himself, bracing his body over her, and his thrusts began to come harder, faster. She felt her breasts start to bounce on her chest with the force of his body claiming hers. She gasped his name, which emerged broken and sweet on her lips. He leaned in and licked his way into her mouth and kissed her, the short sharp strokes of his tongue echoing the motion of his cock filling her body.

Her fists twisted into the sheets, and she couldn't stay still, writhing and lifting her hips to meet him, her heels restless on the sheets. He began panting, his skin slick with sweat. He bent his head and nestled into her throat as his hips jerked feverishly, then the thrusts stopped, his cock pushing deep, his whole body shuddering as he spent himself inside her.

Alex murmured tenderly into his ear as he collapsed on her, gasping for breath. She spoke love words, reassurance, anything and everything in her heart. He clung to her as he gentled, and she stroked his back, loving his weight, loving how vulnerable he was and how much he wanted her.

She never wanted to be without this. This was like finding cool water in a desert when she was near dead from thirst.

Alex stroked Holden's spine softly as he lay atop her, spent, half dozing. His hand curved around her breast, and his lips nuzzled lazily at her throat. She could feel his cock softening, gradually slipping out of her. She hated to lose him.

She wanted to stay in his bed, to love him again and again and again, but the guards would be patient for only so long, and there were things she must do.

She let herself lie next to him for a long time in spite of that, too blissfully content to move. She had come too far to second-guess herself, or to regret. She simply luxuriated in feeling his skin against hers, and stroked her fingers through the unruly, sweat-damp strands of his hair.

At last she stirred, reluctant, but the angle of the light from the window told her the day was nearing its peak. He made a low sound of protest, reaching for her again. She climbed to her knees and began to make her way across the bed.

"Oh no you don't. Not so soon," he purred, and came up behind her, catching her waist in both hands. She glanced over her shoulder to protest, but the sly smile on his face caught the words in her throat, and she let him stop her, watching as he quickly stroked himself to hardness. He settled behind her and pulled her back onto his cock, sliding in easily.

She moaned and braced herself to push back on him, and they came together sharply, making him gasp. His fingers sank into her hips and he rode her hard. She cried out in unison with him, feeling sweat gather on her own skin as she surged back and forth to meet him, matching his passion. He bent over her, catching her breasts in his hands, and licked the blade of her shoulder, then hoisted her into his lap.

"Like this." He settled his arms against her sides, cupping his palms over her shoulders, and thrust with a slight circular motion. She raised herself on her knees, arching her back, and gasped when the angle pushed his cock just so inside her, rousing a flare of sensation that ignited a glowing coal of pleasure.

"Mmmm, yes," he growled, nipping her shoulder. "Right there..." He rocked against the sweet spot again, and her head fell forward. She moaned, tightening herself around him, and he brought one of his hands down, sliding between her legs and setting his fingertips against her again.

She rocked there, caught between his fingers and his cock, and went up in a swelling crescendo of bliss as each sensation intensified the other until she was wailing, riding him in short, rapid bursts of motion, her long dark hair plastered to the sweat on both their skins. He nipped the flesh of her throat between his teeth, and the unexpected sting of the bite transmuted to ecstasy, more than her nerves could withstand. She came hard for him, shouting, clenching on his cock. He pushed her down to the bed while she was still shivering with aftershocks, cradling her gently in both arms. Her cheek rested on the cool sheets as he thrust to his own completion, his hands stroking her back and sides.

"Wouldn't want you to leave without giving you something to remember me by." He withdrew and slumped down beside her, grinning a little—and there was her brat, the imp of mischief she loved so much dancing in his eyes. But she could see her good man, too, reaching out to her with love and pulling her near so he could kiss her forehead and nuzzle against her cheek.

After a few minutes she rose reluctantly, luxuriating in the sensation of his eyes following her. She took her time as she gathered her crumpled clothes and put them on. He chuckled at her while she struggled to contain her tangled hair beneath the confining wimple. "A clever ruse indeed. If I'm as treacherous as Gavin says, then I learned from the best."

She moved to look in his mirror, adjusting the wimple over her hair. "Prince Gavin is too harsh. You know nothing of treachery, and you had no need to learn cleverness from me." She went to him for a final kiss, lingering, taking a last moment to press herself against his chest and inhale his masculine musk. "I've shared your plan with Carl. We'll send men to scout each encampment you indicated, and I'll have the army at hand, ready to pounce on any sign of Danish treachery."

"I knew I could trust you." He stroked the rough cloth of her dress, tracing the curves of her body through the fabric. "Don't start to regret lying with me after you've gone." He whispered the words in her ear, fierce, almost pleading. "Come back to me as soon as you can."

"I will," she breathed, and pulled him against her firmly, hoping to reassure him. "I won't regret it. We'll carry out your plans. Then…?" She drew a deep breath. Then, she didn't know. Would he want to continue? What would he want from her?

"We may not be able to stop the parley in time, before the trap springs." He stroked his hand over her back and her flank. "Gavin and I will fight to get my father out."

"Then *you* come back to *me*," she whispered. "You were right. I love you, my prince." Her cheeks colored, but she held his gaze firmly. She felt as if she was falling, exhilarated and terrified and giddy. His eyes flared, proud and joyful.

"I'll come back." He squeezed her hand and touched his lips to her knuckles: pledge and promise.

Chapter Thirty-Eight

Alex left Holden with great reluctance, blushing and ducking her face away from the guards when they snickered at her, derisive. She pretended dreadful embarrassment and shyness, covering her features with her hands, and scampered down the hall. Once she was away, she maneuvered herself through the increasingly crowded corridors until she could duck into her room unseen.

Clad once more in her own guard's uniform, she went out to seek General Pelley. She finally found him tucked away in a nook of the dining hall. The shine of his bald head betrayed his identity before she ever neared his place. He seemed morose, sitting over a half-eaten plate of roast pork with rosemary and mustard, staring into a flagon of ale that looked largely untouched.

She went into the kitchen and scavenged a platter of cold mutton and an apple, then went in to join him.

"General." She slid onto the bench across from him and returned his sober nod. "How fare you?"

"A man of war fares poorly in these days of parley." His thick mustache drooped as he lifted his face to stare at her. "As I suppose you can see for yourself, if you care to."

"I wonder if you'd do me the favor of reviewing my new troops." She put her hand on his arm. "My father is too busy preparing for the parley, but they'd benefit from a career officer's presence."

He drew himself up, puffing a little with pride. "My pleasure, Captain."

They went down to the stables together, Pelley scanning the halls with a scowl on his face, though his greetings to everyone they passed were courteous and polite. He contained himself until they were well onto the plain, then turned to her, his face grave.

"This peace treaty troubles me, Captain." He exhaled forcefully, blowing out the ends of his mustache, and passed his hand over the crown of his bare head. The sunlight caught on the chased steel pauldrons he wore over his leather mail, momentarily dazzling Alex's vision. "Everything smacks of poor planning and nonexistent strategy."

"Carelessness is not like King Anselm," she agreed, wondering what he knew of the intrigue in the castle and how much he would risk telling her.

"King Anselm isn't responsible at all. Nor is your father. That bounder Fakenham is behind this." Pelley scowled. "Whenever he's not primping in a mirror or having his hair curled, he's hanging about the king at all hours of the day and night, whispering flattery and foolishness in his ear." He gave her a sharp look. "Though if you go running to King Anselm, I suppose I'll lose my rank for speaking ill of his steward."

"No, I won't be doing that," she said quietly. She'd witnessed far too many of the Duke of Fakenham's manipulative tactics since her return. Hearing the truth of his maneuvers came as no great surprise. She'd always disliked him on general principles. He was as two-faced as he was vain, and he'd always been prone to betray his allies and their confidences.

"Tell me. Do you see my father's corporal, the man called Walter, in company with Fakenham often?" She asked him, keeping her tone casual.

"I despise that little weasel. I don't know what your father sees in him." Pelley spat to the left side of his horse, away from Alex. "Always snooping about and eavesdropping, making malice any way he can. The answer to your question is yes. Whenever he isn't with your father, he and Fakenham have their heads together. You wouldn't think Roger would give a tinker's curse for him, but they're thick as thieves."

Alex groaned ruefully. "I should have tried to warn my father about him long ago."

"Walter doesn't concern me half as much as Fakenham himself. I don't know what the man's purpose is, but this treaty is entirely his idea. I've heard him speak on the subject all too often." Pelley scratched his ear, and the plumes on his hat blew back, fluttering in the breeze. "If I dared speak treason, there is much I might say."

"If you dared speak truth?" Alex encouraged him.

"I would say he is steering the king into a trap for his own reasons. I know not what." He stared down at the reins, seeming to regret his open speech.

Alex hastened to reassure him. "You may be especially interested to see Prince Holden's encampment and drills, then." She led him away from the main road, directing her horse off through the fields toward the wood. "My plan is to send our men out to scout the Danes for evidence of treachery, and bring early warning back to the king so he won't be caught in the jaws of the trap Fakenham has set. It seems everyone can see it except King Anselm, but no one can make his majesty listen."

"I was under the impression you were training Prince Gavin's men."

"In stealth tactics well-suited for spying and sneak attack," Alex led him beneath the shades of the wood. "They're learning how to creep up on a camp without being seen, and how to sabotage enemies in a small way, picking off men without directly engaging them in battle. I mean to tell Carl to teach them how to estimate an enemy force's strength and aggression, as well. Stealth attack tactics are the ones Prince Holden had such success with before returning to Norwich." She would not implicate him any further than she had to, not even to Pelley.

"To a less than enthusiastic welcome," Pelley huffed. "When I saw those wagons full of Danish gear, I thought for a moment we had a bit of hope to go on with. Better than a plan to halve the kingdom and abandon our good citizens to the poor mercy of those foreign ruffians."

It took a lot to move a man as loyal and steadfast as Pelley to speak so critically of his king, Alex knew. That he would do so said volumes about the state of the kingdom, even though he was speaking in terms of Duke Roger having bewitched King Anselm rather than directly gainsaying the king himself.

"We're here," she said quietly, and dismounted to hold his horse for him as he dismounted. She gestured to the low row of tents. Since she left, they'd been smeared with dirt and leaves, and they blended in well with the surrounding forest. "The men are probably out in the wood, scouting."

"Some of us are right behind you watching, Captain." Edgar stepped out of nowhere, saluting them. "My shadow and I have been following you for the last half-mile, begging your pardon." He gestured another man out of the trees. The soldier was one of Prince Gavin's, a fair-haired lad so skinny he was barely there, with narrow eyes and a sly demeanor.

Pelley blinked at them, impressed. "Very good, soldiers. I'd no idea you were about."

"That's our job." Edgar moved into the camp proper. "I'll build up the fire, Captain, and brew a pot of that mint stuff you drink, if you like. Lieutenant Carl and the rest of the squad should be back soon to help make supper."

He put on the kettle and began the preparations for stew while other pairs gradually began fading in from the forest to assist. Several fires were lit and the men began to peel and chop carrots and onions. The vegetables went into the big communal kettle with most of a deer, and the camp soon filled with the savory smell of cooking as various pots started to simmer. In places, rabbits and pheasants and other birds turned on spits, and rough camp bread was set to bake in Dutch ovens nestled at the fringes of the coals.

"General," Alex spoke quietly, her hands curled around a mug of mint infusion. "I've been asked to take command of the city defense while the parley occurs. I will be in charge of the army, too, assuming the absence of any superior officer. All the generals are to be dispatched to the parley, but I would ask you to find a reason to stay behind. I want you to command the army in my stead."

Pelley considered her shrewdly. He might look a bit of a fool with his fancy plumes and the awkward, bushy mustache he affected, but he was anything rather than stupid.

"To free you to command this force."

"To use Prince Holden's men and the army to maximum effect in protecting both King Anselm and the two princes." She looked at him levelly. "I have the authority, as designated commander, to delegate responsibilities as I see fit. I want to delegate this one to you. I do this in service to the king and to the realm."

"If I did not believe that were so, I would not be listening to you." He considered the sixty men who sat around the fire, ladling stew into their bowls or gnawing on meat-filled bones. "Show me what they can do."

"It will be my pleasure."

After supper, Pelley sat scowling, watching intently as the men raided their own camp with merciless efficiency, melting noiselessly in and out of invisibility in the forest. In the end he turned to Alex and slapped his knees, his face lighting up with reluctant admiration. "I've never seen anything like it," he admitted. "I think you're onto something, Captain. I'll agree to your plan."

Relieved, Alex extended her hand and they shook on their pact. Pelley called for his horse and prepared to ride back to the city. "Proceed apace, Captain. You don't have much time." He looked down soberly from the back of his bay charger. "Messengers have already begun to come in announcing various factions' acceptance of the proposed meeting. The parley will likely take place in less than a week."

"Yes, sir." She saluted. "We'll need to agree on signals and communications."

"I'll have the army ready to swoop in. If there is to be an immediate ambush, have the monks at the abbey sound their bell. If there is more time,

227

send messengers to me with specific details. I suppose you'll also dispatch them to Prince Holden so he can warn the honor guard." His eyes fixed her, shrewd, despite her deliberate failure to disclose the extent of the prince's involvement.

"Yes, sir." She drew herself up straight. "Someone with the king's party will need to know."

"Indeed." He clucked to his mount. "Success, Captain."

Forced to work with such an abbreviated timetable, Alex and Carl had to stick close to their troops and focus intently on their training. Alex threw herself into the work with a will, but even so, part of her yearned to return to Prince Holden, and she often wondered how he was faring back at the castle.

She worried, too, whether he might believe she had abandoned him due to the regret he worried she might feel.

Pelley soon sent a messenger with the date of the peace talks, and Alex grimaced, folding the parchment and tucking the message in her pocket. The parley would occur two days hence, even sooner than they'd expected. If they hoped to have any news in hand before the parley began, training would have to be cut short and scouting parties dispatched immediately.

She had Carl call the men to gather around the fire, and she pulled out Holden's map. She gave her orders crisply, directing her best pairs to go to the most crucial encampments.

"Shall we try sabotage, or just gather information?" Edgar asked, his face wry.

"King Anselm does not wish a sabotage of the Danish camps," she said slowly. "If you have proof of ill-intent or hostile action, a judicious effort to slow their advance would not be amiss. Provided, of course, one of you comes homeward at speed to deliver the news you've gathered. Getting your information out is of the utmost importance, and should take precedence over sabotage in this case. When you have your information, one of you should travel toward Norwich and find the army and the other should go directly to the site of the parley." She tapped the map. "Ask to see General Pelley when you contact the army, or Prince Holden's aide if you go to the parley. Tell them you have an urgent message from me, and try to deliver your news discreetly. Don't let the Danes know what you're up to."

"Yes, Captain." Edgar saluted, and all the men chorused agreement.

They departed in pairs, melting into the night noiselessly, until Alex stood in the empty camp with no more than Carl and their two horses for company. She put her foot in the stirrup and hoisted herself into the saddle, trying to banish her nerves. This part of the plan was irrevocably set in motion, and was likely to cost more men than all their other encounters put together.

She would deal with that when the time came. Now she had to focus on carrying out the most challenging part of her plan.

Chapter Thirty-Nine

Alex sent Carl along to join Pelley's troops and sneaked up on one of the army encampments near the city. She turned up her collar to hide her face and worked her way in without being recognized. She tethered her horse alongside a number of others, where it would be cared for. Then she slunk into an empty provisions wagon and concealed herself under a tarp while the drivers were about their business. They returned after a time, and she lay hidden among the empty barrels and boxes as the wagon returned into the city for a new load. Her wagon rattled over the drawbridge late in the afternoon, and she slid off as soon as she was well within the twisting warren of streets that made up the outer layer of the city.

Now she was inside the city wall again, and nobody knew she was there. Her men were dispatched with their orders, including Carl. Pelley stood ready to take command of the army in her stead, and everything was as ready as she could arrange it to be.

She made her roundabout way up through the layers of the city and into the castle. She knew the schedule of the guards, none better, and would try to avoid them. Even if she was recognized, she would not be stopped.

She made the most of her knowledge, infiltrating the castle quietly by joining a gang of roustabouts who were helping carry a delivery of food and ale in through the kitchens. That allowed her access to the armory, where she misappropriated the livery of a master sergeant in the army. She took a soup-bowl helm, a breastplate, pauldron, cuisses, a gray cloak embellished with black thread, a blue shirt, and a brown leather tunic with matching trousers.

Triumphant, she stowed the items in a sack and slipped up to her room, sticking to the servants' passages as much as possible. She hid herself away inside, sighing with relief. As far as she could tell, she'd managed to gain her room without ever being recognized.

She would rather spend the rest of the night there, or better yet, go to Holden's room and surprise him. Unfortunately, she didn't dare wait until morning to set out on the next phase of her plan.

Alex stretched and scratched her neck, then undressed, gathering the pieces of her stolen sergeant's uniform. She put on the breeches and sat down on her bed to pull on her boots, but something crackled under her, and she blinked, reaching and finding a folded square of parchment.

She retrieved a candle and touched its flame to the wick of a lamp, then sat down at her desk to examine the parchment.

The letter was from Holden. His seal had been pressed into dark red wax, holding the letter shut in discreet folds. She reached for a letter opener with hands that wanted to tremble. Finding one, she gently pried up the hardened wax, unfolding the parchment to read what lay within.

His handwriting was well formed but unpretentious, utilitarian, his words courtly and sweet. Her heart fluttered as she read.

My dear Alex,

I cannot express how happy your visit and declaration have made me. You have honored me with a great gift. To have your love is the realization of my heart's deepest desire.

We stand poised on the edge of a terrible risk, and though I may go now to face my fate with joy and courage as I carry the certainty and the memory of your love to sustain me, I am not willing to go leaving the rest of my heart unspoken.

You have long doubted my love, my seriousness, and my purpose in pursuing you. If I do not survive, I would not have you look back on our short time together with these questions still in your mind.

I must confess my initial interest in you was born of a young man's rebellion and base lust, but the time I have spent in your company through the years, especially this summer, has tempered the feeling, deepened it, and made it a rich and precious thing. My love for you is the most important and cherished feeling I have ever possessed. I would keep it always.

Though I cannot guess how you may answer, my purpose is this: if I survive this parley, I mean to ask you to wed me. I am only a younger son, with no wealth or estates of my own, and I hold little favor in the king's eyes. But such as I have, I would share with none other.

When I return, I pray I may taste 'yes' on your lips, my beautiful captain.
Until then I remain,
Faithfully your own devoted servant,
Holden, Prince of East Anglia

The letter dropped from her nerveless fingers, drifting onto the desktop. Her hands flew to cover her mouth as she struggled to comprehend and believe. In all her wildest imaginings, she'd never dared dream of marrying him. She had no idea what to expect afterward, but wedding the prince would change her life beyond recognition. They would share a bed every night. That would be glorious. She would carry his children, legitimately, and raise them with him. In the unlikely event she ever became queen of the land, she would be expected to give him children. Rulers could not do without heirs.

Alex sagged into a chair, her legs giving way. She'd never seriously considered marriage or children; she'd never met a man who inspired her to want them…at least, not until Holden. She tried to remember how to breathe, overwhelmed with anticipation and sudden fright. Would she be a good wife to Prince Holden? She'd never spent any time around married couples. Living in the palace, the wife of a prince, she wouldn't have to cook fancy meals or clean house or make soap or do laundry or learn any of the ten thousand other domestic skills she'd always vaguely believed a wife must know to keep her husband happy.

That was a relief, but the one duty she couldn't escape as a royal would be childbearing. Could she be a good mother to Holden's children? She'd rarely dealt with anyone younger than fifteen. The few times she'd attempted to hold a baby, it had begun to wail immediately and she'd hastily shoved it back into its mother's arms. The single time she'd managed to keep a small child from crying by bouncing it on her knee, the infant had managed to vomit all over her armor before she could succeed in giving it away. To have her own children…she laughed a little, feeling quite hysterical. To think she'd believed it would be a challenge for Holden to grow into a good man. Now he expected her to give up being a soldier and become a good wife and a good mother, all in one swift step.

Those were fears talking, the sort of fears she guessed every woman must feel when a man proposed marriage. She would have to discuss her worries with Holden, but she already knew she didn't have it in her to refuse his offer. She loved him too much.

Whatever duties and trials, whatever joys she might have as his wife, Holden would share them with her. When the war was over, they would dine and sleep and make a life together. The babies she bore would belong to them both. After seeing him react so tenderly to his unclaimed child, she suspected he might become a fine father. He would share in the satisfying challenge of raising and loving their children. He would sit at her side during the long evenings. They would read aloud or play cards, or possibly Nine Men's Morris. She might try to learn to sew. Doubtless her clumsy efforts would make him laugh. He would tease her gently and take her needlework from her hands, toss it aside, then draw her into his arms and love her within an inch of her life. She would waken every morning to the sight of his tousled head lying on the pillow beside her. She would need only to turn her head to see him smile.

It was wondrous and terrifying to see the unexpected possibilities opening before her, the future spreading its petals like a rose. Her eyes filled with tears and she felt as if a thousand birds had been set free inside her chest, fluttering and singing all at once.

The letter humbled her after all her hesitation and her fears. She was sorely tempted to hurry to see Holden, his guards be damned, but she had to put her plan in motion immediately if she had any hope of success.

She winced. Her father would be appalled when he learned of her liaison with the prince. It wasn't hard to predict his fury, his disappointment, and his worry. He would not understand. She'd just have to hope Holden could convince him, over time.

Before that could happen, she and Holden had to survive the battle they both knew was coming, and her time to prepare was running short.

Alex read the letter several times, until she could remember every phrase, then folded the parchment tenderly and carried it to the lockbox where she kept her most precious things. She fetched the key, held the letter to her lips, and tucked it away, turning the key in the lock. She returned the key into hiding between two stones in the wall and tucked the box back under her bed.

Then she returned to her original purpose, disciplining herself to a semblance of calm. The uniform waited. She put the rest on hastily, binding her hair up on top of her head as discreetly as possible. The hair helped pad her skull and hold the too-large helm in place.

She went down to the barracks, which were their usual cordial melee of masculine camaraderie, with soldiers joking, playing at dice, cleaning and sharpening their swords, and tending their armor. Everything was in disarray from the assembly of the honor guard. She sought their elite group out and calmly commandeered a spare bunk, sitting down on her cot and taking out her sword to buff away any rust and sharpen the blade. She knew how to fit in from long experience associating with the rank and file. All she had to do was give a hearty laugh at a jest, then make one of her own, before she was friendly with everyone around her.

A few of the men teased her for her voice not having changed yet, and she manufactured a blush to satisfy them, glad her breasts were small enough she could pass for a young lad in her loose shirt.

Since the honor guard was a new group, not an established squadron, her presence went unremarked. She bedded down with them and ate breakfast as one of their number, and she waited for them to be summoned. The word came shortly after the noon meal, and when they mustered, Alex simply gathered her gear and went with them as if she had every right to be among the chosen few. No one seemed to notice, count, or question. She made a wry grimace. Peace had become such an ingrained habit in Norwich that no one even thought to check for the possibility of spies.

She stood in her place among the ranks, waiting in the courtyard as the honor guard packed up their supplies and she was given a ceremonial tabard to wear to the parley. The thing hung on her like a tent, but she accepted it anyway, giving the sergeant a crisp salute.

The guard marched out before the king and his sons in the late afternoon, and they made their bivouac in the open field between the road and the wood where the parley would take place. She stared in disbelief when she discovered no sentries were being set. The group merely set up camp and began to cook for the night. A nominal force of six men was sent to stand around the royal tents, which stood slightly apart from the others at one edge of the group, almost under the eave of the wood.

If Holden's trained force were to attack this camp, they could easily do away with all the leaders, possibly without ever alerting the main body of men.

Alex chuckled without humor, knowing Holden, too, must be chafing at such a foolhardy and careless arrangement.

She arranged to bed down as near to the royal pavilion as she might, which was not as close as she would like. As she laid out her bedroll and put up her tent, she glimpsed Holden standing at the door of his father's tent, looking out, his chin tilted up so far he must have been studying the stars. Her heart warmed. She longed to go to him and take him in her arms. She longed to give him her 'yes.' She wondered what he was thinking, and noted he was wearing fine plate armor and a well-made sword. Good. She'd never had the chance to return the one he'd carried on the road with her and Carl.

He turned away, and she saw a man appear in the doorway next to him. It was Duke Roger, who spoke briefly, his lip curling with contempt. Holden went back inside, and Fakenham followed closely. She bristled a little, worried. She didn't like that the duke was taking an interest in Holden. She had no proof, but she firmly believed he was to blame for Holden's state of house arrest.

Alex had a gut feeling. If she traced all the wrongs in Norwich to their source, every trail would converge firmly on Duke Roger of Fakenham and his political maneuvering. She wished, too late, that she'd dared to warn her men there might be problems within the command hierarchy of their own homeland.

She lay down in her blankets and stared up at the peak of her tent until sleep came for her and interrupted her prayers for all to go well.

Chapter Forty

The honor guard marched before dawn. Danish scouts could be seen here and there along the road, and they faded back into the forest, presumably to notify their superiors the talks were set to proceed. The men of Norwich arrived at the site of the parley as the sun peeped above the horizon. They set to work speedily, erecting pavilion tents and staking out the perimeter of the area.

Alex made the most of her opportunity to scan the forest, walking the edge of the clearing and looking for the best places to bring in an enemy force intent on ambush. There were a distressing number of possibilities. The parley field lay at the center of a deep hollow in the land, and men could be hiding behind the crest of the bowl on at least three sides.

Three roads converged in the nearby plain, giving easy access from anywhere in East Anglia, and one of them led past the clearing as it wound through the forest, taking a sharp eastward turn just beyond its edge. Of course, little of the east road could be seen. She remembered from Holden's maps of the Broads that there was a navigable curve of the Yare a few furlongs to the east, with a deep channel quite close to the shore, providing a good landing for the broad-hulled, shallow-drafted Danish boats. Most of the river's length was shielded by impassable marshland full of trees and brush, where no scouts could usefully be posted to warn of an approach from the sea.

By now, her men should be in motion. Some should even be returning from their scouting assignments at any time with intelligence for General Pelley and Prince Holden.

She saw no evidence of her scouts yet, but a flurry of activity from the road heralded the Danish ambassadors emerging from the forest. Their leaders rode horses, and the procession stirred a cloud of dust as they clopped forward cautiously under the white flag of parley.

She decided Sweyn Thorssen must be the man who led the procession. He was tall and burly, with a cruel, harshly chiseled face, blunt and handsome. He wore intricately tooled, gleaming plate mail over his broad shoulders, and his long dark-blond beard was neatly parted and hung in a braid on each side of his chin. A strip of rawhide tied his long hair back from his forehead. He noticed her scrutiny, giving her a narrow-lipped, condescending smirk, and she hated the sight of him immediately.

He showed not a little amusement as he surveyed King Anselm's preparations. His hard eyes noted every point of security, then fixed on the pavilion tent, and his smile sank deeper into his face at the sight. Uneasy, Alex observed he and his retinue were extremely well armed and armored by comparison to the other Danes she'd faced in battle. That might give credence to his claim he was a chief among chiefs, but to Alex, it seemed he was more prepared for warfare than for peace.

She slipped away from the road and subtly followed alongside Thorssen's group as they passed through the honor guard toward the royal pavilion. King Anselm emerged to greet Thorssen, flanked by Gavin on his right and Holden on his left. There was no sign of Roger, and that bothered her more than anything she'd yet seen.

The parties greeted each other with handclasps, exchanging names, and went inside. Alex fretted. She couldn't get any closer to the pavilion than she already was. She chose a place to stand where she could keep an eye on the tent and assumed a position as if she were one of the guards. She tried to appear responsible and alert in hopes she could forestall inquiry about exactly what she thought she was doing there.

The talks had not been in progress for long when a man staggered out of the woods, winded and gasping from running, and stumbled hastily into the clearing. She recognized him as one of her scouts and abandoned her post to meet him, but he was already approaching the guards who watched the entry of the pavilion.

"I need a word with Prince Holden's aide." Her man saluted. Hal, she thought his name was, one who had joined the group with Gavin's men. "I have an urgent message from Captain Bonham."

They refused him entry, but Alex interposed, taking his shoulder and drawing him away. "Here, now. Come with me. You can't be troubling the great while they're in conference." She hastened him away. "What news?"

"Danish troops are massing at the river. I sent Alfred on to ring the bell," he gasped, still trying to catch his breath, his eyes wild. "Everyone was heavily armed, many are armored, and the camps are well-supplied. More than a thousand of them were already on land and ready to march when we left, Captain, with more arriving on ships. We saw siege engines and catapults, too, being poled up the river on barges. I met with Edgar and Rafe. They were headed further in. They meant to try sabotage, to slow some of the troops down."

Alex bit back a curse. "We must stop the talks at once."

"There isn't much time. I ran as hard as I might, but I had to dodge around their squadrons. The entire wood is crawling with Danes."

"We'll have to warn the king," she started, but the abbey bells interrupted her, tolling with a low and sonorous sound. Guards frowned and lifted their heads, muttering. In all her days, Alex had never heard the bells rung. They were not to be struck except in cases of the greatest emergency, such as a Danish invasion and a massive ambush of the king's ambassadorial party.

"That'll be Alfred. They'll not waste time in attacking now the alarm has gone up." His hand went to his sword. Since he was Gavin's man, he knew how to use it…a damned good thing, given how fast the situation was deteriorating.

"They'll attack right away," Alex agreed, trying to decide what to do. "We mustn't be caught off-guard. Raise the alarm for an ambush, and order the men to form up at the perimeter." Better for him to do it; she knew her soprano voice would startle rather than command.

"*Ambush!*" Hal bellowed, and a few voices took up the cry. Swords rasped out of sheaths. "*Guard the king! To the perimeter, form up!*"

"Now join the defense," Alex directed him, and headed for the pavilion tent at a trot.

Before she could come close, all hell broke loose. Three hundred or more Danes poured out of the woods as if conjured by wizards, howling and brandishing swords and axes.

The door flap of the tent flew open. Her father stared out, wild-eyed, with sword in hand. He took stock of the situation and immediately turned on his heel. "Treachery!" he bellowed, but sounds of melee began to erupt before the word was fully out of his mouth.

The Danes and the honor guard clashed, and the roar of battle overwhelmed her. She rushed forward, but before she could reach the tent, Duke Roger emerged from under a side flap, smiling a little. He lifted a small tin whistle to his lips and blew.

Its sharp tone pierced the air, penetrating through the sounds of battle, and disaster turned to catastrophe. Guardsman after guardsman lowered his weapons, and the Danes poured into the camp unchecked, screaming in triumph.

Alex darted back to snatch Hal's arm. "Fight free and get to General Pelley if you can. Have him send in as many loyal troops as he has, as quickly as possible."

She barely managed to deliver her orders before she was forced to engage an attacker, her blade clashing with his. They were already too late to summon Pelley's troops. The surrender of the honor guard could only result in a crushing defeat. Even if the General's forces set out immediately from a mile or two away, they couldn't arrive before this was over.

None of the royal family had yet emerged from the tent, which concerned Alex greatly. The battle swept around her, enclosing her within a wall of swords. She managed to get her back against a loyal soldier, one of a scant dozen or two who hadn't laid down his arms when Fakenham blew his whistle. Perhaps he was one of Prince Gavin's handpicked men. She craned her neck and glimpsed Prince Holden slashing through the canvas of the tent, his face grim. The duke saw him also and took to his heels. Then she lost track; she snatched her attention back to her foes and fought for her life.

The next time she had a moment to look the royal tent had toppled, and she caught a glimpse of her father briefly through the melee, wielding his sword with a grim expression. A crimson stain marred the cloth on his sword-arm. The fighting seemed hottest there by the collapsed tent, Danes converging on the king's retinue with bloodthirsty efficiency.

The tides of battle swept her away from where she wanted to go, and she could not fight free no matter how she struggled to make headway. She saw no more of Holden or of her father. Alex cursed as a man fell, bearing her down half-under him. She squirmed sideways to escape his weight, and the front of the battle surged over and past her, more Danes closing in on the beleaguered royal party.

She leaped up, furious and desperate, but she couldn't see anything other than flashing swords and Danish helmets. Panicking, she tried to shove through the press to reach the center of the action. She meant to fight to the death at Holden's side, if she could locate him.

A horn rang out, low and insistent, and she jerked her head around. Blue and gray clad soldiers of Norwich poured into the clearing, arriving faster than she ever could have hoped, fighting their way along the road. They overwhelmed the outer fringe of the Danes easily with the force of their numbers, pushing forward fiercely to reach and aid their king. Alex grinned; Pelley was a daring old bastard, and he'd hedged his bets brilliantly by refusing to wait for the bell before ordering his advance.

There were more Danes than anyone could have reckoned on. Hordes of them kept pouring in, arriving through the woods from the direction of the river. She spied Pelley dispatching men to meet them. He made a fine target for archers where he sat mounted on his horse, and as she watched an arrow sprang back, bouncing off his mail. He raised his sword and gestured the left flank of his troops forward to charge the new arrivals while the right flank kept pressing through the clearing toward the king's men.

Alex joined the rush, sprinting over bodies slippery with blood, batting aside axes and swords. Through a momentary gap she saw Prince Gavin go down with a spear through his gut, and she screamed her rage, lopping the arm right off a Dane who didn't see her coming.

But then there was a sound as if the world had exploded, and everything went dark.

Chapter Forty-One

Alex woke on a litter with several people bending over her, their faces eclipsing the bright sky. The back of her head ached fiercely and she blinked, struggling to clear her blurred vision. The foremost face resolved, familiar. Iron-gray hair shaded to white at the man's temples. He had patrician features, a long thin face with a straight nose and narrow lips in a somber blue-eyed face.

"She's awake," he spoke.

Ellis, Earl of Lowestofte. His name filtered fuzzily into her mind: the king's brother-in-law.

"How did you come by this?" His hand rose into her field of vision, holding up her ring, which still hung from its chain. She tried to lift her arm to snatch the ring from him, but her body felt as heavy as lead, and she missed.

"Prince Holden gave it to me." Her tongue slurred the words. "Where is he?"

"This is definitely a woman. Where did you find her?" The earl turned his head to address someone she couldn't see.

"Near the royal pavilion. We found the prince's token on her and brought her out with the remains of the royal party. We thought her dead, I confess, until she started to moan." The voice was a young man's, with enough squeak to indicate a new recruit.

"That's Captain Bonham," another voice spoke. "We thought she stayed in the city, commanding the army there in case of a siege, but I'd know her anywhere."

"Captain Bon...?" The earl's voice sharpened. "Get her off the field and carry her to safety. To my estate," the earl snapped. "She'll be needed."

"Holden?" She tried to insist, but they were already lifting her, and the wave of nausea that followed ate away her vision and left gray nothingness behind.

~ * ~

When Alex came to again, she found herself lying in a bed so soft the pillows nearly suffocated her. Bandages had been wrapped tightly around her head. The air stank of wood smoke. She struggled to sit up, but a nurse bustled over and pressed her back down into the soft pillow.

The woman offered her water, and Alex realized she was desperately thirsty. She drank until the nurse withdrew the glass.

"Not too much. Let it settle a bit first, or you'll sick it all up again."

"Where is Prince Holden?"

"Hush and rest."

She didn't like the sound of that. "Tell me, or bring someone who can. Else I'm walking out of here." She threw off the coverlet and struggled to a sitting position, ignoring her dizziness and the burning ache at the back of her skull. She tried to rise to her feet, but her knees wouldn't hold her, and she fell onto the mattress again.

"Lord Henry, please help me." The nurse caught Alex's wrists and began to wrestle her back down to the bed.

Together, the nurse and Lord Henry prevailed, getting Alex back onto the mattress and pulling the coverlet up over her again. "They haven't found him yet," the man called Henry told her quietly. He had the look of Earl Ellis, and was likely the man's son. He was lame in his left leg, which she supposed would account for him not being part of the battle.

"Who have they found?" She remembered seeing Prince Gavin fall to what was surely a fatal wound. "Who is dead?"

"The king was beheaded by his foe at the bargaining table, it seems. Prince Gavin, fighting Thorssen. General B..." he paused, his eyes troubled.

"My father."

"Yes."

Alex felt tears begin to gather, and impatiently lifted her hand to wipe them away as they began leaking out of the corners of her eyes.

"Many of the honor guard died, also, and a number of the regular army. General Pelley survived, and he led the retreat. He gathered the wounded and withdrew to Norwich with the army after confirming the king and his men were lost." Lord Henry looked somber, drawing the sign of the cross on his chest.

"For the time being, we aren't in jeopardy here. Thorssen has set the city under siege, and his troops will trouble our estate eventually." He fluffed her pillow. "Rest so you will be well enough to travel when they do. My grandfather had an underground passage dug between the existing caves, to connect this estate to the abbey. We can collapse the entrance behind us and go to join the monks, then descend into the caves and come up inside the catacombs under the palace."

"What is the smoke from?"

"The woods are burning." Henry waved vaguely in the direction of the window. "Someone set fire to them during the battle. We don't know who or why. We can't retrieve any more of the dead from the parley clearing until the fire has died. I don't know how many we'll get even then. Danes are crawling all over the area, thick as fleas."

"If the king and Prince Gavin are dead, Prince Holden is the king now," she mumbled.

Henry traded a look with the nurse. "Perhaps you're right."

"He's alive," she insisted stubbornly. "You'd have found him with the others, if he weren't."

"Possibly, yes." He reached for the cup the nurse was stirring. Steam and a scent of herbs wafted to her nose. "Drink this, Captain."

She did, but when the cloying sweetness of the honey faded, she was left with the telltale, bitter aftertaste of a sleeping draught. She cursed thickly as her vision swam and she sank away from consciousness for the third time in one day.

Chapter Forty-Two

When Alex came to again, she was lying in a soft bed in an unfamiliar room she guessed had to be somewhere inside the castle in Norwich. She knew the city and the castle by scent as well as by sight, even though the sounds weren't right. Shouting echoed in the distance, and an occasional dull thudding noise rattled the stones and made mortar dust sift into the air. The earl sat by her bedstead with his head buried in his hands, and when she stirred, he looked up. He gestured, and Lord Henry came over to her bedside, offering a glass of wine.

"Not drinking anything you give me. Not this time." She put her hand to the back of her head and managed to sit up. The earl adjusted pillows to support her back. Alex blinked and focused on the same nurse she remembered from before; the woman stood in a corner, fussing over a table laden with various medicaments.

Alex felt a good bit better. Her vision was clear, and she could talk plainly. Her head still hurt, though.

"Where is Prince Holden?" She vaguely remembered nobody knew, before. Surely he must have appeared by now. He was too sneaky to die, her prince. Too stubborn. "King Holden, I should say, if what I was told is accurate."

Henry glanced to his father, who looked grave.

"We're in the castle. General Pelley is leading the defense against the Danes. We're under siege, or at least they think we are, but at present, the catacomb tunnels to the abbey are still open."

"That's not what I asked." Her heart sank and she reached for Holden's ring, glad to find it still hanging about her throat.

"You're fortunate to have that." The earl pointed toward her hand. "You'd have been left among the dead if you didn't. Fire swept the field soon after you were brought out with the corpses of the king's party, so you'd never have recovered. Nobody quite knew what to make of a common foot soldier wearing a Stuart token, and it wasn't until after you woke that we were sure you were a woman instead of a beardless boy."

"You sent me to your estate," she remembered fuzzily.

"Yes. Given the circumstances, I thought it best to have you put somewhere secluded and safe. Not just from the Danes." He exchanged another glance with Henry. "Matters of government are rather unsettled in Norwich at present."

"I'd imagine so, with King Holden missing."

Again the earl exchanged a glance with his son. "Holden Stuart is presumed dead." The earl tried to speak gently. "This means you are next in line for the succession, Your Majesty."

She shook her head vehemently and winced, hand flying to the bandage wrapping her skull. "No."

"We must have a monarch, and rumors of treason among the king's highest advisers run rampant."

"Fakenham." She spat the word like a curse, sudden memory assailing her. "He arranged the ambush. I saw him command the honor guard to drop their arms against the Danes. He signaled them with a whistle. He must have meant to take the throne."

"Yes. Those soldiers from the guard who survived are in custody, and they await the question at the queen's convenience."

"You say that as if my taking the crown is a *fait accompli*." She eyed the earl with annoyance. "Holden will return."

"If he does, he will be dealt with in good time." The earl refused to yield. "For the time being, I am supporting your claim to the throne. The law is behind us, Your Majesty, but it isn't safe to assume there will be no opposition to your succession. We don't know who in Norwich may hold secret allegiance to Fakenham. That includes members of the castle staff. I've entrusted my own family and servants with your care."

"Duke Roger's body has also not been found, I take it."

"No." The earl's face pulled into a scowl. "We found no sign of him."

Walter. Walter would have information, and he could be dangerous. If anyone was loyal to Fakenham and deep in his counsels, Walter was the man.

"Walter, my father's aide, is one of Fakenham's men, possibly chief among them. He's a corporal, the thin one with the harelip. Don't let him know you're aware of his association with Duke Roger." Her head hurt, but strategy came naturally to someone with her training. "Have him watched day and night. We may learn much of value from watching whom he meets and what he does. He might even lead us to the duke."

"Yes, Your Majesty."

"Take me to see my father." Her eyes stung. Part of her would not believe he was gone, not until she had seen his body.

Chapter Forty-Three

The earl summoned servants, who carried Alex down to the chapel on a litter despite her protests she could walk. Earl Ellis remained adamant, and he also dispatched a group of guards to accompany them. She felt a proper fool riding through the corridors of the castle surrounded by men who fairly bristled with blades, the wide eyes of every single servant and courtier following them as they passed.

King Anselm and Prince Gavin lay in state on a raised dais. Their corpses had been washed and dressed in their brightest ceremonial armor. Their faces were absolutely still and waxy pale. Her father lay near them, his bier a single step down from the others. He still wore his battle armor, and across his chest lay the sword he'd wielded as he died in defense of his king. Other soldiers from the honor guard, judged worthy by their deaths, lay arrayed in rows at her father's feet. The chapel was still except for a few sniffling mourners, the atmosphere heavy, oppressive with the scent of death and decay.

A third bier sat next to Anselm's and Gavin's, empty, covered in spotless blue velvet, awaiting occupation.

The sight of the place prepared to receive Holden's corpse drove a gale of terror and grief through Alex, as if its existence transformed an unlikely possibility into an inevitable fact. Her tears welled up and spilled over her cheeks. She walked to the edge of the bier, resting her palms on the soft velvet, and wept silently, wiping her cheeks with a kerchief one of the earl's guards handed to her. What if Holden *was* dead? His body might be lying burned in the woods, perhaps unrecognizable. She might never know. She might never be sure of his fate. Her heart felt like a shriveled walnut.

"I want to go up to my old rooms," she said, her voice shaking.

They carried her there, and she gathered a few of her possessions, walking unsteadily with Henry hovering anxiously at her side. She directed the servants to pack up her best clothing and retrieved her valuables, including her journals, her money, and her box of jewelry with Holden's letter tucked inside. She put the key in her pocket as she gazed miserably at her old armor, which was neatly arrayed on a stand. If Holden were dead, she would never be his guardian again. She would never guard her prince again in any case, even if he was alive. He would be king if he returned.

She wiped furtively at her face.

He might never return, and he would want her to do her duty to the kingdom now.

She drew her spine straight and tucked the box under her arm. "I'm ready."

They whisked Alex away to the secured room where she had awakened, and she laid her things down atop the wide desk waiting there. Belatedly, she realized these were King Anselm's chambers, cleared in haste for a new occupant, with new linens put on the bed and new hangings on the walls. She gazed around, studying the place. The entire room showed signs of hasty renovation. The space was too large for the furniture inside, hollow and echoing, with clean spots still showing in the dust on empty shelves and on the writing table where the king's personal possessions and ornaments once rested. Alex's few articles of clothing looked shabby and lost in the spacious closet and ornate garderobe. The sitting area was the one place that had not been denuded. It held a variety of ornate furniture in carved wood and blue velvet.

Her fists drew tight with misery. After a moment she went to the wall and tugged the bell-pull to summon the major domo. A few minutes later, the guards admitted a harried-looking woman of around thirty-five, wearing a drab gray dress and starched white apron. The major domo bowed to her deeply. Many times Alex had seen the woman bustling around the castle, issuing efficient orders to the domestic staff, but she'd never made the time to speak with her directly before.

"I appreciate your effort to redecorate for me," she said, trying to begin the interview on a pleasant footing.

"Thank you, Your Majesty." The woman's stiff spine relaxed a little.

"I like the blue velvet in particular. But you need to have the maids return to dust the shelves properly," Alex requested quietly. "Surely there is more spare furniture in the castle? I want some chairs and a table, a few more lamps, and a rug or two. It's very empty in here. I need a new bedstead immediately, at the very least."

"Yes, Your Majesty." The major domo bowed low. "I fear it will have to be a smaller one. The existing bed and mattress were made especially for this room."

"That's fine. Have the footmen bring up the small one from my old room, if you wish, and I'll use it for the time being. I'm not going to sleep in a dead man's bed." Alex kept her voice firm, maintaining her authority even though she felt sympathy for the other woman's position. The job of managing the castle's domestic staff could not be an easy one, especially in the midst of a siege.

"Yes, Your Majesty."

"Have the maids bring up the rest of my clothing, as well. I know it isn't suitable for my position, but it will have to do until I can arrange for more regal attire." Alex didn't actually care what she wore as long as she didn't have to wander around the castle in her shift. However, the citizens of East Anglia needed her to represent dignified authority, so she would have to present the image of a confident and competent ruler as well as she could.

"The castle seamstresses are already working around the clock to create a wardrobe for you, Your Majesty."

"I'm grateful for their efforts. What's your name?" Alex asked suddenly, acting on instinct.

"Berthe," she replied, giving Alex a nervous glance, wringing her hands. "Berthe Weaver, if it please you, ma'am."

"It does. Thank you, Berthe." Alex mustered a smile and went to lay her hand on the servant's shoulder, trying to calm her. She would have spoken further, but a tap at the door interrupted them.

"General Pelley asks for an audience," the earl announced quietly as Berthe hurried out.

"Send him in." She found no leisure for grief. She had to go on as if her heart was not broken, as if she was not as hollow and gutted as this room. She would spend her life wondering whether things might have been different if she could have reached Holden on the battlefield.

Pelley reported at great length. He carried parchments bearing tallies of men lost, supply levels, intelligence on the state of the enemy, and a summary of the type of siege engines the Danes used in their assault.

Fortunately, the defenders could sustain themselves for a respectable amount of time on supplies already stored in the city. At present, more were being smuggled in nightly through the caves. The process would continue until the Danes destroyed the abbey, discovered the cave system, or stopped the procession of small supply barges the locals poled along the river silently by dark of night. Assuredly they would halt the supply chain sooner rather than later.

She ordered the beacons atop the castle towers lit to notify their neighboring nations East Anglia was in distress. She hoped the nearby kingdoms would answer, but she knew they had problems of their own. They might choose not to come.

Pelley had things well in hand. He kept the moat aflame, and the Danes didn't have the strength or the necessary equipment to drag down the drawbridge. The ballistae and archers atop the battlements were presently keeping their camps at a respectful distance. As long as the city defenders had ammunition and food, things would be well. However, there were more Danes than she had men in the city. Victory would be in doubt unless their neighbors came to their aid.

Pelley had little information about the fate of the parley, none she didn't already know. He revealed most of Prince Holden's and Prince Gavin's special troops had been reassembled. Those who'd survived their missions were present, anyway. Edgar was not among them, but his partner reported he'd managed to use belladonna berries to poison any number of the enemy in their riverside camps. He reported that Edgar went slinking straight into the enemy camps disguised in Danish clothing and dropped handfuls of the poisonous fruit into their supper kettles. He'd never returned from his last attempt.

Nevertheless, Edgar's actions were instrumental in disrupting the operation of key installations at the riverside, where extra Danish soldiers were badly delayed and their numbers thinned by his efforts. If not for him, Pelley's army might not have survived to regain the city walls.

Alex decreed Edgar was to be commended posthumously, though her heart wasn't in anything she did or said.

Walter accompanied Pelley to the meeting, skulking about the sitting area during his report. Because of his presence, she cut the interview short when the general would have delved into confidential matters. She thought it best not to confront the corporal or demote him, at least not yet. Let him think he had the run of the place, in hopes he would make a mistake and reveal valuable information.

She flicked her fingers at Lord Henry, casually summoning him. "Bring Prince Holden's remaining men into the castle. I want to see them and discuss their ventures. We will go to a sealed room, to exclude all others so we may speak without fear of spies."

"Yes, Your Majesty."

Her subordinates scampered to do as she commanded, and Carl soon paraded the men into the room to stand before her, including both Holden's original troops and Prince Gavin's new additions. Only half of the men remained, not including either Hal or Alfred, and some of those had been injured. All looked ragged, their eyes dazed and weary from battling against the Danes as they fought their way back to the city and took up positions on the ramparts to help repel the siege. None of them could report having seen the prince.

"You have all done well," she spoke quietly. "The failure to save the king was not your doing. Our plans would have worked, but none of us anticipated the treachery that undid him would be so audacious and so swift. It was impossible to guess one of his most trusted advisers was collaborating with the enemy." She gave no more explanation.

"Prince Holden has not been found." She looked from face to face soberly. "Many of you knew him well. I ask, not command, you to go out through the caves and seek him in the field, should you be willing. The fires in the forest will have moved on or died by now. Start your search in the clearing where the parley was held. He wore plate mail embellished with gold, and he had a fine sword." She had to force herself to go on. "If Prince Holden is dead and his body has burned, his gear should help you identify him. Assuming his corpse has not been looted." She closed her eyes in pain.

"I will richly reward the man who finds him and returns him to me. He will have a purse of two hundred sovereigns." The sum was a veritable fortune to men of peasant ancestry. "Likewise, I will give a bounty of two hundred sovereigns to anyone who gives information leading to the capture or proof of death of Roger, Duke of Fakenham, who is a traitor to East Anglia."

Many faces openly revealed their sorrow, while others displayed eagerness. "Yes, Your Majesty."

"Travel cautiously, concealing your mission, and return in good health," she said to conclude the interview. "I must rebuild the king's guards. They are the queen's guards, now. You among all the soldiers in Norwich are the ones I trust most. You have proven faithful to the crown, your actions heroic. There will be a place in the queen's guards for each of you."

They went out in a file, except for Carl, who hesitated by the door. His eyes were filled with a terrible sorrow as he bowed to her and went out to see the men off, unspeaking.

Drained, she subsided into a chair. Lord Henry handed her a kerchief and she wiped her eyes.

"The ring you bear was a love token, wasn't it." Henry limped behind her and touched her shoulder, kind and hesitant. "I am sorry for your loss."

"The ring meant many things." Her voice emerged harshly from her throat. "But none of them kept me from failing him." She waved Henry out of her rooms. "I'd like to be alone now."

Chapter Forty-Four

Alex didn't let herself weep in her bedroom for long. She had many matters to attend. She needed to appear in the square and on the ramparts to encourage the soldiers of her army. She must confer with Pelley frequently over the best ways to defend the city. She had to check to see whether any allies' beacons were lit in answer to theirs, so she would know who might be coming to join in the battle.

She presided at the funerals of the king, his eldest son, and her father, walking silently into the crypts behind the priests and watching the dead laid to rest one by one in their stone tombs. Her official coronation was scheduled to take place in less than a week, and though she would gladly have deferred the event, she could not.

The day marched steadily closer with no word or sign of Holden. She felt as if she were a hollow shell, her body and bones walking about the castle, functioning in spite of her absence. She consulted her advisers and made decisions by rote from deep within a cold, empty void.

The spies assigned to trail Walter reported nothing of use, though she consulted them daily. If he had orders, he was biding his time and keeping his head low.

Even worse, the men she'd sent to seek Prince Holden returned one by one, empty-handed. None had news of his fate.

The morning of her coronation dawned in due time despite everything she could do to forestall the inevitable. Waking early, Alex slipped away from her guards, sneaking down the hall and into the prince's empty rooms, which she'd forbidden anyone to enter.

The place lay before her, unchanged. Even the tumbled sheets were the very same ones they'd made love on together. His writing desk was still cluttered with parchment maps, quill and ink, and the blotting sand he'd used when he wrote her letter. His night clothing lay on the floor where he'd tossed it when he dressed. Servants had never come in after he left to straighten his things and lay them out ready to put on again.

She sat down on the mattress and inhaled his scent, then collapsed onto the bed where she had known the most love she'd ever felt. She wept into Holden's pillow, giving in to the deep, wrenching sobs of grief she'd forestalled for so long. Bitterly she reproached herself for every instant of love they might have shared if not for her own stubbornness and lack of foresight.

There was nothing to be done to mend that now. All she could do was to honor him by going on, and by being the best ruler she could.

She rose after a time, shaky on her legs, and moved to the window, opening the casement to allow the breeze to dry her face. She ignored the oily smoke from the moat. Its presence was all but constant in the city now. She could see troops mustering out on the plain, filling the entire area south of the Yare, which gleamed golden-amber in the morning sunlight. She had no hope they were allies preparing to assault the Danish siege. She was facing east, in quite the wrong direction to see anything but an endless sea of Danes.

She shut the window again before any archers could see and target her, and she went to the prince's writing desk.

She sat down and trimmed the quill, then wrote to her beloved, saying all the things she'd never dared to say when he was with her. She told him how much she loved him, how much she missed him, and how wished he were still with her. She apologized for failing him, and for taking his throne. She told him yes.

When she'd finished, she dried her eyes and straightened her shoulders, leaving the letter behind.

Alex, uncrowned Queen of East Anglia, returned to her room and put on her coronation gown, a lavish and heavy affair of ivory brocade, French lace, and blue velvet insets, with elaborate gold beadwork and trim and a thoroughly impractical train forming a complete circle around her feet. She ignored the distressed flutter of both her guards and her servants. Passive and indifferent, she let the maids paint her face and arrange her hair. They artfully covered both her pallor and the pink around her eyes. When she looked out at herself from the mirror, she was surprised by the cool serenity of the image, by the absence of swollen eyes and blotchy cheeks.

Pursued doggedly by the Earl of Lowestofte's guards and half a dozen young pages, Alex went out. The pageboys fluttered around her, laboring to keep her elaborate train from touching the dirty floor as she made her slow and tedious way down to the foyer of the Grand Hall. Carl awaited her there, decked out in ceremonial armor so new it squeaked every time he moved. His promotion had already been arranged. He was to be her Captain of the Queen's Elite Guard. He smiled at her with eyes full of sorrow, and she smiled back, fighting tears.

She drew as deep a breath as her corset would permit and let herself be led out through the Grand Hall. She glided along the aisle, accepting Carl's hand as she stepped up onto the dais at the front of the room. The assembled court stood waiting, expectant, every eye fixed on her. They were mostly men, army officers and nobles of the court, with the occasional wife hovering at the side of one or another. After the passing of princes Gavin and Holden, most of the single ladies of the court had fled the city, slipping out through the caves via the abbey by dead of night before the siege closed in.

She gazed out across her subjects, forcing herself not to turn and run. She did not belong here. She should not wear the crown that lay waiting for her on a richly embroidered pillow. Some part of her still believed Holden was alive. They should wait until the siege was over and scour the countryside for him.

That was not feasible. East Anglia must have a ruler, especially in times of war.

Alex walked forward with Carl at her side, trailing pages and lace. She was to stand before the podium where the abbot awaited, holding the crown. As she arrived at her assigned place, a stir in the balcony drew her eye. With a sense of heavy inevitability she saw Walter appear beside a pillar, a gleaming crossbow cradled in his hands.

The world slowed to a crawl. Alex's limbs refused to move in response to her panic. The crossbow rose and leveled. A blur of motion erupted behind Walter. It must be one of the earl's spies, but she didn't think he could act in time.

Then the world exploded into motion again. Carl's body struck hers and the spy tackled Walter at the same moment, just as the quarrel flew. Carl uttered a low grunt of pain and Alex hit the floor hard, the wind knocked out of her lungs by the unyielding, cold marble and by the crush of Carl's weight on top of her. The court panicked, shouts and screams ringing out everywhere, but she didn't care. She struggled out from under Carl's body and rolled him over to check how badly he was shot.

"Carl!" She levered him onto her lap, gasping. He blinked up at her with a rueful grimace. The quarrel protruded from his armor immediately above the elbow. "Summon a physician," Alex snapped to anyone who might be listening. Slowed by his armor, the bolt shouldn't have gone deep. With any luck, his wound would not be fatal.

"You're not badly wounded," she told him. She'd have to wait until his armor was off to know more, but there wasn't much blood, and that was a hopeful sign.

The doctor arrived after what felt like an age, and began cutting away the leather and cloth. When he did, she sagged with relief. The quarrel hadn't left even a puncture wound, merely a shallow furrow across the front of Carl's upper arm, with the shaft caught fast in the leather.

"You should be right as rain in a fortnight. I've seen you take worse on the training ground." She smiled at him through tears of relief; she could not bear to lose another loved one. Not now.

"Hurts like a bugger, though." He grimaced, meaning to smile. The physician led him away for treatment and Alex stood. There was a spatter of blood on her dress, but she didn't care.

She heard scuffling in the balcony and glanced up, seeing Walter had been pushed face-first against a column. He was waiting with his arms immobilized behind him, pinned by half a dozen soldiers.

"Put Corporal Walter in chains," she pointed. "Then take him to the questioning room and have him await my pleasure there." Her voice was cold as ice. It was probably not a good omen that her first act as the crowned Queen of East Anglia would be to put a man to the question, but Walter had a great deal to answer for.

She turned back to the abbot, who stood trembling on the dais, half in shock. "Continue," she commanded, and after he dithered and stammered his way through a few courtesies, the coronation resumed as scheduled.

She felt no different after the ceremony was done, other than consciousness of the weight of the crown resting on her head. The Earl of Lowestofte stood at her right in Carl's place, his son by his side. No further disturbance seemed to be forthcoming. Walter's was the single open objection to her taking the throne.

She gazed out over the courtiers, who went down on bent knees before her. "Arise and be about your business," she ordered them. "Our allies have been summoned in the south and in the west. When they arrive, we will go forth and crush the Danes between us." If they ever came. There was still no response to the beacons.

She turned to the earl. "I thank you for your support. Your loyalty will not be forgotten." She addressed her guards next. "Escort me to the questioning chamber."

She hated the torture room, and she always had. The place smelled of voided bowels and death. Walter was waiting for her there, as she had commanded, shackled into an iron chair of unpleasant construction. Alex stared at the thing with distaste.

The chair was not a Judas chair. There were no spikes to pierce its occupant. Instead the seat and back were smooth, but shackles fastened around Walter's ankles, wrists, waist, and throat held the torture victim exactly in place. The bottom of the chair was made of iron, and a pit under the seat waited for a fire to be built there. If no such drastic measures were called for, the chair had openings in the back for hot irons and other instruments to be inserted. Merely sitting in the abominable device had Walter in a lather of sweat. His face gleamed and his lank hair hung plastered to his cheeks as he squirmed, desperate to escape.

Alex glanced about. She did not know how to begin to use even half of the wicked-looking instruments hanging ominously on hooks set into the mortar of the walls.

She would start the torture mildly and hope he broke before she sickened. Fortunately, she had little opinion of his resolve. He would likely break very quickly.

"Light the brazier; we'll need plenty of coals. Set irons in the fire to heat, and lay a fire ready under his seat, but do not light it yet," she instructed the torturer briskly. "We'll begin by pushing spikes of iron under his nails." She made her voice cold and implacable, remembering her rage at Holden's fate. "For every question he does not answer to my satisfaction, add another spike."

She turned her attention to Walter, her face hard. "What do you know of the Duke of Fakenham's plans?"

"Mercy!" Walter screamed, writhing against the chair as the torturer approached, a spike held firm in a pair of pincers, and snatched his hand.

One spiked nail was all the torture required to break him, and the spike barely penetrated his flesh before he began screaming information.

He was a poor choice of confidante, but unfortunately, Roger seemed to have anticipated Walter's weakness, and he did not know much.

"Fakenham planned ahead with Thorssen," Walter babbled, sweat standing out on his brow. "They meant to halve the kingdom between them after the king and his sons were disposed of. I helped him pick the honor guard. Most of them were loyal to him, and the others didn't believe we could defeat the Danes even if we fought them."

"What about your assassination attempt?"

"He told me to get rid of you. We expected General Bonham to die defending the king, leaving you as the last of Wilhelm's line. After you, there wouldn't be anyone in a position to stop him from taking the throne." Walter drew back as far as he could, his eyes rolling as the torturer approached him with another spike. "Please, I don't know any more. I was just carrying out my orders!"

They couldn't extract any more useful information from him, and after the third spike, Alex ordered the torturer to stop. She judged Walter's assassination attempt originated purely out of his fear that Fakenham would one day return and be displeased with his failure. Maybe he'd hoped to maneuver his way onto the throne himself in Fakenham's absence. He was a callow young fool, barely able to grow enough beard to shave.

Alex drew herself up straight, refusing to pity him. She knew the penalty the law prescribed as a response to his crimes.

"Walter, you have collaborated knowingly in acts of treason resulting in the deaths of the king, his heirs, and my father, not to mention countless other soldiers of East Anglia. You are party to a conspiracy to usurp the throne and you personally attempted to assassinate the queen. You are hereby stripped of your rank and privileges. I sentence you to be hanged by the neck in the city square at dawn. Your head will then be removed and placed on a pike at the city gate, to serve as a warning to traitors."

He began to squeal and sob, begging again for mercy, but Alex merely gestured for the torturer to silence him. The burly man stuffed a rag into Walter's mouth, and he raised his streaming eyes to her, pleading silently.

"This *is* mercy," she told him coldly. "If you were Fakenham, you'd never leave that chair. I'd have you roasted alive."

She left.

Chapter Forty-Five

Sentencing a man to death felt very different from killing a foe in battle. Speaking the sentence left Alex with a horrible sickened lump in the pit of her stomach. Thick and heavy, her disgust interrupted the blank emptiness inside her where her love for Holden resided uneasily in its tomb.

She attended the execution personally, standing straight and giving the headsman his orders with her eyes dry. She waited until Walter's head had been mounted according to her command before returning to the castle.

When she re-entered, she was dismayed to see a seemingly endless file of monks streaming out of the catacomb bolthole and filing into the Grand Hall.

"Your Majesty," Lord Henry approached her, anxious. "My father wished me to report the abbey has been overrun by Danes. The holy brothers have fled and collapsed the tunnels behind them."

With the tunnel collapsed, there was no more chance for news of Holden, no chance for him to return to her.

She sighed. Bad news upon bad news, with no good news to be had, and she was stuck ruling over the slow collapse of everything. She gritted her teeth. Her personal concerns were painful, but as queen, she had no leisure to indulge them. "That was the right action for them to take," she told him. "Find them lodgings somewhere in the city."

"They're being housed in the Grand Hall," he explained. "General Pelley says there is nowhere to put them except the palace, unless they care to bed down in the streets."

Alex accepted the inevitable. "Very well. I'll go in and address them. Call the major domo. They will have to be attended."

She hastened into the Grand Hall, where an alarming number of monks were already milling about nervously, their bald pates shining. They were distraught, their normal nervous behavior even worse than usual due to their agitation. Alex stepped up onto the dais and clapped for attention. No one paid her any mind. She pursed her lips and snatched a ceremonial sword from the gauntlet of an empty suit of armor. She beat the flat of the blade against a column until every startled eye was fixed on her.

"Now, then, if you would be so good as to listen. You may stay here for the time being. I've called for the major domo to meet with you regarding sanitation, meals, blankets, and off-limits areas. You'll be strictly subject to the rules of courtesy." She became aware of a whisper among the men and a stir at the back.

"I command silence," she snapped, tart. "You are here on sufferance."

The whisper fell to a hush, but the monks parted to allow two cloaked men to make their way down the hall toward the dais. Their hoods were pulled low, covering their faces. Alex glanced to her guards, who closed in protectively. Carl was still not recovered sufficiently to rejoin her, and all of a sudden she felt his absence keenly. She missed her armor nearly as much. Fighting would be difficult in her cumbersome, heavy dress, and the cloth would not protect her at all.

The two men stepped through the last layers of the crowd, and Alex saw the foremost one held something suspended from his hand. She frowned at the object. She might not have recognized what he held if she hadn't attended an execution that very morning and seen Walter's head treated similarly. If the hair on this head were black, she would have thought someone had fetched Walter down from his pike at the gate to remonstrate with her, but the hair in the man's fist was blond.

Lord Henry drew his sword and stepped forward, protective despite his lame leg. Alex looked around hastily for a guard with a sword she could snatch. She was ready to fight if needed, but the stranger's calm stride reassured her; he did not seem set to attack.

Perhaps the men came in with the monks, she thought, and meant to offer her the head in order to ask for a bounty. Maybe she could accept it in exchange for giving them shelter within the city. The trophy looked to be from a Danish soldier. They were almost all fair-haired.

"Greetings, strangers. Why have you entered the city?" Alex spoke as the foremost man reached the foot of the dais. He dropped the head, which rolled and stared horribly at the ceiling with distorted but familiar features. Her eyes went wide. Even bloated with decay, the face clearly belonged to Duke Roger.

"To claim my bounty from the queen." Now empty-handed, the man pushed back his hood, smiling: Edgar. Alex's eyes flew open wide.

"Edgar!" She rushed down to hug him, overwhelmed by joy. "We thought you dead among the Danes. A bounty you shall have indeed. And you, sir, will share in the reward for helping to bring in the head of the traitor, the Duke of Fakenham." She remembered Edgar's companion and turned to him as an afterthought.

"I need no bounty. The joy of the queen is reward enough," he declared.

Alex's legs threatened to give way. She dropped her sword, which clattered to the floor, the point digging a chip out of the polished marble surface. She moved forward a hesitant step, then another.

Hands rose and threw back the hood, revealing twinkling eyes and a mischievous smile. "I've returned, as I promised."

"Holden!" Alex launched herself at him like a catapult. He caught her with a startled grunt and toppled over, laughing. They landed heavily on the stone. Alex kissed him within an inch of his life, ignoring the audience of scandalized, tittering monks and Fakenham's gruesome, disembodied head staring at the ceiling a mere foot away.

"But if you're alive, I'm not the queen at all." She blinked down into Holden's eyes in consternation.

"Oh, but you are." He glanced at the crown she still wore. He made no move to escape, but Alex suddenly realized their position. Sandals and brown robes filled the floor around them. She flushed and slipped off him, getting to her feet and offering him her hand.

"We'll sort that out," she promised him, surveying him from head to toe. He looked weary, the skin beneath his eyes hanging swollen and dark. He had plenty of scratches on him, both fresh and half-healed, and bruises, and no small amount of soot. She frowned, scanning him for more serious injuries.

The major domo arrived, all a-bustle, and Alex turned to her. "Prince Holden has returned to us. Have fires lit in his room. Get the servants to carry him up a bath. Have the best physicians attend him. Give him food. Provide these things for Edgar, too." She descended on the woman like a whirlwind, barking orders. "Then house these dratted monks." She couldn't think clearly enough to be diplomatic. Her hands shook.

"Yes, Your Majesty."

Half the servants in the castle were soon scuttling hither and yon. Alex asked Lord Henry to deal with Fakenham's head exactly as she'd dealt with Walter's, then led Holden up the stair herself. "Call for the Earl of Lowestofte," she commanded a random guard. "He will want to see his nephew. Consult the college of heralds, too. There is a question of succession."

She ushered Holden to his room and was still standing there, issuing a torrent of orders, when a guardsman rushed up and saluted in haste. "Please, Your Majesty. We've received a coded message from the ruler of Mercia. General Pelley requests your presence."

Alex dithered for a moment, but Holden touched her arm.

"Go," he said softly, his voice husky with all the words there wasn't time to say. He went down on one knee before her, bending his head. Taking her hand, he pressed his lips to her fingers as if he were her loyal knight. "Edgar and I haven't slept in two days. I'll bide here until you return."

She clasped his hand, then pressed her palm to his cheek, her heart full. Reluctantly she let herself be led away.

Chapter Forty-Six

Fed up with her dress, Alex detoured hastily to her own room and put on a decidedly unregal tunic and breeches before she went up to the signal tower, where the general sat poring over scraps of parchment. He raised his face to her, sober.

"We've received a signal, an answer from Mercia." His voice sounded dull and heavy. "They won't be coming to our aid, Your Majesty. They don't have any coastal lands, and they believe the Danes are our problem."

"They'll soon be more than our problem once they take East Anglia and establish a foothold on this continent," she said sharply.

"Perhaps the Mercian king expects us to win. He merely prefers for us to win without cost to his troops." Pelley rubbed his shining forehead with a kerchief. "Or more likely, they think the Danes will be satisfied with taking East Anglia and won't be a trouble to them after. The Mercian monarch is new to the throne and inexperienced, Your Majesty. His advisors are old men, fearful ones. Perhaps if King Anselm had lived he could have been more persuasive. He spent his lifetime developing political alliances. You have only begun."

Alex bowed her head and gave him a curt nod. "Thank you for your report, general. We will wait to hear from our other neighbors. Perhaps their news will be better." She did not believe so. Coastal Essex had their own problems with the Danes, Sussex was so far away as not to be concerned, and the smaller nations to the north and west would follow Mercia's lead. Mercia's caution would cost East Anglia dearly. "We should revisit our strategy in light of this intelligence."

After the bad news, the rest of the day proved interminable. Alex spent half the afternoon pondering strategy options with Pelley and her best counselors. Then she reviewed her troops, working to build their morale. The rumor of Prince Holden's return had run rampant through the city. On top of the rumors that no aid was coming, none of the men were sure who would rule them in the morning. She assured them such questions would be set aside until the siege was ended, and her leadership would remain strong.

She inspected several areas damaged by missiles from the Danish trebuchets and catapults, and was whisked away in haste when another one screamed through the sky and crashed into the city, leveling a storage warehouse not far from her procession.

When she was able to return to the castle, a laundry list of executive matters waited for her attention. She hashed through them all with her assistants, pausing to gulp down a glass of wine as she worked. By the time she finished, she'd missed the formal meal served each evening in the dining hall.

She went down to the kitchens, causing a flurry of anxiety when she appeared in person to ask for a bowl of stew or a meat pie. The head cook hovered anxiously as she ate her simple meal at a table set against the wall in a quiet corner. Before she could finish, the Earl of Lowestofte came in and sought her out.

"Prince Holden is sleeping. The heralds' lore shows you are rightfully queen and will remain so. You were crowned because he was believed dead, and you have the right of Wilhelm's blood. He has made a statement before witnesses. He does not wish to challenge your coronation."

She disagreed, chewing and swallowing a last bite in haste. "Holden is the rightful king."

Ellis looked at her gravely. "Your Majesty, if I may set aside tact, there is some question regarding whether he would have the proper temperament for the job. There is little question you do."

Her mouth pinched tight. "You do not know him as I do."

He looked at her neutrally, folding his hands in his lap, skepticism written over every line of his face.

"He and I will settle the matter between us," she said, and set her plate aside. She hoped her words were true. "Where is Edgar lodged?"

"We put him in with Carl, for the time being."

"Excellent." She was glad he wasn't bunking with the prince. That would be exceedingly inconvenient. "I've had a long day, Ellis. I'll retire now."

She left him fretting, not much caring what he thought. Every step came a little faster until she was all but running down the hall to the prince's rooms, leaving her guards lagging behind. She stopped outside Holden's door, breathing rapidly, and tried to calm herself. She nearly wept for relief and joy. The emotions she'd deferred throughout her long day of duties threatened to overwhelm her.

The prince's pair of guards looked at her doubtfully, and she gave them an austere glower in return. "The prince is free to come and go as he pleases," she instructed, in case they were under the misapprehension he was still a prisoner.

"Yes, Your Majesty." One saluted her.

She returned the salute and put her hand on the door, but remembered in time the prince was sleeping. She did not tap, but pushed the door open quietly instead and let herself inside.

The lamps were out, but the fire still burned high enough to cast a ruddy glow, just enough to see by. Holden lay abed, hidden by the drawn curtains. His rasping snore filled the room, and the familiar sound undid Alex completely. She slumped onto his couch and her tears flowed unchecked. She let them. They were tears of joy as much as of deferred sorrow, releasing tension. She sobbed quietly until her emotions were spent, then calmed herself by listening to his breathing. Her hands twisted in her tunic for a moment before she could force them to be still.

She rose and stripped off her clothes, then managed to unpin her hair and extracted the crown. She set her hairpins on Holden's writing table. She then realized she'd left her letter there, the one she wrote in hopeless response to his when she'd first thought him lost. She blushed a little, thinking of all the things she'd written. She had been overwrought when she wrote, but she'd meant them all.

The letter was not where she'd left it, and she glanced to the bed, then went to the fire and lit a taper, shielding the flame with her hand as she returned to the bed and pulled the curtains back so she could look in. Her letter lay cradled on the prince's chest, his hand resting protectively on top.

Alex smiled down at him. She combed her hair with her fingers and braided it loosely, tossing it over her shoulder to lie along her spine. Finishing, she went to him and very gently lifted his hand, taking the letter. She set it back on the writing table, then raised the coverlet and slipped into the bed at his side, trying not to disturb him.

He was so weary he never woke. He murmured low in his throat and turned to nestle against her. She laid her head on his shoulder and wrapped her arms around him. He felt warm and solid and real. He was alive and infinitely precious.

She didn't give a damn who wore the crown, and she very much hoped they wouldn't find her position a problem going forward.

Chapter Forty-Seven

Alex woke early, blinking to find herself in unfamiliar surroundings, but she knew Holden at once by his scent and the feel of him in her arms.

She smiled and kissed her way down his chest and belly, where she woke him by taking him in her mouth, sucking softly and stroking him with her tongue.

"I died," he murmured, his voice thick with sleep. "I died, and I went to Heaven." His fingers caressed her hair. His cock lengthened and firmed quickly between her lips.

She wouldn't ever tell him Li taught her how to do this as well as how to fight. However, in both things, he'd been a very good teacher.

She sank down on Holden, taking his cock inside her throat, which made him whimper. She rose and fell leisurely, watching him writhe, his Adam's apple bobbing as he swallowed. She swirled her tongue around the crown of him, tasting salt, and sucked hard, sliding down. She ran her hands over his lean, taut belly and tweaked his nipples.

He was easy to please, gasping and groaning for her, his hips straining upward despite his best efforts to stay still. She laid her arm over him to still his thrusting and slid her fingers between his legs, playing gently with his balls. They were already drawn high and tight. He would be close to climax.

She backed off a little, easing up on the suction, then withdrew and put her finger in her mouth, licking to wet it.

He lifted his head to stare at her, wide-eyed. She trailed her fingers down along his taint, smiling wickedly, tickling lightly when she reached her goal. He parted his legs to show willing, letting her have access. His eyes remained fixed on her, wide and dark.

She went all the way down on him slowly, sucking hard, as she carefully worked her finger into his body.

He bucked, moaning. His eyes slid shut and his fingers dug into the sheets.

She curled her finger, searching, and let him push up into her mouth. She knew she had him when he gasped, sharp and urgent, and she pressed there again, bobbing up and down on his cock and lashing it with her tongue.

He came in her mouth with a combination of growl and wail. His hips hitched and his body twisted frantically. Through it all, she kept sucking, swallowing him down. When he stilled, she released him and he stared hazily at her, blinking in disbelief. She swallowed a last time, savoring his bitter gift. Licking her lips, she gave him a predatory smile.

She stood up, naked in the cool air, and cleaned her hand in his washbasin. She could feel his eyes on her, though he didn't speak. When she was finished, she returned to him, glad to climb back into the warm bed. He inhaled sharply at the feel of her cool skin, but wrapped her up anyway, nuzzling a kiss against her mouth.

"Where in the world did you learn *that?*" He was still gratifyingly breathless.

"How in the world did you survive the ambush?"

That was a question more worth answering. She watched with fond amusement as he tried to gather his scattered wits enough to do so. She didn't make things easy for him, bending her head to suckle and bite at his nipple.

"I should wait. Edgar must be here to tell his part." He sank his teeth in his lip as she tormented his nipple. "Stop that. Come up here." He tugged at her, positioning her with his hands until she was kneeling over him. She blushed as he urged her to move forward until she knelt over his face so he could reach her with his mouth.

He opened her with his fingers and his tongue pressed in, slow liquid strokes that set her nerves aflame. His eyes sought hers, gleaming with desire, so she made a show of her pleasure for him, caressing herself. She imagined the path his hands might have taken if they were free, stroking along her arms and shoulders, teasing herself with light caresses. She stroked her palms over her throat and her face, moaning.

His bright eyes watched her while his mouth worked, his hands moving to support her, resting firmly on her backside. She lifted her breasts and pinched her nipples, whispering his name. His hands stirred, wandering to knead her back and her bottom.

His tongue never paused in its wicked magic, swift and delicate, circling and darting against her, his eyes locked with hers. She could feel him purring against her, and she shuddered for him, whimpering, starting to buck in spite of herself.

His hands settled on her thighs, holding her still.

"Holden," she writhed, gasping for breath, her nails starting to leave red marks on her flesh as she caressed her body, half-maddened with pleasure. When she came, her cheeks were wet and she sank down exhausted to curl against him, pressing her face against his.

"I won't hold you to words you wrote while you believed me dead." He spoke very softly.

"I meant them all." She kissed his cheek, his beard tickling at her lips.

"I wish our fathers had lived to see us wed." His hand slid along her back, tucking her in tightly against him. His eyes looked sad.

"Mine would have been appalled to hear the news of the engagement." Alex smiled at him wryly.

"Did you know my father once warned me if I seduced you, he'd have General Bonham thrash me with a horse-whip?"

"Yet you persisted."

"Some things are worth a whipping." His fingertips traced wandering curves along her back. "I wish they were here to scold us now."

Alex did, too. She petted his chest lightly, sharing wordless comfort. What was done could not be undone.

"Did you tell anyone where you were going when you came here?" He asked at length, his voice sleepy.

She shook her head. "Your guards saw me in, but not out again." Her voice was wry. That news would be all over the castle in short order.

"Your own guards will be beside themselves with worry if you don't keep them apprised of your whereabouts at all times."

"As I was whenever you chose to disappear?" She laughed softly. "I'm still using Lowestofte's men. I haven't chosen my own guards yet. Carl will know exactly where I am without having to ask, and he won't let anyone trouble us."

"Point." He curled her comfortably against his side, pillowing her on his shoulder. "Do you have duties this morning?"

"A hundred, I'm sure."

"Urgent ones?"

"Not unless Thorssen assails the drawbridge again." She hesitated. "Our allies have declined to aid us in repelling the siege."

Holden reached to draw her close. "That's bad news." He stroked her shoulders lightly. "I'd like to see the end of that bastard Thorssen." His voice tightened with hatred.

"You and all of East Anglia."

"Carl will knock if you're needed."

"Yes."

They lay together and drowsed for a time. When he recovered, Holden roused her with kisses. She lifted her mouth to him, nuzzling at his face. He pressed her over onto her back and covered her. He sank between her thighs and gently slid inside her body.

She made a soft sound of welcome, but she could feel tears threatening. She'd come so close to losing this, to never knowing the tenderness of unhurried lovemaking with him.

"Do you often cry during sex?" His voice was tender, his eyes soft, and she laughed a little, wiping her face with the heel of her hand.

"Only with someone I love, it seems." She managed a wobbly smile, reaching to wrap her arms around his ribs and lifting her mouth, asking for a kiss, which he willingly gave.

They rocked together for a long time, slow and luxuriant, mouthing soft kisses anywhere they could reach. Neither of them seemed in a hurry to find climax, preferring, instead, to enjoy the closeness of flesh and breath, so nearly lost.

Alex took exquisite pleasure in holding him and watching him shiver and gasp as he came, sinking his teeth in his lip, his eyes closing as he shuddered, his long lashes lying on his cheeks. She wondered if lovemaking could always be so good. She cradled him in her arms when he collapsed, running her fingers through his sweat-soaked hair and licking salt from his throat.

Some part of her was still afraid one thing or another would snatch him from her, such as death, time, or fading love. However, she'd made her choice, and she would face whatever came to pass.

Chapter Forty-Eight

Eventually Holden and Alex arose and dressed, a lengthy process much interrupted by kisses. She mended her hair as well as she could and as soon as she was presentable, they called for food to be brought up.

The servants' eyes were inquisitive, but they didn't seem surprised to find her there in Holden's rooms. The guards who saw her enter had clearly let their tongues wag as soon as they went off-duty. She sat up straight, refusing to be embarrassed. It was none of their business where she spent her nights, or with whom.

After they ate Holden called for Edgar, and both he and Carl answered the summons. Carl dared to give Alex a broad wink. His teasing grin made her blush. Holden chuckled at her, and she shook her finger at him.

They settled into the seating area before the fire and Holden stared into his mug of cider, pondering how best to begin.

"I suppose I should start with Thorssen's first move," he said after a moment. "We invited him into the tent and sat down to bargain. I thought he wasn't paying much attention. My father and Gavin were laying out the terms of the proposed deal, but his eyes wandered continually, and he had a damnable smirk on his face."

"I saw that smirk as he rode up," Alex muttered. "Smug bastard."

"Indeed." Holden's eyes turned hard. "If I'd been presiding at the parley, I'd have insisted nobody could bear arms into the tent, but my father wouldn't listen to any such talk. He certainly wanted to carry his own sword, little good though it did him." He bit his lip, his eyes clouded by memory.

"When the bell rang, the noise startled father. It startled us all, really. General Bonham went to look out, and he shouted something I couldn't hear. The whole tent erupted into a panic. Thorssen didn't let the commotion faze him, though. He took advantage of the confusion to draw steel and swing. The table was between us, and before I could engage him, my father was dead."

He put aside his mug and laced his fingers, his knuckles white and his face grim. "Gavin was closer than I, and they clashed. I saw Fakenham duck out under the wall of the tent. I wasn't about to let him escape. I went after him, and saw him blowing some infernal sort of whistle. The honor guard started laying down their swords straight away, refusing to give battle.

"I decided he was my quarry. His treachery killed my father as surely as that bastard Thorssen. He didn't expect anyone to follow him. He ran when I challenged him, and I pursued him into the woods. Once we were beyond the clearing, there were only the two of us. The duke was no sprinter, but before I could catch up to him, he found a horse. He couldn't ride fast in the woods, luckily. I stayed near behind and could easily track his passage.

"Duke Roger may have been a traitor, but I'd never say he wasn't a smart man. He must have had flint and tinder, or maybe he located an abandoned campfire. Whichever, he kindled the bracken behind him, hoping to finish me. The gambit very nearly worked. I had to climb into the treetops to avoid the fire. If the forest had been pine or fir, I'd have been for it. As it was, the smoke and the heat nearly choked me." He looked at Alex wryly. "We seem to make a habit of that, do we not?"

She reached out to clasp his hand, reassuring, and he resumed his tale.

"As soon as the worst of the fire passed out from under me, I climbed back down and scouted until I picked up his trail beyond the path of the burn. I hung back to let him think he'd succeeded in putting me off. I had a good idea by then of where he was headed. He made straight for Thorssen's main camp. He thought he'd find his allies there and wait to be apprised of the success of his plot, though I'll warrant Thorssen would have been glad to be rid of him in addition to the others.

"I didn't give him a chance to test Thorssen's gratitude." Holden's mouth firmed and he lifted his chin. "I caught a Danish sentry by surprise and stole his clothes, then I followed Fakenham's trail into their camp. The place was quite a scene of chaos. He was most displeased." He cut a grin at Edgar, who chuckled.

"I've been spending my time in the woods profitably," Edgar confessed. "I've been gathering belladonna ever since I joined the company, getting as much as I could whenever I found some. I did much the same as the prince. I stole a suit of clothes and hid my dark hair under a helm and went into their camps as one of them. I managed to poison the stew in three key camps before I was caught."

Alex smiled her approval. "Hal told me you'd sabotaged the Danes," she nodded to him. "Your courage saved many of our men."

"The Danes who ate that stew were no longer fit to act as foes to the citizens of East Anglia," Holden confirmed wryly. "The camp was full of foulness and corpses, and those few who didn't die of the poison wouldn't move far from the privies. Fakenham could get little response out of them, for all his chivvying.

"I crept up on him unawares and cut off his head, the same way Thorssen removed my father's." Holden's face pinched with hate, looking alien in his wrath. "He deserved no more honorable death. I put his head in a sack, then I freed Edgar from his shackles. There were few Danes left there who were well enough to oppose us. We cut through those who tried and set out for the abbey together. We had a time of it in spite of our stolen gear. The journey lasted for days more than it ought because we had to detour nearly halfway to Sussex. The woods were still afire in places and we couldn't pass through the Danish camps or checkpoints without knowing their filthy language."

Edgar agreed. "We were barely in time when we finally reached the abbey. We joined the Danish raiders who were sacking the place, and as soon as we made our way inside, we threw off our disguises and had barely climbed down into the caves when the monks dropped the deadfalls to seal the passage. Very nearly on our heads."

Alex winced. For Holden to come so close to returning, only to be lost in such a pointless way? If that had happened, she would have driven every living monk from East Anglia and put a sentence of death on any who dared return.

"If Edgar hadn't neutralized those key installations, I believe Pelley's army would have encountered considerably more difficulty getting to the parley clearing and regaining the city afterward," Alex commented. Holden glanced to her, and she knew they were both thinking Edgar deserved a reward.

"You bought us the time we needed. You'll receive the bounty I promised for Holden's return, Edgar. You've earned two hundred sovereigns for bringing him back to me." She smiled. "For your brave service to Norwich in helping to dispatch Fakenham and settle the Danes, as many more. I'll also give you a position among the queen's guards. As a sergeant to Captain Carl, I think."

Holden beamed, pleased. "Exactly what I would have suggested."

Carl clapped Edgar on the shoulder and beamed at him. "Welcome aboard, lad."

Alex summoned a seneschal and commanded the four hundred sovereign bounty to be awarded to Edgar, then led Holden away to the planning room, where they reviewed Pelley's plans for breaking the siege.

Holden frowned down at them. "Now is the time we most need Gavin." Pain pinched his face, and he looked lost for a moment.

"We have General Pelley to advise us," Alex stood firm. "We're well-armed and supplied. We'll wait for winter to bite down hard, then we'll make a sortie to drive the Danes off when their morale is lowest."

"I'm not sure that will work," Holden demurred, scratching at his bearded cheek. "We don't have enough men to be assured of victory. Plus the Danes are used to the cold. Denmark has a much harsher climate than we do."

"A direct attack is our best hope, if the neighboring kingdoms won't come to our aid."

"I should ride out to negotiate with Mercia. King Harold and I used to play together as lads during state visits. I could persuade him to send troops to aid us."

Alex hesitated. "It's too dangerous. You'd have to get out somehow and make your way through the Danish lines."

"I've done so before." He squared his shoulders. "I can make it."

"We should consider all our options first." Alex rubbed her chin. "I don't like your plan, Holden. Maybe if the tunnels to the abbey were still open, but they aren't."

"Going for help makes sense, Alex. I could save the city, not to mention hundreds of our men." He paused, his voice quieting. "I could save you."

"We could send someone else, maybe one of the generals, with a few of our special troops to support him. Maybe Carl or Edgar, whichever you think best."

"They won't be able to persuade the king. I can." His jaw set with determination.

"You can't go, Holden." Alex folded her arms over her chest. "The city needs you."

"Not here," he disagreed, reaching to take her hand. "Not anymore. Norwich needs you. You're the queen. I'm merely another soldier now, Alex."

"Not to me." Her voice nearly broke, but she forced herself to straighten her spine, holding his gaze.

"We must put aside our feelings and do what's best for East Anglia." Holden insisted, stroking her fingers with one hard-callused thumb.

"You can't abandon your people to do what you want, and I won't have you waste your life foolishly." Alex knew she wasn't being fair, but grasping at straws was all she had left if she wanted to keep him with her. She could not bear to think of losing him, not so soon after he returned to her intact.

"You did exactly the same thing when you ignored my orders and abandoned the city to attend the parley." Holden did not relent, his voice reproachful. "You admitted you were there."

Alex flushed. "Yes."

"You won't agree if I ask you to remain in the city instead of riding out to war with the troops when we battle Thorssen, will you."

"Would you agree if you were in my position, and I asked such a thing of you?"

"No, but matters are different with you."

"Because I'm a woman? There is no difference!" Alex slapped her palm on the table, sensing the track of his thought; she was determined to nip this in the bud. "I've been a soldier all my life, Holden. I'm an experienced swordfighter. I'm more likely to survive a pitched battle than you. Your father the king would have fought, you will fight, and I will fight at your side. If anyone should ask aid of Mercia, it should be the monarch, but I can't go."

He frowned at her, and she could see the calculation behind his eyes. He stepped forward, meaning to soothe her, and put his hand on her belly. "You shouldn't go out into battle, either. What if you were…are…carrying a child? Then you'd risk two lives at once."

"We've no idea I am." Even her best mental arithmetic would be inconclusive so soon after their first joining. "We've shared only two rendezvous, Holden." She set her jaw firmly. "The troops need their monarch to rally them, to lead by example. I have a grudge to settle with Sweyn Thorssen."

He looked at her unhappily. "If you're determined to seek him out and challenge him because you're the queen now, then for the first time I have cause to regret your coronation."

"I appreciate what you're trying to do. However, I will not sit in the city and do needlework while others fight the Danish invaders." She realized that was exactly what was in his mind when he arranged his plans as he had for the parley, and she felt her temper start to fray in spite of herself.

"When I am your husband, things will be different."

That was the wrong thing to say. "You'll force me to do as you wish?" Alex's heart sank. She should have guessed her happiness was too good to last. "I think not, my love. I simply won't be able to marry you, if that is your intention."

He drew up sharply, his eyes wounded. "Alexandra, you are free to marry me or not. You have the right to choose. Still, I warn you, Thorssen is dangerous. You're no match for him. His sword killed both of our fathers and my brother in battle. I don't want to lose you to him as well. We need you safe as much as we need the Mercians to aid us."

"You can't make my choices for me. I'm the queen. As such, I have a responsibility to confront any aggressors who challenge the state. I also have a duty to avenge my father."

"Don't be a fool." Holden pursed his lips with annoyance.

"Very well, I won't be." Alex could have wept. She pulled away when he went to clasp her in his arms to soothe her. "I'll have no husband at all."

Holden drew back, his face pale. "If that is truly your wish, I'll withdraw my suit, but I won't stand idly by and watch you commit suicide."

"I will do my duty to East Anglia."

"So will I."

Alex rose to go, trembling with distress, but he did not release her gaze. Feeling as if she'd been kicked in the stomach, she turned her back and took leave of him.

Still feeling perversely defiant, she went down to the armory and inspected her plate mail, the ceremonial suit from her days in the king's guards. The heavy plate she'd had fitted after her promotion to captain was always kept ready there. Since East Anglia had not gone to war in decades, her armor had been used solely for special state occasions. The mail was not covered in gilt and embellished as a proper queen's armor should be, but she ordered it polished and sent up to her dressing area anyway. She sent up her best broadsword, too, so she would be ready whenever she needed to fight.

She went to meet with Pelley soon after, who reported their preparations to withstand new assaults on the city were progressing on schedule. There were no shortages yet, and morale remained high. The occasional shot from a trebuchet or catapult kept people under cover, but so far the casualties were largely superficial.

"We can expect offensives at any time," General Pelley warned. "They know winter is coming, and they'll hope to have a victory before bad weather settles in."

"I'm particularly concerned about the security of the caves and tunnels connected to the burial catacombs under the castle," Alex admitted. "The Danes have intelligence from the Duke of Fakenham, which means they probably know many of our tactical secrets. It's a wonder we were able to use the caves as long as we did; perhaps they don't know about them. But if they dig an entry into the cave system, they could be among us before we ever know they've broken in."

"I agree. I've already stationed sentries at key junctions belowground in order to monitor the situation. I'll increase their numbers and ensure they're ready to fight."

"I wonder if we could use the caves to take advantage of the Danes ourselves. We might come up behind their lines or inside their camps."

"Those are good ideas." Pelley made a note. "I'll consider them."

"General." Alex hesitated. "I mean to lead our men into battle when the time comes."

He raised his head and studied her wearily. "I'd expected you to. It's traditional for the reigning monarch to lead the troops into battle."

"Good." She suddenly found the wood grain in the arm of her chair fascinating. "The prince thinks otherwise."

"Ah." Pelley frowned. "Well, I suppose he's entitled to his opinion." He puffed out his mustache. "Of course, he has no authority to tell the rightful queen what she may or may not do."

She exhaled, relieved. "Holden always loved wandering about underground. He knows the caverns better than anyone else in the castle. Consult with him regarding a possible route through the caves. Inquire into any other ideas he might have, too. As long as we understand my role in the proceedings, General."

"Yes, Your Majesty."

Chapter Forty-Nine

Alex had begun her day late, so her duties preoccupied her long into the evening. She never would have dreamed there was so much administrative work associated with governing over a siege, but every day more duties cropped up. She had to authorize disbursement from food and materiel stores, handle criminal proceedings, review the troops and the defenses, and take care of various other urgent matters.

By the time she was through, she wasn't sure whether to go back to Holden's room or off to her own. She was too tired to continue their argument, but she didn't want to go to bed with matters unresolved, either. The thought of climbing into her cold, empty bed in the unfamiliar chamber decided her: she would go to him, even if it meant a renewal of their disagreement.

She began to climb the stair to the family level, but she spied Carl approaching, and a flutter of unease formed in her belly as he came to her.

"Where is…?"

"Have you seen…?" they each began together, then stopped.

"Prince Holden?" They both spoke at once again, but Alex was too worried to laugh about it.

"I don't like how neither of us knows where he is." Carl frowned. "I'd not thought we'd need to watch over him, but he left his rooms at midday and I can't find any trace of him since. The guards said you'd commanded he was not to be restricted to his rooms. Maybe I should have had him watched."

"He always used to hide away in the caves when he wanted to think, or sometimes he'd run off to pickle himself in the stews in the southeast quarter of the city. Of course, I don't think he'd be there now." He'd best not be...if she found him dallying with some barmaid in a filthy pub, she'd damn well *geld* him.

That was not the case, and she knew it. Given their argument, there was only one likely answer.

"We checked the upper portions of the caves, and none of the guards had seen him. Of course, he might have gone through an unguarded passage. Sometimes I think we haven't mapped half of what's down there."

That was true. Nobody knew how far the caverns extended, and none of the guards were as familiar with the prince's hiding places as she. "Did you find Edgar?"

"Prince Holden sent him out to join the soldiers manning armaments in the city."

Alex cursed to herself. Holden had gone off to Mercia alone, without a doubt.

"I'm going up to my room to change into something a little more appropriate for catacomb-crawling. Meet me at the main trapdoor in ten minutes."

She stalked up the stair like a thunderstorm in the making, and both courtiers and servants alike scampered for safety when they saw her coming. She ignored them, slamming into her room and pulling on a tunic and breeches. She wrapped her braid into a coil on the back of her head and jammed a hair-stick through the bun, then added a pair of heavy gloves to the outfit.

She hesitated for a moment and went into the hall, letting herself into Holden's empty room. There was little information there. The room was tidy, and she didn't know his closets well enough to tell what was missing. On his writing desk, she discovered a piece of parchment weighed down by his inkwell.

"Gone to negotiate with Mercia. Await reinforcements." The final two words were underlined heavily, and were followed by his seal.

Alex picked the letter up, furious, resisting the urge to crumple it in her fist, and went out to meet Carl.

"I know where he went." She showed him the note and he whistled in dismay.

"He can't get out. Can he?"

"Yes, and I think I know how." Alex lit the torch and set out firmly. The corridors were well known to her, and she scanned them keenly, seeking Holden's prints.

The sentries had been back and forth, obscuring any marks in the main catacombs, but she found Holden's tracks in a little-used side passage, one she had followed him through a time or two in the past. She led Carl along, pursuing the prince's footprints as they led downward.

"This will take us under the moat," she gestured at the water-stained rock. "It's treacherous. The stonework of the moat leaks, and water seeps in. Usually this passage stands full of water during wet weather." She gave a nervous look at the ceiling. "I don't like these tunnels even a little. One of these days they're sure to cave in. This one comes out under the watchtower on the west side of the castle, well hidden under the slab where the sentries make their fire. Fakenham should not have been able to tell the Danes. He didn't know it exists. I don't think anyone does, other than the prince and me. Now you." She stared down the corridor, finding the standing water she'd expected. "Given how dry the summer has been, that won't be much more than knee deep," she judged. "He didn't have to swim. Luckily for him, the rains are still holding off."

"Holden will take weeks to get to Leicester. Then he'll have the job of convincing the Mercians to come and fight."

"Three weeks to get there, maybe four, then days in talks, and at least a month and a half coming back." Alex tried to calculate how fast he might move without a good horse while trying to hide himself. "Armies move slowly. The New Year will come before he can get them back here. It might be February before he arrives."

"It's a dreadful risk." Carl took the torch and they returned to the catacombs, sober.

"Yes," she said slowly. "His mission is a risk, but he's our best hope of help. I meant to send other men to try, but he believed he had the best chance of moving King Harold to send aid. Maybe he's right." The words tasted bitter in her mouth. "He's done the right thing, though he went about departing in the wrong way." That was mostly her fault.

Alex rubbed her forehead, trying to ease the headache forming between her eyes. "We can't do anything to aid him now, but we can continue with our own plans in case his don't bear fruit."

"Can we hold off the siege so long?"

Her mind was already racing. "We'll have to ration supplies with even more care, starting tomorrow."

Carl swallowed hard and squared his shoulders. "We'll tighten our belts." He pivoted to follow her as she turned an unexpected corner, and caught up with her after a few steps, though she was setting a brisk pace. "He should've told you."

"He did. We argued over his plans this morning." She cut him off, curt. "I ordered him not to go." She drew herself up straight, trying not to let her distress show. "I should have known he wouldn't listen, but there's nothing to be done to change things now. We may as well return to the castle and rouse General Pelley. Then we'll need to adapt our rationing plans."

They did, though tempers within the city grew hotter after food became harder to get. More fights erupted, and the courts were forced to sentence anyone involved to serve a punitive tour of duty carrying slop buckets to the middens.

The siege dragged on, and Thorssen experimented with new methods of attack alongside the tried and true. The defenders' supplies of oil and pitch soon ran short. Alex dreaded the day when there would be no more oil to fire the moat and make flaming arrows, or pitch to catapult over the walls to burn the Danish siege engines.

The moat kept the Danish forces from employing siege towers to assail the walls, but their catapults and trebuchets kept up a constant and costly assault on the city. Unfortunately, there was no shortage of wood outside the city walls for the Danes to use. The hammers and saws of their carpenters could constantly be heard, the soldiers and craftsmen hard at work producing new catapults and wagons. They replaced the burned ones nearly as fast as the defenders could destroy them.

Within a month all the pitch was launched, and after their supply was gone, Danish missiles fell unchecked in the outer layers of the city. The oil looked to run out next.

The Danes tunneled into the cave system before that could happen, and a raiding party nearly sneaked into the city in spite of the sentinels who'd been set to keep them out. Alex was forced to triple the watch underground, but there were so many uncharted passages in the caves it proved impossible to guard them all. Ultimately, she decided to divert the river and flood the entire subterranean passage system. If she had done so before Holden left, he'd still be in the city with her. She tried not to regret having failed to think of it in time.

The Danes seemed to breed like rats. Every time they killed one, a dozen others popped up somewhere else. Perhaps they weren't like rats after all. The rank and file of Alex's soldiers had been eating all the rats they could catch, and now there was not a one to be had anywhere within the city walls. The same was true of dogs and cats, and the less said about that the better. The mere thought of eating a family pet made Alex's skin crawl.

Worse, Pelley warned her disease might soon arise within their walls. As the winter drew on, sickness would spread quickly among people packed in so tightly, unable to find privacy or dispose of their waste or find an adequate supply of wood and coal to burn to keep warm.

Alex stalked through the castle, scattering ruffled, flustered monks in her wake and trying to ignore the unpleasant smell of their unwashed bodies. Water was too scarce for washing while the river was diverted into the caves.

"General, I don't care what Lord Dunstan wants. We haven't the food to spare for him to hold a feast. He should spend his son's birthday being glad the lad is still alive." She shuffled through parchments. "If he doesn't like that, he's welcome to try to swim out through the caves, but the drawbridge doesn't go down for anyone." She put the fool's request on the bottom of the pile. "I have more urgent concerns. Lowestofte says some of the nobles have been solicited to meet in secret to discuss whether they should demand a new ruler. What intelligence do you have there?"

"We're working with the earl to see if the group can be infiltrated, but they're cagey. None of them want to share Walter's fate, or Duke Roger's, either." He rubbed his eye, and she noticed he needed a shave. His bristled jowls looked untidy under his helm, and his mustache badly wanted trimming. "Some of them think we should make a sortie now. They don't believe aid will ever come from Mercia. They don't want to wait for the depths of winter."

The calendar count had barely reached the middle of December, still too soon to expect aid from Holden and the Mercians. Alex sighed so deeply she shuddered all the way to the tips of her toes.

"Holden will bring the Mercian troops." She was too stubborn to consider any other possibility, such as Holden lying dead in the field outside the castle, having been apprehended and stopped as soon as he emerged from the caves. "If he doesn't bring them within a reasonable time, I'll consider a sortie." They'd hoped to receive word long ago indicating his arrival in Mercia, but the signal towers remained dark.

"We haven't had any messages at all for more than two weeks now," Pelley looked grave. "We have to assume Thorssen has found and destroyed the relay towers, Your Majesty."

"Likely." Alex set her jaw. "Messages or no, we have to give Holden more time."

"Your Majesty." A page ran up to her, puffing. "I apologize for interrupting, but General Pelley is needed on the ramparts. The Danes have brought up a siege tower, a new kind."

They rushed up after him and Alex accepted a spyglass from an adjutant, putting it to her eye and gazing out over the plain. The Danes had yoked up teams of oxen, which were pushing a wall forward. It was not the usual sort, not one intended to overtop the castle walls. Instead of sporting arrow loops and ladders, the wall had a featureless armored surface that slanted at an angle with its bottom belled out well beyond the supporting wheels. Carts filled with stone and earth trundled along behind.

"They mean to push that up and hang the lip over the moat, then dump earth into the water and fill up the trench so they can send the siege tower across and overtop the wall," Pelley muttered. "I'll send up the archers and have them wrap their arrows in oily rags. We need to set the tower afire."

"We won't kindle that thing without a good deal of luck," Alex racked her brains for an answer, without success. "Not without pitch or something that clings."

"You know as well as I. There's none left." Pelley grimaced bitterly. "Your Majesty, we must reconsider waiting for aid from Mercia."

Alex collapsed her spyglass and handed it to the captain who waited at her side. "Very well, Pelley. You're right." She drew a deep breath. "Prepare the men for a sortie. We'll assemble at first light and ride out to battle. We can even use their own siege engine against them. At least with that wall positioned next to the drawbridge, half the battlefield won't be able to shoot at us as we ride out." She squared her shoulders. "I'll lead my knights to Thorssen. Killing their leader ought to take some of the fight out of them."

It would also let her fulfill her vow to avenge her father.

Chapter Fifty

Morning light revealed the clutter of rubble scattered within the outer rings of the city. People milled about, sorting through the mess in spite of the occasional falling missile, trying to pick up the few unburned pieces of their lives, or simply working to clear roadways so they could pass. Unfortunately, dawn also revealed a wide swath of the moat had been filled, and the Danes were ready to cross, their oxen yoked to siege towers. Their foot soldiers waited, massed in ranks, prepared for the impending attack.

Even as Alex watched from her window, a horn call resounded over the plain and the army began to march forward, their siege engines shielded behind metal plates and safe from flame arrows. The men seemed oblivious to fire from the defenders as they dug in for the day's attacks.

Alex heard the first thump of catapulted missiles striking the stone walls of the castle as she called for a squire and hastily donned her armor with his help. She was nearly dressed by the time a runner arrived to summon her, and she hurried down, still braiding her hair.

"They've brought up catapults and trebuchets behind the front lines," the young soldier who carried her helmet hastily reported. "They're mounting a full assault."

"Go to the west tower and have the code master signal our allies," Alex instructed. "Tell them we are beset, and we need their aid, but we plan to send out a sortie to drive the Danes back and give them time to arrive."

"A sortie?" He looked doubtful. "What allies?"

"Just have that sent." If Holden was within range, he might see the signal and find a way to hurry his men. She finished buckling on her sword and plucked a bun and an apple from the platter being borne past by a serving girl. She ate them hastily on her way out to the courtyard.

The Danish catapults launched a seemingly endless barrage of flaming pitch into the city. Living in the woods as they were, the Danes had no shortage of it. Several fires already roared unchecked where shots had fallen within the courtyard. Alex winced. It looked as though any wooden structures still remaining in the outer part of the city would be destroyed by nightfall. The city folk were already packed into every remaining structure, and it looked like more would be sleeping inside the castle by the time night fell, piled up and down the stone hallways on top of one another like cordwood.

She rode out with her newly appointed queen's guards to find General Pelley on the battlements, defending the drawbridge. He had the archers keeping up a staggered volley. Boys scuttled about, rescuing and reclaiming any arrows the Danes fired into the city so they could be shot right back out again. A bucket brigade labored to control the worst fires, and the moat was ablaze with nearly the last of their reserves of oil to keep the Danish grappling hooks at bay, the flames sending up a pall of thick oily smoke that clawed at Alex's lungs. Soldiers and citizens scurried everywhere, carrying arrows to the archers, shooting through crenellations on the parapet, or bringing water to their brothers-in-arms and to the firefighters. Workers bustled around clearing debris out of the streets and alleys wherever crumbling buildings had created a blockage.

The cooperation reminded Alex of an intricate maypole dance, every person in his place, and the sight brought tears to her eyes. The threat had brought out the very best in the people of Norwich. Her people.

She lifted her chin. Time to put some backbone into them, if she could.

"General, we can't squat in here any longer like a badger in its sett, waiting to be dug out. Waiting is costing us dearly, though it costs the Danes next to nothing. We will make a sortie and push our enemies back even as they charge." She gazed about the assembly, meeting her men's eyes squarely. "We will repel them on every front. Heat the kettles for the murder holes, and be ready to fight sword to sword with climbers on the ramparts. Place a double guard on the winch room. Don't let them in there to put down the drawbridge, or we'll be fighting in the streets. Have those who are wounded or weak sent to the palace and house them there."

He saluted briskly. "I'll order my knights to assemble, and the foot soldiers behind them. We have reserves who'll remain inside, waiting to spell their companions on the walls. I assume you want them to remain."

"Yes. They'll need to cover our exit and our return." She pointed crisply to the ramparts. "For now, bring down all the yeomen you can spare from the ramparts and lay down a cover fire on either side of the drawbridge to keep them from charging in as we ride out."

"Yes, Your Majesty."

Alex watched as the muster began, then climbed up to the parapet above the drawbridge. Edgar stood among the men who were tending fires heating boiling oil and molten lead at stations near the drawbridge. She gave him a nod and went to nestle between two archers. She peeked through the crenellation there to orient herself to the layout of the battlefield. She noted a handful of bannermen scattered about. She recalled Thorssen's device from the parley and made sure to mark his location carefully.

Regardless what Holden thought, she and that Danish bastard had unfinished business regarding her father.

Alex returned to the courtyard and mounted her horse, which danced as a ball of pitch landed nearby and skittered across the square, shedding liquid fire and scattering men. "Steady," she admonished. "Regroup."

Pelley gestured to the men who controlled the winch. The portcullis rose and the drawbridge began to descend, flames from the burning moat licking up around its armored edges. As the bridge opened, the queen's yeomen began their volley, arrows and quarrels sizzling out to block the Danish advance.

"Stay to the center of the road for as long as you can," Alex called to her men. She looked to her left, where Carl sat on a chestnut warhorse, and to her right, where his second waited, riding on a roan. All her guards rode clustered around her, bristling with swords, resplendent in their silvery plate, their horses similarly armored and shining, dancing about as they caught their masters' eagerness for battle. "For East Anglia, gentlemen. Raise the shield wall."

The soldiers raised the cry and the foot soldiers held their shields up, linking the edges together to form a protective wall over their heads as they clattered forth, their iron shoes rattling and striking sparks on the cobbles, then thudding over the wooden surface of the bridge. Alex brandished her sword, her heart racing. An arrow struck her belly and sprang back off her mail. She spurred her horse forward, and soon she was among the Danes, her warhorse rearing and kicking, bearing men down, doing his job even as she hacked and chopped at anyone within reach.

Together, the horsemen cleared a path for the foot soldiers. She saw a charger go down from an axe to the foreleg, and kept her momentum going so her foes would not have time to set and prepare a blow. The Danes weren't expecting horses. None of them had pole-arms, and the cavalry trampled over rank after rank of men.

She spied Thorssen's standard and pointed it out to Carl. Together, she and her guards angled their progress toward him once they were far enough from the walls to be out of range of their archers' protective fire. Bringing Thorssen down should take some of the starch out of the others. Maybe his death would disarrange the Danes so much her men could drive their army into the river.

Alex struck out, cutting down a Dane who was trying to seize her horse's bridle, and dodged the ball of a mace swinging wildly near her head.

"Your Majesty!" She could hear Carl bellowing for her, and turned till she found him, riding a bit back on her left flank. He looked excited. "Can you hear it?"

She listened, tilting her head, but the din of battle was all she could hear.

"It's a horn." Carl swung his sword, forced to defend himself, wheeling his horse about and bringing an enemy under its hooves.

A few minutes later she heard the horn herself, a faraway, mellow note, a rallying cry. The pattern was distinct, three short notes and a long.

"Mercia!" Alex shouted shrilly, and Carl's joyful affirmation echoed her cry. She pushed up the visor of her helmet and squinted to the horizon. A dust cloud billowed above the woods, gilded by the rising sun. Her heart swelled. Holden had brought the aid he promised.

Spurred to optimism by the sight, Alex wheeled her horse, seeking Thorssen's banner. The coward was lurking well back from the front lines, which placed him in danger of attack from the Mercians, who would march in on the west flank whenever they arrived. She glanced at the horizon again, trying to gauge the distance of the smudge of dust. How long before the reinforcements arrived?

Their arrival would split the Danish army, forcing them to fight on two fronts. She could already see the rearmost ranks turning about, making ready to face the Mercians. Bless Holden. The Mercian infantry were bursting out of the woods already, charging forward, arriving faster than she'd dared hope. They plowed into the ill-prepared Danes, and screams began to erupt from the entire width of the field.

Heartened by the sight, Alex spurred forward. "Thorssen, are you afraid to face a woman? Come out and fight!" Her shrill voice penetrated the din and was whirled away. Carl and a dozen guards still rode close to her, their horses' hooves lashing out, taking down leather-clad Danes and trampling them underfoot.

The drawbridge had been winched back up after all their men emerged, though a line of Danes who'd managed to land a grappling hook on the top were struggling to drag the bridge back down even as the men of Norwich attacked to stop them. That was all she could glimpse before a hand grasped her ankle, demanding her immediate attention. She stabbed even as her horse turned its head to bite, and the man fell with a scream. She realized there were arrows lodged in her cloak, but none had yet touched her skin.

She cried out her challenge again and spied Thorssen amidst the swirl of combat. He heard her, and their eyes connected for a moment. He scowled, turning toward her, his sword in his fist.

The soldiers between them parted at his command. She sized him up as he stepped forward, reining in her horse. He held a long, heavy sword, almost a claymore, but the quillons were straight, after the Danish fashion. He scowled at her, wiping a trickle of blood from his cheek.

"Very well then. Climb down and fight, woman." His English was thickly accented and nearly unintelligible over the roar of battle.

Alex swallowed hard, considering her strategy. He would wear her strength down fast, battering at her with his heavy blade. She would need all her skill and some of Holden's tricks, as well. She'd still be able to move faster than Thorssen in plate, though she would tire sooner than usual.

A solid ring of Danes enclosed her and her knights now, but they stood back at Thorssen's gesture. If she dismounted, she would not be able to re-mount her horse when the duel was done, even if she survived. She'd have to fight them all on foot with her knights' support. The gain would be worth the risk, though, if she could rid the world of Thorssen.

Carl gave her a look that said he didn't think much of their chances, but he held her horse's bridle as she slithered gracelessly off and stood in front of Thorssen, suddenly feeling small.

"We have killed so many men they have sent their women out to fight us." Thorssen's contemptuous glance included Carl. His taunts were in English, meant for them more than his own troops. "Prepare to die, girl, or be taken prisoner." He leered at her, his mouth cruel. "I think you would enjoy meeting a real man under the blankets."

Alex drew her sword and waited for his attack, refusing to respond to his taunts.

He lunged in and she danced aside, circling out of the radius of his sweeping stroke. His sword had a good deal more reach than hers, and that would help compensate for his lack of speed. Alex sidestepped, keeping the man moving, keeping him on the chase.

The first real clash of blades nearly shivered her sword from her hands. He laughed and straightened up, holding his heavy sword in one fist. He barked to the other Danes in his own language, and they chuckled together derisively.

"You are like a kitten trying to fight a mastiff."

He was more right than she cared to admit. He waded in, pummeling at her defenses, and his men pressed close, forcing her inward and keeping her within range of his blade. She ducked a sweeping slice and jabbed at his ankles, but the angle was poor and his steel-clad leather boot turned her blade. She rolled, using her momentum to come up again. If she fell flat, she'd have the devil's own time getting back up. She'd be crushed on her back like an insect.

Alex feigned a weakness in her left flank, trying to bait him. When he responded, she danced around him to get more running room. He laughed at her. "You cannot run forever."

He was right again. She spared a second of numb regret for Holden, who'd probably had precisely such a scene in his mind when he tried to forbid her to ride out. She was forced to admit she should have listened to him instead of insisting on confronting Thorssen, duty or no.

She managed to score a hit with the tip of her blade on the next exchange, jabbing through a hole in the left elbow of Thorssen's armor. He grimaced and backed off, glowering at her.

"Even a kitten has claws and teeth," Alex told him. She had only false bravado, but she played her cards for all they were worth. "A smart mastiff will back off before the kitten flays his nose." All she needed was the right opening. All she needed was a stroke of luck.

"Then that same dog will break the kitten's neck." He charged her, and again his men blocked her retreat. His sword clattered against the side of her mail, bruising her ribs and leaving a dent. He jostled up against her, trying to knock her to the ground. Alex managed to stay upright, but he caught her by the sword-arm with his injured left, and he very nearly managed to bring his blade back around for a fatal blow before she could twist away.

"You are a coward, using your men to interfere." She spat on the ground at his feet, and his eyes narrowed.

"Your father the general died squealing, girl."

Alex saw red, and in her fury, she lost sight of her strategy. She sliced at him with all her strength, again targeting his injured arm. He stepped back, then lunged forward with a brutal riposte. The tip of his blade squealed across her armor, leaving a deep dent, and her boot turned on a stone as she stumbled back. She toppled off her feet onto her back, and she heard Carl groan in despair.

She stared up into the clouds, hearing more horn-calls, loud and clear. More Mercian infantry were arriving. She was lost, but perhaps she'd bought enough time for her men.

The flash of Thorssen's blade dragged her hastily back to the present, and she rolled desperately, avoiding a two-handed chop that would have cleaved her from stem to stern. Thorssen put his foot on her sword, trapping it atop a rock on the stony ground. Her blade bent under his heavy boot, and she released the hilt. Carl was off his horse now, surging forward to attack the Danish king from behind. The Danes closed in on him, thwarting her mounted knights and barring them from their leader.

"I will have you for my prisoner until I tire of you, girl." Thorssen snarled a laugh. "Then I will leave you to my men for raping."

One of his men gave a shout, and Thorssen turned, blinking, as a fresh wave of horses burst through the ranks, bearing down on him. The foremost rider thrust a long, wicked spear at him, and he slapped at the ironclad haft with his sword, battering the weapon aside. One of his men screamed, trampled beneath flashing hooves, and the others broke ranks, trying to bring their weapons to bear.

The knights of East Anglia rallied, shouting triumph, and Alex struggled to climb to her feet. A helpful arm caught her. Carl hauled her up, his temple and one leg bloodied. One arm hung limp at his side, but he was still alive. He nearly went down himself as he raised her to her feet. Her knights spurred forward, circling about them, spears and swords at the ready.

Thorssen seemed to have forgotten her challenge, shouting orders in Danish and working to rally his men, who had been scattered by the charge. Alex cast about frantically, weaponless, and snatched a discarded short sword from the ground, wrapping her fingers about the hilt. Very well. She would fight on foot. She darted out of the protective circle of horses, stabbing at an inattentive Dane, who fell where he stood.

"Drive them off!" She heard a familiar voice shouting, and her eyes sought frantically among the melee, finding the very horseman who'd nearly speared Thorssen. His bay Frisian shuffled alongside her, and he flipped up his visor. The rider was Holden, sweating and dirty, but his eyes twinkled.

"In the nick of time?" He reached down for her, and she clasped his arm. With Carl boosting her arse quite indelicately from behind, she struggled up into the saddle behind the prince.

"Get Carl!" Holden shouted at another horseman, pointing to Carl to identify him, and reined his beast around. "We'll soon have them on the run. For East Anglia!" He raised his sword, and the men of Norwich who saw him gave a ragged cheer, then a stronger one. Others around them took up the cry and raised it until the sky rang as they celebrated that Holden and their queen survived.

Holden waited until the noise died away. "Form ranks. To me, East Anglia! Rally, Mercia!" The men heard him, and the cry went round. Troops began to form ranks, driving forward as the Danes faltered.

"The queen!" Alex heard her men raise a second shout. "The queen lives!"

So she did.

She and Holden rode forth past an abandoned catapult. She tugged at his shoulder. "Stop. Men?" She raised her voice. "Take the catapult. Take any abandoned Danish gear you can find and turn it against them."

A group of foot soldiers hastened to obey her, and she wrapped her arms around Holden again. "Now let's go get that bastard. Together." She leaned in against his helmet as he spurred forward, following Thorssen's standard. "Here's what we'll do."

Chapter Fifty-One

Thorssen did not flee far before re-forming his command center, this time from near the back edge of the field. He paused to regroup amidst the tents of his camp at the base of a tall tree, an oak with branches stripped bare by winter. The camp was far enough from Norwich the archers on the ramparts could not reach the tents, and no arrows stuck out of the tree's broad trunk, only the forearm-thick shaft of a single stray ballista bolt.

Alex could see Thorssen gesturing toward the camps, where reserves of fresh men waited, no doubt directing his subordinates to go for reinforcements. She hung on as Holden spurred his mount through a line of Danes, scattering them, and drew up before him. In the distance, the abandoned catapult began to trundle around, its arm winched back and ready to fly.

"I'm calling you out, Thorssen. For my father, King Anselm of Norwich, and my brother, Prince Gavin, both killed by your treachery and lies," Holden snarled, ignoring the threatening array of bows and blades rising to focus on him as he forced his mount forward.

"Does East Anglia have a king after all, or are you merely a spoiled princeling, clinging to his lover's skirts?" Thorssen blustered, and drew his sword. "Not strong enough to claim the throne on your own?"

"Strong enough to do for you." Holden vaulted off the horse and Alex scrambled down after him. He drew his blade and Alex clutched the sword she'd picked up off the battlefield.

The familiar ring of Danes closed around them, many fewer this time. Most had been drawn into direct combat with the Mercian army, but enough lingered to be a nuisance. "They'll cheat," Alex warned Holden. "They'll close in during the battle and close off your retreat."

"Noted." Holden moved to one side and after a moment Alex moved to the other, splitting Thorssen's attention between them.

"You cheat also. Two at once?" Thorssen bared his teeth and spat to one side, contemptuous.

Alex felt a man paw at her arm, trying to catch her and drag her out of the battle. She brought her blade around savagely and he fell back, whimpering, clutching half a hand.

"Frightened?" Holden's voice mocked Thorssen.

"Not in the least." Thorssen lunged, testing Holden's strength, and he parried the blow, dancing back. Alex pressed in, trying to find an opening before Thorssen could re-set, but he anticipated her, raising his shield to block.

"You call this a man, girl-queen? He fights even more like a woman than you." Thorssen pushed forward, battering at Holden's defenses. She knew Holden was in trouble. He might have defeated Gavin, but Gavin had been blinded by preconceived notions and by the kindness of brotherhood.

Thorssen had neither of these weaknesses, and to pretend to less skill than he actually had would swiftly prove fatal for Holden. The tall Dane was in deadly earnest, each swing meant to separate his opponent's head from his shoulders.

She darted in again, a gadfly, forcing Thorssen to pull short on a savage attack. He reversed, turning to her as the greater threat. Holden tried to slip behind him, but one of the Danes stuck out a boot and he nearly fell over. A gust of laughter went up, but the laughter died as a huge stone struck the ground nearby, shattering on impact and sending shrapnel knifing through the air.

Two men screamed and fell. A few bits of gravel pelted Alex and a shard penetrated her visor to cut her cheek, but neither she nor Holden was seriously hurt. Unfortunately, neither was Thorssen. He scowled and cursed, but he kept coming at her, pushing her back. Holden darted in and out, working to distract him, but Thorssen's armor was good and his shield-work even better, holding at bay the attacks he could not block. Alex noticed the dried blood on his armor from her earlier attack, and she tried to target the same weak spot again, managing to drive him back a little.

She stepped in, pressing her attack, hope surging in her heart, but then another stone careened into the ground and shattered behind them. She felt an impact against her armor like a punch to the kidney. She fell forward, winded, and lay still. Holden gave a shriek of rage and metal scraped as he intercepted Thorssen's sword. This wasn't exactly what they'd planned, but Alex played her role to the hilt nonetheless. She lay still as Thorssen's feet buffeted her, glad none of the shrapnel had caught Holden and grateful her armor protected her from the worst of the impact.

"Who will you hide behind now, princeling?" Thorssen taunted Holden, his voice triumphant. "Your wet-nurse is gone."

He pushed forward, battering at Holden with a flurry of blows, forcing him back. Alex lay very still, trying not to panic. Holden gave way, keeping himself out of range of the deadly sword, but was in danger of being driven too far from her for their original plan to work. She did not dare risk giving him a signal to show she lived.

He began to circle, drawing Thorssen after him, and she breathed a quiet sigh of relief as they approached her again. Disregarded, she began to inch her hand down, reaching to her belt for her dagger. She wrapped her fingers around it, easing the weapon from its sheath.

Holden gave a cry, and she forced herself not to jerk her head up to look. He kept moving, the sound of his leather boots a softer scuffle in contrast to the heavy clatter of Thorssen's armor.

"First blood." Thorssen gloated. "I almost hope the woman isn't slain. If she isn't, I'll bind her and put her on the ships. I'll have her sent to Denmark to work as a slave for my tribe. First I'll show her what she's missing, wasting her time with a worthless pup like you."

"Every time you open your mouth, you're boasting of rape. Are you ashamed of something?" Holden panted, and she could hear pain in his voice. "That's a hell of a sword. It wouldn't surprise me at all to learn you're overcompensating for a deficiency inside your breeches."

Thorssen renewed his attack in grim silence and the two men circled farther, their breath coming in harsh gasps. Now she could see them out of the tail of her eye. Holden darted in and retreated, and she spied a ribbon of blood staining his left sleeve. He was fighting one-handed now, with no shield. She hissed softly, hatred swelling in her heart. A little farther, a little more, and Thorssen was hers.

Another bolt struck and a rain of stone pattered down. The catapult was definitely targeting Thorssen's standard.

Thorssen snarled a few incomprehensible words over his shoulder, and men scrambled to lower the banner so the catapult would have no mark to aim at.

The momentary distraction was all they needed. Holden lunged forward, forcing the king back, and as he stumbled over her, Alex surged up, driving her knife into the seam behind the knee of his armor, slashing back and forth with all her might.

Thorssen screamed as his leg crumpled under him, and Holden was ready, his sword scraping at the steel coif around the Dane's neck. Alex pulled out her blade and stabbed again, higher. Thorssen screamed and blood gushed from his groin. He dropped his sword, clutching at his inner thigh.

"Nice choice of target," Holden puffed, turning the point of his blade and piercing the coif. Thorssen gave a gurgling cry and slumped to the side, groping weakly at his neck. "Not surprised you missed your chance to geld him, though. He seems to have some well-founded issues."

Alex snorted and pulled away from the Dane's death-throes, rolling to her feet with her dagger in her hand. The other Danes stood dumbfounded for a heartbeat, staring at their stricken leader.

Another catapulted missile whistled through the air. Alex and Holden ducked as the stone slammed against the tree, shattering branches and sending a deadly rain of splinters scything through the air. The men flinched back, and without their leader, their courage evaporated. They swiftly took to their heels, headed for the forest.

"He even struck his standard so we wouldn't have to," Holden laughed shortly. His face was pale, his arm bloody. "Thanks for the help," he called to the dying Thorssen, who was bleeding out too rapidly to launch any further attacks, his face already turning white as he struggled in vain to stanch the wound.

They paused long enough for Alex to bind Holden's arm. The cut was ugly but not too deep, inside the bend of his elbow. She stopped the bleeding as best she could, tying a crude sling to hold his arm immobile against his chest.

"We should return you to the city."

"No, they're on the run. Time for that later." He glanced about. "My horse." The beast still stood waiting a few yards away in the lee of what remained of the thick tree-trunk, miraculously unharmed by the battering fire of the catapult. "Come on."

They struggled up onto the charger with a good deal of difficulty, and Holden raised the rallying cry to Mercia while Alex's shrill soprano mustered the men of East Anglia. The nucleus of their forces regrouped on the shambles of Thorssen's camp and drove forward, commandeering Danish oxen and catapults as they went.

The rout occupied most of the rest of the day, but they pushed the leaderless Danes back down to their camps on the Yare and onto their ships, then peppered them with fire from their own siege weapons, sinking many ships as the Danes rowed down the river and tried in vain to catch enough wind to fill their sails.

When dusk drew near, Alex called for the leaders of their combined forces to assemble, marshaling them together and issuing orders to sweep through the woods and dispatch the stragglers, then press on to the coast and ensure the surviving boats all departed. She watched as the majority of her army dispersed to begin combing the forest and the field for enemy soldiers. She kept a few of them in reserve, though, to search the battlefield for wounded men and return them to Norwich for treatment.

"That lot will soon be riding the waves back to Denmark as fast as the wind will carry them. I doubt they'll trouble East Anglia again." Holden looked to her as they once again clambered up onto his horse. His face was pinched with weariness and pain, and the set of his mouth was grim. Alex knew he regretted the death he had seen and caused on the battlefield.

She wrapped her arms around his waist as they spurred forward. He tied the reins around his belt and his hand sought hers, their fingers twining together. They rode back along the battlefield to the city, where they paused to await the lowering of the drawbridge, watching as soldiers carried wounded men from the field to the medical tents.

"You are a good man, Holden Stuart, and a clever one. You will make a fine King of Norwich," Alex said softly.

He turned to glance back at her, his eyes alight with hope. "Have you forgiven me, then?"

"Well. I might not go so far as that." Alex bit her lip. "I'm furious with you for going off without leave. Not because we fought beforehand, but because you made a major move without planning first. You needed to consult with me and Pelley beforehand on tactics and timing and signals."

"I didn't think you'd let me go if I did," he admitted.

"I didn't want to, I admit, but I would have seen reason in time." Alex reached out to him, putting her hand on his shoulder. "Even though I didn't like to." She gave him an apologetic smile. "I suspect both of us will have to learn to let the other do things we don't like, when the situation demands."

They rode on slowly, crossing the battered drawbridge and gaining the interior of the city, where Edgar jumped out from the milling crowd to greet them. Holden stopped the weary horse and waited while Edgar helped Alex down, embracing her in his joy at seeing her alive again.

"They never entered the city, Your Majesty. The sortie worked," He beamed. "General Pelley sent more of our men out through the drawbridge after Mercia arrived and drew the Danes off. I think I could have held the battlements all by myself thereafter. We never even had to use the murder-holes. The archers were enough."

"Have you seen Carl?"

"He came through a while back, walking alongside one of the knights on a shutter. He said he'd seen you headed for the Broads, driving the Danes in front of you."

"We sent them on their way with a few parting gifts from their own catapults." She pressed his hand, glad to see him again, glad to know Carl also survived. "Go and help bring in the wounded, Edgar. We need as many able-bodied men as we can muster. Take the horse, too. It may be of help to those who can't walk."

"Yes, Your Majesty." He shouldered his unstrung bow and trotted out, leading the charger behind him.

Alex turned to Holden.

He covered her hand with his own as they began to walk in through the city streets together, heading slowly toward the castle. "You're right about one thing. We have to do a better job of talking things through." His voice was gruff. He lifted her hand and stripped off her gauntlet, then kissed her palm. "I tried, but you wouldn't listen. You didn't just mean to lead the troops. You wanted to do exactly what my brother did. You carried the fight straight to Thorssen and demanded a contest of strength. That kind of thinking cost Gavin his life."

Alex drew a deep breath. "Yes, and I should have listened to you instead of letting my temper and my pride rule me. I was right to lead the charge, but not to call Thorssen out for a duel." She gave him a wry look. "Don't think it's escaped my notice. You, too, came straight in to confront Thorssen despite knowing he was your better with a sword." She touched his lips with her fingertip.

"I went for him because I knew you'd be there, but yes." He dropped his gaze, then lifted it to her again, amusement and chagrin mingled on his face. "We seem to be two of a kind, reckless and headstrong."

"That we are." She stepped close to him. "As such, I think perhaps we should marry after all." She gave him a wry grin, then raised her hand to his chest, stopping him before he could sweep her up and kiss her. "If we are to wed, Holden, we must both agree always to listen to one another. No commands issued to the other without due discussion, no running off on impulse without talking things through first."

"Agreed." He reached and moved her hand, then pulled her to him, taking her mouth joyfully, without caring who might see.

"So how were you doing against Thorssen when I rode in?" His eyes danced.

"I was about to take him down." She would have, too, if she hadn't stepped on that stone and fallen. She knew what Holden must have seen as he charged. She'd been flat on her arse in the dirt with a bent sword in her fist. However, just because he had a point didn't mean she had to let him rub it in. "I had things well in hand. I only had a little bad luck, that's all."

"I'll ask Carl to verify your tale and get the truth."

"You go right ahead. He'll tell you the same."

They went into the castle together, laughing, his arm about her waist.

Epilogue

In the aftermath of the battle, Alex and Holden were finally free to wed.

They planned to marry at Beltaine, though they already shared the prince's rooms. No one dared to gainsay them on either the sharing or the marriage, though the Earl of Lowestofte raised an eyebrow at Alex and pursed his lips with a visible touch of worry.

She knew better, and trusted the courtiers would soon learn the truth of their future king. He'd already captured the love and admiration of the people by bringing the Mercians to end the siege and ousting the Danes from their land; the nobility would not lag far behind.

Alex and Holden rarely spoke openly of their fathers, but they went together every now and then to visit the new tombs in the catacombs. Alex rested her hand on the lid of her father's sepulcher and thought of what she would say to him if he were alive. "You were wrong. He loves me. He changed. Our line is back on the throne again, the way you always dreamed." Maybe he had begun to believe the prince was changing even before he died. She regretted she would never know.

Holden's feelings about his own father seemed even more troubled. When they went down to visit the tombs together, he sat silently and stared at his father's name, which masons had carved into the cold marble lid of the king's tomb. He was sometimes pensive for many hours after. Alex was glad that at least Prince Gavin had come to see his younger brother's value before he was slain. Gavin's respect gave Holden more peace with the loss of his brother than of his father.

She went to Holden where he sat, brooding over King Anselm's tomb, and wrapped him in her cloak to warm him when she'd finished her silent conversation with her own father. He slid his arm around her, holding her close, but otherwise remained still. She guided him away when she judged he had sat there in silence for long enough.

The nights after those visits were sweet. He always made love to her slowly, looking into her eyes, his hips barely moving until they both grew so aroused they couldn't bear waiting any longer. They soon accelerated out of control, clutching and writhing. They rolled over and over in the prince's wide bed, wrestling for the top until they couldn't delay their pleasure any longer. Then they came, sometimes together, always frantic, moaning, and sweating. Finally they collapsed tangled together to sleep.

Alex refused an elaborate white dress, and she wed her husband wearing armor instead. They walked up the aisle of the Grand Hall together, resplendent in gilt plate mail, trailing purple velvet cloaks trimmed in ermine. As soon as they were married, Holden was crowned King of East Anglia. Alex smiled at him as he turned to the court, lifting his chin with pride and a hint of defiance. She clasped his hand and they received their applause together. Edgar and Carl stood on their left while the Earl of Lowestofte and General Pelley waited on the right, as their most trusted friends should. Alex thought Edgar looked a little wistful during the wedding, but he bore up well.

The royal couple presided at their wedding feast, polite and friendly to all the courtiers. Nearly every member of their court returned from their extended retreat to the countryside in order to attend the wedding and coronation. The women stared at Alex with open amazement, some of them with envy, their faces disgruntled. Prince Gavin's one-time admirers seemed listless, their pretty faces sad. She smiled at them all regardless, gracious and kind even to those who did not welcome her as their queen.

She planned to work at making friends among the ones who seemed willing.

Holden remained attentive to Alex through the night, vanishing for a few moments at a time and returning rapidly to her elbow with a cup of wine or a tidbit of some particularly fine delicacy. He invariably lifted the dainty morsels to her mouth rather than handing them to her, and she laughed and accepted, her lips touching his fingers, her eyes meeting his and kindling heat there.

The evening grew late before they excused themselves. Before they went up, Holden directed the servants to send wine and brandy around again for all the guests. A little tipsy from too much wine of their own, giddy with joy, they could hardly manage to make it upstairs before he began tugging off her armor.

She laughed and fled down the corridor with him in hot pursuit, and they slammed the door behind them, flustering the embarrassed guards dreadfully. Each of them wrestled with the other's armor at the same time, hindering rather than helping one another, but they eventually managed to remove it all, leaving the pieces scattered in wild disarray across the floor.

When the armor was gone, Alex tackled Holden and pushed him onto the bed on his back, then climbed onto him, pushing his shirt up and tangling it about his arms while she kissed him and fondled his chest. He groaned, arching under her hands; she rather thought she liked him like that, hot-eyed and helpless.

"Ahhh, my handsome lad. So innocent and helpless and virginal, trapped at the mercy of a terrible, brazen hussy." She grinned at him and pinched his nipples. He grinned back, then widened his eyes as if he would plead for mercy.

"Be gentle with me?"

"Not even a little."

True to her word, she leaned in, kissing and biting his lips and his neck. He moaned and squirmed, the perfect picture of reluctant arousal, not bothering to free himself from the confining shirt. She dragged her nails along his chest and belly, watching his muscles tense in automatic response, watching his cock swell and fill. She wrapped her hand around him and gave him tight, rough strokes that made his tongue dart out to lick his lips.

"I think you like this rather more than you're admitting," she purred, running her thumb over the leaking tip of his cock, then lifted her hand to her mouth for a taste and let him watch her suck it clean.

He whimpered for her, closing his eyes and turning his face to the side, and she bit softly at his jaw and earlobe, laying herself along his belly and rubbing her hip against his hard cock. She ran her hands along his outstretched arms, catching her fists in the cloth that bound him, and writhed until he turned breathless.

"Please," he begged, but she showed no mercy. She reached to steady his cock and mounted him. He gave a breathless cry, fists clutching at the bedstead above his head.

She tightened her body and rode him, slow and hard and deliberate. He bit his lip and his head thrashed from side to side, restless. He moaned, his hips pushing up against her.

"Mmmm, conflicting signals," she murmured, and leaned in to nip at his mouth playfully. "I'm certain you quite like this after all." She nipped his earlobe. "So you should," she breathed in his ear. "Because you're all mine now." She reached up to catch hold of his shirt, twisting it tight around his arms and knotting the sleeves. She liked having him at her mercy like this, watching him want her helplessly for just a little longer.

He hissed softly and his hips bucked, lifting her. She kept her seat easily and watched him swallow. Beautiful. His eyes gleamed at her for a moment, wicked and merry. She laughed and speeded her pace. This time her hands on him coaxed forth any response she could, tickling at his sensitive nipples. She stopped moving after a few quick strokes, tightening and loosening her body on him. Sweat broke out on his brow and he struggled with himself, a losing battle.

"Please," he moaned again, hoarse and husky, a plea for her to go on, for her to move, for her to stop the torment and let him come.

She obliged him. He groaned with appreciation as she lifted and impaled herself on his hard cock. His throat worked and his muscles tightened. He rose up sturdily to meet her, but she was still in control, still moving slower than he liked.

"Want more?" Alex murmured, daring him. "Take me, if you want me."

His eyes lit up in response to her challenge. His muscles worked as he fought the linen shirt, twisting and pulling. She watched, still riding him lazily, and licked her lips. The fabric started to rip with a low purring sound, her single warning before he finally worked his way out of the tangle of cloth and grinned at her, wicked good humor lighting his eyes.

"I think I will." He flipped her over rapidly, still inside her. She squeaked with surprise and he laughed, triumphant. She reached for him, but he pulled back, slipping out of her, a demon of mischief dancing in his eyes. He slid his arms beneath her knees and lifted them toward her chest, pulling her body downward, and she gasped, eyes going wide, as his weight came down on her, forcing the breath from her lungs. He plunged back in hard.

Alex whimpered, lifting to meet him. She could feel every inch of him as he drove in, feel the power of his muscles as he pulled back and filled her again.

She reached up, bracing her palms against the headboard, and he gave a low growl of pleasure when she met him sturdily as he thrust home. She cried out again, writhing, her head tossing against the pillow.

Each smooth, brutal thrust left her gasping, whimpering, and pleading as he claimed her roughly, sweat gleaming on his face and throat, his teeth clenched with effort. She dug her nails into the carved wood of the bedstead, struggling for breath. His fierce thrusts continued, igniting a melting flame at the core of her body, and she squirmed. She was sweating now, too, straining under him, her head swimming as she tried to breathe.

Pleasure swelled and built inside her as he continued, relentless, his breath hissing through his teeth. He shifted his grip, pressing her thighs farther up, and she cried out as the angle changed and his cock hit exactly the right spot midway through every stroke.

She couldn't last. She shattered beneath him, a choked shriek echoing inside the bedchamber. He followed her after only a half-dozen more strokes, making a hoarse, barking cry of his own, and collapsed on her, releasing her legs.

They lay entwined, recovering slowly, until she had to move to ease a cramp. She pushed at him and he shifted, rolling half off her. He returned after she was comfortable, pulling her loosely to him. His skin was hot and slick. Even though she was overheated, she slid her arms around him, running her hand along his spine.

"You're a succubus," he stroked her back and breasts, still a little breathless. He smiled, his eyes warm. "Still, I rather like being yours, I admit."

After they rested, he stirred again, nuzzling a kiss on her mouth, and covered her body with kisses as he worked his way down between her thighs. He made her believe his words all over again with his lips and tongue and fingers.

~ * ~

So matters remained between them as the days passed. They didn't always see eye to eye, but they managed to listen to one another. They moved swiftly to end their differences when they fought. They talked and argued. They laughed, cried, and loved.

Not long after their wedding, Alex found herself with child. Holden was beside himself with joy at the news. He smothered her with care and caution until she was ready to scream, offering her chairs at every possible moment, fretting when she insisted she would ride her horse during the early stages. He put his foot down and forbade her to do sword drill with Carl from the very first moment he learned she was pregnant. However, his care was welcome when he held her forehead while she vomited into a basin every morning, or when he curled around her in the evening, resting his hand on her belly to feel their baby kick.

317

He took over more of the duties of governing while she was indisposed with morning sickness and needed to remain in bed. Though he was initially met with skepticism, he remained patient. He slowly gained respect from the nobles of his court and the adjoining rulers, including those who had not come to the aid of East Anglia in their contest against the Danes. He improved his diplomatic skills steadily. His decisions were usually clever. When he was unsure, he listened to his advisors carefully, then decided whether or not he would heed them. The Earl of Lowestofte and General Pelley worked with him daily, helping him learn to handle the difficult task of diplomacy.

She knew he was making good headway when she chanced to pass through the Grand Hall one day and saw Ellis cover a smile while helping him work through a tricky business of negotiating territorial boundaries with Essex. She asked him later how he'd managed to get such favorable terms for East Anglia. He laughed, teasing, and told her he had ignored all his advisers' well-intentioned advice about tact and threatened to call for his pregnant and irritable warrior queen to mediate the talks if Essex wanted to learn how much land they truly stood to lose.

She could sometimes see Holden's memory of his other son in his eyes when he looked at her belly, and she was aware of his regret, even his grief. His sorrow touched her, but also made her secretly glad, for she knew their child would be deeply cherished.

That knowledge didn't keep her from cursing him and swearing she'd never let him touch her again when she was tormented by the extremity of her pain during the birth. Despite her words he stood helplessly by, refusing to leave while the midwife tended her. He held her hand as she sweated and panted and screamed. When their son was born, he accepted the howling, purple, linen-wrapped bundle with trembling hands and looked into the baby's face with so much wonder and love in his eyes she was moved to forgive him for the ordeal she'd undergone.

Watching him standing there, holding their baby, she could see into the future as if she had already lived it. She could foresee Holden tucking their son into bed after reading to him from a book of fairy-stories, showing the boy how to buckle on a vambrace and shoot a bow, or the two of them riding out on their horses together, laughing, the sun kindling red flame in their hair.

He balanced the baby carefully over his arm and brought him to her. He settled him into her arms and helped her open her shirt to give the child her breast.

He asked her if they could name their son Gavin, and she agreed.

About the Author

Olivia Fields is a grader of papers, herder of dogs, knitter of scarves, and keeper of fish. Her favorite authors are J. R. R. Tolkien, Geoffrey Chaucer, T. S. Eliot, and Terry Pratchett. She spends her spare time watering flowers, admiring her favorite celebrities, hoarding movie memorabilia, hiking, making crafts, and watching cartoons.

VISIT OUR WEBSITE
FOR THE FULL INVENTORY
OF QUALITY BOOKS:
http://www.roguephoenixpress.com

Rogue Phoenix Press
Representing Excellence in Publishing

Quality trade paperbacks and downloads

in multiple formats,

in genres ranging from historical to contemporary romance, mystery and science fiction.

Visit the website then bookmark it.

We add new titles each month!

www.ingramcontent.com/pod-product-compliance
Lightning Source LLC
Chambersburg PA
CBHW070646180626
46817CB00006B/2258